THE COMPLETE
PORRIDGE

THE COMPLETE
PORRIDGE

Dick Clement and Ian La Frenais

Based on the
classic BBC TV comedy series

BBC BOOKS

Porridge was first published in Great Britain in 1975 by the British Broadcasting Corporation
© 1975 Dick Clement and Ian La Frenais
Adapted from the TV series by Jonathan Marshall
© 1975

Another Stretch of Porridge was first published in Great Britain in 1976 by the British Broadcasting Corporation
© 1976 Dick Clement and Ian La Frenais
Adapted from the TV series by Paul Victor
© 1976

A Further Stir of Porridge was first published in Great Britain in 1977 by the British Broadcasting Corporation
© 1977 Dick Clement and Ian La Frenais
Adapted from the TV series by Paul Victor
© 1977

Published by BBC Books,
a division of BBC Enterprises Limited,
Woodlands, 80 Wood Lane,
London W12 0TT

First published in one volume 1990

ISBN 0 563 36054 2

Printed and bound in Great Britain by
Richard Clay Ltd, Bungay, Suffolk
Cover Printed by Richard Clay Ltd, Norwich

CONTENTS

PORRIDGE

Adapted from the TV series by
Jonathan Marshall

Contents

Prisoner and Escort

Here I am ensconced in my old flowery-dell; that means cell for the uninitiated, contemplating the pros and cons of serving a five stretch. No central heating, a stone floor, a small barred window and no handle on the inside of the door. What you might call a prison.

On the other hand, according to the *Law Society Gazette*, sentences are going to get longer. And, if we go by what the *Daily Mirror* reports, unemployment is rising, petrol is due to rise and so are Manchester United, an' that *can* be bad. I mean, think of all them grotty United supporters infesting dear old Highbury. Looking at it in that light, I reckon there is something in doing a bit of porridge in the winter.

Now, I must be honest – and that's going to break the habit of a lifetime. When old Justice Fraser, known by the criminal fraternity as Big Nose, gave me five years I didn't actually leap up and down with shouts of jollification. No, as I recall it I said, 'Charmless nurk', and went on down the steps for my cocoa and a limp bun. Old Fraser didn't look too pleased with my comments but then he hadn't looked pleased at all during the trial. Course being a Scotsman doesn't help. It's not that I'm racially prejudiced or anything but I've always noticed that Scots are not much bottle in the way of having a giggle. Now me, I like a joke, and try to inject a note of levity into most situations such as weddings, funerals or court appearances.

I nicked this lorry, see. That's not really my game. A sort of impulse steal you might say. There I was minding my own business waiting for the labour exchange to open, not that I was looking for work, oh dear no. Just waiting to collect my rightful state assistance, when I noticed this lorry, with the glamorous words Johnny Walker painted on the side, pull up at the Ace café. In 'e goes, double egg and chips, and a large tea. Right, I thought, he's there for the next half-hour. Should have been a right old doddle.

Can you believe it? The brakes failed! There I was, belting down the Archway with six ton of scotch on my back. I said to Mr Fraser, I said, 'It's criminal the way some people let their vehicles get in such a condition.' In court, I asked for leniency on the grounds that my only thought at the time was to avoid injury to pedestrians. I done a quick double-declutch, and swerving to avoid a bollard, I hit a Rolls-Royce, went through two back gardens, demolished a tool shed, six chicken runs, a green-house, and finished up going clean through a brick wall.

Well, when they reads that little lot out in court, old Fraser did his nut. 'Oi, Fletcher,' he said, 'you can't go round nicking people's motors that are loaded up with gear like scotch, and knocking down walls. How do you plead?'

'Guilty,' I said. 'And I ask for six other fences to be taken into consideration.'

Well, I laughed. I mean who wouldn't? Mr Fraser for one. He had a quick butchers around the court, a scratch under his wig and robes, took two tablets, a swig of water and opened Archbalds. That's the book they use when they are not sure, or when they want to play for time. Little things like that all go to show that you've got a heavy sentence coming.

So, it's New Year's Eve and there I am travelling from Brixton to Slade Prison. A new one to me. For some un-known reason the Home Office likes putting up nicks in outlandish places. Adds to the tourist attraction, I suppose. Anyway, there I was with two right old screws, the like you'd never seen before. One I knew all about though. MacKay. A Scot. And a right cocky Scot as well. He could have been spending Hogmanay with all those other lunatic Scots. Instead there he was huddled over the latest copy of *Penthouse,* devouring the centre page pin-ups. He was not a happy looking nurk at the best of times. Walked as though he had a poker stuck up his backside. And, to top it all he had a Ronald Colman moustache. His head had a funny habit of jerking forward like a chicken, and when he talked his body remained still. Come to think of it, he looked more like a turkey.

Now the other screw, oops, they don't like that word, do they? Officer, gives them that feeling of power. Any rate, this other screw looked if anything even more miserable than MacKay. About six foot three, droopy shoulders and an air of ultra misery. Put upon, that's how he looked. Right away I sussed out that he was going to be a soft touch. You can always tell them.

I was grumbling that they hadn't let me have a slash before we left the station. I didn't fancy using the bog on the train, I don't like train bogs, full of British Rail bog paper, graffiti and stodgy dog-ends.

'Would you like to read my *Angling Times*?' said Mr Barrowclough. He was the other screw.

Now that was an opening I couldn't refuse. I could see the headlines screaming at me from the front page. 'And now – The 2p Lugworm!' Full of full-frontal salmons and the price of cod inside no doubt. I reached across to take the magazine. As I did the Scottish nurk snatched it out of my hand.

'God Almighty,' he says. 'Molly-coddling him already. You seem, Mr Barrowclough, to forget what prison is for. He's got a debt to pay to society, and that debt doesn't include reading informative magazines.'

With that he settles back into his seat with a last jerk of his neck. Yes, just like a turkey.

The other screw looked just as surprised as I did. I fell silent for a minute or two and gazed out of the window at North London's back gardens. Then I thought of the long journey ahead with no reading material or television and I thought, Well, we have got to do something to pass the time, haven't we? I looked at MacKay out of the corner of my eye and said very casually, 'I spy with my little eye something beginning with C.' Now for some unknown reason he took that very personal. Leaning across and wagging a finger he said, 'Watch it, Fletcher, watch it,' he says.

'It was cuffs, handcuffs I had in mind, Mr MacKay. Oh, sorry, I should have said HC, that would have been more fair.'

'Don't come the old soldier with me,' he says.

'Wouldn't dream of it, I says.'

'Any more trouble with you and I'll . . .'

'Let me guess,' I says. 'You'll wait till we pick up speed at, say, Hemel Hempstead and chuck me out of the window. Then put it down to attempting to escape.'

This offended the other one's sense of fairness. 'Oh, he wouldn't do that,' he says.

'I suppose you're right,' I says. 'Couldn't spell Hemel Hempstead. He'd wait till we got to Rugby.'

I felt sure that MacKay and I were going to have a right old game with each other in the months to come. I could tell by the look he was giving me that I was going to be one of his favourite targets.

'Look,' said Barrowclough. 'There's a long journey ahead, let us not conduct it in a feeling of hostility and aggression. Why don't we all have a nice cup of tea?'

'Oh yes,' I says. 'A cup of tea solves all nasty experiences as my old Mother used to say. And I'll have one of those individual fruit pies if they've got any.'

Rob Roy gave me a hard look, he wasn't sure whether I was in fact having a go at him or not. Anyway, he decided that it is a good idea and off he strutted leaving us alone in our first-class compartment with the blinds pulled down so as not to offend the eyes of the gentry with a glimpse of a convicted felon.

I thought, this should give me an opportunity to find out some valuable information about old misery-guts. The number one priority in dealing with two screws is to inject a little bit of bother between them. Divide and rule. So nodding towards the door I says, 'He's a laugh, ain't he? Sort of casual like. He plays it careful, won't be drawn.'

'I expect it's with him being a Scotsman and having to miss Hogmanay,' he says.

'Scot is he? I'd never have guessed,' I replied. But the sarcasm goes right over his head.

'Oh yes, and they do take it very seriously, the Scots.'

'Yeah, well they'd take any excuse for drinking seriously, wouldn't they? Nothing social about their drinking habits, is there? With them, it's like a religion. They don't enjoy a few glasses of the old vino, oh, no, they drink to get drunk. And, whereas other people having reached that state get a little warm and sentimental, or as in my case, randy, your Scot, all he wants is to fight and smash a glass in someone's boat-race. Only one thing worse than a drunken Scot and that's a sober one, an' we've just seen one of them, haven't we?'

I settled back in my seat feeling the power of having got that off my chest. He sat there blinking through his spectacles, sucking his teeth before saying unhappily, 'I'm Scots on my mother's side.'

Well I couldn't let that pass, could I? 'Oh yes?' I said.

'Yes, Scots, Polish, Irish and English . . .'

'She got about a bit, didn't she?'

'Who?'

'Your mother.'

He didn't get it. He just leaned further forward in his seat and blinked.

'No, I didn't mean that. It was my father, that side of the family. He was the mixture you see.'

I decided to get off the subject of his family tree and on to more profitable ground.

'I'm pure London myself. In fact pure North London. You could go to Muswell Hill Cemetery and see all my ancestors. Full of Fletchers, it is. There's always been a Fletcher, right back to . . . oh, I should think Henry the Fourth Part Two. Oh yes, we Fletchers have always put it about.'

He seemed very impressed with that so I decided to give him a little more of the Fletcher history.

'Now my great grandfather, William Wellington Fletcher, was the last man to be hung for sheep stealing. An' Paddington Jarvis Fletcher was in Newgate with Jack Shepherd, wun he? In fact he also has the honour of being the last man to have been hung, drawn and quartered, at Shepherds Bush. Named a district of London after him, didn't they?'

'Runs in the family then, does it?' he said.

'Wot, naming districts?'

'No, crime,' he says.

'Well, I know there's a lot of Fletchers in Australia.'

'You could say that it's hereditary,' he said.

Here we go, I thought. There's always someone trying to get to the bottom of why you went to prison. Social workers an' the like. You know, they come in the cell and ask stupid pointless questions about your background, family life. Whether you hated your father and fancied your **Aunt** Olga, which I did when I was young and stupid. Mind you, she was only my Aunt by marriage and worked as a part-time stripper in the Chez Susan night club in Bow, and you had to be blind or a Tory not to have fancied her. No, the point is, they're always trying to get you to say that you came from a broken home, and that your Dad beat you and your Mother every night before going up the Green Man for his twenty-two pints. Or that your Dad smashed up your favourite toy train on your fifth birthday or something stupid like that. Then, after you have told them all that cobblers, they go away and write it all down in their case-folders, just to prove that the textbooks are correct. No, they get none of that toffee from me. I did it because I was greedy, and lazy. Anyway, my old man's still happily married to his old girl, diamond wedding in fact this year.

'Before you go any further,' I says to Barrowclough. 'Before you go any further, let me make it quite clear that I turned to crime 'cause I fancied it, didn't I?'

'Did you?' he said, quite taken aback.

'Certainly. When I left school I went around to the local labour exchange and appraised the professional opportunities open to me. Now unfortunately my lack of schoolistic achievements prevented me from doing the things I really wanted to, like being a stockbroker or teaching tennis in a girls' school, and I found nothing really exciting about hosing down the local brewers' horses nor working in a cardboard-box factory. So I robbed this sub-post office on the North Circular. I thought, if I can't get in that girls' school, I might get the job as bathhouse cleaner in Holloway if ever I have the unfortunate experience to get caught by the local fuzz.'

'And you've never looked back since, so to speak?' he asked.

'No, nor have I been short of postage stamps.'

'You may find yourself changing at Slade Prison. We're quite modern, you see. Not the buildings but the attitude, so to speak. The Governor, Mr Venables, he's only been there two years, but in that time he's really instituted some amazing occupational and recreational facilities.'

'Like what?' I said, vaguely interested just in case it came in handy at some later stage.

'Well, you could come out as an intermediate welder, or an accomplished trombone player.'

'Oh yes,' I says, my voice brimming with apathy. 'Bird's bird though, in' it.'

'I'm a bit of an amateur botanist myself. Sometimes I take some of the prisoners out on the fells to explore the natural phenomena of our countryside.'

'Out on the fells?'

'Yes, lovely views.'

'I might put down for that. That might interest me. Natural phenomena of our countryside . . . How far's the nearest railway station?'

'Oh that's the beauty of it, you see, we're miles from anywhere. Pity you're not in longer,' he goes on. 'You could take up civil engineering or become a master builder.'

'Oh pity.' Hoping to knock him over with my sensitivity. 'Yes, that is a pity. If I had've known I'd have asked old Judge Fraser for a ten stretch, then I could have taken my welding finals or been a doctor of biology. Come to think of it, that would have been interesting. The biology bit I mean. Imagine all that research!'

'I'm just saying that Mr Venables' approach is based on sympathy and understanding and not correction and punishment alone.'

Oh gawd, I thought. That's the worst kind. Never know where you are with that type. Next thing, we'll have the screws having a vote of no confidence in the Governor.

'Leave it off, mate,' I says. 'I sees through all that Home Office cobblers, all part of the new technique to turn us into zombies and non-thinking individuals. Then when they kick us out into the brave new world, we'll all be like clockwork orange characters. Spending the rest of our lives playing the trombone or happily welding away at new prisons. No, I don't want none of that.'

The moment I finished that little speech I felt as though I'd kicked a spaniel, you know, all sad eyes and long ears. Then the door opened and some air of normality returned.

'I forgot if you take milk or sugar or not but it doesn't matter, 'cos I spilt most of yours battling with the swaying of the locomotive,' he says to me.

He hands Barrowclough his tea and gives me a quarter-full cardboard cup.

'Where's all that sympathy and understanding?' I says indignantly. 'I bet he'd bring back the birch at the drop of a ball and chain. Typical candidate for the post of Secretary to the Lord Chief Justice Goddard Appreciation Society.'

He surprised me, he took that one well. He leaned forward and I soon could sense that he'd had a couple of quick whiskies at the bar.

'Just keep your nose clean, Fletcher. Show me a little respect and I'll treat you all right. Right? I'm hard but fair.'

'Like Leeds United?'

'If you like. You play ball with me, and I'll play ball with you, and you'll find me a reasonable man.'

'Could I have a shufty at your *Penthouse* then?'

'Could you hell.'

You've got to admire consistency. Least I knew where I was with that one. I dozed off and when I awoke we were on the outskirts of Stoke. The train was motionless.

I had time to study the town as we were there for about twenty minutes. They fed me just outside of Preston. Now there's an awful town to get lumbered in, they still talk about Tom Finney as though he were God. Come to think of it, he wasn't bad. The food? One of those plastic sandwiches with orange plastic filling allegedly called cheese. Several more trips were made to the buffet by old MacKay. The smell got stronger each trip.

By the time we got to Carlisle it had just gone two o'clock. So they bung the cuffs back on. Me to Barrowclough. Then MacKay slung a raincoat over the cuffs. This was to hide the fact that we were in fact prisoner and escort. Mind you, the sight of two middle-aged men linking arm and arm is guaranteed to attract anyone's attention. They were wearing sports jackets and flat hats. They thought they looked like two gentlemen out for a day's racing. To me they looked like two screws escorting a prisoner from Brixton to Slade Prison. We walked to the car park and there it was, the unobtrusive-looking green prison van, tarted up to look like a mini-bus. It was set apart from the rest of the cars. There was a bitter wind blowing and stretching my legs made the wind go straight to my bladder. So just as we were about to get into the van I asked, quite politely, if I could have a slash.

'You should have thought of that earlier,' said MacKay.

'How far is it to the nick?' I said.

'About an hour and a half across the Fells.'

'I'll never make it.'

'God Almighty.'

Amazing how often he calls to the Almighty for help. The other one butts in.

'You'd better let him go. We can't stop in transit.'

Reluctantly MacKay agrees. He takes off the cuffs first and then points to the far side of the bus.

'What, out here? Why can't I go inside like any other human being?'

'Because I say you do it out here, that's why.'

Well, orders is orders. Round I nip to the back, old eagle-eye MacKay watching my every move. My hand moves to the zip of my fly, and I look up. MacKay turns away in embarrassment. As he does I notice, at crotch level, the petrol cap. I swear that I had no plans at all when I asked to go for a slash. I have asked myself on many occasions why I did it and the answer is always the same. Because it was there. About two inches away. Had it been locked of course . . . But it wasn't.

We all climbed into the bus, and off we went out of town over the moors. Quite beautiful, if you like heather, peat and wind-swept barren moors. Which I don't. Totally uncivilised.

Roads in Britain are classified as A, B and others. We were on one of the others. Not a building in sight. Then the engine coughs.

I looks at Barrowclough, he looked at me. We both looked at MacKay. Who in turn looked uncomfortable.

'What do you think it is, Mr MacKay?' I said in all innocence.

He got out of the van and lifted up the bonnet.

'Is it plugs?' says Barrowclough.

'How the hell should I know, I'm a Senior Prison Officer not a bloody mechanic.'

'Sounds like the big end's gone,' I says.

'Put the cuffs on him, Mr Barrowclough.'

Barrowclough starts to comply with the order.

'Don't think that fate has given you a chance to have it on your toes over the Fells, Fletcher. I've got my eye on you, laddy.'

He got back into the bus and tried the starter.

'I don't believe in fate.' By now the starter was making horrible noises.

'I think it sounds like the carburettor,' says Barrowclough, helpful like.

'Why don't we catch the bus then?' I said.

'Don't be stupid, man, there are no buses out here,' said MacKay.

'Hitch a lift then.'

'Fletcher, for your information no one drives around here, this place is like Outer Mongolia, no petrol stations, no tea shops or good pull-ins for drivers, and the mail still gets delivered by pony express.'

'Mr MacKay's right, you know, Fletcher. Two hikers died last year of exposure. It's getting a bit cold.'

I thought it was time I stuck my oar in again. 'Getting dark, too.'

'God Almighty!'

'Don't you know how to fix it?' I said. 'Hasn't your training as a Principal Prison Officer taught you how to cope with any situation?'

'It is getting dark,' said Barrowclough. By now, the darkness was creeping up on us fast. I could imagine all the locals, if there were any for miles, calling in the pigs and having a last look at the Bible.

'They forecast snow too.'

'Pull yourself together, Mr Barrowclough. Look, there's only one thing for it, one of us has to go for assistance.'

'Right,' I said.

With that I tried to make my way to the door, but the lure of the handcuffs was stronger than my arm.

MacKay pulled himself up to his puny five foot eight and said, 'Now listen to me, Fletcher. You do not move. You stay there. And you Mr Barrowclough, do not, I repeat, do not take the cuffs off him. Right?'

'Right, Mr MacKay,' said Barrowclough.

'Right Bwana.'

'Fletcher, I'm warning you.'

The hero made off down the road. We could see him disappear like Doctor Livingstone with a touch of the piles into the damp misty darkness. It was a bit parky and I was beginning to have doubts whether my piddling little encounter with the petrol cap was in fact a good idea.

'Fletcher, do you think if we put my coat over our knees it would help to keep us warm?'

'As long as you keep your hand to yourself.'

'Fletcher!'

'No, Mr Barrowclough, I was only joking, I mean, you have to put one hand under, don't you?' I held up the hand that was cuffed to his, raising his hand at the same time.

'Oh, sorry.' Right now I wished that I was locked up in my warm cell.

We sat there for some time. I tried flapping my arms across my chest but that wasn't too successful owing to the restraining umbilical cord between Mr Barrowclough and me.

'By the time they find us we'll be dead with exposure,' I said. 'Like Robert Taylor at the end of that picture.'

'What picture was that, Fletcher?'

'You remember. Western about buffalo hunting. In the deep frozen north. He had to spend the night out in the open. Summer clothing he wore, just like us. Up a tree he was, right up a tree.'

'Why was he up a tree?'

'Well, I expect he was avoiding the marauding buffalo, driven half-crazy by the extreme cold.'

I could see he was getting a belt of the jitters. Rub it in hard mate, I thought.

'Marauding buffalo?'

'Yes, driven half-crazy by the intense cold, much as we

will be in an hour or two. Ain't there no houses or farms near?'

He thought for a moment or two. I wasn't sure if he were trying to remember or make up his mind as to whether we could take the chance. The fear of MacKay was still predominant.

'There's a cottage not too far.'

'Well, let's go there then.'

'Mr MacKay said that we were not to move from the van.'

'Yeah, I know that but ...'

'But what?' he says.

'All right, we'll die in the van.'

He looked around as though he were looking for the marauding buffalo to appear. The night really was dark.

'It'll be locked up, they only use it in the summer.'

'So what,' I said. 'That's what we need, an empty house.'

'Yes, if it is empty, we could ... no, there is a problem.'

'Yes, what's that?' I said.

'It'll be locked up.'

Cor, what a nurk, what a twenty-two carat nurk. With a sigh of resignation I said, 'Mr Barrowclough,' I said.

'Yes?'

'I'm only a professional housebreaker, ain't I?'

'All right, Fletcher, but you must promise me that you will respect the trust I am about to place in you.'

'Mr Barrowclough,' says I with indignation, 'Mr Barrowclough, my old Borstal's motto was "Never let a mate down". Do you really think I'd do that?'

'Fletcher, you can't really claim that we are mates, can you?'

'Well, no, but in times of trouble comrades 'ave to stick with each other, don't they?'

'Yes. We'd better lock the van up.'

After locking the van we walked along the road. Because it was quite dark we found ourselves stumbling a lot. Mind you, I wasn't helping, I mean who wants to walk in the country with the cuffs on.

'Sorry,' I said as I helped him up. 'I think that we'd be better off if the cuffs were not on. I have given my word, Mr Barrowclough.'

'All right, Fletcher, but they have to go back on when we get to the cottage.'

After walking about two miles we eventually came to the cottage. I could just make out the name as we went up to the door. Dunromin.

Now there was an omen.

'How do we get in?' he said.

'Got any celluloid on you? No, don't suppose you have. Still, never mind. I can always ring up the local locksmith.'

'Fletcher,' he said as he shivered. 'You said you could open that door!'

'Course I can, just wanted to keep your spirits up. Right?' I said, as I stood back and looked at the lock like one of them geezers on the telly, you know, them who open any lock with an 'airpin. 'Right, you stay here and keep watch while I go around the back.' It was all coming back, just like the old days when I was at the housebreaking game.

'Fletcher!'

'Mr Barrowclough, I promised.'

I left him there looking like a virgin going to Hampstead Heath for the first time. The back was the same as most cottage rears, and sure enough I found the back door key under the mat. They never learn, do they? I opened the door, but before I opened the front door I had a quick butchers in the dim light around the cottage. I found two packets of cigarettes and a bottle of whisky. Shoving the fags in my pocket I took two large gulps of whisky. God, it was like virgin's water. Quickly taking another slurp I went to the front door. As I did I could hear Barrowclough calling.

'Fletcher, Fletcher, are you there? Are you all right? Come on, Fletcher, answer me. If you don't I'll, I'll, I'll blow my whistle.'

'Mr Barrowclough,' I said as I opened the front door, 'I thought we'd made a pact?'

'What took you so long?' he replied.

'Well, they have one of the new Sturmey-Archer anti-burglar locks on the door. Very difficult they are too. I'm the only man who has mastered them so far. Although I think there is someone in America who can open them. Certainly no one over here, though.'

'You amaze me, Fletcher,' he said as he entered the small living-room.

'Right, you sit down and I'll rustle up some tea, you'd like a cup of tea, wouldn't you?' With that I went into the kitchen. Not bad. In the neon strip-lighting I was faced with a split-level cooker and all the other trappings that go with a modern kitchen. I opened the cupboard in front of me and there staring at me were tins and tins of food. At least I was going to have a good meal before I got to Slade Nick. I rustled up some scotch broth, opened a tin of jellied turkey, and made a pot of tea.

Barrowclough was sitting staring into space as I entered.

'Fletcher, what have you got there?' he asked.

'What's it look like? Scotch mist? Well, you're nearly right, it's scotch broth.'

'Are you sure that we should be eating their food?'

'What the eye doesn't see!'

'It's very good,' he said as he started to get stuck into the soup. 'Quite like the food in the officers' mess at the prison.'

'Really? You mean they've already got a good cook?'

'Well, he did take some lessons when he was at Dartmoor. You see, Fletcher, there are opportunities if you take them.'

'Yeah, we've been through all that already, haven't we? I mean, only nurks fall for all that cobblers. Here, have a drink.'

I hands him the bottle of whisky I'd found.

'I don't drink. What is it?'

'I'm not sure.'

He takes the bottle, opens the top and has a sniff.

'It's scotch. Oh no, I couldn't. Anyway, I'm on duty.'

'It's medicinal,' I says. 'Help to revive us. Take the chill out of our numbed bodies.'

He looked at me with that sad spaniel look he had.

'Where did you get it?'

'It was in the first aid box.'

'You stole it!'

'I didn't, I told you it was in the first aid box.' With that I took it out of his hand and took a long pull of it. He looked at me.

'Is whisky medicinal?'

'Yes. I always feel a lot better after I've had a few.'

With that I poured a large tot into his teacup.

Suddenly all hell broke loose, well, in the peace and coldness of the night it seemed like a cacophony of bells. In fact it was a clock striking. We counted the chimes.

'Hey, it's twelve o'clock. Happy New Year, Mr Barrowclough.'

'Is it?' he said. 'All the best then.'

I leaned back on the soft settee.

'Like the Defiant Ones, ain't it?'

'I beg your pardon, Fletcher?'

'You know, that picture. The Defiant Ones, 'bout these two cons on the run, one was black and the other white.

Fact, if you had a bit of black blood in you, 'stead of all the Polish rubbish you've got, you could have played Sidney Poitier to my Tony Curtis.'

'We have a cinema club at the prison. Only last Thursday we showed Irrigation in the Gobi Desert. On the same bill with Rotational Farming.'

'Standing room only, was it?' I said.

'No, we didn't have much of a turn out that night.'

'I'm amazed.'

He leaned across and poured himself a large cup of whisky.

'My wife likes the pictures. But we don't go much these days.'

'No wonder, Mr Barrowclough – it's so blooming remote. Stuck right out in the middle of Cumberland, where you going to find a cinema? I should think it would be impossible to find an AA box.'

'That's the trouble.'

'What, that you can't find an AA box?'

'No, it's my wife. She feels very bad about being deprived of the excitement and amenities that a city can offer. She's always terribly unsettled every time we come back from our monthly day-trip to Workington.'

'Oh yes,' I said. 'I can see how the lights of Workington would turn a young girl's head.'

'How do you mean?' he said, as I leant across and filled his cup again with the whisky.

'Well, come on, mate. Surely you, as one of life's intelligencier, will appreciate that the amenities in Workington ain't up to scratch. They ain't got no christianity up there yet, so you can't even go to a church function, not even for tea.'

'Different for you Londoners. My wife's always wanted to be gay and cosmopolitan. Should have put in for a posting to Wandsworth or Brixton.'

'No, if you was going to Brixton, mate, you'd have to be Sidney Poitier.'

'Too late now,' he said as he leaned back and finished off the cup of whisky.

Hallo, I thought, hallo. 'So er, your old lady, she er feels . . . deprived, eh?' His eyes were beginning to close.

'She sees a future of frustrated ambitions stretching before her. She doesn't like what I do, or where we live. So over the years she's grown bitter and unsettled, full of restless urges. Which have manifested themselves in various ways, like a bad temper, spots and sleeping with the postman.'

'Huh!'

'And there were liasons with other men. We started rowing all the time. Things went from bad to worse. Eventually she went to a Marriage Guidance Counsellor.'

'That help, did it?'

'It helped her. She ran off with him.'

Poor old sod, typical of the underdog type of screw. Conned into becoming a prison officer by the lure of the word Officer, imagining smart uniforms and a posting to the glamorous Head Office, then promotion to Governor in two years. When all they ever do is supervise slopping out, and if they're lucky get to count the stitches on a mailbag.

'Well,' I said, 'you're well out of it, aren't you, mate? You're well out of a slag like that.'

'She came back.'

'Oh, I see. Well, people do change, the leopard an' all that.'

I could see that the drink was having its desired effect. He leaned further back and put his feet up on the coffee table. 'I blame myself really. I'm a failure. I'm only hanging on to my job by the skin of my teeth. I get so depressed. I even contemplated taking advantage of the prison psychiatric unit.'

'Aw come on, leave it out. Look, mate, I don't know you very well. But I can tell that you're a man of kindness, compassion and humanity. Now listen to me, mate. You can't buy things like that, can you? Would you swop them for a colour telly and a penthouse in Workington? Course you wouldn't.'

'I suppose not.'

I got up and walked over to him. 'Here, have this cushion for your head. You can't go through life thinking that you should have been something else. You're doing the job you've always wanted to do. You have to say to yourself, this is what I am. I am what I am. Then, when it's all over you can look at God straight in the eyes and say, I done it my way.'

'I done it my way,' he mumbled.

'Confidence in yourself,' I said.

'Confidence.'

'Trust your own judgment and initiative.'

'Initiative.'

'Here, why don't you get some kip?'

'D'you know, I've never talked to anyone before – never really talked.'

'Yeah, yeah, why don't you try and get some kip, mate?'

'That's a good idea, but I'll have to put the cuffs back on.'

'What!'

'It's the rules, Fletcher. Our lives are bounded by rules.'

'Yes I know, but what about the judgment and initiative. Are you going to do it their way, or are you going to do it your way. Confidence in yourself.'

'You know, you're right. I am not going to replace the handcuffs because in doing so, I would be breaking the principles of Slade Prison and my own, in approaching those placed in our care with sympathy and understanding.'

I couldn't believe my ears . . . Hold on, there was more to come.

'Fletcher, you are a criminal, habitual and hereditary. But until we show you trust, how can we expect you to understand what trust is.'

'Oh yes. That is irrefutably true, Mr Barrowclough. What more can I say?'

'Made me quite sleepy that whisky has.'

'Another good reason for having a kip, Mr Barrowclough. I mean, we couldn't have had a kip with the cuffs on, could we?' I said. 'Be like Babes in the flaming wood.'

'I can hardly keep my eyes open. You will respect the trust I've placed in you?'

'That's it, you close your old mince pies, my old mate.'

'Right,' I said to myself. 'Right. As soon as the silly nurk has gone to the land of bo-peep I'll be on my toes. Back to the bright lights and gaiety of Muswell Hill.'

'Fletcher?'

'Yes, Mr Barrowclough?'

'You know, I do hope that you join in my botany class.'

'I'll give it serious consideration, squire.'

'I feel a better man for tonight, I don't feel a failure. I feel that for the first time since I've been at Slade I've been allowed to use my own judgment. And I'm right.'

'Right?' I said.

'Right about you, Fletcher.' With that he starts to snore like a pig, and a great big one at that.

'Mr Barrowclough?' I had a hard look at him. 'Mr Barrowclough.' This time I whispered it. No reply. He definitely was in the land of nod. London here we come. I got up from the settee, very quietly so as not to disturb him.

That night was going to be one I'd remember for the

rest of my life. I started running as soon as I left the cottage. Up hill and down dale, as my wife's great uncle once said to his housemaster at Eton, when asked how he'd managed to get there.

Over flaming fields. And through farmyards. Eventually I came to make my way to what appeared to be a main road. Soon I'd find a telephone box, then I would reverse the jolly old charge to London and the good wife would organise the rest of the well-planned and well-carried-out 'escape plot'. I'd be able to drink for free in the local for the next six months on the strength of this escape. I must have walked for about six miles along that road without a telephone box in sight, nor for that matter a house or any sign of civilisation.

Eventually, I saw a small cottage surrounded by a low wall. I couldn't see any sign of a telephone cable leading to the cottage but at least it would keep me off the road, and seeing that it was quite light by now, I knew that old Barrowclough would be waking. I could picture the look on his face when he found me gone. All part of life's ups and downs. Divide and rule, them were the rules of the game.

I approached the cottage in the prescribed manner. Walk, stop, look, listen. No sign of life, and thank God no bloody dogs. One thing I can't stand is dogs when out trying to do an honest night's thieving.

I made my way to the back door. Hallo, some nurk has forgotten to lock it. I opened the door and crept in. The curtains were still pulled in the kitchen and it was still dark inside. I moved to the door leading off the kitchen. Then I heard it. Someone was up already. Having successfully escaped, no one was going to take me back now. I picked up a large saucepan and hid behind the door. Suddenly the door opened.

'Fletcher, are you out here?'

There was nothing else I could do except drop the saucepan.

'Mr Barrowclough!' I said.

'What a shock you gave me, Fletcher. What are you doing out here?'

'That's what I'd like to know,' I said.

'What were you doing with that saucepan?'

'Milk, er, yes, that's it, milk. I thought I'd try and get some milk, thought I might find a stray cow floating around.'

'You look terrible,' he said. 'As if you'd been up all night.'

'True, true, I couldn't sleep, could I?'

'That was a very nice thought, Fletcher, thinking of getting some milk. But you shouldn't have done it.'

'You're right,' I said.

'You could have got lost. People are always getting lost out here on the Fells. Wander around in circles they do.'

'Do they?'

Well, to cut a long story short, we walked back to the van. I suppose we'd been there about ten minutes when old Rob Roy himself turned up. The journey to Slade took us about an hour and MacKay didn't say a word all the time, just kept giving me funny looks.

Eventually we arrived at Slade Prison. God Almighty! Now I knew why MacKay used that term all the time. The sight of the nick was enough to make anyone call for help.

So, as I said, here I am sitting in my cell, contemplating the thrill of slopping out. Then the door opens.

'So, whose good behaviour has made him the Governor's blue-eyed boy?'

'I must be the first man to have got remission before he even got to a nick.'

'Don't give me any of that officious lip, Fletcher,' he says as he jerks his chin out. 'I know that you were trying to pull something last night.'

'On what do you base that supposition, Mr MacKay?'

'On the evidence of the motor mechanic.'

'Oh yes,' I say. 'How's that?'

'It appears that the petrol tank had more in it at the end of the journey than before . . .'

'Good God,' I reply. 'Good God.'

'And for your information, it certainly was not 5-Star. Now I'm going to watch you all of the time. Like a hawk. No one, I repeat no one, goes over the wall from this prison.'

'No, Mr McKay, no one takes the petrol out of you.' With that he exits strutting like a turkey.

New Faces, Old Hands

I remember one guy writing that a 'prison cell was like a hole in the wall, like an optical illusion. A place where men die and men are born, but that it always takes something away from you, mostly that which is good.' I think he had something there. Anyway – here I am waiting for the Reception Board. You know, the dehumanising bit that we all go through.

I had thought of asking to see the Prison Governor and telling him all about last night. 'Sir, any naughty thoughts that I'd had about escaping were quickly dispelled by the cool authority of Officer Barrowclough. A man to whom I later owed my life, owing to the fact that he forced me, against my will, to leave the vehicle and take shelter against the cruel elements, supporting and half-carrying my exhausted body across several miles of rough terrain.' But that would have been pure cobblers so I gave it a miss.

The three of us were sitting there in the Reception waiting for the doctor. Three? Well, there was Heslop, Cyril, aged 42. Three years robbery, third time he's been in the nick. Thick as two short planks, about to become Slade's number one nurk. The next was Godber, Leonard Arthur, aged 23. First offender, two years for housebreaking. Seemed somewhat naïve. But a nice looking boy. Then there's me. Fletcher, Norman Stanley, aged 42. Five years, you already know what for.

Suddenly as the door opened we heard that voice.

'What a beautiful day.' In entered MacKay. 'For the time of year, quite astonishing. Beautiful day.'

'Oh lovely,' I said. 'Perhaps later on we can all go out for a cycle ride?'

He walked across to where we were sitting.

'Stand up.'

We stood in a line.

'Know what they say about New Year's day? What you do on the first day of the year, you do all the year round. In the case of you three gentlemen that's perfectly true. You laddie, you, Mr Godber, first time in, isn't it? You must be wondering what an average day inside is like. Tell him, Mr Fletcher.'

'Exactly like the day before, Mr MacKay.'

'The voice of experience. Now tell him how the average day begins, Fletcher.'

Hallo, I thought, the mister bit has gone already. 'Begins at seven. You'll be woken by a persistent and deafening bell. Then the screws will come around . . .'

That was too much for MacKay. His neck went in and out double time. 'I beg your pardon !'

'Sorry, Mr MacKay. The Prison Officers will come around, offering such encouragements as "Wakey, wakey, get your socks on, move, you 'orrible creatures." We shall respond to this badinage with such gems as, "Good Morning, Sir", "Good Lord, is that the time?" or "Who's been sleeping with your old woman while you've been on night duty?" '

To which he replied, 'Very comical, Fletcher. Eight o'clock slop out. Eight ten, breakfast. Eight fifteen, return to cells. Nine o'clock, yes, Fletcher?'

'Slop out again, Mr MacKay, followed by work until eleven fifteen when we . . .'

'Exercise.'

Quickly heating up to being the centre of attraction he went on, 'Walking in pairs, five yards apart, no con-

36

versing with the man in front or behind. This is followed by the highlight of the day. Heslop, what is that?'

Oh, my gawd, I thought, here we go.

'Huh?' muttered Heslop.

'You've been inside before, Heslop, what is the highlight of the day?'

He stood there, bald head, you could see his brain trying to cope with the question.

'Er . . . visiting hours?'

This was too much for MacKay.

'We're in Cumberland, man! A barren, windswept fell north of the Pennines. We are two weeks from Euston! When you see your loved ones it will be the highlight of the year.'

I turned to young Godber. 'Glad you came?' He looked lost.

'Fletcher, you tell us what the highlight of the day is.'

'Highlight of the day, sir? Dinner.'

'Which is,' he said.

'Nourishing,' I replied.

'Nourishing it is not,' said MacKay.

'Can't wait,' says I.

'Midday, bang up,' said MacKay.

Straight away Godber rises to the occasion.

'Bang up?'

'Not what you think, laddie, bang up means back to your cell. Thirteen hundred, slop out. Work, tea, evening association, which means in principle that you can follow a wide range of recreational activities. Which in practice means television and ping-pong.'

'Telly?' said Heslop.

'Yeah,' I replied. 'But only until seven. That means News and kids' stuff. So if you're a devotee of "Z cars", my old son, forget it. You'll have to get your kicks from the Wombles of bleedin' Wimbledon.'

'Seven thirty, slop out, supper. Seven forty-five, lights out. Any questions?'

'Any point?' I said.

'None whatsoever. At ease,' said MacKay as he went over to the reception desk.

Young Lenny Godber looked at MacKay in disbelief.

'So this is Colditz?' he said, in a doleful Birmingham voice.

'Colditz! You've gotta be joking. Compared with this place, Colditz was a doddle,' I said. 'Load of public school-boys playing leap-frog and digging tunnels. This is a nick this is. We spend our days slopping out and sewing mail-bags. And by seven forty-five our lights are out. Here, all you do is think about it, get frustrated and then go to sleep. In Colditz when the lights went out they started brewing cocoa and having pillow fights. No, my old cocker, this is doing porridge, I promise.'

Poor old Godber, you could see the look of despair on his face. He took a packet of cigarettes out of his pocket and put one in his mouth. MacKay looked up and said :

'Godber, who said you could smoke? Did I say you could smoke?'

'Don't think he wants you to smoke,' I said as I took the fag from his mouth and put it in my pocket.

'I was trying to give 'em up anyway,' he replied.

'Good, I'll help you,' I said.

The door opened and in walked Mr Barrowclough.

'I'm leaving you with Mr Barrowclough,' said Mac-Kay. 'Oh, one more thing. Nice to have you with us.' And he left the reception.

'My wife was coming next week.'

'What?' I said. 'Who said that?'

'Me,' said Heslop. 'He says once a year. My wife was coming next week. Wrote to me, she did. Staying overnight with her cousin in Barrow-in-Furness. It's not fair. Not fair that she might have to stay there indefinitely.'

'Not fair for anyone to have to stay in Barrow-in-Furness,' I said.

'Heslop!' said Barrowclough.

'Who?' said Heslop.

'Will you kindly step up here?' Heslop walked over to the reception desk where Mr Barrowclough was sitting.

'Christian name, please.'

'Cyril.'

'Date of birth?'

'April 1st, 1933.'

'That figures,' I said as we all looked at him.

'What's happening now?' said Godber.

'We're about to be dehumanised. First they take away our names and give us a number. Then they give us a medical check-up, and we 'ave a bath in six inches of luke-warm water. Watch out for the bath-house cleaners though.'

'Why?' he asked.

'Lot of trustee poofs work in the bath-house, don't they,' I said as I walked over to the bench and sat down. Godber followed.

'You know all the form, don't you?' he said as he sat beside me. 'Been here before?'

'Not here,' I said. 'They're all the same though, ain't they? Porridge is porridge.'

'First time for me. Don't know how I'll get through it.'

'Cheer up,' I said. 'Could be worse. State this country's in, could be free. Think about it. Out there with no work, a crumbling economy and inflation pricing us honest thieves out of business. Christ, what would you do if you were out there now? Go to bed and increase the population.'

'Won't be doing that for a while, will I?' he said.

'Oh, no, course not. Tasteless joke. Shouldn't have said it.'

He looked down at the floor.

'I'm going to feel ever so deprived. I had this fiancée, Denise, she was very active in that direction.'

'Oh,' I said. 'You'll have to drink a lot of tea, won't you?'

'What good's tea going to do me?'

'It's what they put in it,' I said.

'Oh yes?' he replied.

'Yes,' I said. 'Something that will moderate your desires for Denise.'

'But I don't drink tea!'

'You are in trouble. Come to think of it, so's the bloke you share a cell with.'

'I'll have to throw myself into my mailbags, won't I?'

'Depends. Word of advice, son. What you tell 'em today can decide how tolerable your life in this nick is going to be. I mean, if you want to work somewhere cushy and warm, like the kitchens or the library or get the job as tea-boy in the main offices, then you've got to invent yourself a new career.'

I could see that Heslop was just about finished with Barrowclough so I thought I'd show young Godber a thing or two.

'All right, let's have one of you,' he said.

'Me, Mr Barrowclough.' I went to the desk.

'It's Fletcher, of course, isn't it?'

'Yes, that's right, Mr Barrowclough.'

'Christian names?'

'Norman Stanley.'

'Date of birth?'

'2.2.32.'

'Next of kin?'

'My beloved Isobel. The little woman. Well, she ain't

40

so little. I said to her just before I surrendered to my bail, I said to her, Isobel, I said. I'll never get over you, I'll have to get up and go round.'

'Address?'

'107 Alexander Park Crescent, London N5.'

'Occupation?'

'Librarian during the day.'

'During the day?'

'Yeah, at night I was a chef. Library or the kitchen, I don't mind,' I said as I looked at young Godber. Honestly, I don't know what's coming to the younger element, they don't seem prepared to learn. There he was reading the prison rule book. I mean what's he going to learn from that?

Anyway, we were processed and bathed, them's their terms. And we sat waiting for the medical officer to arrive. I honestly don't know where they dig their medics from. Most of them are alcoholics or skiing fanatics, always going off breaking a leg somewhere. I thought I'd put Godber in the picture a little bit more.

'Look, I meant to tell you, when the doctor comes in, tell him that you've got dodgy plates.'

'What do you mean?' he said.

'Plates of meat, feet. Tell him that they're sweaty or something, then you might get to wear your brothel creepers. Otherwise you'll have to wear the prison issue shoes. Guarantee you bad feet for the rest of your life, they will.'

'Oh, I see,' he said.

That stupid nurk Heslop started to laugh.

'Look, mate, I'm not joking. Perfectly true, you'll see.'

'I don't mean that. I mean your wife. That's funny about your wife. You know, what you said about her being a big woman and you having to get up and go round her.'

'Gawd help us. Take no notice, Godber. Just you remember what I've said about your feet. By the way, what religion are you?'

'C of E, I suppose,' he said.

'That's no good. You get no perks with C of E. What you have to do is think of a nice new one, like Sikh. Now if you was a Sikh you could grow your hair long. Or if you was a Muslim you could have special grub sent in by your loved ones.'

'I don't like Chinese food,' said Godber.

'Muslim ain't Chinese,' I replied.

'Well, what is it?' he asked.

'What? Well, er, it's, it's more erotic than the rubbish they serve up here.'

'Don't you mean exotic? The other means sex.'

'Godber,' I said. 'Godber, that's the trouble with you, you've got sex on the brain. I tell you, you'll have to drink more tea. Now, where was I? Oh yes, it's gotta be better than the filth they eat here otherwise the Muslims wouldn't eat it would they, stands to reason. Or you could say that you were Jewish. Yeah, say that you were Jewish. No, come to think of it you couldn't, could you? Doctor will be here in half a moment and he'd spot the evidence.'

'Evidence?' said Godber. 'What evidence?'

'Well,' I said, 'with Jews it's circumstantial. They been circumstanted.'

The door opened again and in walked this skinny runt with a dirty white coat on. He looked like he worked in the meat market. He was coughing all over the place.

'Tropical fish,' he said.

'Pardon?' I replies.

'Nothing, I'm the medical officer.'

I looked at the others. 'That's reassuring, in'it.'

'Now look,' he said. 'I have to give you men a stringent medical. It's important that we ascertain your medical history and state of health.' He proceeded to cough his guts out. 'Right, Fletcher, you're first.'

I limped forward to where the doctor stood. The conversation after that proceeded at a fast pace.

'Have you ever had crabs?' he said.

'No, I don't eat fish.'

'Lice?'

'No.'

'VD?'

'Not so's you'd notice.'

'Suffer from any illness?'

'Bad feet.'

'Paid a recent visit to a doctor?'

'Only for my bad feet.'

'Are you now or have you been at any time a practising homosexual?'

'What, with these feet!'

'Right, you're A1.'

With that he stamps my record with the appropriate stamp.

'A1? Hang on, mate. What about my bad feet? I can hardly walk.'

'Soak them in hot soapy water.'

'What?' I said.

'Look, Fletcher, everyone's trying to pull something in this prison, lying about their feet or their teeth or eyesight. Do you know they even eat light bulbs and razor blades? On top of all the crap I have to take from you I've got a Governor that's got fin rot.'

'Got wot rot?' I says.

'Fish, tropical bloody fish, they've got fin rot.'

'Oh,' I says. 'Interest of the Governor's is it?'

'Yes, Fletcher,' he replies. 'It's an obsession. That and pigs.'

'Pigs?'

'He's started a prison farm to indulge his interest in livestock. Only it's the rest of us who have to look after it. His pigs and his fish and his favourite Jersey cow. I'm a man of medicine not a flaming vet.' He started to pull boxes out of his bag. 'Half the pills in this bag are for his animals. A prisoner came in here yesterday for earache and I gave him pills to dry up his milk. And now the Governor's four-eyed butterfly fish has got fin rot, and he wants me to isolate it.'

By now the poor old sod was in a right old two and eight. He took two tablets from a box, put them in his mouth, and rinsed them down with a glass of water.

'You must be rushed off your feet, doc,' I said.

'I can't cope, man.'

'Good job they ain't bad feet like mine.'

'Look, Fletcher, you're A1, I told you so, all right? Now you see that specimen jar over there?' He points to three specimen jars lined up on the table the other side of the room. 'Well, I want you to fill one of them up.'

'What, from here?'

'Behind the screen, man. Now where's Heslop?'

I walked over to the screen. As I did Godber said, 'You didn't pull that one off, did you, Fletch?'

Stupid brummy nurk. 'What did you say?'

'Prison shoes for you, eh?'

'All right, sonny, win a few, lose a few. But my little chat might prove invaluable. Know something about our Governor, don't I? That's another priority for your first day in the nick. Know your Governor.'

'Here, Fletch,' he said, slightly taken aback. 'What's he mean, a practising homosexual?'

'One who hasn't quite got it right yet,' I said as I made my way behind the screen to fill up.

After the other two had been to see the doctor and we'd had our fingerprints taken we were taken to the kitchen to get our midday meal. I gave the kitchen a good suss out while we were there. I knew one or two of the faces that I saw, but didn't want to let on just yet, thought I'd save that for later. Typical prison meal, gritty spuds, thin slice of what the cook called meat, soup that was like old socks and a mug of tea. By the time we had got to the dining-room all the other cons had gone back to work, so we sat down on our own with just old Barrowclough in attendance. He turned the telly on and sat and watched 'Listen with Mother'.

As soon as we were seated both Godber and Heslop started to get stuck into the food.

'Will we eat with everyone else tonight?' said Godber.

'Don't,' I said, picking out the tasty bits of food from the rubbish, 'don't be in too much of a hurry to get thrown in with the others. Nothing but a bunch of criminals they are. And don't eat too much of that stuff. Otherwise it'll ruin your palate for tonight's piss-de-resistance.'

'What will it be, Fletch?' said Heslop.

'Lumpy, lukewarm, grey and gritty. Told you to say you were a Muslim.'

'Sheep's eyes,' he said.

Both Godber and I looked at him with amazement.

'What Muslims eat. Figs. Desert. Wadis and things,' he continued.

'Oh, I see. Yeah, we all thank you, Lawrence of Arabia,' I said.

'Why didn't you put down as a Muslim then, Fletch?'

'I don't need to, do I? Going to be working in the kitchens, ain't I?'

'But they haven't allocated us jobs yet,' said Godber.

'Now listen, you see that screw sitting watching telly? Looks like Arthur Askey on stilts. He'll see me all right.'

'How come?'

'Brought me up from Brixton, didn't he. Stands to

reason when you're handcuffed to a screw for that long you develop a sort of rapport.'

'Suppose you must do, specially when you go to the lavatory.'

'Oh, Godber, I see that you've got a sense of humour. Come in handy during the grim nightmare of your next two years.'

'Will it be that bad?' he said.

'Listen, Godber, it's a waste of time talking to Heslop, but you, I think, will take heed of the advice I'm about to give you. The important thing is to remember who you once was. Keep a bit of that person intact up here. In the head. Don't get bitter, or militant, or even try and screw the system, 'cos it will only screw you. Just keep your nose clean, bide your time and do your porridge, do it on your pot as they say.'

He looked at Heslop then at Barrowclough.

'I'm only here due to unforeseen circumstances.'

'Which were?'

'I got caught.'

'Oh yes,' I said. 'I've had a few unfortunate tragedies like that myself.'

'It was my fiancée, Denise. She has this nice flat in a tower block in Smethwick. Well, it's her mum's, like. Very nice. Overlooks the M6. Anyway, I thought I'd get her some nice things for it. But I didn't want to carry the loot too far, so I did the flat next door. I knew he'd be away, like 'cos he's a long-distance lorry driver. He drives a juggernaut from West Bromwich to Brussels. Only thing was, he got a puncture outside Coventry and came back quick like.'

'What did he do? Report you to the police?' I said.

'Not before he kicked my head in.'

'Ramsgate.'

'I beg your pardon, Heslop?'

'Took the wife.'

'Took the wife **where, Mr Heslop?**'

'To see Lawrence of Arabia. It was raining, see. We couldn't go on the beach, could we? So I took her to the pictures to see Lawrence of Arabia.'

'Yes,' I said. 'Rains a lot in Ramsgate.'

'Rained the next day,' he replied.

'Told you it would,' I said.

'She'd seen the film on at the other cinema, so we come home. Though we did stop for a cup of tea at her sister's in Sidcup.'

'Here, Heslop. Why don't you put that on a postcard and send it to Tony Blackburn's magic moments?'

'Don't like him much, prefer Ronnie Corbett.'

I sat back and surveyed the field. What a right lot they were.

'Tell you what,' I said. 'Tell you what, I shall miss the cut and thrust of your intellectual conversation.'

'Why, Fletch?' said Godber.

'Well, not sharing a cell with you.'

'How come?' he said.

'Well, I'm having a single cell, ain't I? I like my privacy. I prefers to be alone, see. Don't like sharing really. Don't like dominoes, chess, cribbage, ludo or other people's sweaty feet.'

'I prefer a single cell myself. I'd really like to take the opportunity of this enforced confinement to study.'

'Study, Godber?' I said.

'Yes, I've had an education. I've got an O level in geography.'

'Oh that'll come in handy that will. I can see you now. The escape committee will be calling for your assistance all the time. I mean, they're bound to need you, 'cause you'll help them find the way to Carlisle station.'

'Fletch, you should have tried it, you know. It's very interesting is geography, very educational.'

'Yeah,' I said. 'But it's not the sort of subject you can make a career out of, is it? No, the only reason people learn about geography is so that they can teach others about it. You tell me what's the use of knowing the capital of Siam, or what an isthumus is.'

Mr Barrowclough looked over to where we were sitting.

'Good lunch, lads?'

'Oh yes. Cordon Bleu, I'd say.'

'Yes, I think I'd agree with you, Fletcher. Still, mustn't interfere with your meal,' he said as he turned back to the telly.

'Now where was I?' I said. 'Oh yes, now in principle you could learn a trade in here. I mean you could come out with a diploma in, say, house decoration or shoe repairing. Or you might like to be a welder. That's a riveting profession.'

'What?' said Heslop.

'Riveting? No, don't matter, forget it.'

'Do you mean that I won't be able to learn a profession here, Fletch?'

'Course you can, oh yes. There are trades you can learn in here. For starters you could become an expert at how to open a safe, steal a car, forge a banknote. Oh yes, many's the trade you can learn. Bloke I was in Maidstone with, Charlie Mossop, first offender he was, by the time he come out he was a brilliant forger. But brilliant. And he only went in for reckless driving.'

'Do you know, Fletch,' said Godber, 'I really want to finish with this thieving game. I'm fed up with it. There's no profit in it really.'

'How old are you, son?' I was taken back by what he'd just said.

'Twenty-three.'

'Twenty-three and you want to turn it in? What sort of attitude is that? You're at the start of what could be a promising career. Think about it. Where did the train robbers start? Not at the top I can promise you, no, they went in right at the bottom. Then as they progressed, they became more what you might call adventurous. No, old son, you can't throw away the chance of a lifetime. I could teach you so much, how to nick only the best, how not to get caught...'

'How come you got caught?'

'Tragic misdirection of the jury by a biased judge.'

'What's an isthmus?' said Heslop.

'What's what? What is it now, Einstein?'

'What you said, an isthmus?'

I knew he was thick, you could tell by the shape of his head.

'An isthmus. Well, it's a thing ain't it. A thing in geography. A geographical expression.'

'It's a strip of land joining together two larger pieces of land,' said cocky Godber.

'Yeah, strip of land, right,' I said.

'There's something in education isn't there, Fletch?'

'Right, young Godber. True, very true. Hang about. I'm not saying don't put down for educational classes. Education, that's different. Current affairs, pottery, archaeology. I'll be putting down for some. Can't beat it. An hour every night in a warm classroom. With a bit of luck you might get a female teacher. Then, with a bit more luck, she might drop the chalk and wallop! There you are, a quick flash of a nylon-clad thigh. Oh yes, I've nothing against educational classes.'

By now we'd finished our meal. Young Lenny Godber took a packet of cigarettes out of his pocket and offered the packet to me and Heslop. We quickly took one each and put it in our pockets.

'Why'd you do that?' he asked.

'We're not being impolite, Lenny, my son. It's just that Heslop and me have been inside before, an' you see, inside, snout is like gold. You was mad to give us a fag.'

'But you took them.'

'Ah, yes, you gotta learn the hard way, haven't you? Learn not to be lavish, you're not Paul Getty! Should have just lit one and shared it.' And I lean over and takes his fag and has a puff before passing it to Heslop.

'Right, lads,' said Barrowclough, as he turned off the telly and walked over to where we were sitting. 'Drink up, lads.'

'What's next on the agenda, Mr Barrowclough?'

'You should know, Fletcher, all the time you've spent inside.'

'Oh yes,' I said. 'It's the Governor we see now.'

Lenny and Heslop collected up their trays and walked over to the sink to wash them. This gave me the chance I'd been waiting for.

'Did you get what I asked for, Mr Barrowclough?'

'Well, there isn't much in the library in the way of what you want. Just this booklet. *Know your Tropical Fish*.'

'Oh good, it's my hobby you see.'

'Do you know, Fletcher, by an extraordinary coincidence that's the Governor's hobby too.'

'Is it?' I said.

'Oh yes, he likes all animals. He's on the local RSPCA. Between ourselves though, I think he'd be much better off looking after a zoo than a prison.'

'True, but when you think about it, Mr Barrowclough, we're all caged animals, ain't we? Talking of cages, you will get me one on the south side on my own? I'm not a sharer really. I mean, the boy's all right, but his feet smell. And Heslop, well, you can't say that he's on my intellectual level, is he? Don't think he's on anybody's level really. If the Governor did open a zoo, Heslop'd be a big attraction.'

'Fletcher, you must understand that I'm a Prison Officer and you are a prisoner. You must recognise that relationship. I am not here to be coerced or cajoled into doing what you want, when you want it.'

'Mr Barrowclough, please. Would I ever? Here, give this a rinse out while I go and have a slash,' I said as I handed him my tray and mug.

Have you ever had to walk from one building to another with an ex-corporal from the last world war? Well, if you haven't it's an experience you should miss if you can. We had to go from the mess to the main office block. You can guess who took charge. Yes, that's right, Old Mac-Kay. There he was, three of us in single file.

'Right,' said MacKay. 'By the centre. Wait for it . . . By the centre. Quick . . . March!'

Christ, you could almost hear the drums and pipes playing.

'Left right left right left right. Keep up there, Heslop! Chin in, Fletcher. Nicely now. That's it, nice and smooth.'

What a state he looked. Come to think of it, what a state we all looked. There were cons all over the place, work parties going about their work. They all stopped and looked at us.

'Don't stand there, man,' shouted MacKay to one party of men as we went by. 'Move! Right. Party halt! Right turn! Mr Barrowclough,' he said as his neck jerked in and out, 'Mr Barrowclough. Take charge of the party while I ascertain as to whether the Governor is ready to interview the receptions.'

After we'd stood there for ten minutes or so, we were taken into the main office building.

'Fetch them in, Mr Barrowclough.'

We went into the Governor's office, and the three of us stood in line.

'Stand up straight in front of the Governor,' said MacKay. 'Heslop, Godber and Fletcher, SIR !'

'Thank you, Mr MacKay,' said Mr Venables the Governor. 'Now you men have been sent here for varying offences and varying terms of imprisonment. This is not a maximum security prison, you are in a "C" Class establishment. However, if any of you abuse the less stringent security measures we have here, you will quickly find that we will be on you like a ton of bricks.'

By now I had located the fish tank.

'Are you listening to me, Fletcher?' he said.

'Face the front !' shouted MacKay.

'I'm sorry Mr Venables, sir. I just couldn't help but notice your aquarium. It's an interest of mine, you see. Indoor fish, tropical fish.'

'Is it really?'

'All right, Fletcher, face the front,' butted in MacKay.

'I'm sorry, Mr MacKay. Sorry, Sir. I couldn't help but notice. But something is bothering me.'

'What's that?' said the Governor.

By now I was really into it. I leaned over so that I could see into the fish tank.

'Well, sir. This is only a first impression but . . . I think your four-eyed butterfly fish has got fin rot.'

That ended it. MacKay couldn't believe what was happening. The three of us went back to the wing. They put us all into a three cell until we'd been allocated jobs.

'Crafty old nurk aren't you, Fletch?'

'Hang about, young Godber. I'm finishing off the *Farmer's Weekly*. There's this marvellous article on Artificial Insemination that the Governor said I should read.'

'He fell for it, didn't he? He really believed that you had a deep interest in fish and livestock.'

'It ain't been a bad day all around. I told you this was the day that conditioned how tolerable your life'll become here. No, old son. Porridge is porridge.'

'I think he was impressed by my O level in geography.'

'Oh, I could see that, you'll probably work in the mailbags.'

'Why, Fletch?'

'Well, they'll need someone to understand all them foreign names they have to stencil on the air mailbags.'

The cell door opened and in walked Mr MacKay.

'All right, lads, on your feet. Exam results. It's been a full and exciting day, hasn't it? Right, Godber, you're first, here they are.' With that he hands young Godber a pair of civvy shoes. 'Courtesy of the Medical Officer.'

'How'd you work that?' I said.

'I told him that I had flat feet, didn't I?'

'Which he believed, Fletcher,' said MacKay. 'Young Godber still has a certain amount of credibility, unlike yourself. I'm afraid we're going to have to split this little threesome up. One of you's going to a sing.'

With that I started to pack my kit.

'Oh yes, only right, Mr MacKay,' I said.

'Not so fast, Fletcher.'

'Whot'yer mean?'

'Get your things together, Godber.'

'Godber! Him! A cell on his own?' I said.

'Yes, that's right, the Governor thought it would be more conducive to his studies.'

'Oh, that's lovely, I didn't fancy sharing. No offence, Fletch.'

'You didn't fancy sharing? What about me, you leave me here with the "Brain of Britain"!'

'There'll be three of you. Don't worry, Fletcher, we're moving Evans in here.'

'Evans,' I cried. 'That Welsh lunatic who eats light bulbs.'

'Only when he can't get razor blades,' said MacKay.

'Oh, wonderful. Just bloody wonderful. Can I have permission to grow a beard?'

'Right, now it's jobs. Godber ... Kitchen.'

Godber grinned. 'Oh that'll be nice. All warm and second helpings.'

'Heslop ... Library.'

'Library! Him! He's illiterate.'

'I read a book once,' said Heslop indignantly. 'It was green.'

'Look, Mr MacKay. Tell me, what's Godber got the kitchen for? God Almighty, he should be breaking rocks or something. He's gotta pay his dues. This is victimisation. Mr MacKay, sir, look, sir, I'm an old hand. I've been in before, you know me. I should have something befitting my seniority.'

'And you have, Fletcher, you have.'

'I have?'

'Oh yes, oh yes.'

'What?' I asked.

'Special duties.'

'Special duties, Mr MacKay? What special duties?'

'Who's the Governor's blue-eyed boy then?'

'Well,' I said. 'Well we did have a sort of rapport. Cemented by our common interest in all things bright and beautiful, all creatures great and small.'

'The Governor said you're just the man he's been waiting for.'

'What is it, Mr MacKay. Is it fish?'

'Well...' said MacKay.

'Fish?'

'Not quite, Fletcher, not quite.'

'What is it then, sir? Come on, tell me.'

'Pigs!' said MacKay with a smarmy smart look on his face.

'Pigs?' I said.

'Yes, pigs,' he answered.

'What about pigs?' I said.

'They're your pigs,' he said.

'My pigs?' I said. 'How are they my pigs?'

'Well, laddie, you showed such a great interest in livestock that the Governor thought you would be the ideal chap to look after the pig farm.'

'But I don't even like the taste of bacon.'

'You'll soon get used to it. Come on, man, time to collect your wellies. You'll need them in the pigsty.'

There I was the next morning up to my neck in . . . Well, there I was. 'Get out of the way, you great big brute.'

'Morning, Fletcher.'

'Morning, sir.'

'It always gives me great pleasure to place a man in a job which gives him real fulfilment.'

'Oh, yes, Mr Venables. Oh yes.'

'Oh, by the way. Have you finished that article in the *Farmer's Weekly* I gave you?'

'I'm afraid I didn't, sir. I would have done, only Evans ate it.'

The Hustler

Eventually my good work with the pigs impressed the Governor so much that he gave me more of the farm to look after. You could say that I was immersed in my work. Then on the other hand, you could say that I was up to my neck in it.

Anyway, Ives, a grotty little man of dubious parentage and an uncontrollable habit for gambling, had challenged me to an egg-laying competition. Not that I had to lay the eggs. Oh, no. Ives, maybe!

'Come on, come on. You can do it, my love!' said Ives to his choice of chicken.

'Come on, gel, come on, gel. Force it out!' I said to my chicken. 'Effort! Effort!' I looked at Ives – he was bent over his hen.

'Come on, my son,' he said.

'Hang about. It's a girl, you nurk. My son!'

'How'd you know, Fletcher?'

'Hens is all girls, ain't they?'

'Are they?' he said, in his stupid dim way.

'Course they are. All hens are females. Your male is your cock.'

'Oh, yes. 'Ere, listen, there's a hell of a lot more females than males.'

'Course there are, Swede head. That's why your cock always looks so smug. Always knows it's there. Hence the expression cocksure.'

With that subtle little bit of knowledge I'd implanted into his bonce we started back to encouraging our respective birds.

'Come on, gel. Force it out.'

'Mine's looking imminent,' said Ives.

So are you, I thought. 'Nodded off, she has,' I said.

' 'Ere, listen. Want to double the bet?'

'Certainly!' What a berk – he'd fall for the three-card trick.

'Right, done,' he said.

'You certainly have been.'

'Why?' With a look of amazement on his face.

With that, my chicken produced the long-awaited egg. It rolled down the little channel I'd set up under both chickens. I picked the egg up with pride. 'Jackpot. Thanks, gel. And thank you, Ives.'

He took out two hand-rolled snouts from his pocket and was about to hand them over. 'Listen, Fletcher. Double or quits?' He picked up the egg and placed both hands behind his back. 'Which hand's it in, then? Go on, fair's fair. Double or quits.'

'All right,' I said. He had both hands out in front. I took a good look. 'That one,' I said, as I touched his right hand.

'Ha! You missed out that time, didn't you, Fletcher,' he shouts and opens his empty hand.

'Oh, oh that one, was it?' I said as I squeezed the other hand, the one with the egg in it.

'Oh, Fletcher, very funny. Very funny.'

'I thought so too. Trouble with some people is, they can't take a yolk.'

'Ives!' someone shouted from outside the chicken run.

'I've gotta go, Fletcher. But just you wait.' With that he left at a hurry, rubbing his hand down his overalls.

Poor old Ives, I thought. Poor old Ives. If Elizabeth Taylor had triplets and he was one of them, he'd be the one in the middle on the bottle. A permanent loser.

I crossed over to Ives's chicken. 'You're not a loser, are you, old gel?' I said, as I took a small piece of rag from under her. With that an egg rolled down. 'You'd have won by rights, if I hadn't cut off your access, wouldn't you?'

I collected all the other eggs that the hens had produced that morning and quickly put them into a bag that was half filled with grain. 'This, girls,' I said to the chickens, 'is what you might call one of life's little perks. With these eggs I can get myself a quarter ounce of shag, or two tubes of toothpaste, or three bars of fruit and nut, or I could take them over to E wing to Smutty Garland, King of the Porn. Trade 'em in for one of his dirty books. Filled with full-frontal, naked nubiles . . . No, thinking about it, I'd rather have the fruit and nut.'

I went down to the sty. The worst job I had to do was to feed the grotty pigs. I filled up the troughs. I can't imagine what pigs think about when they eat the garbage they are given. Gawd, they're messy, I thought, and they eat like pigs. I wondered if they could run. Yeah, that's a thought. Pig Racing! That would make a nice little attraction in Slade Prison. Pig Racing. We could have the Slade Prison Selling Stakes. The Royal Cheltenham Pork Cup. Yes, I could run a book. Have my own stable . . . sty. Thought appealed. Cor blimey, think about it. The Bacon Handicap.

I had to nip back to the henhouse to collect my eggs. As I entered I saw Barrowclough.

'Morning, Fletcher.'

'Morning, Mr Barrowclough. How's things?'

'That man Ives, what was he doing round here?'

'Ives? Oh, er, he was, he just dropped in on his way to the silos,' I said.

'He wasn't taking bets was he, Fletcher?'

'Bets?' I said with all the innocence I could muster.

'Yes, it has been suspected that Ives is Harry Grout's runner.'

'Runner, Mr Barrowclough? Runner?' Harry Grout, the bookmaker in D wing, was Smutty Garland's brother-in-law.

'Taking bets.'

'You don't say!'

'Yes I do. Harry Grout's a long-termer and he's not the pleasantest of men. In fact he seems to exert a lot of unhealthy influence in the prison. We're fairly sure that he controls both the gambling and most other illegal goings-on in Slade. I – I'm telling you this, Fletcher, in strictest of confidence of course, because, well, you're a good chap really, and I wouldn't want you to get sucked into that subversive subculture.'

'What?'

'Fletcher, I'm trying to help you.'

'Yes, I know that, Mr Barrowclough. You must have no fear on that score. No, I was appalled with the fact you obviously thought I'd got involved in gambling. Good Lord no. Gambling appals me. I've seen the consequences too often.'

'It's like a plague in this prison, Fletcher. I am so very pleased that you appear to be taking every opportunity to use this period of time to enhance yourself.'

'Mr Barrowclough, sir, I am pleased that you think that. 'Ere, do you think pigs could run?'

'Run?' he said.

'Yes, run. Do you think they could be trained to run?'

'I suppose so . . . Why?'

'Well, I just thought it would make a change for them, something different from just walking around in the pigsty.'

'It is good to see that you're taking an interest in your fellow creatures, Fletcher.'

'You can say that again. When I was first assigned to the farm I took offence at the dirty habits of the animals. I mean, I've never been a rural man. Always had a deep mistrust of animals.' Screws, policemen and judges as well, I thought to myself.

'But I thought that you told the Governor you had a keen interest in farming and livestock.'

Honestly, if he was in the Thames he would miss a battleship. 'Oh yes, that. Farming and livestock, yes. It's just that I ain't so keen on the animal end of it.'

'You know, Fletcher, you're very lucky to be working on the farm alone. Normally only a Red Band or Trusty gets a job like this. You are in a very privileged position.'

'Don't think that I don't appreciate it, Mr Barrowclough. I'm sure that you had something to do with it, sir, knowing your kind and generous nature.'

'No,' he said, 'I had nothing to do with it.'

'Say no more, say no more. When are you going to get me a single cell then?'

'It's not in my power, Fletcher.'

'Look, sir, I'm not a sharer. And those two I'm in with, well, Heslop, I mean. And take Evans. There's no intellectual rapport there, no stimulus. Know what I mean?'

'Evans, yes, is he still eating light bulbs?'

'No,' I said, 'he's got a taste for other things now. Ate my shaving mirror yesterday.'

'I'm afraid there's very little I can do about it. And it's wrong of you to ask me.'

'Oh no, wait, Mr Barrowclough. Please, sir. You mustn't think that . . . you must *not* think that I'd try and influence you . . . to coerce you to . . . dare I say the words . . . to bribe you !'

'Quite right,' he said.

'What, sir, you, a prison officer? Bribe a person that's been specially chosen by the Home Office for his integrity and honesty. Oh no, I couldn't do that. Would a dozen eggs make any difference?'

That was enough. He told me to collect my stuff together and it was time to go in for lunch. I had to deliver the rest of the eggs I was nicking to the kitchen. Barrowclough helped me load up the handcart.

We eventually arrived at the gate. Old Bread and Water Smith was on gate duty. 'Lovely day for it,' I said as we entered.

'You won't be getting it for a long time,' he said.

'You obviously ain't had it for a long time,' I replied. Which didn't go down well.

The first person I saw when I got into the kitchen was Lenny Godber, who was washing down the hot plate. Alongside him was Lukewarm, nicknamed after his cooking, just one of the many poofs who didn't make it into the bath-house cleaner's job.

'There you are, Lukewarm, three dozen and two,' I said.

'What? Only three dozen. What's wrong with those duckies since you took over? Shell shock?'

'Hens, Lukewarm, not duckies.'

'Thieving again, are you, Fletcher?' said the voice of Mr Appleton, the Cook and Baker Screw, six foot eight, thirty stone and dirty finger nails.

'There's no need for that, Mr Appleton. No need for that sort of defamatory.'

'You're always pilfering, the whole lot of you.'

'Now listen, Mr Appleton. I resent that. I may have done some bad things in my life, wouldn't be here if I hadn't, but I ain't a petty sneak thief like some I know. That's not my style at all.'

'All right, Fletcher, but don't let me catch you, that's all.'

He left us alone and went into his office. As he did I put half a pound of marge into my pocket.

'Er, Lenny. Anyone left a message for me?' I said.

'Yes, a bloke from D Wing came in and said Harry Grout said permission granted.'

'Did he? Oh good.'

'Permission for what, Fletcher?'

'Permission to hold a game,' I replied.

'What game?' he said.

'A game of chance,' I said.

'How do you mean?'

'Oh, for gawd's sake, Godber. A spiel, a gamble, a flutter.'

'But gambling's not allowed,' he said.

'I know. That's precisely why we're doing it.'

'Tell me, Fletch, why do you have to get permission from Harry Grout?'

'Godber, Lenny, my old son, you've been here a week. Ain't you learned nothing yet? Officially this hotel is run by a Governor appointed by the Home Office, Mr Venables. But in practice of course we knows different. In practice Harry Grout runs the nick. He can bring it to a standstill any moment he likes.'

'What do you play for, big stakes, is it?'

'Yes,' I said, 'we will do if Lukewarm can nick us some from the meat safe. We play for anything negotiable. Snout mostly. But we don't play for chicken feed. Pity really, 'cos I got bags of that.'

'I've noticed people are always betting on something,' he said. 'I suppose it's their way of generating excitement to counter the misery of their monotonous existence.'

'What? Oh yes, right. It ain't just the excitement of the game, what you win or what you lose. It's the pleasure what you get from doing it under their noses, surreptitious like.'

'There's two blokes next door to me who've had a bet on how many bricks there are in their cell.'

'Oh yes,' I said. 'Commonplace, that.'

'I can't think or study. It's driving me mad listening to them. Recount after recount. Three hundred and forty-one, three hundred and forty-two . . .'

'Blokes doing stir'll bet on anything. Two flies going up a wall, hymn numbers in the chapel, two flies going down a wall. I even laid a bet on an egg today. There was a big game last night in D Wing. Weren't you aware of the atmosphere in the air? It was electric, the tension.'

'Tension, I noticed that. But I thought that was because the female social worker comes round Tuesday.'

'What, gruesome Glenda? Her with the brogues and the bicycle? You'd be hard pushed to have an erotic fancy about that one.'

'I dunno. Nifty Small's in love with her. He stole her bicycle saddle.'

'Really? Gawd, the ride back must have been painful for her. He won't have that long. They'll soon find it.'

'What, under his pillow? I bet they won't.'

'All right,' I said, 'you're on. How much? Two fags?'

' 'Ere, I'm not gambling. My mother said gambling will get you into trouble.'

'Godber, my old son, it may have escaped your notice but you're in prison. Your mother was too late. You is in trouble.'

'Yeah, well nevertheless I'm not gambling. I'm not counting bricks or watching flies. Gambling's one thing I'm going to resist inside.'

'Bet you can't,' I said.

'Oh yes I can,' he replied.

'Bet you a bar of soap you can't.'

'Bet I can.'

'There you are. You bet me you wouldn't bet me. So

you just lost your first bet. That's a bar of soap you owe me. Work that out.'

Ives came into the kitchen and dumped a sack of spuds on the floor.

'What are you doing, Ives?' said Mr Appleton, coming out of his office.

'Just brought the spuds in, sir.'

Appleton went over and started to talk to Lukewarm.

'Got the spuds, eh?' I said.

' 'Ere, listen, Fletcher. How much do you think they weigh then?'

'You know already,' I said.

'Course I don't, there ain't no scales out there.'

'What's the bet then, Ives?'

'All the eggs you've got there in that bag.'

'You crafty nurk, Ives. Against what?'

'Ounce of snout,' he replied.

'You're on,' I said.

'Are you in, son?' he said to Lenny.

'No, I'm not,' said Lenny.

I picked up the bag and tested it. 'Nearest one, eh?'

'Nearest one.'

'Twenty-three pounds about, I'd say.'

Ives took the bag in one hand, lifted it and said, 'Twenty-seven pounds. Just over.'

'Gave that a lot of thought, didn't you?' I said.

He put the bag on the scales. 'Well I never. Would you believe it, just over twenty-seven pounds.'

I gave him a long hard look. 'Ives, you are a grotty, nurkish git. You knew, didn't you?'

' 'Ere, Fletcher, I ain't no cheat.'

'What?' I replied. 'You're in this flaming nick for fraudulent conversion. It's your stinking career, you're a natural cheat.'

'Lose gracefully, Fletcher. Come on 'ere, listen.'

I gave him the eggs. 'I'm listening.'

'I needed them eggs. I owes Grout, don't I?'

'That's right, don't do to owe Grout, do it? Now naff off.'

He left my side as Mr MacKay entered the kitchen.

'Good day, Mr Appleton,' said MacKay.

I decided to disappear quick like.

'Fletcher. Where are you going?'

'Pig swill.'

'What!'

'See about the pig swill, Mr MacKay. Little fellows need their swill this time of day.'

'Come here, laddy.' Neck in and out. 'I'm told, Mr Fletcher, that your chickens are on short time. I am also told that since you took the farm over the egg production has fallen drastically.' He was strutting as he spoke. 'Am I not right in my presumptions?'

'No, Mr MacKay,' I said, 'you are wrong. Don't blame me, perhaps they are in a fowl mood.'

'Don't come the old soldier with me, Fletcher.' He picked up the sack I'd brought the eggs in. 'Now, what have we here?'

'Chicken meal, Mr MacKay.'

'Empty it,' he says. Ives started to leave the kitchen, but MacKay saw him. 'Stand still, Ives! Now Fletcher, do as I say and empty the bag.'

'Empty it?'

'Empty it.'

I tipped the bag of grain all over the floor, and MacKay sifted through it with his truncheon. He was very unhappy not to have caught me with anything.

'All right, Fletcher, but if I catch you thieving at all, your feet won't touch.'

'No, sir, you won't catch me, I promise.'

'Ives, come here, you horrible man,' said MacKay.

'Who me, sir?' Ives said.

'Yes you, sir.'

'But I'm behind, Mr MacKay. I've got my turnips to...'

'Don't give me any of that insipid verbiage, Mr Ives. When I say here, I mean *here*.' You could see that old MacKay was on tip-top form. 'Bit of a jackdaw yourself, aren't you, Ives? Last time we caught you in the kitchens, you were trying to steal a meat cleaver.'

'Only to sharpen my pencil, Mr MacKay,' said Ives.

'No, it was not, Mr Ives. It was used to persuade your cell-mate to part with his Pirelli calendar. Now what have we picked up today? A meat skewer?'

He gives Ives a quick rub down. You could see the extreme look of anguish on Ives's face as he felt the eggs break in his pockets. 'Yes, yes, yes,' said MacKay as he proceeded to mash the eggs deeper into the lining of Ives's coat. 'Oh yes. Now, Mr Ives, perhaps you would be so kind as to come with me?'

With that they both left for the Governor's office. Poor old Ives...

There we were, sat in a three cell, Heslop, Evans and me. Decor not by G-Plan I can assure you. The furniture, if you can call it that, consisted of a two-tier bunk and a single bed. That's right, I had the single bed. I mean, who'd want to lay in the same bunk as Heslop? He picks his toes and has falling dandruff. No, it's the single for me. I'd just had a slight altercation with Evans about the pros and cons of eating my shoe polish. Naturally he denied it, but when I put the question a little more forceful he admitted eating it to help my shaving mirror go down easier.

Sure enough Ives made his appearance. I'd just settled down to reading the latest edition of the *Law Society*

Gazette. It pays to keep up with the latest information in the legal profession. You never know, you might be able to hire yourself out as a legal authority in the nick. Jailhouse Lawyers they call them. You know, advising on an appeal or divorce case pending. One little way to supplement the snout situation.

'Don't we knock?' I said as he hovered in the doorway.

' 'Ere, listen.'

'Ere, listen. That's all he ever said. I could feel the next question coming before he thought about it. I hear you've got a game going, I thought. 'I hear you've got a game going,' he said. Shouted it, in fact, so that all the screws in the nick could hear.

'Oh say it a bit louder. Few people in E Wing didn't catch that. Why don't you bellow it from the bleedin' rooftops?'

'No listen, is that gen? You got a game put together?'

'Yeah.'

'When is it?' Ives asked.

'Saturday afternoon. When the world is watching Grandstand, and the screws are playing E Wing at football.'

'Can I be in?'

'Sorry, Ives, old son. Full house.'

'Who's in then?' he said.

'Myself. Mr Heslop, here. Lukewarm from the kitchen. And Mr Evans – providing he don't eat the dice.'

'Oh it's dice, is it?'

'What? Oh well, possibly, possibly. Said enough, said enough.'

'You can make room for one more, Fletcher.'

'Not your sort, Ives.'

' 'Ere, listen — '

'It's all been arranged, it's all set up, right? So naff off,' I said.

'You telling me you got a game set up? In this place? You ain't got a snowball's.'

'Same in any nick. Question of integrity. Where there's a will there's a way.'

'MacKay'll have your guts for garters if he sees you gambling with anything. Draughts, dominoes. Even that whatsit, that game with the wooden spelling . . .'

'Scribble?'

'Yeah, that's it. Scribble. Venables'd come down like the clappers, he would. Ever since the Earwig Derby.'

'The what?'

'The Earwig Derby.'

'Earwig Derby . . . yes, tragic that,' said Evans.

'When was this, Ives?' I asked.

'Last earwig season, wasn't it? Organised by Grouty, of course. Very much on the lines of the Jockey Club. There was handicaps, eliminators, and then in September the Grand Final – well, the Derby. Over eight yards across the laundry floor. Whole prison was on. Then MacKay finds out, doesn't he? How we never knew.'

'What did he do?'

'Put his foot down. Right on top of 'em.'

'It's dice, is it?' said Heslop.

'Oh you're with us, are you, Mr Heslop?'

'You never told me it was dice, Fletcher,' he went on.

'I did, I told you Saturday, only it's obviously just permutated.'

'Listen, Fletcher,' said Ives. 'Where d'you get the dice then?'

'Lukewarm made them in the kitchen. Out of pastry. He baked them.'

'Won't they break?'

'Not his pastry.'

' 'Ere, listen. You'll never pull it off.'

'What you talking about?'

'Organise this game and get away with it.'

'It's already organised.' Now I saw what was in his little bird brain. 'Mr Ives,' I said, 'would you like to take part in a little gentlemanly wager?'

'Right, Fletcher, let's have a bet.'

'Go on then.'

'How much?' he said.

'Try me,' I said.

'A biggy.'

'Big as you like.'

'How big?'

'Try me.'

'Snout.'

'Obviously.'

'All right then. Half a pound.'

'Fair enough,' I said calmly.

'Did you hear me, Fletcher? I said half a pound.'

'I heard you.'

'That's eight ounces.'

'Nice one, Einstein.'

'Now let's get this perfectly clear. I'm betting you eight ounces of snout that you don't get away with a game. I bet you get caught.'

'You're on.'

'All right then. I'll be off then.' Ives left, looking somewhat shaken at the size of the bet.

'When I was doing bird in Shepton Mallet,' said Heslop, 'we used to bet on the number of bricks in a cell.'

'Oh original yes. How did you get on?'

'All I know is there was over thirty-seven.'

'Oh roomy, wasn't it? When I was in Maidstone, we only had a roulette game going, that's all. With a dart board, see. People bet on it. You could bet on red or black, evens or odds, sequences or individual numbers. Your croupier was blindfolded and threw the dart. We used to play in association and we bribed this screw to turn a blind eye. Big game it was, mammoth.'

'Oh crafty that, roulette.'

'Yeah. Pity it came to such a tragic end.'

'What happened?'

'One night the croupier got a bit careless. Now the screw turns a blind eye to everything.'

The next hour was taken up with organising things just in case we did get captured by MacKay and Co. I had to have a get out. So there we were, sitting in the Boiler House. Me, Heslop, Evans and Lukewarm. The rest of the nick were watching the football match.

'You sure they won't find us in here?' asked Heslop.

'Lukewarm here assures me they won't. He, being a trusty, happens to have access to the coke store key. Cosy, ain't it?'

'They'll never look down here today,' said Lukewarm.

'Mind you, I did try to persuade Tommy Macready to put forward his escape attempt to today, 'cos knowing Tommy he'll cock it up and the diversion would have come in very handy. However, he couldn't be swayed as he pointed out, quite rightly, state this country's in you can't rely on trains at the weekend.'

'I didn't know Tommy was going over the wall,' said Heslop.

'Oh yes, common knowledge. Domestic problems. Wife's got nerves or something.'

'Things are getting on top of her, are they?' said Lukewarm.

'Quite the reverse. She's sleeping with a limbo dancer.'

'A limbo dancer? Is he black?'

'Black and blue, I should think, knowing her.'

Old Lukewarm came up trumps, to coin a phrase, and produced four nice steak sandwiches.

'Can I eat mine?' said Heslop.

'No you can't. You're like a big kid, aren't you. Soon as you get outside the front door, you want to start the picnic. Just wait. Now the rules of the game, gentlemen,' I said, as I produced a pack of cards. 'Minimum bet is one fag. You can't raise more than half the kitty, and losers divvy up within twenty-four hours. Otherwise Mr Heslop here will come round with a reminder – just like the Post Office.'

'The Post Office?' said Evans.

'Yeah, he'll stick one on you.'

As you can guess, we got captured by MacKay and Co. The first we knew was when a load of coke came down the chute into the boiler house. There was coke and dust all over the place. MacKay had the time of his life. 'Welcome to the Black and White Minstrel Show,' he said as we came out choking and spluttering.

Eventually they escorted us all back to our cells. As we were walking along MacKay was spouting off to one of the other screws about cracking down on gambling. Then in the paranoiac fashion he adopts so well, he started shouting about gambling leading to debts, ill-feeling and antagonism. His neck was really doing twenty dozen to the minute.

The next morning we all had to go in front of the Governor, you know, the adjudication bit. Left, right, left, right. Stand on the white line and face the Governor. Full name and number. Two screws standing either side of you. Just like the army. The Guv'nor told me that I had abused his trust and that I'd lost my privileged position on the farm. Also said that I was an evil influence on Heslop and Evans. Me! A bad influence?

I was collecting my kit in the cell when in walked Ives. 'Morning, Fletcher.'

I ignored the little man.

'Morning, Fletcher. I hear the coke's on you.'

'What? Oh, yes, Ives, you're a very witty man. Full of that irrepressible Liverpudlian wit, no doubt.'

'What'd the Governor say then?'

'Among other things, he said that I was a bad influence on my two cell mates, and that I was to move into a single cell forthwith.'

He liked that. You could see the sneering look on his face as he said, 'Oh dear, how tragic. I am sorry.'

'All right, don't give me all that. I know you grassed, Ives. As does the entire prison. As you will find out when you take your first run round the recreation yard. I'm not saying there'll be any unpleasantness, but if I were you I'd try and borrow some shin pads from the PTI.'

' 'Ere, listen, Fletcher.'

'Not that I bears you any ill-feeling, you 'orrible contemptuous despicable nurkish git, you. Oh no, you was just a pawn in my grand strategy.'

'Never mind that, Fletcher. There's still the bet. You owe me eight ounces of snout.'

'Very true, very true,' I said. 'And that eight ounces of snout may provide some consolation to you in the nightmare days that lie ahead.'

I turned my back on him and finished off collecting the rest of my cell kit. He kept on dodging around the cell trying to catch my eye.

' 'Ere, listen, Fletcher, you take the heat off me, okay, and we'll forget about the bet. I mean, you're never going to raise eight ounces, are you?'

'No? Well as a matter of fact, I shall take it out of my winnings.' With that I started to leave the cell.

'Winnings? What winnings?'

'Lose a few, win a few. You see, you little git, while you were running about grassing to all and sundry, I was betting the whole landing that I'd be in a single cell by Sunday. Oh yes, Ives, I shall be rolling in it,' I said as I made my exit. Quite grand like, in fact quite regal.

An Evening In

I'd been in my single cell for about three weeks. Getting quite used to the peace and quiet of living alone, I'd adopted a nice little routine for myself. Evans came and cleaned out the flowery during association time for the grand fee of half an ounce a week. I had to keep my shaving mirror out of his way, though. Still, part of the joy of having done a bit of porridge before, sort of having served my apprenticeship you might say, was that you soon got into the little fiddles that were part and parcel of doing your bird. Doing it this way was 'Doing it on your Pot'. Simple. Anyway there I was doing it the easy way, sipping my nightly cup of coffee, courtesy of Luke-warm and the Officers' Mess, when in walks young Godber.

'Hallo, Fletch.'

I chose to ignore his greeting.

'I said hallo, Fletch. They told you, didn't they?'

'Yes, they told me,' I replied.

'Only temporary though. They'll move me out as soon as my cell has been repainted.'

I decided to put the position on its rightful note. 'You bet your sweet life that it's temporary, young Godber. This is a single cell by rights. Mine.'

He looked a bit down at that. 'It's not my fault, Fletch, they said it was either with you or share with Heslop and Evans.'

'Well, I don't blame you on that account, Godber. Heslop and Evans! Neither could really say, "Mirror mirror on the wall," could they?'

'No?'

'Forget it, son.'

He looked around the cell. I was on the top bunk, status the top bunk is. I didn't really feel in the mood for polite conversation or the like so I just let him get on with what he wanted to.

After a while he'd laid all his kit out on the small three-cornered table that every cell has, tooth-brush, shaving kit, a tin of throat-lozenges, a box of liquorice all-sorts, and a photograph of his fiancée. He then lay on the bottom bunk and picked up the paper that had dropped from my hands.

'Oy, Godber, there are certain rules that you have to abide by in this cell. Number one is that you do not read the newspaper until I have finished with it.' He handed me the *Sun*.

'What's mutism?' he said.

'What's what?'

'Mutism. It's in the crossword you started in the paper.'

'How the hell should I know? Hold on, it's, it's er, oh yes, it's something to do with a religion – I think.'

'No. I'm sure it's not that. More like sheep.'

'Why waste your time thinking about things like that? I mean, where's your education now, eh?'

He looked at me and smiled. 'Fletch, you're an old con man, d'you know that? You con most of the people in here, but the one person who you con all the time is yourself.'

'Wotcher mean, Godber? Anyway, who are you to tell me that I'm a con man? Eh?'

I won't admit to getting hot under the collar, but the little man had me over the barrel so to speak. I decided to change the subject quickly.

'How come they've moved you then?'

He then told me the story all over again. I mean the

story that everyone in the nick had been talking about. They'd had a riot on his landing. His cell-mate Banks had been one of the ringleaders.

'Head case, that Banks,' I said.

'He wasn't a bad bloke to share a cell with. He was always very nice to me. He showed me the ropes and taught me cribbage. And he never displayed no violence. He was the gentlest of men. He found this kitten and smuggled it into the cell. From the way he handled it you could see the gentle side of his nature.'

'You what? Before he set fire to his mattress I heard he threw a screw off the top landing.'

'Well, he weren't hurt. He hit the safety net.'

'That, Godber, is somewhat academic. The point is that a fifteen-stone prison officer was hurled from a top landing by your cell-mate, mighty Joe Banks.'

'Only because he said he couldn't keep the kitten.'

'Hardly an excuse, sonny. Hardly an excuse. Can't see that cutting much ice with his parole board.'

'Where's the harm in keeping a kitten?'

'It's not allowed, that's the point. It's against prison procedure. Cage birds, well yes, sometimes they'll let you keep caged birds. Insects in a match-box. But you can't keep cats. And Banks knows that, the porridge he's done.'

'It was only a little kitten.'

'A kitten differs from a cat only in scale. They share the same lavatorial tendencies, they pee on your blankets.'

'Just don't see the harm,' he said.

'There are rules.'

'You're rule-mad, Fletch.'

'Yes, that's right, and here are some more rules relating to this cell. Well, not so much rules as standards. This is my cell, in which you are a temporary resident, and as such you will honour those standards.'

'Which are?'

'You don't rabbit, snore, or pick your nose.'

'I don't do any of them, Fletch.'

'Good. Then we should get on passably well.'

I took off my shoes and settled back to my paper.

'I've got some grey darning thread,' he said.

'What?'

'I've got some grey darning thread if you want that hole in your sock darned up.'

'What? Oh yes, thanks – yes,' and I took off my sock and handed it to him.

'Your standards don't include sweaty feet, I notice,' he said.

'Man who don't sweat, young Godber, ain't healthy. Like a dog with a dry nose.'

He said nothing and began darning my sock. One of the worst things about doing porridge is that there are no birds around – not the feathered ones, the female type. Of course, you've got your social workers, all garters and passion killers, but you don't count them. No, it's bloody diabolical without a woman. You start to think. You try and remember names and faces. The longer you are locked up the harder it becomes to relate back to the sanity of what is, after all, the holiday period of your life – that's if you're like me, in and out.

'Unnatural, ain't it, men in cages,' he said, as though he knew instinctively what I was thinking about.

We sat in silence for a while. Then a screw came and slammed and locked the door.

'This is the bit I can't stand, Fletch,' he said. 'It's only eight o'clock. Not even dark yet. If I was home now, I'd be going out for the evening.'

'That's the point, son, we're here to be punished, ain't we? Deprived of all our creature comforts, the little things you've been taking for granted all these years – a clean shirt, an open fire, records. Still, we could have a night out.'

He looked at me. 'A night out?'

'Yes, Godber, a night out. We could find a couple of birds, you know like them birds on Top of the Pops. Pan's People. What's her name, the big one with the – with the blonde hair. We could arrange to meet them in some little secluded Italian restaurant in Soho. Then we could go to some night club and dance till dawn, then back to their luxury apartment in Mayfair, and wallop! The trouble is I done all that last night so I'm a bit knackered.' I looked down from the top bunk at his face. He was gone, eyes all glassy and breathing heavy like. 'Why don't we have a quiet night in. All right?'

'If you say so, Fletch. Trouble is, I've got six hundred and ninety-eight quiet nights to go.'

'Do it night by night, mate.'

'Do you think she'll wait?'

'Who?' I said.

'Denise. My fiancée.'

'I dunno. I shouldn't think she'll wait *in* for six hundred and ninety-eight nights!'

'She is my fiancée!'

'Yes, I know. But when she said she'd love you for ever, she didn't know you were going to get put away for two years, did she?'

'I do miss her. I can't sleep for thinking about her.'

'That don't do no good. Don't do no good lying awake at night brooding and twitching about what you ain't going to get for a long time. Carnal thoughts – well, best to give them the big E, the elbow. Less you think about women the better.' I turned back to the paper. 'Cor, look at that. "Beauty Queen shocks Council. Lovely Sharon Spencer, 22, shocked members of her town council when she played the title role in the new sexsational film 'The

Virgin and the Vicar'. 'Had we known,' said a council spokesman, 'we would never have crowned her Floral Queen.' 'I don't know what all the fuss is about,' said Sharon, a former convent girl, whose hobbies include water-skiing and carpentry. 'I am proud of my body, and what I do with it in my spare time is none of the Council's business.'" She'd never get planning permission for that ... Sorry, what was I saying?'

'You were saying the less you think about women the better.'

'Oh yes, yes, carnal thoughts. Yes, fatal.'

'That girl reminds me of Denise a bit. Not that they're similar in appearance, but they're both . . . physical. Know what I mean?'

'You're not telling me that Denise is a star of the silver screen, are you? Or a model?'

'Oh no, nothing like that.' His voice got soft, as though he were reminiscing to himself. 'Though I did once take some provocating polaroids of her when we were caravanning on the Gower Peninsula. I don't mean mucky like, but she was sort of expressing herself . . . posing, like.' With that he ups and starts to pose like a model, you know, bent legs, shoulders back and a simpering look on his face.

'Oy, come off it, son. Leave it off! What will the neighbours think? I'm not worried about me, Godber, they know which side my bread's buttered. It's you. You carry on like that and you'll have all the fairies round here in a frenzy.'

'But I'm engaged to Denise,' he said, all innocent.

'That means naff all to them, my son. They're all engaged – to each other. Look, Denise is a thing of the past, a letter in your top pocket, a photograph under your pillow, a warm tingle in your loins.'

'In me what?' he said.

'Your loins.'

'What are loins?'

'Loins is . . . look, when you thinks about Denise in the still of night, thinks of the times you had together, don't you ever get a warm tingle?'

'Oh – yes.'

'Well, them's your loins.'

'I thought they were my . . .'

'Well, there's lots of words for them,' I said from behind my paper.

He went back to his reminiscing again. 'Very physical girl, Denise. She was a beauty queen, you know. At the Office Equipment Exhibition. Miss Duplicating she was. Her picture was in the local paper. She became the pin-up of two thousand sailors on an aircraft carrier in the Pacific. They were on a world tour. They wrote to her and said she was the girl they'd like most to get shipwrecked with.'

God, I thought, they do still breed them. 'That must have made you very proud,' I said.

'Oh, I didn't know her then. She was going out with a footballer. Platonic like, it was. He said he liked her as a sister. That was before she moved to Smethwick, before that never-to-be-forgotten day when I met her at the supermarket. She was stamping "Special Offer" on giant-sized jars of pickled onions and my wire basket ran over her foot. It was a magic moment. We both knew. I said to her straight off, "Will you meet me outside?" And she said, "All right, but I've got six dozen more jars to go." And I waited, even though she was longer than she said she'd be, 'cos the manager made her stack a pyramid of luncheon meat.'

'God preserve us, Godber. You might have picked a more romantic setting for your first meeting.'

'How'd you mean, Fletch? I told you it was beautiful.'

'I know, son, but a supermarket!'

'Was your courtship any more romantic?' he asked.

'Well no, to tell the truth it wasn't really. I'm a city boy like yourself. And it was just after the war. We had a bit more space in those days, you know, bomb sites and the like. There was the pictures too, the Muswell Hill Odeon, or the back seat of a car, that's if I could open one. Somehow we had more room to manoeuvre, not like today. Bloody great big office blocks, housing estates with all mod cons, like shops and laundrettes. Can't make love in a laundrette.'

'We did.'

'What?'

'Well, we had these three big bagfuls to do, and it was bitter out,' he said.

I don't know what the younger generation is coming to. In a laundrette, I ask you. 'That hardly entitles you,' I said. 'It's not decent. Course, I don't know Birmingham.'

'It was very quiet at the time.'

'That's a relief. Now my eldest Ingrid — '

'Who?'

I got out of bed and sat on the chair, rolled myself a snout and sat back. I liked a good rabbit.

'Ingrid is my eldest daughter. My old lady called her after Ingrid Bergman what was a famous film star who was sweeping the country at the time. *For Whom the Bell Tolls, Casablanca, Spellbound.* I don't suppose you remember them.'

'Didn't I see *Spellbound* on the telly? Wasn't it the one about the scientists in the secret laboratory in Arizona and this man drinks this substance by mistake and turns into a werewolf, and carries off the doctor's beautiful daughter and does things to her in the catacombs?'

'No,' I said. 'No, that definitely wasn't one of Ingrid's. I can say without fear of contradiction that she was never in no catacomb with a werewolf. My daughter Ingrid might have been, but certainly not the lovely Miss Bergman.'

'You were saying about Ingrid.'

'What? Was I? Oh yes, my point was that my eldest was – this is between ourselves, Godber – she was conceived in Highgate Cemetery. You see we weren't married at the time. Of course we got married when we realised young Ingrid was on the way. But at the time we wasn't. And we needed somewhere flat to consummate the passion we felt for each other.'

'But a cemetery!'

'Oh yes, but a very famous and historic cemetery.'

'Still seems a bit indecent to me,' he said.

'No more indecent than your local laundrette. Anyhow it wasn't premeditated, 'cos we'd gone there to see Karl Marx's tomb. I was politically minded at the time, and very randy. Mind you, my political career never got beyond painting slogans on viaduct walls.'

'I've done that,' he said. 'Last thing I painted was Lennie Godber loves Denise Shorter on a warehouse wall.'

'Denise Shorter?'

'My fiancée.'

'Oh that Denise Shorter.'

'I wrote to her during association hour. Helped to pass the time. I didn't have a class.'

'What class are you on?'

'Shoe repairing.'

'Oh, that's useful, yes. Very elevating.' Load of old cobblers, I thought.

'Helps kill the time. Anything to take me mind off the monotony of this place.'

'Listen,' I said, 'this ain't so bad, this nick. Compared to Leicester, Parkhurst, high security places like that. Got closed-circuit cameras there. Can't even go to the lavatory without it being on television. Not that that would worry an exhibitionist like yourself, of course. Someone who makes love in laundrettes.'

The lights were suddenly switched off. That's the way it goes in the nick, lights out with no prior warning. Just an eye looking through the judge's hole.

'Oh, I ain't got me things off yet.'

'Move over will you, son . . . Owww!' I yelled.

'What's the matter?'

'Something stuck in me foot.'

'That must be me darning needle.'

'Well, what's it doing there?'

'I was darning your sock.'

'Well, do it in the morning. Watch it, now you're standing on me other foot.'

'Oh. Sorry.'

'Just go to bed, son.' I climbed up onto the top bunk.

'D'you want a liquorice all-sort?' he asked suddenly.

'No, I don't . . . How d'you get liquorice all-sorts?'

'I swopped them for a pound of marge I whipped from the kitchen.'

'Learning, aren't you?'

'Little victories, you told me that, Fletch. I'll tell you something, though. D'you know what I've found useful since I've been inside?'

'What have you found useful, Godber?'

'I've started to do something which I haven't done since I was a kiddy. I find it helps.'

My mind boggled. 'I bet it does,' I said.

'Do you know what I do?'

'I dread to think.'

'I pray.'

'God preserve us.'

'That's what I keep asking him. So, if you don't mind . . .'

'If you must.'

'Dear God, thank you for getting me through another day. Thank you for the letter from Denise and the liquorice all-sorts. Please look after Denise in your infinite wisdom. And the same applies to me Mum, Dad – where-ever he is – and me Aunty Vi and Uncle Donald, Uncle Les and Aunty Con, me Aunty Rita in Newport Pagnall, and Cousin Rita in Walsall. And Cissie, and Stu, and Vic, and all the lads in the darts team at the Bell and Dragon; and Norma and her husband who emigrated to Melbourne.'

He paused long enough for me to get a word in. 'Is this a prayer? Or a dedication on the Jimmy Young show?'

'And please, God, look after Fletcher and forgive him for being such a bad-tempered, evil-minded, cantankerous old git.'

After that we dropped off to sleep. Well, I did and assumed that he did too. I suppose I'd been asleep about an hour when something disturbed me.

'You awake, Fletch?'

'No.'

'Oh.'

'Why?'

'Nor me neither.'

'Your God in his infinite wisdom isn't giving you a peaceful night then.'

'Wasn't one of the things I asked for.'

'That's true. He won't be getting much kip neither, the list you gave him.'

'Don't be irreverent.'

'You've changed your spots, ain't you? Day we came

in, when we went through reception, you didn't even know if you was C of E, Pressed Beef, or a flaming Buddhist.'

'Don't think it matters much. I just believe in God. Doesn't matter which lot you support. I admit my belief's only been revived since I come in here. I prayed when I was a kid, like. When I was up in Juvenile Court and when Villa looked like doing well in the Cup. But I became disillusioned when I got probation and Villa got knocked out by Rotherham one-nothing.'

'That's typical, isn't it? Most people never give a second thought, do they? When things are going well, ticking along with scant regard for the ten commandments. Stealing, committing adultery, coveting each other's oxen. Then, wallop. In the face of adversity, "Please God, please help your loyal and trusted servant".'

'You're right. But I am in the face of adversity. I hate prison, Fletch. It makes me depressed and it makes me afraid. I hate the air of defeat and the smell of disinfectant. I hate the shouting and the keys. And I hate not having a handle on the inside of that door.'

'Kids like you shouldn't be in prison, son. It's the system, see. You ain't here to be reformed or rehabilitated. You're here because of public revenge. Now it's different for me. Occupational hazard, being as my occupation's breaking the law. But my family ain't gone short, most years. Three kids and my old lady. Show you their pictures when it's light. Now my youngest, he just got into Grammar School.'

'Has he?'

'Yes, lovely school. Costs a bit you know. Books, equipment. But when my son showed up first day he weren't short of nothing. Rugby boots, blazer, scarf, the lot. Now he wouldn't have had all that if his dad had been a strug-

D

gling clerk. Or a shoe repairer. No. The reason he had all that was that his dad robbed a school outfitters.'

'What would your son think if he knew the truth.'

'He'd think, Oh so that's why the blazer's a bit big. But he'll grow into it.'

'So you only do it for your family then, Fletch.'

'And my old lady, yes. Twenty-four years we been together. Married at nineteen, see. That was Highgate Cemetery for you.'

'You must love her very much.'

'Yeah, well . . .'

' 'Cos when you were asleep, you were calling out her name.'

'I was?'

'Yes, you were saying her name over and over again, "Gloria, my love – oh Glor, Glor, my dearest Glor".'

'That's funny. My old lady's called Isobel.'

'Who's Gloria, then?'

'You may well ask. You sure it was Gloria?' I was puzzled. 'Gloria. I remember. There *was* a Gloria once – well more than once in fact – many times.'

'Was that before you met your Isobel?'

'In truth, er, it wasn't, Lennie. That was a little indiscretion round about 1955. I remember that 'cos I was King of the Teds in Muswell Hill at the time, and Gloria was a machinist in the clothing factory. So I used to go round to her place, get me evil way, and get me trousers narrowed at the same time.'

'I could never be unfaithful to Denise.'

'Now, listen. Don't get no wrong impressions. This was an indiscretion. You must imagine my position. You can't be King of the Teds and say at ten o'clock I've got to go home to the wife. Not after you've just smashed up an Amusement Arcade.'

'So you don't make a habit of indiscretions?' he asked.

'Course not. Look, Isobel's my old lady and she knows it.'

'Then who's Sharon?'

'Sharon?'

'After Gloria you was moaning about a Sharon.'

'I couldn't have been, I don't know no Sharon . . . here, wait a mo. She was the girl in the *Sun*, weren't she? "Beauty Queen Shocks Council".'

'Carnal thoughts.'

'Listen, Godber. No one asked you to eavesdrop on my dreams. It's about the only place you have any privacy – inside your head. You want to remember that, son. Dreams is freedom.'

'That's true, Fletch, that's really true.'

'Well, I'm getting back to mine and I suggest you do the same. Goodnight.'

When I opened my eyes again, the sun was streaming through the window and the screws were banging their keys against the doors to wake everyone up. Definitely not the day to be in the nick, I thought. Slop out, breakfast, slop out, then work. No morning papers delivered, no fresh eggs, no handle on the inside of the door. I swung my legs over the edge of the bunk and banged young Godber's head.

'Oops. Sorry, son.'

'No, no, it's your cell. Sorry if my head hit your foot.'

'How d'you sleep then?'

'Very well since our chat.'

'Did you dream? Did you find that freedom I promised you, that land of exotic fantasy.'

'Oh yes, I had this dream about Denise. We were in this laundrette and we got through five bagfuls without stopping. Trouble is this bloke came in and spoilt it.'

'Oh what a pity.'

'It was you.'

'Couldn't have been. I was with Sharon Spencer all night up at the Hilton.'

We had a bit of a laugh about our night out. When I thought about it, young Godber wasn't too bad, that's if you did have to have a cell mate.

'Fletch,' he said. 'Thanks.'

'What for?'

'For helping me out. With advice, like. You know, it's like that song – "Help me make it through the night". Don't suppose you'd know it, though. More contemporary than your era. Suppose as King of the Teds your tastes were more Eddie Cochran and Conway Twitty.'

'No, my tastes were a bit more mellow. What was it I used to like? Kay Starr. Rosemary Clooney. Jo Stafford.'

'Don't know him.'

'He was a girl, you nurk. Jo's a girl's name. They don't write songs like that now. Had a bit of melody in them days.'

'Go on. You're a sentimentalist at heart. Under that gruff exterior there's a kind man with feelings.'

'Yes, well — ' I said gruffly, as I got down from the bunk. 'Bloody hell! That ruddy darning needle again.'

'Here, you can have these,' he said, offering me the liquorice all-sorts.

'What?'

'Go on – all of them. Present, like.'

'Oh all right, then. Not say no, son.'

'It's meant as a thank you. 'Cos when the door's locked I'm depressed and afraid, and you – you know – just make it a bit more tolerable.'

'You'll get used to it, Lenny. And the night's not so long, is it? It's your human spirit, see. They can't break that, those nurks. We'll be all right, you and me, son.' I thought for a moment. 'Tell you what, we'll go out tonight if you like.'

'With those dancers?'

'If you like. Or I could ring Miss Sharon Spencer, eh? She's sure to have a girl friend. Bound to. Soft lights, music, night clubs . . .'

'It's discos now.'

He started to leave the cell. 'Oy,' I said.

'Yes, Fletch?'

'Haven't you forgotten something?'

'Sorry. Yes, you're right, we could go out. Then on the other hand, we could have a night in.'

'I don't mean that,' I said. 'It's your turn to empty the pot.'

A Day Out

Spring by now had turned to summer. The smell of the green grass and hay filtered through the prison corridors and into the cells. I had got myself back in favour with the Governor and he'd let me work outside the prison. In fact today was the first day of a new working party.

Godber was still sharing my cell at this time. Now you might think that was stupid of me after all the strokes I'd pulled to get into a single cell, but the truth is Godber was very handy with the housework. Anyway, this morning when I woke he was almost finished dressing.

'Oh yes, what's your rush? Getting release, are you?'

'Been looking forward to today.'

'What's so special about today? Only one good thing about a new day in here, it replaces the old one. Crossed one off, haven't we?'

'But we're going out today,' he said. 'Aren't we? Breath of fresh air. Trees. Walking on grass. The sounds of birds in the branches.'

'Don't get so flaming lyrical, Wordsworth. All we're going to do is dig drains for the council. Stooped six hours over a shovel. Doing a job they'd only give to prisoners, seeing as any civilised geezer would tell 'em to stuff it.'

'I don't care what they make us do,' he said. 'We're going outside, that's all I care. A whole day out of here.'

'You're like a kid on a school trip, son, aren't you?'

'You don't fool me, Fletch. You just mask your enthusiasm, you do. But if you were that indifferent why would you have gone to the trouble of bribing yourself onto the party?'

'Yeah, well . . .'

'Yeah, well.'

'Well, I can't deny the thought of fresh air appeals. Get the smell of disinfectant out of me nostrils. Not to mention your festering feet.'

'I change my socks every day, Fletch.'

'Pity you can't change your feet.'

'If it's not one thing it's another. I don't complain about your personal habits.'

'What personal habits? I don't have any personal habits. Like what?' I said.

'You talk with your mouth full and you whistle out of tune, and you snore and you spit.'

'How dare you. I do not whistle out of tune. What a flaming nerve. This is my cell, you know, my cell. And you've got a nerve to talk about my personal habits – you – the product of some Birmingham back street.'

'I had a very good upbringing. Never had much money, but my mother kept us spotless.'

'Yeah. Well you ain't spotless now. Your clothes are covered in gravy, so don't give me no stick about table manners.'

'Everyone at our table's covered in gravy. It's your gravy. You talk with your mouth full.'

'You'd better watch it, Godber. I'm warning you. I do not talk with my mouth full.'

'Look, you're doing it now. I'm covered in toothpaste.'

'Cheeky young nurk.'

'Don't let's fall out, Fletch. We don't want to spoil things this early. Today's the big day.'

'It ain't that big a day, son. Ain't a coach trip to Southend. Not a day at the seaside, with a trip up the pier and a big nosh up and reduced rates at the local knocking shop. We're only going across a remote Cumberland moor to a remote Cumberland village to dig drains. Sustained by the remote possibility that the District Nurse might pass by on her bicycle and give us all an exciting glimpse of stocking top.'

'Cor, a woman. A woman on her bicycle.'

'Maybe, maybe,' I said.

'No, Fletch, I can see her. Clear as day. In her uniform, on her bicycle.'

'District nurse, huh. Some old spinster with brogues and bike rider's buttocks.'

'No, she's young, Fletch, honest. Young and nice-looking. Well, more than that, beautiful really. And the prim uniform which she so proudly wears can barely conceal the voluptuous figure within.'

'Oh, voluptuous figure within, is it?'

'Yeah. Which her prim uniform cannot conceal.'

'Barely.'

'Her face is at once innocent and knowing.'

'I know them innocent faces.'

'Obviously primitive passions are stirring deep within her breast.'

'Oh, deep one, is it?' I said.

'Oh definitely.'

'Here, hang on,' I said. 'What's this gorgeous, deep-chested, thigh-flashing bit of nooky doing up this neck of the woods?'

Young Godber hardly hesitated. 'Well, you see she come home to nurse her Dad what's been sick with a fatal tropical disease.'

'Fatal, is it? That could kill you.'

'She turned her back on the bright lights, out of duty.'

'Of course she did, didn't she? Could've been a model, girl like that, cover girl, chased by playboys and Arab princes.'

'Instead of which — ' he went on.

'Instead of which,' I said, 'she returns to nurse her ailing Dad, trying hard to subdue her primitive stirrings. Until the day of course when fate decrees she has a puncture right next to the drain I'm digging.'

'Here, hang on, Fletch, I saw her first.'

'Naff off, Godber. Age before beauty. I'm at her side, picking her up, dusting her down, and not failing to notice as I do so her proud, firm body. She's sprained her perfectly-formed ankle, and I carries her over several miles of ploughed sludge, staggering at last, exhausted, into her lonely cottage miles from anywhere, leaving the two of us thrown together as night falls.'

'What about Dad then?'

'Oh he's dead. There's just us. Me and her. Together. Alone. And she pours me a drink, after slipping out of her wet uniform. Slip, slip. Then she gets me some grub. And I eat and we talk.'

'There you go again, Fletch,' he said.

'What?' I asked.

'Talking with your mouth full.'

As I said, today was the first day of a new working party. Working party? I must be joking. The lot we had there would have put the League of Work is Bad for your Health Union to shame. I mean, Navyrum, Ives, Scrounger, Godber and, wait for it, Dylan! Dylan was a long-haired anarchist git from Huddersfield, King of the Huddersfield Hippies, who called everyone Man. His definition of being sent was to be stoned out of his mind. He should have been stoned at birth.

We were waiting in the large Departure Room near the Main Gate. Navyrum and me had been in Maidstone together. I introduced him to young Godber. 'When he gets to know you a bit better, son,' I told him, 'he might let you read his tattoos.'

Navyrum and Ives had already had a hell of an argument as to who was the senior con and should have the job of making the tea. The job of tea-boy was considered one of the Working Party perks. Navyrum won the argument with a short right-hander.

'Listen, Ives, you bird-boned, skiving little git,' he said, 'I'm a working man. Always have been. Stoker. Worked my way through the seven seas. Paid my dues in the Persian Gulf. Tankers. That was a big sweat, I tell you.'

'I had a job once,' said Scrounger. 'Worked on a road gang. Motorway. Naffing job that was. Had to live on a caravan site with the old woman and two nippers. Always mud. Work in mud, come home to mud.'

'Should feel at home today, then,' I said.

'What we waiting for then?' said Navyrum.

'We're waiting for Mr MacKay,' said Mr Barrowclough.

'Oh dear. Scotland the brave. Is he coming?' I said.

'Mr MacKay's in charge, yes.'

You should have heard the moans and cries from the rest of the Working Party.

'Git,' said Navyrum.

'Pig,' said Dylan.

'Charmless nurk,' said I.

' 'Ere, listen,' said Ives.

'On your feet,' said Mr MacKay.

'Oh, morning, Mr MacKay. Just voted you man of the year.'

'None of your facetious lip, Fletcher.'

'You'll get none of it today, Mr MacKay.'

'Right now, men. As this work party is comprised of a group of spineless, delinquent, obstreperous rabble, let's make a few things crystal clear. There will be no skiving, no fraternising with members of the public, no kipping in the long grass, and no visits to the nearest pub masquerading as Irish labourers working on a mythical motorway extension. Any questions?'

'Yeah, I've got a question,' I said.

'What?'

'Is the ball and chain worn inside or outside our wellies?'

'Right, all of you, get into the van. Mr Barrowclough, sit at the back please, and I'll drive.'

With that we made our way to the small wicker gate that every prison has, the door to freedom, and piled into the small mini-van the prison used to run prisoners about. The same van I'd put out of operation when I first arrived. When we arrived at the site, we found that our task was to clean out half a mile of ditch along the north side of the small B road that led to the next village. I suppose we'd been working about a couple of hours when the district nurse cycled past. She must have been sixty if she was a day, but we all stopped work to look.

'Get on with your work, the lot of you,' said MacKay. 'Ives, put some effort into it.'

' 'Ere, listen. Everyone picks on me.'

'I think you'd have us in chains, wouldn't you, Mr MacKay, if you had your way?' I said.

'With the greatest of pleasure.'

'Can we sing?' asked Godber.

'Sing?'

'What we got to sing about?' I said.

'No, but it would help like,' he said. 'Keep our spirits up. Like the negro slaves on the plantations in the deep South. Work songs, things like that, kept their spirits up, didn't it? We're working in a gang just like them.'

'If you chuck much more mud about we'll look like them an' all,' I said.

MacKay turned to Mr Barrowclough. 'I'm just popping down to the village to ... er ... to get a small part for my lawn mower, Mr Barrowclough.'

'You won't be long, will you?'

They then had a long chat about Prison Officers being capable of taking control of any situation. Take control? Poor old Barrowclough couldn't control a children's school-crossing. Anyway, eventually MacKay convinced Barrowclough that everything would be all right and that he wouldn't be too long getting the lawn mower part. We all watched him drive off down the road. The moment he was out of sight, work stopped and we all sat down for a fag.

Poor old Barrowclough didn't like that. 'Now come on, men,' he said. 'Let's knuckle down. My approach to the inmates in Slade Prison may not be as strict as Mr Mac-Kay's but there's work to be done and I'm here to see it gets done. Mr MacKay has left me in charge and we should respect the trust that both he and the Governor have placed in all of us. So no shirking or slacking, lads, and no taking advantage of my good nature.'

As he said that, the rain started. And since the mini-van had gone we had nowhere to shelter.

' 'Ere, listen,' said Ives.

'Oh, shut up, you little snivelling rat,' said Navyrum.

'Hold on, hold on,' I said. 'We can't stay out here all day in this rain. That wasn't in the parole papers we signed. All we said was that we wouldn't run away or scarper. No, it didn't say anything about sitting in the rain.'

By now the rain was getting heavier. After a short while we all decided that the only place we could get shelter was in the local church.

Someone once said that churches were places of refuge and help. In our case they were right. There we were sitting in the peace and quiet of the small country church, smoking. Young Godber had been rabbiting on about how nice it was to be out of the nick.

'Oh yes, well makes a change,' I said. 'Get a bit more exercise. Mind you, I'd like today to be a bit more to write home about. Pub just down the road. Wouldn't half like to be in it. Pop in the village shop. Get some sweets, and a *Reveille*.'

'Ain't possible, is it?'

'It's been done.'

Barrowclough looked in through the church door. 'Right, men, come along. You've had enough time for a smoke, time we all got back to work. We shouldn't be smoking in here at all.'

'We had to have somewhere to sit,' I said. 'Couldn't sit on the damp grass, could we? 'Cos it's bad for you, very bad for you.'

'It's usual to sit on the earth you dig out. Form little piles,' he said.

'Exactly, that's what I'm worried about, forming little piles.'

'That's enough, Fletcher. Now we really must knuckle down.' He started to count up to see if we were all there. 'One, two, three ... Where's Ives?'

'He's outside, desecrating the holy ground, ain't he?' I said.

'How do you mean?' said Barrowclough.

'Gone for a slash in the churchyard.'

As I said that, Ives reappeared. ' 'Ere, listen, 'elp. I've been stung !'

We all laughed including Mr Barrowclough. 'Obviously the Lord's retribution, you vulgar nurk,' I said. 'Bee was it?'

He was rubbing his 'arris. 'I don't know what it was. What d'yer think I am? A flaming zoologist?'

'Maybe it was a wasp, or a hornet,' said Godber.

Poor old Ives, he couldn't stop rubbing the sore part. 'What difference does that make?'

'Makes a lot of difference, Ives. Stands to reason. Difference in the degree of pain and poison,' I said.

He started to look very unhappy, that's if Ives could be any more unhappy than he already was. 'It was a great big thing, Fletcher.'

'Oh yes,' I said, 'that's an 'ornet. Can be fatal.'

Mr Barrowclough looked aghast. 'What do you mean, fatal?'

'Well, Mr Barrowclough, if one of us don't suck out the poison from Ives's, er, system, well, if it don't happen lively like, he's going to die.'

There was absolute silence. No one moved or said a thing.

'You're going to die, old son,' I said.

' 'Ere, listen. That's not funny.'

'You mustn't joke, Fletcher,' said Barrowclough. 'The man's obviously in some distress. Don't worry, Ives, it's almost certainly just a wasp sting.'

'I'm dying,' said Ives.

'Permission to make a suggestion, Mr Barrowclough?' I asked.

'What?'

'Why don't someone go down the village and get some ointment or TCP. Then the only problem's getting a volunteer to rub it on. I'd be willing to go and get some.'

'Go to the village?' he said.

'I'd be willing to take that long walk on this mission of mercy.'

'Well, I suppose, if you went straight there and back.'

'What else, Mr Barrowclough? Man's life at stake. Need money of course. Expensive those antibiotics.'

'All right. Well here, I've only got a pound.'

'That should cover it.'

'Now look, Fletcher . . .'

'Mr Barrowclough, please, every second counts.'

The Rowbarge pub was owned by a geezer called Horatio Septimus Hoddinott and his wife Enid Mabel, salt of the earth. I was standing in the corner of the small bar finishing off a pint of bitter in record time. The journey from the church was only half a mile, so it didn't take me too long to find the pub.

'You needed that,' said Horatio Septimus.

'You're right. First I've had for ages. Well, I'm not allowed to, am I? Doctor says I'm not to drink. Ulcer, you see. I can't take it any more, but just occasionally I have one to be sociable. Just a little sip, so to speak.'

There was just one other geezer in the pub so I chatted up the landlord for a while, just to get the feel of the place. Not bad, really. Darts, not that I play, oh no. I like a good game of spoof or chatting up the birds. And the Rowbarge didn't look like that type of place.

He asked me if I wanted another. So I agreed that one more wouldn't hurt. 'Oh, and six packets of crisps.'

'With an ulcer?' he said.

'No – cheese and onion.'

'But if you've got an ulcer, what are you doing buying crisps?'

'They're not for me. They're for the lads.'

'Oh yes? And what lads would they be?' he said, inquiring like.

'What lads? Oh, er, we're working on the motorway, aren't we?'

He nearly fell through the floor. 'What motorway?'

'The new by-pass,' I told him.

'But we've never heard of no new by-pass!'

Blimey I thought. Why don't I keep my big mouth

shut! 'No, it's that new, that's why you ain't heard of it. I've only just heard of it myself.'

'But this is an outrage. This whole area's National Trust. What's the use in having a by-pass through here?'

Get out of it, Fletcher, I thought. 'Look, mate, it's none of my doing, is it? I see your point, despoiling England's green and pleasant land and all that, but it's the law, ain't it? I mean, once it's passed, well. That's how I got my ulcer, worrying about it.'

Just then the local sky pilot came into the pub with another geezer, all collar and gaiters. It's amazing, ain't it, how vicars and that lot always seem to have lots of time off. I mean, they only do a one-day week, don't they?

'Good morning, all,' he said in a vicarified way.

'Vicar, just the man we want to see. Have you heard of the new by-pass they're building?' said Horatio Septimus.

'Good Lord. Where?' he said. They all looked at me.

'Where?' I says. 'Oh, well, over there, ain't it?'

'But just what is the point of a by-pass? There's nothing to by-pass, except the Prison, of course.'

'What prison, eh?' I asked, thinking it was typical of the middle-class git, that wants to be above the trials and tribulations of the suffering prisoner. We are sent to prison for guidance, not to be jumped on and ignored by the thinking masses of this world. I mean, think of all the people who have been in the nick and have made a success of life after. Yeah, go on, think of them. There's, well, there's Hitler. Come to think of it, he got bunkered in the end.

'Six hundred bloody convicts on our doorsteps,' said our genial host.

'Now now, Horatio, you mustn't prejudge these men. The poor souls are serving their penance.'

Typical do-gooder, this one, I thought. 'Quite right,

Rev. It's all public revenge, ain't it? I mean, an eye for an eye, a tooth for a nail, an' all that.'

'No, no,' he said. 'We must treat our unfortunate brethren with compassion and tolerance. I don't mean to sound pious, but people must keep an open mind. My mind, like the doors of my church, is always open.'

'Well spoken, Rev. Greater joy in heaven over a sinner what repenteth.' I thought I'd give it a bit of help.

'Repenteth? Yes, indeed. I was wondering – would you like to . . .'

'Thanks, I would. A pint please,' I said, quick as a flash.

He hummed and arred for a second or so, then asked Horatio Septimus to do the honours. 'In fact I was going to ask you if you'd like to bring your chums over to evensong on Sunday evening.'

'Oh? What? Well, much as we'd like to we may not be able to get out, er, across. Tell you what, we'll come if we're free. All right? Cheers.'

At that moment MacKay walked in through the other door and propped himself up at the bar. Christ, I thought. I slid down to the floor as though I was tying up my shoelace. How the hell was I going to get out of this?

'Ah, here's a man with a different outlook on life,' said the Rev. I looked over the top of the bar. There he stood. Neck in and out.

'Good morning, Padre, sir.'

'Good morning, Mr MacKay. What are you drinking?'

'Whisky with a pint chaser, please. Different point of view to what?'

'To our friend here,' he said, turning towards me as I ducked down again. 'Oh, he's gone.' There was silence while MacKay downed his whisky.

'On duty?' asked Horatio Septimus.

'Well, half. Got a work party down the road.'

I started to crawl out from the bar. I got to the back door and waited outside. I had to know what they were going to tell MacKay.

'Work party?' said the vicar.

'Yes, they're digging out the ditches down at Felton Bank.'

'Prisoners?' The vicar's voice again.

'Oh yes.'

'Verger, why don't you pop down to the Church?'

'But it's going to pour again any minute.'

'You've got your bike, pop down and lock the church door.'

'But why?'

'You heard what he said. There's a bunch of criminals loose in the area.'

I nipped round the front and borrowed a bike what was standing there, and belted it down the road to the church. I bet I beat Banister, Chattaway and Wilson – you know, that geezer who always runs in his black underwear, the geezer in the *Dandy*.

When I got into the church I saw Navyrum chatting to Lennie Godber, showing him his tattoos. Stupid Ives was still standing with his trousers around his ankles and the rest were sitting about. That's apart from Barrow-clough. He was trying to show Dylan how to keep his balance whilst standing on one foot.

'This one was done in Valparaiso,' said Navyrum. 'That's in South America. Chile. Very Catholic country, Chile. Hence the religious overtones.'

'What's her name? Doris? Doesn't sound very Chilean.'

'No, she weren't. She were from Bootle. Stranded there with a juggling act. What with me being from the Pool, that's how we got on so well, hence the affectionate over-tones.'

' "I'll always . . ." ' young Godber read out.

'Don't read it out loud, son. Not in here.'

'Ah, Fletcher,' said Barrowclough. 'Did you get the ointment?'

'Ointment?'

' 'Ere, listen,' said Ives. 'I'm dying.'

'Oh yes, the ointment. No. Thing is, see, the village shop was closed, wasn't it? Closed for lunch.'

'But it's only half past eleven,' said Barrowclough.

'Yeah, well, that's not my fault, is it? They close for lunch earlier in the country, don't they, 'cos they get up earlier and they get hungry quicker. Stands to reason.'

'Oh come on,' said Ives, 'I'm in agony. I'm ablaze.'

'Stick it in the font, then.'

'I might die.'

'Anyone know the burial service?' I asked.

'I buried a bloke at sea once,' said Navyrum.

'Oh, you're all right, Ives, then. There's a reservoir up the road.'

'Oh dear, oh dear,' said Barrowclough, 'this day's turning into a disaster. Come on, there's not going to be any storm. It's passed over. We should be getting that ditch dug.'

'Hold on, Mr Barrowclough,' I said, as I gave out the packets of crisps. 'We have to have our nourishment.'

'You crafty nurk, Fletch,' said Godber. 'You've been down the pub, ain't you?'

'Don't think I'd forget the lads, do you?'

'Did you buy those crisps out of my pound, Fletcher?'

'Yes, Mr Barrowclough, and the lads thank you very much.'

'Thank you, Mr Barrowclough,' said Godber and Scrounger together.

'You're a toff, Mr Barrowclough,' said Navyrum.

'Here, where's mine?' said Ives.

'You don't get none, Ives,' I said. 'Salt's bad for stings.

The rest of you, eat up. Now we've got all that protein inside us we can get on with the digging.'

'Digging, yes, there's been precious little done so far,' said Barrowclough. 'Come on, lads.'

Lennie Godber seemed to be having some difficulty in opening the church door. 'It's locked,' he said.

We all had a try, but no luck, it certainly was locked. I went into the vestry and tried the door there, no luck. Obviously the verger had been quicker than I thought without his bike.

' 'Ere, listen, we could break a window,' said Ives.

'Break a window? That window's four hundred years old,' I said. 'This is a church, you nurk. Have you got no sense of reverence? You're a Palestine, that's what you are, a Palestine.'

'Philistine, I think you mean, Fletcher. Philistine,' said Barrowclough.

'Yeah well, depends on your religion, don't it?'

'Man, let's ring the bell, some cat might hear it,' said Dylan.

'They never use the bell,' said Barrowclough. 'It's ancient, you see, like the tower. Last time the bell was used in these parts was to warn the villagers of marauding Scots.'

'Marauding Scots, was it?' I said.

'In the sixteenth century, yes. They came over the border, pillaging the crops and, well, ravishing the local womenfolk and all that.'

'Yes, I can see that ringing the bell would put the wind up their vests. They'd probably all flee south with their possessions strapped to the back of their Vauxhall Vivas. Mind you, I reckon a few of the womenfolk might stay. I mean, it's been four hundred years since they had a good ravishing.'

'Wait a moment, Fletch, there's someone outside,' said Scrounger.

We all jumped up on the pews to have a butcher's. There stood MacKay and the Vicar. 'A good idea to have locked the door, Mr MacKay, under the circumstances.'

'Well, it may be a good idea for you, Padre, but what about me? Not only have my prisoners absconded, so also has my number two officer. How can I face the Governor. In fifteen years of service I've never had a man get away from me. I'll kill them when I find them, and find them I will. This will put the kibosh on my good-conduct medal. I worked hard for it, too. That's what comes of showing kindness and consideration towards those placed in your care.'

'Yes, I do understand. But where can they have got to?'

'I don't know. But I shall have to report it to the prison authorities. I'll use the phone in the church if I may?'

'I'm sorry, Mr MacKay, but we don't run to such luxuries in this parish. However, there is a public telephone box about half a mile up the road.'

With that, they both walked off in the direction of the phone-box.

'We must get out,' said Barrowclough. 'Can't you do something, Fletcher? You've been convicted for breaking and entering.'

'Breaking and entering, yes. Entering is the operative word. I ain't never been convicted for breaking out of nowhere.'

'Flippin' hell,' said Godber. 'We get one day out from nick and what happens. We get locked in.'

We obviously had to get out of the church a bit lively before old MacKay got back with the heavy mob. Talk about Dragnet, it would be nothing to what MacKay would organise as soon as he got to the phone. I mean, we couldn't let old Barrowclough down after he'd given us the crisps. Using what expertise I had, I managed to pick the lock without leaving any signs of having done it. We all made a mad rush up to where we were supposed to be working. Sure enough, within half an hour they arrived. There were ten police cars, dogs, and practically every prison officer from the nick.

We were all deep down in the ditch when they arrived, out of sight.

'There, what did I tell you, Governor? All gone,' said MacKay.

'Right, Chief. Get on to the local . . .'

Mr Barrowclough stood up. 'All present and correct, sir.'

Well, you should have seen the look on old MacKay's face. If looks could kill, then the whole working party would have been dead there and then.

'Mr MacKay,' said the Governor in a very quiet way, 'Mr MacKay, I think that you and I should have a little talk. Don't you?'

'But, sir.'

'Don't "but, sir" me. I want to see you in my office in one hour's time. Right, Mr Barrowclough, continue with the good work.'

With that, the whole lot left and drove away.

We all started to laugh, even Ives, miserable gittish Ives. ' 'Ere, listen,' he said. ' 'Ere, did you see old MacKay's face when he discovered we were here. Cor blimey.'

Later that day me and young Lennie were in my cell when MacKay stuck his head around the door. Here it comes, I thought. 'The Edinburgh Tornado.'

'I have been dropped in it, have I not, Fletcher? I have been put upon from a great height.'

'Oh dear, Mr MacKay. I'm sorry to hear that, Mr MacKay. Anything we can do to alleviate it, as it were?'

'When I am in it, Fletcher, I absorb it with a stiff upper lip.'

'No choice, have you, if you're up to here in it.' I put my hand under my chin to show him what I meant.

'Yes, I can see you think you're clever, laddie. But mark my words, Fletcher, I absorb it all with cool Celtic calm, like a man. And then I relieve my frustrations by making sure that everyone down the line below me suffers.'

'Hey, that's not fair,' said young Godber.

'Fair?'

'Yeah. Why take it out on us? Nobody's fault we got locked in the Church.'

'Why were you in the Church to begin with, if you weren't skiving. Abusing our trust. Taking advantage of Barrowclough's laxity.'

'I didn't know Mr Barrowclough had laxity,' I said. 'Did you, Lennie?'

'No, poor fellow. 'Cos we were miles from anywhere.'

'Godber, do not imagine that you will be excluded from my spiteful resentment. Over the next few weeks you'll both suffer some terrible indignities. Your feet, Fletcher, your dinky little size sevens, will not touch the floor. I harbour grudges.'

He seemed very pleased with himself, as he strutted out. For someone who had just been in the karzy up to his neck, he seemed all right. Still, as long as I stayed out of his way, I'd survive. You get the pecking order in or out of the nick, so it don't really matter, does it, as long as you don't let 'em give you a baby.

'It was worth it, weren't it, Fletch?' said Godber.

'Course it was, son. A day out. Pint of beer, bag of

crisps. Ives in agony. All that and MacKay being dropped in, wallop ! We did all right, son.'

'You did better than most, Fletch.'

'Yeah, well naturally.'

'I got something out the day meself.'

'Oh yes? What?'

'Something I nicked from the Church. A surplice.'

'You stole? From the Church?'

'It's the only place you can get 'em.'

'Yeah, but what do you want it for anyway?'

'It'll satisfy a need I've had for some time, this will.'

'What you talking about?'

'It's to cover me from the gravy when you talk with your mouth full.'

Ways and Means

MacKay did eventually have his evil way with us. Not that he was able to get me put on report, or any of us for that matter. No, what he did was to drop a note in the prison letter-box saying that the whole of the work party had taken part in the killing of a sheep and that we had eaten the evidence. The cunning git got some sheep bones from somewhere and hid them so that the Governor could easily find them. As you can guess, Mr Venables did his nut. 'Fletcher,' he says, 'Fletcher, I placed my trust in you on two occasions, both times you have let me down. Now you'll have to suffer like any other prisoner in this establishment. You will work under close security. There will be no more trips to the local pub, oh yes, I know all about that too. I'm sick of trying to help people like you who only take kindness for a weakness. You will work in the Net-shop until I see fit to put you elsewhere.'

Not only was I working in the Net-shop making fishing nets, but young Godber, who I'd got to like a bit, had moved back into his old cell. You get to know people in the nick, really know them. I mean, if you spend three or four years kipping and slashing with the same old faces, you've just gotta know something about them, ain't you?

I suppose I'd been in the Net-shop about three weeks. Boring job. The game was to think of something else all the time. You know, like what job you're going to do when you get out, like whether it will be the Post Office or the local Co-op. The Co-op would be better, they don't have as much security as the PO. You could do a course in mental relaxation. Anyway, there's always plenty to think about. Just take a butcher's around the workshop. Everyone in it's being punished for same trivial thing. Take McLaren, for instance. He had a cushy job in the kitchen, but he was victimised. As I said to Mr Barrowclough. 'What chance has a man got, when all the establishment forces are aligned against him? We know society's extracting its revenge on those who never had a chance to begin with. Look at McLaren here. Never had a chance, did he?'

'Cowing used to it, ain't I?' McLaren murmured.

'What did you do, son?'

'I spoilt the stinking soup.'

'He spoilt the soup! And for that he has to pay the penance. Well, what chance has any of us got?'

'McLaren, that's not the whole truth and well you know,' said Barrowclough. 'You spoilt the soup because you held a prison officer's head under it for two minutes.'

'Yeah, well . . .' he said.

'You tried to drown that prison officer, McLaren. It was a vicious and unprovoked attack.'

'Tried to drown him?' I said. 'Who was it?'

'Parker. He cowing asked for it.'

'What, Hang'em and Flog'em Parker, that fascist git of a screw?'

'You could have severely scalded him,' said Barrowclough.

'Not in this nick, you couldn't,' I said. 'Not with the lukewarm soup we get. Poisoned him possibly, yeah, could have poisoned him.'

'What sort of soup was it?' asked Ives.

'Mixed vegetable.'

'Mixed vegetable?' I said. 'Stone me. I bet he was furious. All those bits of barley and carrot up his nose.'

'It's not funny, Fletcher,' said Barrowclough. 'It was a vicious attack, and that's why McLaren's here. And your attitude makes it quite clear why you're here.'

'Oh, I see. Yes, well, I see. Yes, well.'

'I was provoked,' McLaren put in.

'I bet you were, my son.'

'He called me a black bastard.'

'Now if that were true,' said Barrowclough, 'if he really did say that, you could have gone straight to the Governor, McLaren.'

'Oh yeah? Fat chance,' I said. 'I mean technically he ain't got a leg to stand on. Technically the facts as stated by the Prison Officer are not wholly inaccurate, being as how he is a) negro and b) illegitimate.'

'It was the way he said it.'

'I know that. You know that. He'll probably tell the Governor that in the course of conversation he simply observed that you were non-Caucasian and born out of wedlock.'

'Now that's enough talking, all of you,' said Barrowclough. 'There's work to be done.'

'Work?' I laughed. 'Knitting string vests for hippopotamuses. This probably won't fit me anyway. They're cunning, ain't they? 'Cos giving you a job like this they knows that we won't cock it up. They knows we wouldn't do nothing slipshod, 'cos we'd be screwing up those brave fishermen of England, wouldn't we? Leave a few holes in here and they'd be back half a top of cod short, and the price of fish fingers would rocket. Not to mention cod pieces. Whereas of course mailbags, well – don't care if we do a sloppy job there, do we? Makes it easier for our mates that rob mail trains.'

Naturally old Barrowclough reacted. 'Fletcher,' he said, 'one just has to listen to you for a matter of minutes to know your type. When you first came here I had high hopes for you, I won't pretend I didn't. It has to be said, you're surly and hostile.'

'Yeah well, years of prison hardens you, doesn't it? Well-known fact.'

'But you've only been here six weeks.'

'I'm not really hostile, I'm just resentful. Well, when I first came in here I thought between the two of us there was some sort of rapport there, you know?'

'You mean you thought I was in your pocket?'

'What a terrible thing to say! Just 'cos I asked you one or two little favours. What a terrible thing to say! In themselves they was meaningless, but they would just have made life that little bit more tolerable.'

He looked at me in a strange way. 'Your little favours were supposed to include a single cell, with a window facing south, not to mention the extra blankets and the bit of carpet, the special soap, extra tobacco, carpet slippers, a set of darts, and a roll of soft toilet paper and some back copies of *Playboy*.'

'There's no need to exaggerate, Mr Barrowclough. I said you needn't bother with the darts if you were pushed.'

'Now I haven't forgotten that you've given me very helpful advice on . . . on, domestic matters. You mustn't think that Mrs Barrowclough and I don't appreciate that, because we do. But I'll be damned if I'll let you treat me like some glorified batman.'

'No? I mean, no,' I said.

'Well, as long as we've got that right.'

'I wasn't just referring to your . . . marital problems. Though one can't help reflect that there's been some change in your old lady's attitude . . .'

'How can you tell that?'

'Oh, just little things. In the morning your general demeanour. A spring in your step. That certain smile that plays around your lips when you comes round ordering us to slop out.'

'What certain smile?'

'The smile of a man who's getting his oats.'

'Fletcher!'

'Are you denying it, then?'

'Look, I've said I'm grateful,' he said, moving away.

'Oh yes, well yes. I don't want your gratitude, Mr Barrowclough. I've learnt my lesson. It's them and us.'

'Look, Fletcher — '

'Now if you'll excuse me, I must get back to my knitting, Mr Barrowclough. Talking to you I'm getting all behind like a donkey's tail. I might not get my full 60p this week, and I won't have enough to buy my wintergreen.' I gave him a sly look. Was he going to bite or not?

He did. 'Wintergreen, Fletcher?'

'Yeah, all my money goes on medicaments. I've never been a well man, you see. Always been suspect to lumbago and rheumatics. All those illnesses what are caused by not having enough blankets, having a cold draughty cell facing north, and walking around on concrete floors without carpet slippers. Anything like that.'

'All right, Fletcher. I'll see about the extra blanket.'

You're in, Fletch, I thought. Get in further. 'No, no, no. I don't want any favours from you, sir, I don't want nothing at all.'

'Oh come on, Fletcher.'

'Well, if you insist, Mr Barrowclough, there is one thing that wouldn't go amiss. Only 'cos you insist that is. It's a small thing really.'

'What's that?' he asked.

'I want a job in the library.'

I didn't get it as you could imagine. Never mind, do it a

little bit at a time. It comes to those who wait, and are cunning enough. Later that night as I was walking down to the recess I accidentally bumped into McLaren. Apples and other things went everywhere, he'd just been to the prison canteen.

'Cowing hell.'

'Sorry, son, sorry,' I said.

'Can't you watch where you're cowing well going, Fletcher.'

'Look, I said I'm sorry, son. My fault. Won't happen again. Promise you.'

He stood there, thickset and tough. You could see the aggression pouring out of his eyes. 'Watch it, that's all.'

'I will, son. I promise. No bovva, eh?'

He picked up the apples and the rest of the stuff he'd dropped. I waited until he was right by my cell and then kicked him hard on his 'arris. He fell across the table and I grabbed him by the collar and pulled his face close to mine. 'Now, I know you're an 'ard case, son. We all do. We know you're full of nasty militant feelings with no thought for others, only yourself. But if you ever speaks to me like that again, I shall twist your black head round like a cork in a bottle of Beaujolais, and give it to Clarence, that poof in B wing, to keep his wigs on.'

After a few more choice words of wisdom, we decided that he was sorry. I offered him a snout and we sat on the bed.

'You know, son, you're your own worst enemy, ain't you?'

'What makes you say that, Fletch?'

'Look, I know that things ain't all that easy for you. Seeing as you're black with a Scottish father. I mean, it's an unfortunate mixture. It's the Scottish side that brings out all that aggression in you, ain't it?'

'Is it?' he said. Poor kid, he looked a bit lost.

'Yeah, course it is. I mean, it subdues your basic West Indian personality. Which is one of exuberant high spirits. All them steel bands, Jamaican rum and carnivals, like. You know, all that lordy lordy bit. I mean, it only takes someone to score a boundary in a Test match and they have a firework display.'

'What you on about, Fletch? I ain't never set foot in the West Indies. I was born in Greenock. Or at least found. Some copper found me up an alley wrapped in the *Glasgow Herald*.'

'Yeah well, I did admit, didn't I, you ain't had it easy.'

'I never knew my father. A Mam who didn't want me. Flaming orphanage and I'm black with a Scottish accent. What you want me to be, Fletcher, happy-go-bloody-lucky?'

'It could be worse, son, couldn't it? I mean, the Scottish part could have been MacKay! But you don't want to let that illegitimate tag worry you. Lots of famous people was illegitimate. Royalty like. And Lawrence of Arabia . . . Michelangelo . . . Marco Polo . . . Napper Wainwright.'

'Who's Napper Wainwright?' he asked.

'He was a screw in Brixton. Mind you, he was a right bastard.'

'Never let you forget.'

'It ain't a stigma no more. Not these days, in these liberated times. Out of fashion, marriage is. All these glamour people, these trend-setters, your pop stars and television personalities, well all their offspring's outa wedlock, isn't it? Frankly, in a few years' time, illegitimates is going to be fashionable figures. Like homosexuals are at the moment. In fact, being an illegitimate black poof's about as chic as you could get.'

'I'm not a — '

'Oh come on, I knows that.'

'If anyone suggests — '

'Course no one won't. See the way you fly off the handle? Own worst enemy. Come the hard man, where's it get you?'

'Got me pride.'

'Oh yes, pride is it? Listen, we ain't even got privacy in here, and where's a man's pride when he ain't got no privacy. You have to learn to turn the other cheek. Yes, sir, no, sir, three bags full, sir.'

'Makes me sick to my guts. You obviously had no reason to hate the law like me.'

'That don't mean I don't despise them. But I beat them by more subtle methods. Let me give you an example. I've got a bit of garden back of my house. Flower bed, bit of lawn, some rhubarb and gooseberries. It's not much but it's a lot for my old lady Isobel to do when I'm inside. Anyway, I was on remand in Brixton. I done this job – a jewellers in Southwark. They got me, but they didn't get the stuff, see. You know what I mean. Anyway, I'm in Brixton, and I writes to Isobel and says, "Please dig in the back garden." Course, next morning there's twelve police round there, with shovels, being as they'd read my mail, the devious nurks.'

'Did they find the stuff?'

'There weren't no stuff to find. It was hidden elsewhere. Just my way of getting the garden turned over. All Isobel had to do then was plant the geraniums. They was a riot of colour when I come out.'

'Crafty nurk.'

'Subtle. Certainly more subtle than immersing a screw in the soup of the day.'

'Wait till it's pea soup next time. Drown quicker in pea soup. Or maybe semolina pudding.'

'How long you in for, son?'

'Three years.'

'You ain't going to be out for ten, the way you're going.'

'I ain't hit a screw for three months. That's if you don't count Parker and the soup.'

I laughed. 'Not actually hit one, no. But apart from the soup incident, you've tripped one down a flight of stairs, locked one in the deep freeze, caught one in the goolies with a football, and put cascara in the Padre's cocoa.'

'Got a lot of pleasure out of that.'

'Yeah, and a lot of solitary. Not as much as the Padre got. He was shut in the bog all week.'

We had another snout and sat there in the old flowery-dell contemplating the joys of doing a bit of porridge in what wasn't a bad nick. In a way it reminded me of Branksome Prison in Dorset. That was the nick that the Home Office had forgotten about. The Governor only had five cons there at one stage and he was copping two fifty quid per head for three hundred cons he hadn't got. Then the Home Office tumbled that they'd forgotten about the nick and decided to send a Home Office Inspector to check the place out. They got out of it real shrewd like. What happened was that one of the cons, Bennie-the-Mole, came up with this idea that if they got a load of people down from a theatrical agency under the pretence that a TV company was going to do a documentary programme, they would have enough cons for when the Inspector arrived. The Home Office was so pleased with the Governor for carrying on under such diabolical conditions, like being forgot and all that, that they promoted him right away to Head Office and the whole nick got transferred to Dartmoor. I think there are still some actors in the moor wondering how long the programme is going to take.'

'Welfare Officer wants me to see a psychiatrist, Fletch. Observation like. Thinks I need psychiatric help.'

'That's not a bad idea,' I said.

'Course not. I'd be crazy to turn it down. Cushy hospital, better grub, soft bed. But the Governor wouldn't wear it. Said he knew my sort, I was trying it on.'

'Yeah, he's shrewder than we credit him for, that Venables. It's my problem, see. Trying to ingratiate myself back in his good books. I've lost a lot of ground in the credibility stakes. I've been racking my brains to come up with an idea to get out of the Net-shop, and I think we just might be able to work something out. You with your compulsive sloshing of screws and the like and me with my cunning brain.'

We talked over what I had in mind, and then he got up to go.

'Well thanks, Fletch, like. It's been more use than talking to the Welfare Officer. You're straight, you are. Bloke can trust you.'

'Don't forget your things.'

'Oh thanks. Where's me apples?'

'Dunno, son. Aren't they outside on the floor? Someone must've had them. Bunch of criminals in here.'

'Cowing heck. Oh well, tata, Fletch.' And off he went, while I sat back and enjoyed a delicious apple.

The following morning was taken up with normal boring routine work in the Net-shop. Part of the plan was put into operation when McLaren asked to go and see the medical officer. They call it going 'special sick'. What's so special about being sick beats me but that's the way the prison runs, along stupid lines. Anyway, McLaren went sick and had been away for about half an hour when the alarm bell started. Barrowclough was on duty in the Net-shop at the time. 'If that's for me, tell them I'll ring back,' I said.

'Don't be funny, Fletcher,' he said. 'Now, back to your cells, all of you.'

The normal prison routine when the alarm bell goes is for the screws to lock the nick up. It doesn't matter what the trouble is about, 'Lock 'em up and count 'em' is the answer. So there I was, banged up in my flowery.

'What's up?' I said, as Barrowclough came in.

'It's MacLaren.'

'Oh, he's gone over the wall, has he?'

'He's on the roof and he won't come down. Threatening to chuck himself over, unless we answer his demands.'

'Prisoners Rights Union, is it? I don't know what the younger element of convict is coming to, not like that when I first came inside.'

'No, Fletcher, it's not the Prisoners Rights Union. It's McLaren doing his nut on the roof. Threatens to throw himself off if we don't listen to him. Get the prison a bad name, this sort of thing. Next thing we'll know, it'll be on News at Ten.'

'Oh yes. Then *Panorama*. *World in Action*. A six-part series in the *Sunday Times* taking the lid off the penal system. Then questions in the House of Commons. The Howard League for Penal Reform. A right old turn up for the media.'

'It upsets the men, this sort of thing.'

'They'll be playing the anvil chorus on the radiators with their mugs next,' I said. 'You could have a full-scale riot on your hands by tea-time. Though hang about, what day is it?'

'Thursday.'

'Oh no, they won't riot this afternoon. Good tea on a Thursday, in'it? Cauliflower cheese.'

'Fletcher, you take nothing seriously. There's a man's

life in danger, to say nothing of the reputation of Slade Prison.'

'Oh dear, we don't want to lose our good will, do we? Or we won't get any bookings for next year.'

'Your flippancy is in very bad taste at a time like this,' he said.

I could see that Barrowclough was getting upset. If the plan was going to be successful I had to do something. 'Sorry, Mr Barrowclough. It's just that I believe that the only way you can survive in this place is to keep joking. How are they trying to get him down?'

'At the moment the Padre's trying to talk him down through a megaphone.'

'The Padre? Is he sober? I mean the village pub's just closed, hasn't it?'

'He's not alone. The Welfare Officer, Mr Gillespie, is with him.'

'What's he know? The lad's just out of university. Got no experience of the practical. He's probably thumbing his textbooks now. Trying to find the chapter on negro nutters and how to deal with them.'

'I think you're being a bit hard on Mr Gillespie.'

'Mr Barrowclough!' This was it. 'Permission to see the Governor?'

'What? Not now, Fletcher. Perhaps when it's all over.'

'It's about now that I want to talk. About the lad. I think I might be able to help, see.'

'Help the lad?' he said.

'Yeah. Are you going to take me or not?'

'Well, I will if you think it might help. But Mr Mac-Kay's in charge.'

'There you are then. Anything's better than leaving it to Mr MacKay. He'd probably just let the lad jump, then jump on him.'

Old Barrowclough didn't like that, but he took me to

the front office. After a long rabbit the Governor asked me why I thought I could get McLaren down.

'Do you know something we don't?' he said.

'I know something about what makes the lad tick. I'm not saying you're not all experienced in these matters, Mr Venables. But in his mind you all represent the Establishment which only inflames his feelings of hostility and persecution. I mean, the Padre's been out there rabbiting for two hours, and all he's had for his trouble's a brick up his megaphone.'

'How is the Padre?' Venables asked MacKay, who had come along to see what I was up to.

'He's very upset, sir. Very upset that he couldn't get through to the man. Very upset also about losing two front teeth.'

'There'll be no sermon on Sunday,' said Barrowclough.

'Thank heaven for small mercies,' said the Governor.

'You see, it's a question of attitude, isn't it, sir,' I said. 'Last thing the lad wanted was all that preaching and sermonising. Same with our well-meaning intrepid Mr Gillespie. Asked for trouble, didn't he, going up that ladder.'

'How is Gillespie, Mr MacKay?'

'As comfortable as could be expected, sir.'

'We must do something. We can't leave McLaren where he is, sir,' said Barrowclough.

'Why not?' said MacKay. 'Let him sweat it out. Then tonight when that cold wind comes whistling over the Pennines, let him freeze it out. If we give way just one inch, we'll establish a regrettable precedent. We'll have prisoners crawling on every inch of rooftop, clamouring for extra blankets, cleaner sheets, bigger helpings.'

'On the other hand I could go up and talk to the lad,' I said. 'He don't trust you lot, right? And you can't send for friends or family 'cos the lad ain't got none. But maybe he'd respond to the overtures of one of his fellow inmates.'

'That's a very good point, Fletcher,' said the Governor. 'But it could be quite dangerous.'

'Yes, yes, I know, sir. I'm aware that I'm putting life and limb in some jeopardy. But you try not to think about things like that. Try to ignore the tight knot of fear in the stomach, which I ain't had since Kuala Lumpur.'

'Kuala Lumpur?'

'Yes, I was there National Service. Fighting those Malayan bandits for Queen and country. Jungle warfare. Wading through swamps up to here, rifle above your head to keep the barrel dry. Suddenly you're in a clearing. There'd be nothing but the sound of the night creatures in the undergrowth, and Taffy Williams's stomach rumbling.'

'I was in Kuala Lumpur with the Black Watch,' said MacKay. 'What mob was you with, Fletcher?'

'Me? Oh, er . . . well we was on special duties. You know. Like the Dagger Division in the desert at night, slip in and out like . . . rats, that's it, Desert Rats.'

'But I thought the Desert Rats fought against Rommel in Africa in the last war?' said Barrowclough.

'Yes, you're right, but we was special operations like, secret.'

'I was in Singapore for my National Service,' Barrowclough went on. 'RAF Equipment.'

'Oh, Singapore. Doddle, Singapore. All them historical temples and hysterical brothels.'

'Gentlemen, there's a man on the roof,' put in the Governor.

'We cannot let a prisoner go up, sir,' said MacKay. 'We have to deal with our own problems, we can't leave them in the hands of a prisoner.'

'In that case, sir, there is only one alternative,' I said to Venables. 'You'll have to go up.'

In the distance I could hear the sound of a fire engine coming. They were really taking this seriously. We already had the Prison Doctor, three medical screws, half a dozen coppers, and now the fire service. They set the extending ladder up against the side of the building where McLaren was. I looked up the whole length of it. Christ, what a climb. Still, I'd thought of the idea so I had to go through with it. Everyone's eyes were on me as I started up. Step by step I ascended. I didn't dare look down. In fact, now that I thought about it, I'd always hated heights. Slowly but surely I made my way to the top. I could see McLaren sitting there, looking quite pleased with himself.

'Hi, Fletch. Lovely view up here,' he said as I finally got to the top and started to clamber on to the roof. 'Hey, watch out for them slates, they're a bit dodgy.'

I opened my eyes. I'd closed them for the last six feet of the ascent. 'High enough, ain't it?'

'It was your idea,' he said. 'Climb a roof, you said.'

'Did you have to pick such a high one? I'm not a bleedin' steeplejack even if you are.'

'Makes you look more of a hero. Got more dramatic impact.'

'Don't use words like impact, will you? Not at this height.'

'Want a bit of chewing gum?'

'Chewing gum? McLaren, you must be out of your tiny mind. Of course I don't want any bloody chewing gum. All I want is to get down off this roof.' I looked down at the vast crowd who were all standing in the prison exercise yard. I could see all them grotty faces looking up at us. What a right mug I was to have suggested the idea in the first place.

'We can't go yet. You're supposed to talk me out of it. I'm a nutter, remember? We'll be up here at least an hour before I succumb to your eloquent persuasion.'

'An hour? I've got vertigo. I'm sick. I'm dizzy.'

'We'll go down in time for tea. It's cauliflower cheese today, isn't it?'

And we did! I promise you that McLaren had his moment of glory that day, or should I say night, 'cos it was practically nightfall before he allowed me to help him down. Well, not me help him, more like him help me. The truth is I was so petrified that I couldn't move on my own. I mean, there have been lots of other heroes that have suffered with vertigo, haven't there? Take Churchill, for instance. Well-known fact he hated going up high.

The next day saw the results of all my hard work. There I was in the hospital wing, pushing my trolley. 'Ding dong, Fletcher calling. Your friendly mobile library.'

I wheeled the trolley into a small ward. There were three empty beds, and the fourth was occupied by Ives, grotty nurkish Ives lying in bed!

' 'Ere, listen,' he said. Typical Ives.

'Oh, it's you, Ives. How'd you work this number?'

' 'Ere, listen, I'm ill. Gastero-enteritis.'

'Oh, they're not difficult symptoms to fake. Keep running to the bog every five minutes clutching your stomach and screaming in agony.'

'I didn't fake nothing. I really got it. Genuine,' he said.

'Oh, that's unusual. Must be some sort of record, a genuine illness in this hospital.'

'What about you? I heard you had a spot of bother.'

'I have a few bruises, but they say I can still have children.'

'I heard it was shock. They told me you couldn't stop shaking.'

'All right, Ives, wouldn't you be shaking after an heroic ascent like that?'

'Your descent weren't so heroic. The kid had to bring you down on his back.'

'Look, don't needle me, Ives. Otherwise you won't be getting anything worth reading off here at all. I shall be palming you off with *Lamb's Tales from Shakespeare*, without benefit of mint sauce.'

' 'Ere, listen, Fletch. I've never been able to understand you. You've been the biggest villain in the nick. You've caused more trouble than anyone else I know of. Yet you finish up with all the cushy jobs. How do you do it?'

'Simple really, Ives. I work at it. That little rooftop caper was all set up, wasn't it. It was all arranged between McLaren and me. He went up there so I could rescue him. All right, I didn't expect to get a dizzy turn like I did. But at least I goes up a hero and he comes down one. As a result of which I have leapfrogged my way back into the Governor's good books. My slate is clean and all my misdemeanours is writ off. I also have the cushiest job in this nick – assistant librarian. And the kid, McLaren – who they've decided to treat with sympathy and understanding – has the second cushiest. Hospital orderly.'

'You crafty nurk, Fletcher.'

'Crafty as they come, my son.'

' 'Ere, listen, what about a decent book? Know what I mean?'

'You mean something a bit risqué.'

'Won't be risky, I won't tell anyone.'

'Risqué means dirty, you nurk.'

'Oh dirty, yes. That's what I mean, yes.'

I picked up the book I'd been looking at previously.

'Well, I could offer you this one. It's about the sex-starved lady pygmies of the Malaysian Jungle.'

His mouth fell open. 'What's it called?'

'*Little Women*. It's an erotic classic. Don't you remember the trial at the Old Bailey?'

' 'Er vaguely, like. 'Ere, what's it doing in the prison library?'

'Library? Don't be a nurk, Ives. I nicked that from the Governor's private bookshelf. It was concealed next to the tropical fish book for 1973.' I opened the book. 'Here, listen to this. "She came out of the clearing, her flimsy shift soaked by the sudden monsoon. Through it Gilbert could discern the hard and firm contours of her proud young Malaysian body. She was everything that he had imagined on that long train ride from Kuala Lumpur. Suddenly she was standing close to him, and he gazed in awe at her half-naked, uptilted, perfectly formed — " ' I shut the book. His eyeballs were standing out like organ stops. I had him right where I wanted him.

' 'Ere, listen, perfectly formed what, perfectly formed what?'

'I'll give you a clue. There was two of them, and they went up and down when she ran, and I don't mean her kneecaps. Now if you was to borrow this torrid saga of Malaysian love rites, well it could be yours for only two snouts, couldn't it?'

'Right.'

'In advance.'

'Done.'

'You certainly have been.'

I started to wheel my trolley out and bumped into McLaren who was just coming in.

'Just watch it, you clumsy nurk.'

'Hey, hey, hey. Have we learnt nothing? Where did that ever get us?' I said.

'Oh, sorry, Mr Fletcher.'

'That's all right, Mr McLaren. And how's things in the medical world?'

'Fair, Mr Fletcher, fair. And the library?'

'A doddle, Mr McLaren.'

'Did you get me *The Godfather*?'

'Yes, I did. Did you get me my wintergreen ointment?'

Men Without Women

The job in the library went along very very well. What with all the fiddles I could wangle with the kitchen and the hospital I lived like a lord. The Governor was well satisfied with the way that I had changed. No more subversive activities. No more knitting fishing nets or mailbags. Oh yes, life was good.

One day we had a new geezer come to work in the library as my assistant, a nice kid really. The Governor thought that, seeing as I'd made such a good job with McLaren, I could be trusted to look after any other stray body that might turn up. This one was like most other kids that get nicked. Full of aggression and stupidity. But underneath, that's if you could reach him, a nice kid. Anyway, as I was saying, one day he came to me.

'Fletch, can I have a word with you?'

'No. What do you want?'

'Are you doing anything important right now?'

'Yes. I'm thinking.'

'Thinking?'

'Yes, thinking. I realise, Warren,' that's his name by the way, 'that to you and the rest of that lot thinking is an alien pastime. But some of us, more endowed with a bit of grey matter where it matters, namely in the bonce, preserve our identity and sanity in this place by thinking.'

'Yes I can see that, Fletch. But what are you thinking about?'

'At the moment I'm thinking why don't this bloke Warren naff off and leave me alone.'

That's the trouble in the nick. You can't have

moments of peace and quiet when you want them. I know that quite a lot of nicks only have single cells, but even in there you can rarely be alone, even with your thoughts. Something always manages to interrupt what you're thinking. The sound of keys jangling or heavy footsteps on the cell landings. I suppose the worst thing in most nicks is the smell, you know, the smell of fear and hate. It's always there.

'Look, Fletch,' he says, sort of sorry like, 'I realise that you are a man of . . .'

'Intellect.'

'Well, yes . . .'

'And erudition,' I says.

'That too, Fletch, if you say so. But that was why I wanted to have a word. I got this letter.'

He pulled a crumpled purple envelope from his pocket and handed it over to me. I sniffed it.

'From a woman, I would say.'

'That's right. How can you tell?'

'Female handwriting, in'it? And judging by the stationery and the perfume, a woman of little sophistication or class.'

'That's right, it's from the wife.'

'Oh, I don't mean to infer — '

'No, you're a clever bloke, Fletch. That's why I wanted your help really.'

'Oh I see. Another one. My counsel, is it? Advice to the lovelorn. Now you want me to assess the situation and compose an appropriate response.'

'No, it's simpler than that,' he said. 'Just want you to read it to me . . .'

Poor nurk. Like twenty per cent of the nick he couldn't read or write. How he was expected to change his ways I'll never know. They do try and teach the guys who don't read or write, but the trouble is most of them are too ashamed to let on.

'Look, Warren, come and see me at association tonight, okay? I've got a session with some of the others on just this subject.'

Later that night after we'd had our tea, Warren joined the group. There was Heslop, and Tolly, and Lukewarm.

'Now,' I said, 'this letter of Warren's – it's very, very typical. It's your classic wive's letter after you've done eight months to a year – that sort of period. I mean, wives make all those marital vows, but you have to be around to make sure they do love, honour and obey, don't you?' There were murmurs of agreement all round. 'You see, after a while a wife gets restless urges. So having got restless, chances are they weaken and gets naughty. That's when the big elbow comes in. That's when you start getting "Dear John's".'

'I've had one of those,' said Tolly.

'Course you have, you berk,' said Lukewarm. 'Your name's John, ain't it?'

'I'll kill her,' said Warren, thumping his fist on the table.

'Yes . . . that is one solution,' I said, 'but what we're looking for here is something a little more constructive. Besides, you're in here and she's in Bolton.'

'It's visiting day next week.'

'Yes, yes, we know. But if you was to strangle your wife on visiting day there's a good chance you'd lose your remission.'

'I'm just saying.'

'Leave it off, Warren,' said Tolly. 'Leave it to Fletch. He knows, doesn't he?'

'Thank you, Tolly, for the vote of confidence. Now where was I?'

'Just getting to the naughty bit.'

'Oh yes. Now having got naughty she gets guilty, and that's where you step in, or rather I step in. Before it gets to the Dear John stage you sends a letter that points out one or two things. Sort of like what I've written out here in which I have sought to achieve subtlety with strength. An obvious display of affection but carrying beneath it a hint of menace. Sort of like this : "My darling, I realise these are difficult times for you. Here we are, men without women – and you are women without men with all your attendant frustrations." Nice phrase that, isn't it?'

'Well chosen,' said Lukewarm.

'Got it out of *Reader's Digest*. "I realise, my love, that it is a lot to ask, to ask you to wait for me. But I will be upset, dearest one, if I hear about you having a nibble of something you shouldn't. I have friends on the outside, dear heart, who have friends who have friends. And any word from them of you having any hanky-panky will be followed by swift and merciless retribution. I hope the weather is nice and you are feeling well in yourself. Yours etc, blah, blah, blah." '

'Very good, Fletch,' said Tolly. 'I told you, Warren, Fletch knows.'

'My wife's sister lives in Sidcup,' Heslop said suddenly. 'And sometimes we stay there, or drop in for a cuppa when we bin to the coast.'

'What's that got to do with it?'

'Well, once we was there, you see, and while my wife was upstairs powdering her nose prior to going to see *Paint Your Wagon* by the Sidcup Operatic, her sister touched me.'

Heslop relapsed into silence.

'Where, where?' we all said.

'In the kitchen.'

'Oh.'

'She got very . . . heated. Had me pressed up against the Aga.'

' 'Spect you got fairly heated then, didn't you, up against the Aga?' I said.

'She was saying how she'd always fancied me, she knew it was wrong, being as she was the wife's sister, but she couldn't control her true feelings no longer. I had to say now listen, Gwendolyn – that was her name, see – I said, "Listen, Gwendolyn, this is no way to behave. It's not right, it isn't decent and what happened must never happen again." '

'But nothing did happen,' said Warren.

'Yes it did.'

'Doesn't sound like it,' I said. 'All you did was give her a lecture.'

'That was an hour later when we were getting out of bed,' he said.

'Look, look what point is it you're making, Einstein? You're on a different time-scale to all the rest of us. Your head's about twenty minutes slow. Now,' I went on, 'I've done copies of this letter. There's one for each of you. You just have to write 'em out in your own handwriting. I'll do yours, Warren, for a small fee, as you can't write. Of course you must all fill in the names of your loved ones. What are their names?'

'Iris,' said Heslop.

'Norma,' said Tolly.

'Trevor,' said Lukewarm.

'Oh. Well, post these sharp 'cos we want them to read them before they comes up on visiting day. So that they can be duly humble and apprehensive.'

'There's no evidence that my Iris has strayed from the straight and narrow,' said Heslop.

'What? Oh well, post it in any case. A stitch in time saves a hole in the trousers.'

'Oh, right, I'll post it then.'

'You got no problems on this score then, Fletch?' asked Tolly. 'Marriage like.'

'No, no. I been married a bit longer than you lads, ain't I? And she knows her place.'

'Doesn't she get upset that you keep going inside all the time?' said Lukewarm. 'She's got a house and three kids to run, after all. I don't know how she does it.'

'Oh, I'm not saying it ain't hard, obviously. A few weeks ago she had to build a new coal bunker. That's a terrible job for a woman.'

'You mean she had to mix the cement and all that?' asked Lukewarm.

'Oh, no, no. That was all right. Her mother came over and did that.'

We spent the rest of the evening association till the bell went playing cards and darts, that's after they had all coughed up with the snout they had to pay for the lesson in letter writing. As we got up to go back to our flowery-dells Barrowclough came over.

'Come on now, lads. Well, Fletcher, have you enjoyed yourself usefully this evening?'

'Just giving the lads the benefit of my experience, Mr Barrowclough.'

'I – I've heard that your opinion is sought in this prison. Mr Gillespie, the Welfare Officer, he was saying that he's running out of customers.'

'Yeah, well Welfare Officers – like the Padre, they're not to be trusted.'

'I think you're being a bit harsh on a very well-meaning body of men and women,' he said.

'I ain't saying they ain't well-intentioned. But the lads, you know, they bring me their problems, they know I speak their language.' I sat down again. 'By the way, how's things with your old lady?'

'What? Oh well ... difficult, you know, Fletcher, she's been a bit better since you and I had that chat, but, well, things could be easier. She's not an easy woman to live with, my wife.'

'No, no ... not still the postman is it?'

'Oh no, heaven forbid. He's in the sorting office in Carlisle now.'

'Sorted him out, did they?'

'Pardon?'

'Nothing, nothing. Shouldn't joke at your expense.'

'No, no. Well, I'm afraid I'll have to ask you to ...'

'Yeah, I know. Time I turned in.'

'I hate this part of the job, you know, Fletcher. Shutting men up, caging them in.'

'Yes – it is a shame. Just when the good telly's starting an' all. All we ever see's the flaming news. And *Nationwide*. Fat lot of interest to us, that is, locked in here.'

'No,' he said. 'I've never got used to bolting those doors. I think of you in that little cell – and I think of me going out of here, and going home, to my house. To my wife, who's waiting for me.' He stopped.

'What's wrong, Mr Barrowclough?'

'I sometimes wish I was in here with you lot ...'

During the next week, Warren and I had lots of chats about married life and its ups and downs. I told him how I'd met my wife and he told me how he'd met his. On one occasion he confessed that he'd never been out with anybody else. I thought that was great, I mean that's got to be true love, or on the other hand perhaps he couldn't get another woman? There are some like that, I mean take MacKay for starters.

Anyway, one evening I was sitting on my bunk when Warren came in with a slop-bucket.

'Would you do the honours?' he asked, producing another letter.

'All right.' I sniffed it. 'The wife?'

'Yeah, knows her perfume anywhere.'

'Not surprised, Warren. It's very distinctive. Should think it kills ninety-nine per cent of all known germs.'

'Don't you like it? Should I tell her to change it?'

'No no, my son. You're safe from other men as long as she wears this. Now let's see. "My dear Bunny." Bunny?'

'Yes. Bunny Warren.'

'Ah. "I got your letter, for which many thanks. It's wonderful that already prison has taught you to write and spell proper. Who knows what you may come out" – what's this word? Oh "qualified as". It was the k-w that fooled me. "Now, Bunny, about this other thing. I don't know where you've got these doubts from. I spend my nights watching the box on which is placed your picture which I cut out the *Manchester Evening News*. It is the one of you resisting arrest, but I have cut off the two policemen. I've left the Alsatian on as I know how fond of animals you are. I did go out Sunday I admit, but only to see your mother who has had to go into Salford again with her feet." She usually go into Salford without them then?'

'No no, what she means is, er, she's had to go back to the chiropodist like. She's always had these feet you see.'

'Has she? The same ones? Oh. Anyhow. "Never mind the expense, I am coming up visiting day, to put your mind at rest. I will get Saturday morning off at the laundry. I miss you and I think of us when you were at home and you used to take my..." '

'What – used to what?'

'Oh well, this last bit's a bit intimate, Warren, I don't think I should read it aloud in front of me. Personal, isn't it?'

'What is it? What's she say?'

'Er, well, how can I say it? Well, the gist of it is . . . she misses you, er – no. Put it another way . . . which you obviously did. No, it's just that . . . well, she regrets that you're not home providing for her.'

'Oh. Oh good. Anything else?'

'Anything else would be a bit of an anti-climax. It just says, "I wish you were here. Oh well, I must stop and get on my lover" . . . Oh, I see, "must stop and get on, my lover. See you Sat. Elaine.'

'Oh. Yes, she's a good girl Elaine. No problems there – what you think, Fletch?'

'It's a nice letter, Warren. Heartfelt. You can tell. And coming up Saturday, isn't she?'

'Aye. And so is Heslop's missus. All the way from Kent. And Tolly's wife. You're a clever lad, Fletch.'

'Yeah well.'

'Your ole lady coming, is she?'

'She'll be here.'

'You had a letter like?'

'No, I ain't actually . . . but she'll be here.'

'I think Lukewarm's fella's coming up as well.'

'Is he now? Course Lukewarm's got a different sort of problem from the rest of you. His Trevor's the insecure one there, isn't he? I mean there's six hundred men in here. So whereas you're all worried what your wives are up to on the outside, Trevor's worried what Lukewarm's up to on the inside.'

As Warren left MacKay arrived, smirking all over his face.

'Tell me, Fletcher, is it true that this is the office of Slade Prison's Miss Lonelyhearts?'

'That why you're here then, is it? Problems of that nature?'

'I do not have problems of that nature.'

'Oh come on, Mr MacKay, all screws, beg your pardon, all prison officers have problems in that area. I mean, matrimonially you and me are very similar. 'Cos while we're in here we can't be too sure what our old ladies are getting up to, can we? No difference.'

'There is a major difference, Fletcher. Your wives are criminals' wives. They belong to the criminal classes with all their inherent traits of slovenliness and promiscuity. Our wives are the wives of uniformed men, used to a life of service and duty, decency and moral fibre. My house reflects my wife.'

'Big, is it?'

'It's spotless. And when I get home of an evening my uniform for the next day has been cleaned and pressed, the jacket with its buttons gleaming, the trousers with razor-sharp creases and the shirt crisply laundered.'

'Oh yes? So what's that prove? Your old lady's having it away with the bloke from the dry cleaners?'

'I refuse to rise to your bait, Fletcher. It's obvious that your cynicism derives from some bitter personal experience of your own.'

'No, no, no. Nothing wrong with my marriage. No doubts about my Isobel. My wife and I have always got on very well.'

'You've spent half your married life in prison, man.'

'Yeah well, maybe it's our separation that brings us closer together, isn't it? Absence makes the heart grow fonder in our case. Bet your old lady wouldn't mind a break from all that ironing and cleaning.'

'My wife has never had any desire other than to be by my side. Before Prison Service you know, Fletcher, I was in the Army. I was a drill sergeant in the Black Watch.'

'I'd never have guessed that!'

'And even though I was posted to some far-flung places, Marie would always be with me.'

'I bet she was. Brassing up, polishing, blancoing. Female batman. I can just see you coming in of an evening off the parade ground. "Marie, stand by your bed!"'

'Seventeen years of domestic contentment.' He started to go.

'Er, Mr MacKay? Drill sergeant, was it?' I said.

'That's right, Fletcher, drill sergeant.'

'Do everything by numbers, do you?'

'I am not rising to your bait, Fletcher, and it's naïve of you to assume that I would.'

'Even with your old lady? Numbers is it? "Marie, we will now make love. Wait for it, woman, wait for it! Two three – knickers down – two three!"'

Of course old MacKay rose to the bait. His neck was going in and out sixteen to the dozen, as he pointed his truncheon at me.

'I'll have you, Fletcher!'

'Don't you hit me!'

Wednesday was visiting day and we all got dressed up in our best gear. You know, clean shirt, uniform pressed and shoes shined. We were all waiting in the visiting room. Two screws were on duty, Barrowclough and MacKay. Come to think of it, they're always on duty.

'There's my girl, there she is,' said Heslop.

'Can't see my Elaine,' said Warren.

'Look at the little darlings,' Heslop went on. 'Don't you want to have a look, Fletch?'

'See her soon enough, won't I? I know what she looks like.'

'Come on now,' said Barrowclough. 'Sit down, let's have some order.'

'Did the trick then, Fletch,' said Tolly.

'Yeah, well.'

'Kent's a long way, you know,' said Heslop.

'Trevor's come all the way from Southport,' said Luke-warm. 'He'll have had to close the shop. He's a watch repairer.'

'I did a watch repairer's once,' said Warren.

'Yeah, and now you're doing time for it,' I said. 'Did you get that, Mr Barrowclough.'

'I beg your pardon?'

'Never mind, it's a second hand joke.'

'Oh yes, very funny, Fletcher, very funny,' he said. 'Nice to see you all in such good spirits.'

Warren thought he could smell his wife's perfume.

'No, that's the sheep dip from the prison farm, that is,' I said.

We took our seats at the table and Barrowclough unlocked the door. In they came.

'Hello, Dad,' said Ingrid, my eldest.

'Where's your Mother, then?'

Ingrid looked around before she replied.

'She couldn't come, Dad.'

'Not ill, is she?'

'No, Dad, she — '

'Come on, girl. What's wrong?'

'She's found another man.'

Everyone in the visiting room had heard what she had said. I didn't know where to put my face. I could see MacKay sniggering. He had that 'I told you so' look on his face.

'What?' I said. 'Found who? Come on, tell me who she's found.' I jumped up and moved around the table. Both Barrowclough and MacKay made a grab for me.

'Okay, laddie, take it easy,' said MacKay.

'Take it easy?' I said. 'You heard what she said. My old woman's found another geezer. How about that, eh? While I'm in here, she finds another geezer.'

Eventually I collected my senses together and sat down

again. Ingrid told me all about the geezer, what had been going on, and how long what was going on had been going on. I didn't look too cheerful, as you can imagine.

After she had left I was taken back to my cell. Old MacKay said that he thought I needed time to sit and reflect on what had happened. Me, sit and reflect? You've got to be joking, I said. Anyway, they left me alone until after tea. Then the cell door was opened, and guess who walked in the old flowery? Yes, that's right, the Governor. Followed by MacKay and Barrowclough.

'Hallo, Fletcher, how are you?'

'All right, sir.'

'I understand from both Mr MacKay and Mr Barrowclough that you've had this domestic . . . well, I suppose crisis isn't too strong a word, is it?'

'My wife's scarpered. Yes, I think crisis is a very good word.'

'She hasn't actually left you yet, Fletcher.'

'She's about to.'

'Look, Fletcher, I know what you must be feeling right now. I don't want you to do anything silly. Now tell me what you know.'

'Well apparently, from what I elicited from my eldest, he's a heating engineer. We was getting new central heating installed. So obviously he was round there quite a while . . . younger man, bit of patter, from what I heard, new Capri in mustard yellow with wing mirrors.'

'Younger man, was it?'

'Yeah, with wing mirrors, bound to turn a woman's head.'

'It couldn't just be an infatuation?'

'Not according to my eldest, Ingrid. She knows the score, my girl. She says they're planning a new life together in Hemel Hempstead.'

'Oh, I know Hemel Hempstead,' said Barrowclough. 'Pass through it on the train – it looks nice there.'

'Yes, yes, Mr Barrowclough,' said the Governor. 'Well now, Fletcher, the Welfare Officer seems to think it would help if we gave compassionate parole.'

'Parole – what get out like?'

'Not so much get out as go out. For forty-eight hours only. You could go on Friday. Report to the local police on arrival, but otherwise the weekend would be your own.'

'My own?'

'As you heard the Governor say, Fletcher,' said Mac-Kay, it's only for a short time.' He turned to the Governor. 'Sir, when I told you of Fletcher's matrimonial problems, I thought that you might give him permission to write an extra letter. I didn't think that you would be such a . . . I mean . . .'

'That's all right, Mr MacKay. I know how you feel, but I do think this is one of the cases where kindness and understanding will show good and rewarding results.'

'Get a decent Sunday dinner, I suppose.'

'Now, Fletcher, if that's your attitude — ' said the Governor.

'No, no, Governor, I'm sorry. My flippancy was only masking my deep wounds. If you see fit, sir, I shall go. For the sake of my marriage and your trust in me I'll go. I wonder if Spurs are playing at home?'

Within twenty-four hours I was on the train to London. The journey took hours, but as travelling time was added on top of the forty-eight-hour leave that didn't really matter. As you can imagine, I got really sloshed on the train. The prison had allowed me ten pounds of my own money to use as pocket money. Talk about a waste of money, there I was in the bar all the journey. I mean, what did I have to buy a ticket for?

When we arrived at Euston I went off to the local police station to report as instructed. Sergeant Norris insisted on coming home with me.

'Look, I've checked in, sarge, you know where I live, you don't have to walk me home.'

'I don't mind, Fletch. Breath of fresh air.'

'I'm going home to see my old lady. It's personal, matters of a personal nature. That's the reason for my parole.'

'It's the personal nature that concerns me, Fletch. Want you to greet your wife with sympathy and understanding. Don't want you to force her head through the mangle.'

As we walked up to the front door it was opened by my Ingrid.

'Hello, dad.'

'Hello, love. Your mother in, is she?'

'In there,' she said nodding towards the living-room.

'You know Sergeant Norris, don't you?'

'Met him in court.'

'Only stopping a minute, love,' he said.

We went into the living-room. Isobel was standing in front of the fireplace. She looked very composed and assured.

'Isobel . . .'

'Norman . . .'

'I got this compassionate parole.'

'So they told us.'

'Yeah, well . . .'

'There's no need for you to stay, Sergeant Norris,' Isobel said. 'Thank you.'

'I just thought that — '

'Yes, well there's no need for worries on that score, is there? So if you'll excuse us?'

'Yeah go on, sarge,' I said. 'Just leave us be, eh?'

'Course, course . . . I hope things will . . . well, you know what I mean.'

He went out. We waited for the front door to close and then embraced.

'Hello, Norman love.'

'Hello, my beauty.'

'It worked then.'

I gave her a kiss. 'Like a flaming charm.'

'I knew it would. It worked in Maidstone. Knew it would again.'

'Like a flaming charm,' I said again.

'Ingrid, go and get your dad's slippers and put the kettle on.'

'And don't be in too much of a hurry to come back, neither,' I said. 'Your mother and I have got a lot to make up.'

'It's just like when I was a kid,' Ingrid said. 'If you give me some money I'll go to the pictures.'

'It's worth it.' I put my hand in my pocket. 'Hang on – that's how your brother was born. Puddle off.'

The weekend went all too fast. Spurs won at home. On the Saturday night we had a party. Sunday was spent breakfast in bed, reading the papers, and down the pub dinner time. Yeah, it was wonderful, but all too soon it was over. I was sitting watching the telly when Isobel came in with my case and a carrier bag.

'You'll have to get ready, I'm afraid, love,' said Isobel. 'Won't take long to get to Euston on a Sunday.'

'Did Sergeant Norris say he'd drive you there?'

'Yeah. It's guilt, in'it? I mean, he was the arresting

officer, wasn't he? Now he sees what he's done to me – to us.'

'I've given you some apples. And a banana. And some tangerines – what a price they are. But you need the fruit, it's good for your complexion. You should get shaved, love. Norris'll be here soon.'

'Yeah, I suppose so.' I got up and turned off the telly.

'It's been lovely having you, Norman.'

'Done me a power of good, Isobel. See you and the kids. Colour telly, home cooking, soft lavatory paper.'

'It's all here when you come out. Just bide your time, love.'

'Tell you what, love. I ain't going back no more.'

'You've got to, Norman. You're on parole.'

'No. I mean I ain't going back after this stretch.'

'You've said that before.'

'I mean it. I've had me fill of porridge. It's full of kids these days. Talk about a generation gap. Father figure I am. No, it's been a mug's game, my life. And seein' you and seein' the kids, and realising I'm missing them growing up. And all the things this weekend gave me. I tell you, the best things in life ain't free, but the best thing in life is bein' free.'

'Oh, Norman, you say lovely things. What made you think of that?'

'I didn't. Randolph Scott said it just before you came in.'

Monday morning saw me sitting in the library reading the paper. Course I felt choked. Who wouldn't? But I knew there'd be more weekends like that, especially if my Isobel used Plan C, the one that we'd used when I was in Wandsworth.

'Morning, Fletch,' said Warren. 'Er . . . you all right?'

'What?'

'Me and the lads just wanted to say we're sorry. I mean, I know we laughed about it last week, but you know. Well, look, the fact that you're not so clever after all just makes you more human like the rest of us. Your problems is just like ours.'

'Oh yeah? Let me ask you something, Warren. What you done this weekend?'

'What? Well — '

'I'll tell you. Same as you did last weekend. Had a freezing shower, cleaned your shoes, washed your vest, had your dinner, had another freezing shower, spent the evening lying on your bunk picking your nose. Now some of us was in the pub, some of us was eating roast beef, or watching Spurs play at home, or having a sing song with their friends and relatives, or lying in a big crisp bed with their crisp old lady.' I reached over to a bag on the table. 'Have a banana.'

ANOTHER STRETCH OF
PORRIDGE

Adapted from the TV series by
Paul Victor

Contents

Just Desserts

Gone! My brain reeled. A moment before, I'd come pattering into my flowery dell – that means cell for the un-initiated – straight from lunch and full of pleasurable anti-cipation. I'd pulled back my pillow, peeled back the loose flap of mattress, plunged my eager hand into the fluffy depths, and found – nothing! It's not that I was sur-prised. Oh no! After spending as many years inside the nick as outside it, I knew the score. It's always the same inside. Something beautiful beckons. You reach out for it – and get a chunk of air! No, I wasn't surprised. I was just very dischuffed!

Could I have put it somewhere else? I rummaged briefly through my possessions and then, just for good measure, through Lennie's – but no, it was gone all right.

A grim smile playing about my lips, I made my way down to Funland, otherwise known as the association area, and seated myself at a scrubbed trestle table upon which a number of convicts were playing draughts and other board games. Some of these unfortunates greeted me with cries of : 'Hello, Fletch,' 'Got any snout?' and suchlike. However, my brooding silence alerted the more sensitive amongst them to the fact that all was not well and finally Warren, a baby-faced villain and former cellmate of mine, inquired :

'What's up, Fletch?'

'What's up? I'll tell you what's up. Are you listening, Ives?'

I had a particular reason for wanting to attract the attention of this nimble but brainless felon. He glanced up from his paper, his lower lip, as usual, curled up like a lily only not as beautiful.

'Oh sorry. Yeah, I'm listening, Fletch.'

'This is a very painful thing for me to have to say, gentlemen, but it appears – there's a thief amongst us.'

When this line is uttered in a film or on television it has a powerful effect. Men draw in their breath sharply and ladies give little cries. Nothing like that happened on this occasion. Instead my auditors exchanged puzzled glances and Warren pointed out :

'There's six hundred thieves amongst us, Fletch.'

But I was prepared for this obtuse response and I swung round on him.

'Very true, Warren. Most of us here, and throughout the nick, have been convicted of stealing. But that was stealing on the outside, wasn't it? Against civilians. That's work, that is. Making a living. But the theft to which I'm referring has been perpetrated within these walls. And that is despicable. A crime which offends the dignity of any normal, law-abiding criminal.'

Banyard, the unfrocked dentist, swung his huge, aristocratic nose in my direction and, in his fruitiest upperclass accent, asked :

'What is the nature of this alleged offence?'

'There's nothing alleged about it, Mr Banyard. Someone has crept into my cell and – ' I paused for a split second both to emphasise the enormity of it and to see if anyone, Ives in particular, might betray a sign of guilt, and then I thundered : ' – lifted a two-pound tin of pineapple chunks !'

Ives was indeed the first to comment but I was unable to determine for sure if his tone had a guilty ring to it or not. He merely repeated, licking his lip :

'Cor, pineapple chunks !'

I raised a warning finger.

'Let's all keep our voices down. We *are* discussing contraband, after all.'

'I see,' nodded Banyard, whose manner is always more impressive than his matter, 'pineapple chunks.'

'Correct. One tin of chunks pineapple. Thickly-cut chunks of delicious pineapple, soaked in a heavy syrup, and steeped in the sunkissed fragrance of Honolulu.'

'Mmm, lovely!' Lukewarm, the chef, murmured appreciatively.

'I trust that blissful look on your face doesn't stem from happy memories, Lukewarm?'

'Course not, Fletch. I haven't had your chunks.'

Banyard, as if he'd put his finger on the crux, asked: 'Have you any idea who took them?'

I sighed. 'I was hoping our little chat might throw some light on that. I don't mind saying that I'm extremely dischuffed about this. Luxuries are few and far between in this neck of the woods. I'd been looking forward to that tin, I had. I'm particularly partial to tinned pineapple. Very fond of all tinned fruits but particularly tinned pineapple – in the absence of tinned pears, that is. Bad enough if I'd had some snout nicked, or a new razor blade. Or even money, God forbid. But never my tin of pineapple chunks.'

Warren asked: 'When did you discover they was missing, Fletch?'

'Just now, you nurk! I was going to have some after my Sunday lunch. For dessert. To supplement your wretched cuisine, Lukewarm.'

Lukewarm shrugged. 'I do the best I can with the materials provided.'

There was an abrupt whirr, like a clockwork toy going into action, and Ives launched into a breathless narrative.

' 'Ere listen, I had something whipped last week. All right, nicked! You remember visiting day when Ronnie

Arkwright's old lady said she weren't coming back no more 'cos she was going to live with a Maltese ponce in Morecambe? And Ronnie went berserk and attempted to strangle her until restrained by that Scottish screw with the hare lip?'

I complimented him : 'You certainly spin a pretty yarn, Ives. They could use you on Jackanory. Go on.'

'Well, during the commotion my missis slipped me a jar of her mother's home-made gooseberry preserve. Now, 'ere listen . . . by the Tuesday, I'd eaten most of it, and d'you know I was only out the cell for half an hour, but in that time some scroat whipped the rest. While I was in the hobby shop making me Bugs Bunny money bank.'

I eyed him narrowly. Ives, a man who wouldn't recognise a scruple if one fell on him, was my number one suspect and therefore I naturally supposed that this Mysterious Affair of the Gooseberry Preserve was just a diversion. But I couldn't be sure. I growled :

'Well, now we're getting somewhere, aren't we? We've narrowed the trail down. The net is closing in. We know the thief has a sweet tooth.'

Banyard, who had been brooding deeply on some of the more disturbing implications of my tragic loss, rose to his feet and proclaimed : 'Look here, Fletcher, you must be aware that any speculation you have about who took your pineapple chunks can hardly apply to me.'

'Oh yes, Mr Banyard? Perhaps you'd be so good as to reseat yourself and elaborate a little on that theme.'

Banyard smiled in a superior way and waved his hand as if dismissing a flunky but he reseated himself. He explained : 'Well, unlike the rest of you I'm not a common criminal.'

'Has it slipped your notice, Mr Banyard, that you're doing porridge and have been for the past eighteen months.'

'You know what I mean, Fletcher. I'm a professional man, a dentist, and consequently – '

'Let's keep the record straight. You *was* a dentist. It's been some time now since they struck you off their list. Following those regrettable incidents with the laughing gas. You may not *consider* yourself a criminal but to the ladies in question it certainly weren't no laughing matter.'

Lukewarm at this point extruded three of his front teeth in a menacing way before sucking them back in and saying mildly : 'He's a good dentist though. He did a lovely job on my bridge once when the old one fell in the soup.'

'I'm not questioning his dental expertise,' I said, 'but that doesn't put him above suspicion. Now all of you listen, I'm going for my shower, to stretch my legs and wash 'em and all. Then I'm going to chapel to contemplate the errors of my ways and make peace with my bookmaker. Round up the others from the landing and meet me in my cell in twenty minutes. Then, if the pineapple has been returned we need proceed no further. If it has not, we'll have to open a full-scale enquiry. A thing like this can spread. I mean, if we can't live 'ere together in mutual trust what kind of men are we?'

'Quite right,' said Warren. 'Here – who's pinched my polos?'

As I'd gloomily anticipated, the delicious morsels did not reappear in the flowery. Instead, a large assortment of villains poured in. Never had the homestead been so populous.

'Pass right down the cell, please,' said Warren, enjoying himself.

'This is not a laughing matter, Bunny.'

'Sorry, Fletch.'

The assembly was, of course, against the rules and so I

called out from my position, squashed against the back wall : 'Who's keeping an eye out?'

Ives's Liverpudlian lilt called back : 'Gay Gordon. He's at the end of the landing.'

'Bit conspicuous, isn't she?' I said, as I struggled to a commanding position near the centre of the throng. 'She's got her hair in curlers.'

Lukewarm reassured me : 'Nifty's at the other end.'

'I take it the pineapple chunks have not been returned?' said Banyard, opening the proceedings.

'No, they haven't. But I know when the crime was committed and each one of you lot had the MMO : means, motive and opportunity.'

Banyard, never one to quail before even the most awe-inspiring implications, asked : 'Are you saying that the thief is one of us here in this very room?'

'That's exactly what I'm saying, Monsieur Poirot, yes. Everyone here was on this landing before bang-up last night.'

'Where were you then?' called a voice from deep in the bank of scowling faces.

'Had to go over and see genial Harry Grout, didn't I? To negotiate the tobacco concession.'

At this point, there was a disturbance similar to what would be produced by a small tank, and McLaren, the Scotch spade, came ploughing into the room.

'Kangaroo court, eh? No need to leave me out, Fletch. We're all in this together. Finger of suspicion points at everyone. Just like to mention, of course, that if anyone points it at me, I'll clobber 'em.'

'Good of you to be so reasonable, McLaren,' I said humbly. 'Now just to recap, I've established that the crime was perpetrated during the fifteen minutes before bang-up last night.'

This produced a torrent of alibis.

'I was in the gym, working on me weights,' offered McLaren.

'I was playing ping-pong,' claimed Lukewarm, 'with Gay Gordon and two others. Mixed doubles.'

'I was teaching Atlas the rudiments of chess.' That was Banyard.

'I was watching telly.' Warren.

And so on. In fact, the occupations possible in a nick are not all that varied and for this reason many of those present made the same claim. Then again your average prison is not fitted out with spacious grounds and pleasant retreats in which people can lose themselves. In other words, if *you're* doing something it's practically certain ten other lags are doing it with you. Thus most of the alibis carried weight. There came a point where I was compelled to admit: 'We don't seem to be getting anywhere.'

'Can you suggest any other procedure?' asked Banyard gravely.

'Yes, I can. There is amongst us one who is notorious for this kind of petty, two-faced gittery. So I propose we grab hold of Ives now and extract a swift confession.'

'But,' exclaimed Banyard, deeply shocked, 'we should adhere to the fundamental principles on which our legal system was founded. Every man is innocent until proven guilty.'

'Certainly,' I said. 'Every man but Ives. So McLaren–'

'Don't you worry, Fletch,' promised the ebony Scot, and he grabbed Ives in a vice-like headlock. 'I'll extract a confession.'

Ives, his voice unnaturally high as a result of oxygen deprivation, squealed, ' 'Ere, listen. It wasn't me, straight up. I was in the hobby room. Making toys, honest.'

'Could anyone use a second head?' asked McLaren, methodically twisting off the one in the possession of

Ives. Then he abruptly stopped and said reflectively : 'Oh, wait. That's true, what he says. Saw him meself. On the way back from the gym. Making a big fluffy panda he was. He's vurra guid at handicrafts. Have you seen his Bugs Bunny money bank? I think you're barking up the wrong tree, Fletch.'

Ives croaked hoarsely : 'Let me go ! Let me go !'

'Shall I, Fletch?'

'Yeah, you'd better. He looks even worse blue. Well if it wasn't Ives we must go on living with the knowledge that there's a thief amongst us.'

'Where did you get the pineapple in the first place?' asked Banyard.

'Stole it from the kitchen, didn't I?'

At this point, a young woman in curlers darted into the flowery dell and hissed : 'MacKay's coming.' It was Gay Gordon. He hastily concealed himself in the throng.

'All right, lads – we all know what we're here for. The initial gathering of the newly-formed Slade Prison Cowboy Club. All together now – '

And with me conducting serenely, everyone burst into a chorus of Home on the Range. The voices swelled out powerfully but were easily outclassed by a bellow from the door : 'Quiet, the lot of you, you horrible rabble !' This request was immediately granted and the same voice inquired : 'What the hell's going on in here?'

I exclaimed enthusiastically. 'What do you know, pardners, it's Mr MacKay?'

A ragged cheer, sprinkled with cries of 'Howdy, Mr MacKay', echoed round the dell. But Mr MacKay seemed, at that moment, indifferent to fame. He asked again, if somewhat less piercingly : 'What *is* going on in here?'

'The cowboy club, sir,' I explained.

'The what?'

'Friends of the West. Kindred spirits, brought together by a mutual love and interest in those far-off days of the new frontier. We plan to meet, sing the great old songs and – '

'Poppycock! This is an unlawful assembly, Fletcher. Prison regulations clearly state that no more than three prisoners will congregate in a cell at any one time.'

'Ah, there you have the advantage of me, Mr MacKay. Try as I might I have been unable to obtain a copy of the current Home Office Regulations.'

MacKay glared around at the gathering: 'On your feet, the lot of you. There are only two rules in this prison. One : you do not write on the walls. Two : you will obey all rules. Now then, back to your cells!'

'All right, lads,' I said, 'you'd better mosey along.' And with such pleasantries as 'Next time I'll bring me Gene Autrey songbook,' and 'Adios, amigos,' the lads trooped away.

MacKay bent small, menacing eyes upon me, and proclaimed: 'Fletcher, there is a growing current of insubordination and laxity in this prison. A definite rise in insolence. And pilfering.'

'Pilfering, yes. I've noticed it myself, Mr MacKay.'

'I'm not referring to petty sneak-thieving amongst yourselves. That's to be expected amongst incorrigible criminals. I'm referring to thefts of prison property. Mark my words, Fletcher, I'll find the culprits.'

Finding it a strain to maintain an innocent look, I was greatly relieved, a moment later, when Lennie entered. He was fresh from the kitchens and still wearing his tall chef's hat. MacKay whirled.

'Well, Godber? What are you up to?'

'Off work, sir. Been up since six this morning.'

I said : 'Lad looks tired, sir. So if you'll excuse us – '

But MacKay's eyes bouncd back and forth from Lennie

to me as if following an invisible tennis ball. He nodded. 'Yes, this is a very unfortunate combination.'

'Oh yes? How's that?'

'Godber with his opportunities to steal from the kitchen. And you with your distribution network.'

'I resent that, Mr MacKay. I don't steal,' said Lennie indignantly.

'Then you won't mind if I frisk you, will you, lad?' And Mr MacKay started patting and poking in the time-honoured way.

Lennie, although he had to put up with it, continued to complain. 'This is not on, Mr MacKay. All right, I'm inside. Certain circumstances brought me here. Environment. Lack of parental guidance. Times were tough and I did go off the rails. I've done wrong but I'm paying my penance. I have a few decent qualities underneath and I've learnt my lesson. I don't grass and I don't cheat and I certainly do not steal.'

Mr MacKay, whose investigations had apparently confirmed the last assertion, nodded grimly: 'All right, sonny Jim, we'll say no more ... for the present.'

Whereupon he turned smartly, in the way he'd picked up serving in the Prussian Guards, and swaggered out of the cell. I congratulated Lennie. 'Well said, son. You even impressed MacKay with your eloquence and obvious sincerity.'

'Should think so. Suspicious old scroat.'

'Good thing you were clean though.'

'Good job he didn't look under me hat,' he said, removing his chef's hat and revealing a pound of butter nestling in his youthful locks.

I was cleaning my teeth that evening, almost recovered from my grievous loss, when Lennie asked: 'Can I have a loan of your black boot polish?'

'Why?'

He sighed patiently. 'Why do you think? My mascara's run out.'

'Now don't be cheeky, young Godber.'

'I just want to clean me shoes, Fletch.'

'Borrow someone else's.'

'It's after lock-up.'

'Then you should have thought of that earlier.'

'You seriously mean you won't give me a measly bit of shoe polish?'

'No. I think that, in the light of recent events, it would be better if in future one keeps what one has to oneself.'

'I take it you decided on this policy after I shared my butter with you?'

'I've done a lot for you, Godber. Boot polish, snout, toothpaste – why, the first night you moved in here I give you my toothpaste.'

'You give me one squeeze.'

'On three successive nights. That adds up to a lot of toothpaste. Moreover, it wasn't no ordinary toothpaste. It had hexochloroform in the stripes. I got that special to match my pyjamas.'

'I gave you liquorice all-sorts for that toothpaste. Fair exchange is no robbery.'

'When you were at death's door last month with your inflamed bronchs, who gave you a TCP throat lozenge?'

'That's right. Lozenge. Singular.'

'And who saved you all those match sticks when you wanted to make a model of the *Cutty Sark*?'

'And who sat on the model?'

'Well, it was a pointless exercise. You need a ten stretch for the *Cutty Sark* in match sticks.'

'Who stole nails for you from carpentry classes so you could stick your pin-ups on the wall. And who gave you half his mother's home-made shortbread?'

'Who loaned you their darning wool then?'

'You did. And whose socks am I darning, you ungrateful nurk?'

I glanced round at this and saw that Lennie really was engaged in replacing the heel of one of my best green woollens. 'Oh. Are they my socks?'

''Course they are.'

'Oh, go on then, there's me shoe polish. Don't take too much.'

Lennie put aside his darning and shook his head morosely. 'You told me when I moved in here that our best protection against the nurks out there was mutual interest. Team spirit.'

'Yes, but my trust has been misplaced, hasn't it, as that missing tin of pineapple has proved. I was careless enough to forget that this is a jungle in here. You can't trust no one.'

'Here, are you including me in that?'

'Look after number one. That's what it's all about.'

'That's not answering my question.'

'What question's that, then?'

'Do you think *I* nicked your chunks?'

'I don't know *who* nicked them.'

But Lennie strode over and confronted me, an unnecessary gesture, I always feel, in a tiny cell. 'Fletcher, don't evade me. This is a very critical point in our relationship. I respect you, Fletch. I owe you a lot, and I'm not talking about stripy toothpaste. I've never pretended to be cool or off-hand about doing stir. It bleeding petrified me. But you made it tolerable. You taught me the right approach and now I can get by. Just about. I'm very grateful as I thought you knew. Do you think I'd repay that by stealing your tin of naffing pineapple chunks? Not even my favourite fruit.'

The lad was upset as I could tell by the fact that his left

eyelid was winking like a semaphore, always a sign that Lennie is in a stew. I said soothingly : 'Here, here, here – such a thought never entered my head, Lennie. If there's one person I know didn't take them, it's you.'

'Well, I just hope – '

'You and me – oppos, ain't we.'

'That's what I thought but – '

'You know we are. Living like this, like caged animals, we're bound to get the needle with each other sometimes. But I trust you, Lennie. I know for certain that you didn't take my pineapple.'

'How can you be sure?'

'I know the kind of person you are, the integrity, the sense of honour. . . . Besides, when you were in the shower, I went through your gear.'

For a moment his face darkened, but then, seeing the funny side and accepting the two squares of fruit and nut I hastily held out to him, he sighed and shook his head. And after that we had a very pleasant evening.

Now in the prison library, where I spend my time a' serving of Her Majesty the Queen, there is an idyllic corner beside the radiator and under the window. Nothing is more pleasant on a winter afternoon than to sit on the radiator, smoke a roll-up and contemplate the tiny section of moorland visible over the grim, grey roof of Slade nick. But there is a curious law which states that, even if I have been diligently at work cataloguing the literary treasures of the place for an hour and a half, no sooner do I extract Lamb's *Tales from Shakespeare*, in which is stored my precious snout, than a key rattles in the lock and a screw barges in.

The next afternoon was no exception. Indeed, I had just glanced up from entering *Collecting Old Silver*, a very popular work incidentally, and fixed my eye on the enticing nook, when the inevitable happened. The key rattled and in barged – but no, that word is too dynamic to describe the entry of anything as placid as Mr Barrowclough. Anyhow, he wore, as usual, the distracted look of a cow that's accidentally been put out to graze on concrete, and, as usual, I felt a genuine urge to cheer him up.

'Have a nice weekend, then, Mr Barrowclough?'

'Not especially.'

'Still, the weather kept nice.'

'Did it? The sun rarely shines in my household.'

Of course, I knew he was referring to his wife who has a slight tendency to succumb to milkmen, dustmen or any other male person that unwisely strays within a hundred yards of the Barrowclough mansion, but I pretended to be ignorant of his drift.

'Maybe you need a skylight?'

'I wasn't referring to the architecture, Fletcher. Still, I haven't come to discuss my domestic situation.'

'All right by me if you had, Mr Barrowclough. Your problems are my problems.'

'I'm aware of that, Fletcher. You've been very helpful with advice in the past, and that's why I've been lenient with you.'

'Lenient?'

'I haven't had a chance to talk to you since I went off duty for the weekend, but on Saturday afternoon when you were all out watching the football match, Mr Malone and I were detailed by Mr MacKay to do an RSC.'

'A what?'

'A random security check.'

'Oh yes. The vocabulary varies from nick to nick, but in practice it's the same thing. I'm sure you agree, Mr Barrowclough, that such practices are a despicable infringement of civil liberties.'

Mr Barrowclough tried to look stern but his face just

isn't adapted to it. 'The practice is justified, Fletcher, when one finds stolen tins of pineapple chunks.'

For some reason, I lost all interest in pursuing the conversation and I busied myself with my work. '*Robinson Crusoe,*' I muttered, as I scrawled down the title on an index card. 'Ever read it, Mr Barrowclough? Full of interesting tips on – '

'Fletcher! Did you hear what I said?'

'Something about a security check, wasn't it, Mr Barrowclough?'

'It was. And in your cell I found a stolen tin of pineapple chunks. By rights, I should have reported it.'

A remarkable feeling of relief swept over me. 'You mean – you didn't?'

'No. As it happened, Mr Malone's attention was distracted. So I was able to conceal it under my jacket. Fletcher, if I had reported it you would have lost this job, had loss of privileges and probably solitary confinement.'

My heart overflowed. 'What can I say, Mr Barrowclough?'

'You can promise to keep your nose clean in future. I felt I owed you a favour but now the slate is clean. We're all square from now on.'

'Absolutely, sir.'

'You've got a very cushy number here. It's a better job than most *trusties* have got.

'Oh, I'm well aware of that, sir, and suitably grateful. Mind you, it's not all skiving. I've got this very complicated index to do.'

'Yes, and you've been at it for five weeks.'

'Well, I want to avoid mistakes.'

'You want to avoid finishing it. Because then you've got to decorate the place which is why you were put here in the first place.'

'Still waiting for the paint, sir.'

'Well, what's happened to it?'

'Stolen.'

Barrowclough shook his head mournfully. 'What is happening to this prison?'

'There's a nasty criminal element in here, sir.'

'There's altogether too much petty pilfering. Mr MacKay is putting pressure on me to stamp it out. Now I've let you off the hook, Fletcher, and in return I want to see a sharp decrease in your block. Understood?'

'Rest assured, sir. . . . By the way, that tin of pineapple? Did you manage to return it to the food store?'

Mr Barrowclough shuffled uneasily, like a cow that's backed into a thorn bush. 'Not exactly. I took it home and the wife made gammon steak Hawaii.'

This was indeed an interesting admission. He continued : 'I hadn't intended to. But the wife found it and . . . I couldn't very well tell her where it had come from. So we – well – '

'Ate it.'

'Under protest.'

'On top of gammon. Well, that puts rather a different light on things, don't it? I mean, if I did commit the alleged offence – which, in the absence of evidence, is a difficult thing to prove – you are unquestionably an accessory before, after and during the fact. You are a felon same as me.'

Poor old Barrowclough winced and shuddered as though the flies were biting.

'I am aware of the situation, Fletcher. I would suggest that we purchase another tin of pineapple and replace it in the food store.'

'What do you mean "we"? I can't just stroll down to the village shop, can I?'

'I realise that, Fletcher. I shall do the purchasing. And you shall pay for it.'

I opened my mouth to protest but Mr Barrowclough, eager to terminate the discussion, sidled to the door and vanished.

Well, of course, when I thought it over and considered the terrible vengeance that MacKay would have wreaked if he'd found that accursed tin, I coughed up and Barrowclough purchased a new tin and found an opportunity to slip it into the stores. And that, I felt and you probably do too, should have been the end of my involvement with tinned pineapple, at least for that stretch. But it was not to be.

The next day I was returning to the old flowery after an unsatisfactory day in the library and found Lennie acting somewhat strangely.

'What's the matter?'

'Nothing's the matter with me. What about you?'

'Some new paint's arrived,' I said.

'So?'

'So it means I've got to decorate that library.'

'Can't you get rid of it, like all the other consignments?' he asked.

'No, not a chance. There's not a screw left who hasn't got a gleaming front fence.'

'Well, never mind, Fletch. Why not have a wash? I've laid out your towel for you.'

I glanced at the bed and saw that my towel, neatly folded, really was laid out. This was unusual, to say the least, since we do not normally go in for these upstairs-downstairs refinements in the nick. However, I nodded and said lightly, 'Yeah – could do with a lemon squash.'

And I removed my shirt. Lennie watched me with a curious,. eager expression as if he couldn't wait to see my tattoos, which I don't happen to have any of, considering tattooing a disgusting habit and one which in any case usually provides a handy identification mark for the law.

'Come on then, Fletch. Get on with it,' Lennie urged.

'You've never shown such interest in my ablutions before, Godber? You're not – '

'What?'

'You haven't forgotten Denise, your fiancée, already, have you?'

'I don't get you, Fletch.'

'Never mind.'

Having bared the manly bosom, I reached for the towel and just then, with all the finesse of a bull out shopping for Wedgwood, MacKay marched into the cell. I relinquished my grasp on the towel and greeted him.

'Hello, Mr MacKay, what can I do for you?'

'Haven't come to see you, Fletcher.'

'Oh dear – well, I'll just have to grin and bear it.'

'I've come to see Godber.' He turned to Lennie. 'Now, Laddie, I don't want you developing a chip. I don't want you to get the idea I'm always picking on you. I have a job to do, but whatever else I am I'm fair. I treat you all with equal contempt.'

Lennie tried to look suitably grateful. 'I appreciate that, Mr MacKay.'

Seeing that it was just flannel hour, I decided to continue with my toilet.

'You won't take offence, Mr MacKay,' I asked lightly, 'if I have a wash? Terrible dusty in that library.'

MacKay did not demean himself by replying but Lennie, to my surprise, exclaimed : 'No !'

'I beg your pardon?'

He said desperately : 'You don't need a wash, Fletch. You're so – so clean.'

'I'm covered in dust. Anyway, a moment ago you was egging me on to get scrubbed.'

'Yeah, but – '

I seized the towel and flipped it over my shoulder. Lennie groaned and covered his eyes with his hands. Puzzled but not deterred I moved towards the door. An instant later I heard a kind of strangled exclamation. I glanced over my shoulder and saw MacKay gazing, pop-eyed, at my bunk. I followed his glance and – me own minces nearly shot out of me head! There, in the exact spot where my towel had been, as large as life and twice as incriminating, sat a whopping great tin of pineapple chunks.

Well, of course, you can guess, as I did in a flash, what had occurred. Godber, still young enough to derive pleasure from giving surprises, had nicked me another tin of chunks from the kitchen where he worked. But then, instead of just handing it to me with perhaps a short, sentimental speech, he'd conceived the fatal idea of hiding it under my towel so he'd be able to enjoy the look of amazement on my face when it came to light. Well, he saw that all right.

'It's a plant,' I said.

'Oh no, it's not,' said MacKay. 'It's a stolen tin of pineapple. Come along with me.'

And that's all young Godber saw of me for the next three days. As I was marched off to solitary, I heard his voice calling out on the landing :

'Anyone got a tin opener?'

Heartbreak Hotel

'Hey!' said Lennie, in an aggrieved tone of voice, 'I was listening to that.'

'You may have been listening,' I conceded, 'but you couldn't have been enjoying it.'

We were both referring to the programme which, a moment before, had been echoing round the old dell. Then I had entered and switched off the transistor. I had with me a pearly-new copy of Peep and craved a peaceful half-hour on my bunk with it.

'Certainly I was,' Lennie insisted.

'The wireless is never off in this nick.'

'I wanted to hear that bit special though,' Lennie grumbled. 'It was the Special Request slot in their "Hello Young Lovers" corner.'

'Sentimental teenage slush.'

'Yeah but I'd written in. For a record. For Denise.'

'Denise?'

'My fiancée.'

'Oh yes, that Denise. Of course.'

'I wanted her to know of my undying feelings of affection and devotion. "Everlasting Love" I asked for.'

'Oh? Not "My Ding-a-Ling"?'

'You got a coarse streak, Fletch.'

'Very likely. Not exactly a school for etty-kett the nick, is it? All right, if you want to play your weeping wireless, go ahead.'

But Lennie shook his head moodily. 'That was the last request of the day. I been listening all week, but it ain't been on yet.'

'Hang about,' I exclaimed. 'Did you write on prison notepaper?'

'Yes. If you remember, I gave you my last sheet of Basildon Bond.'

'That's it then.'

'Why? You mean they're biased against prisoners?'

'Maybe not officially. But I don't recall ever having heard a prisoner's request on the air. Forces yes. Aircraft carriers or ack-ack batteries, but never heard nothing from no one in the nick.'

'It's a disgrace,' complained Lennie. 'We have a rotten enough life in here without having our requests refused. That's discrimination, that is – as well as the postage up the spout.'

'Still,' I pointed out judiciously, 'you can see it from their point of view. The public what pays its radio licence fees regular every year – take offence, wouldn't they? I mean, picture the whole family sitting down to Sunday lunch, with their beloved Family Favourites playing re-assuringly in the background. Suddenly the announcer says: "And now a request from Parkhurst: Tommy 'Mad Dog' Hollister would like to hear 'Clair de Lune'".'

'What was that, Fletcher?' asked Mr MacKay, entering, as usual, without knocking.

'Nothing, Mr MacKay. Just talking about music. Oh, perhaps you could tell us the ruling.'

'What ruling?'

'Miss Lonely Loins here wants to know if the BBC ever play prisoners' requests?'

Mr MacKay chuckled evilly as if personally responsible for the policy. 'No,' he said firmly. 'The answer is definitely no – on the grounds that it would cause embarrassment.'

'Embarrassment?' asked Lennie, puzzled.

'To the prisoners' families. You see, Godber, the family

might have excused the man's absence by telling the neighbours that the felon in question was abroad, say, or working on a North Sea oil rig.'

'Oh, I see.'

MacKay turned to me with the twisted leer which he employs in the belief that it conveys a sense of matiness. 'No doubt your wife, Fletcher, has told your friends that you're on a five-year safari.'

He laughed heartily. I gave him his head and then said casually : 'No, she tells them I'm doing missionary work in Scotland.'

His laugh expired. He turned to Lennie again. 'Moreover, Godber, the practice was open to abuse. There was nothing to stop prisoners sending messages in code through the air.'

This intriguing thought had never occurred to me and I could not help exclaiming enthusiastically :

'Ah, that's a point – yeah, that's really a point. You hear some heartwarming Christmas message from some poor lag, dedicated to his beloved wife and family and dear little Tiny Tim. Could he please hear Harry Secombe singing "The Impossible Dream"? But to those in the know what he really means was "Nobby, have the ladder round the back of E wing, Boxing day". Yeah, very neat.'

'You *would* think so, Fletcher,' growled MacKay.

'How's that, Mr MacKay?'

'Because it's dishonest. You're fascinated by things that are dishonest, aren't you, Fletcher?'

'Not necessarily.'

'How about toilet rolls?'

'I've never known a bent one, Mr MacKay.'

'You know perfectly well what I mean, Fletcher. Six rolls of soft toilet paper have disappeared from the Governor's closet – his own personal water closet.'

I tried to look suitably appalled and Lennie unwisely exclaimed : 'What next?'

MacKay spun round and snapped at him : 'Knowing Fletcher, the seat!'

'Honest, Mr MacKay,' I said earnestly, 'I don't know anything about the Governor's paper.'

'Nor me,' chimed in Lennie. 'It's writing paper I'm short of.'

MacKay glanced keenly about the cell but I could see he wasn't planning a real, mattress-shredding search. He shook his head : 'It's not right. We've had to give the Governor standard prison-issue tissue.'

Neither Lennie nor I could resist that opening.

'That's rough,' from Lennie.

'That'll wipe the smile off his face,' from me.

Whereupon we both had an attack of the giggles. MacKay watched narrowly but failed to erupt. 'Fortune,' he said at last, 'has given you two privileged positions in this prison. You would be foolish to jeopardise them by any infraction of the rules. . . . I'll say no more.' Whereupon the pink-nosed incorruptible turned on his heel and stalked out of the cell.

'Why does he always pick on us?' asked Lennie irritably.

'No imagination. Just because he may once have found some trifling item of contraband in this general area he makes a beeline, or perhaps a vulture-line would be more accurate, for our cell whenever anything goes missing.'

As I spoke, I rummaged in my locker. 'Here, catch.'

'What? Hey, a toilet roll ! So you have got one, Fletch.'

I shrugged modestly. 'I had six.'

'Where's the other five?'

'I traded them, didn't I?'

Lennie shook his head in admiration. 'Who to?'

'There are a few inmates with some middle-class refinement left in this nick who jumped at them. In return I am due to receive a lot of nice middle-class merchandise. I'm promised a cricket sweater, a pair of hush puppies and a box of after-dinner mints. As I've often said before, Godber, you can find a taker for anything in the nick. And now, if you'll belt up for an hour, and if MacKay can refrain from persecuting us for that long, I'm going to have a read.'

'Share and share alike.'

'What?'

'Rule of the house, isn't it?' .

'Share my toilet roll?'

'Only fair. Look at all them darned socks.'

'Oh, all right.' I tore off a piece and handed it to him. 'Mind how you go.'

The high spot of your convict's life is, in most cases, visiting time. Mind you, I have known instances in which the arrival of the loved one is not an unmixed delight. In fact, I recall a bloke I shared a cell with once in Brixton for whom the chance to commune with his nearest and dearest was pure hell. He was a very hard man inside and had everyone, including some of the screws, in a state of abject terror. But when his old woman faced him across the little table he dwindled into a cross between a worm and a jelly. Still, I had no problems along those lines, having an excellent relationship with my wife and a strong paternal affection for my kids. It was thus with keen delight that I saw my eldest girl, Ingrid, swaying down the central aisle towards me.

'Hello, dad,' she called cheerily.

'Hello, Ingrid, love.'

Ingrid seated herself opposite me and gave me a big, warm smile. I returned it but as I did so I became aware that there was something disturbing about her appearance. I was still trying to put my finger on it – mentally, you understand – when someone tapped me on the shoulder and, turning, I found Lennie smiling in a deferential way. He was seated at the next table, opposite a grey-haired old bint. Either that's not Denise, I thought to myself, or young Godber needs straightening out. However, he immediately reassured me by saying : 'Oh – er – this is me mum, Fletch.'

At this, the old mother-of-pearl leaned towards me and smiled primly. I didn't want to waste time on other people's visitors but courtesy demanded some response. So I stood up and said, 'Great pleasure, Mrs Godber. Got a fine lad there. This is my eldest, Ingrid.'

Ingrid also offered a smile but I noticed that it seemed to be aimed more towards Lennie than his mum. Just then a roar like a nearby building collapsing caused us to jump. It turned out to be MacKay registering disapproval at our little social gathering which is against regulations. 'Sit down, Fletcher. And you, Godber. This is not a royal garden party.'

'Who's he then?' asked Ingrid, when the reverberations had subsided.

'That's Mr MacKay. Charmless Celtic nark.'

'And who's the boy?'

'Oh, that's Lennie. Lennie Godber, my temporary cell-mate. He's from Birmingham but he's got an O level in geography. Need to, I should think, to find your way round Birmingham. Well, what's the news? How's your mother then?'

'Oh fine, dad. Sends her love and everything.'

'How's your sister?'

'Oh, Marion's fine. Got a new job.'

I was not surprised by this news but nor was I specially chuffed by it. 'Gawd, can't she never keep a job more than three weeks?'

'It's the bosses she has trouble with. They molest her, she alleges.'

'Well, that's her and her short skirts.' Once again I felt faintly uneasy about some aspect of Ingrid's appearance but I still could not quite decide what it was. 'What's she doing now then?'

'Timothy Whites.'

'Oh well. That's better. She shouldn't get molested there. Qualified pharmacists, aren't they?'

'Her flat fell through.'

'What flat?'

'The one behind Olympia that she shared with six other people.'

'Six? Fell through to the flat below, I should think.'

'The rent went up, so she's home again.'

'And how's young Raymond?'

'He won the mile in the school sports.'

'Did he? Wish I had – might not be in here now.'

'And he came in second in the high jump. And he's swimming for the school. And he's stage manager in the play.'

'He should be acting. Last year he was Yum Yum in the *Mikado*.'

'His voice has gone.'

'Oh?'

'Well, he's on thirty a day.'

'Thirty a day – at fourteen! Shocking – and a waste of money.'

'He saves the coupons, dad. Wants to buy himself an aqualung.'

'He'll need one on thirty a day.'

'He plans to go skin-diving at St Ives.'

'I notice all his achievements seem to be extra-curricular. Isn't he keen on anything *inside* the classroom?'

'Mostly the girls, dad.'

'Yeah, well he'll have to watch that. Tell him I said to curb his appetites. Don't want him getting no girl into trouble.'

Ingrid smiled coyly. 'If you hadn't, dad, I wouldn't be here.'

'Ingrid, there's no call for coarse remarks of that nature. I don't know what modern youth is coming to.'

'There's nothing wrong about it, dad. You and Mum have proved that your love wasn't just a passing infatuation. Silver wedding coming up.'

'Nevertheless, I don't want my adolescent love life held up as a yardstick to young Raymond. He's only fourteen. When what happened happened to your mother and me in Highgate cemetery we was mature responsible sixteen-year-olds. We had something behind us, and I don't mean the tomb of Karl Marx. Your mother had a steady job in Gamages and I had my plastering diploma from Borstal.'

'Yes, dad,' Ingrid said meekly.

'Speaking of Highgate cemetery, how's *your* love life? Not still that Eddie Risley, is it?' Ingrid lowered her eyes, confirming my worst suspicions. I continued sternly : 'I warned you about him, gel. He's a crook is Eddie Risley.'

'Oh, he's straight, dad. It's just he's a tough business man. It's not fair what people keep saying about him, that he'd sell his own mother.'

'I had that story confirmed on very good authority.'

'Who from?'

'The two blokes that bought her.'

Ingrid sighed. 'It's no use talking to you about Eddie, dad. You got a blind spot about him.'

'So have you, my girl. I know he's giving you a bad time. True?'

'I just don't know where I am with him.'

I leaned forward. 'You do pick them, Ingrid. You're

a bonny girl with a lovely nature. You could have anyone you wanted, you could. And time's passing, girl: You're not getting any younger. You're twenty-four. Has to be said.'

'That's not old.'

'It is for a teenager, and a spinster.'

'Oh, dad, things have changed since your day. Girls want to be . . . well, they don't want to be tied down so quick. They feel there's alternatives to marriage.'

'Not in Muswell Hill, they don't. Nothing's changed there.'

'Well, they've twinned the Odeon.'

'I'm talking about standards. Moral standards. All these social commentators – they don't know Britain. They all live within a stone's throw of each other in NW1. They ain't never been north of Hampstead or south of Sloane Square. But in the real world – Birmingham, Bristol, Muswell Hill – the fundamentals haven't changed – ' Suddenly I spotted what it was that had been bothering me about Ingrid's appearance. 'Here, are you wearing a bra?'

'I don't need to, dad.'

'You what?'

'I haven't done for years. My breasts are firm and pliant.'

There was no argument about that as anyone could see and the fact that anyone could see was exactly what I intended to argue about. I leaned forwards and whispered fiercely: 'Ingrid, please. This ain't San Tropay, you know. This is Slade bleeding prison. There's six hundred men in here would go berserk at a fleeting glimpse of unveiled shin, never mind your bouncing unfettered knockers.'

Ingrid bridled. 'Dad! Really!'

'You're very naïve in certain ways, Ingrid. Don't you

know the effect your body could have on the shackled male?'

'Well, I think you're very old-fashioned, dad. I shouldn't think anyone's even noticed.'

With one accord, we turned and surveyed the room. Practically every single con had his popping eyes glued to my Ingrid's buoyant bust.

The pale light of the moon may be romantic by the side of mountain lakes or in the landscaped grounds of stately homes but it don't do nothing for the nick. It just emphasises the cold, dreary nature of the place. I stood beneath the barred window in our cell, thinking troubled thoughts. Finally I moved a few paces and, almost absently, shook the bunk on which Lennie was snoring blissfully.

'Godber!'

There was no response. I shook harder.

'Godber! Are you awake?'

There was a little convulsion on the bed and a series of strangled sounds, reminding me of Tarzan fighting a crocodile, and then Lennie suddenly sat bolt upright.

'What – what – whazzamatter?'

'Are you awake?'

'I am now!'

'Got any snout?'

'Snout? You woke me up for that?'

'Didn't know where it was, did I?'

'I haven't got any snout.'

'Inconsiderate nurk!'

'You've got a – anyway, I thought you'd given it up.'

'Feel like starting again.'

'Me mum bought me some Maltesers.'

'No thanks.'

'Oh. Couldn't you have waited till morning?'

'Things on me mind, ain't there?'

'Like what?'

'My business.'

'Oh, come on! I mean, now you've woken me up, you might as well talk it out.'

'I get depressed at times, that's all. Stinking stir!' And to emphasise the point, I kicked the table.

'That's not like you, Fletch.'

'A father's place is at home, with his kids, giving them affection and parental guidance. I got three of them, you know?'

'Yes, I know.'

'Fourteen, nineteen and twenty-four.'

'Quite a gap between each.'

I sighed deeply. 'Unavoidable in the circumstances.'

'How d'you mean?'

'Kept going in prison for five years, didn't I?'

'Oh.'

'Now take the two youngest – well, that's a terrible age, the teens. You expect trouble then, don't you? But Ingrid, my eldest – you'd think she'd have learned some lessons by now.'

In the gloom, I saw Lennie nodding agreement. Then he brightened. 'She looked a nice girl to me. She had lovely – '

'I know what she's got lovely, Godber,' I said hastily. 'Just remember, it's her father you're talking to.'

'Eyes, I was going to say. She had lovely eyes – big and blue.'

'Oh – '

'And a nice smile too, which seemed to indicate a nice disposition and generous nature.'

'All true, that.'

'Fletch, I hope you don't mind but I couldn't help overhearing some of what you said – '

'Oh yes?'

'Doesn't sound good enough for her, that Eddie Risley, if you ask me.'

I brought my fist down hard on the table. 'He ain't! Used to claim he was in the motor trade, but you know what branch? He forged car log books. Not that she'd believe it.'

'You sure?'

'Certainly I'm sure. I bought two off him. They weren't much cop either. He spelt Citroen with an "s".'

'Well, with a bit of luck he'll get rumbled sooner or later and sent down. Give her a chance to find someone new.'

I nodded. It was comforting to have an oppo to take an interest in my problems. But then Lennie went on like the nine o'clock news : 'And I should think your Marion is awakening to the possibilities of her sex. She'll settle down all right at Timothy Whites. And I wouldn't worry too much about young Raymond either. I was on thirty a day when I was fourteen. Oh and congratulations on your silver wedding.'

'Well – you have been attentive !'

'Sorry, Fletch. Like I said, I couldn't help overhearing – '

'Your poor old mum must have had a thin time.'

'Her fault. She never has much to say for herself, dear Mum, and I get bored with the family ailments.'

'Didn't she bring news of the lovely Denise?'

'No. She doesn't talk about Denise because she don't approve of her.'

'Why not?'

'Because she uses green nail varnish and doesn't wear a bra – Denise, that is, not me mum.'

'Your Denise and my Ingrid seem to have certain things in common.'

Lennie considered this for a moment. Then he said wistfully : 'Your Ingrid's got nicer knockers.'

A couple of days after this exchange, I was engaged in a depressing game of ping-pong with a cracked ball, the only one we had left, when I saw Barrowclough beckoning agitatedly. As soon as I could I joined him on the gallery, whereupon he led me to a relatively secluded spot.

'Sorry to drag you away from your game, Fletcher, but I thought we ought to have a quiet word.'

'At your disposal, Mr Barrowclough.'

'Do you know where Godber is?'

'He'll be at one of his poxy evening classes – let's see, woodwork today, isn't it?'

Barrowclough paused for dramatic effect and then let fly : 'He's up in front of the Governor.'

This was both astonishing and distressing news. 'What? The Kid? What's he done?'

'He attacked another prisoner. At work, in the kitchens. He attacked Jackdaw with a soup ladle.'

My first reaction was disbelief. Jackdaw was the kind of bloke that could provoke you to homicidal fury just by entering a room but Lennie was the most passive of men. 'Come off it, Mr Barrowclough. Lennie wouldn't hurt a fly.'

'Well, he hasn't improved Jackdaw. I thought you might be able to shed some light on the matter?'

'No. Lennie was his usual self this morning. And at lunch he was quite cheerful. Mind you, and no offence intended, Mr Barrowclough, one of your colleagues, Mr Pringle, did slip on some orange peel and hurt his neck, so naturally we was all quite cheerful.'

'This is serious, Fletcher. Godber's in trouble. It's so irrational. I mean, I like that lad. I think he's got a lot of promise.'

I sighed deeply. 'Well, that's prison, isn't it? The system. Already turning a nice quiet lad into a violent criminal. You screws – er, officers – don't realise that you're sitting on a volcano. Any moment it could erupt in an explosion of desperate violence and mayhem.'

Mr Barrowclough's jaw dropped, as if he'd inhaled a hornet with his hay, and he asked nervously : 'Listen, Fletcher, you've got your finger on the pulse. What can be done to avert it?'

'I can think of one thing, Mr Barrowclough, that might help postpone the holocaust.'

'Well – what is it?'

'Get us some new ping-pong balls.'

Naturally, I awaited the arrival of Lennie that evening with some interest and not a little trepidation. As I lounged in our compact, purpose-built flat I tried to imagine possible explanations for his unexpected eruption. But nothing seemed to fit. Would he be changed? Would he now wear the hard, cynical expression of the old lag? In fact it was the same old, or rather young, Lennie who finally slouched despondently into the living quarters. I gave him time to begin the necessary explanations but he didn't seem forthcoming. He just sat down on his bunk and stared gloomily at the slops bucket. Finally I could stand it no longer.

'Well then?' I asked.

'Well then, what?'

'I heard.'

'Heard what?'

'I heard you hit Jackdaw with a ladle.'

'Heard right then, didn't you?'

'I'm sure you had your reasons.'

'Yes. I did.'

This was not the easy flow of confidences that normally passed between us. I tried a different tack. 'Ain't you going to the cooler then?'

'No. I'm not.'

'Well then, you're a lucky lad.'

'Lucky?'

'Assault. Ladling a fellow prisoner. Automatic cooler offence, ladling.'

Lennie grunted moodily and shifted his gaze to the toe of his left shoe. He mumbled : 'Governor gave me a severe reprimand and loss of privileges. He accepted my mitigating circumstances.'

'Oh, mitigating circumstances, was it?'

'Yes.'

More silence. I didn't want to lean on the lad, especially as there were various objects about the dell that might serve him as a substitute for a ladle, but my natural and legitimate curiosity demanded satisfaction. I tried again.

'All right, don't tell me what drove a normal affable lad like yourself to the pitch where he suddenly launches himself on another prisoner with a deadly weapon, to wit a ladle.'

'I won't then.'

'I see.' I paused. 'Doesn't it occur to you that your hitherto blameless record is due in no small part to yours truly. I'm just the bloke who showed you the ropes, helped you get by, kept you on the rails and loaned you his soft toilet paper.'

'I'm not ungrateful, Fletch. Every time I go to the bog I'm not ungrateful.'

'Well then, Godber, remembering that you know more about my private life than Scotland Yard, don't you think I'm entitled to know a bit about yours?'

Lennie transferred his gaze to his right shoe, but for some time that was his only response. Then he sighed and nodded slowly. 'I suppose so. I had some news which upset me. Jackdaw thought it was a joke. He kept taking the mickey. He wouldn't leave off. So finally I hit him. While the balance of my mind was disturbed.'

'News?'

This produced another outburst of silence and I was beginning to contemplate abandoning the quest when he slowly rose to his feet, put a hand into his pocket, withdrew a letter and handed it to me. Of course, as soon as I saw it I had a strong suspicion as to the truth.

'What is it?' I asked. 'A "Dear John" letter?'

'No. It's a "Dear Lennie" letter.'

'Yeah, well – same principle, ain't it? Yours but no longer for ever, signed Denise. Is that it?'

'Just about.'

'Dear, dear. So it's the demise of Denise, is it?'

'Not funny, Fletch.'

'Of course it's not, lad, but it's inevitable. I've seen it happen time and again. Only natural. Least your Denise has been honest enough to write a letter. Because they're all at it like knives while we're in here.'

Lennie began to open up a bit. 'Came out of the blue this, Fletch. No hint of it a fortnight ago in her last letter. Her only concern then was whether we should have a canary or a budgerigar.'

'Well, that's one decision you don't have to make.'

'No.'

There was another long silence and, more to distract him than because I thought the subject was a very pressing one, I resumed :

'Speaking personally, from personal experience, I would say I would always without doubt plump for the budgerigar.'

Lennie surprised me by asking, with apparent interest, 'Oh, why?'

'Budgies is friendlier. And canaries is very prone to draughts – it's the angle of the tail.'

'Oh.'

'I speak from experience, as I say. We had a canary once – surly little bleeder he was.'

But Lennie had lost interest in the topic. 'Don't really matter now, does it?'

This seemed beyond dispute. I reverted to the nub : 'So your Denise has – er – I mean – well, there's another man, is there? I mean, presumably?'

'There is.'

'Do you know him?'

A faint, bitter smile played across Lennie's face but whether that signified 'yes' or 'no' I couldn't be sure. However, he volunteered : 'His name's Kenneth. He's in the Merchant Navy. Third engineer, qualified. So there's no contest, is there?'

No contest? A sailor? It suddenly seemed to me that Lennie was way off course and clouting people with ladles for nothing.

'Jack the lad, is it?' I asked, with an undercurrent of irony. 'The blue-eyed boy with his navy blue uniform and gold braid? And Denise thinks the sun shines out of his porthole, does she? Lennie, that's just temporary, my son, just temporary! If he's a sailor he's got to go back to the sea, hasn't he? He's committed. And then *he'll* be in the Persian Gulf and *you'll* be in – er, with Denise. It's clear now that this is only a temporary setback.'

But Lennie didn't rally the way I had expected. He just shook his head moodily and murmured : 'I don't think so, Fletch.'

'Why not?'

'She's married him.'

This did seem to be an obstacle. Try as I might I could think of nothing further consoling to say. Lennie went on : 'Last Saturday, Smethwick Registry Office. She thought it was my right to know.'

'Well – very thoughtful – '

'Apparently it kept fine for them and the Cross Keys – our local pub – did them proud. Pâté and ham salad.'

'Sounds like a very nice affair. Now listen here, young Godber, it don't do to brood or bean people with ladles. Right now you feel the bottom's dropped out of your life. But believe me, you'll get over it. You're young and before you know where you are you'll have found a new girl and you'll wonder what you ever saw in Denise.'

Lennie lifted his pale face and our eyes met. He said simply : 'Never.'

Well, visiting time crawled round again and there once more was my eldest, Ingrid, sitting smiling at me across the little table. I was a bit miffed because I'd expected the old trouble-and-strife but Ingrid explained :

'Mum's definitely coming up next month. She would have come today but the doctor expressly forbade it.'

'Nothing serious, is it?'

'Scrubbing the surgery. You know she helps him out sometimes.'

'Oh, yes. How's the rest of the family?'

'Marion ain't with Timothy Whites no longer.'

I did not exactly feel giddy with astonishment. 'Dispensed with her services, did they?'

'It wasn't molestation this time. She got a better job, selling shirts. She shows them round the offices.'

'Well, makes a nice change from showing her knickers round the offices.'

'And she's found a flat in Maida Vale, which she's sharing with some nurses.' At this point, Ingrid sort of gulped and then continued. 'And what you'll be most glad to hear is that Eddie and me have split up.'

Naturally, at this heart-warming news, I perked up. I patted her hand. 'Not before time, girl. It's a relief to us all.'

I was none too chuffed, however, to hear a low voice from my left confirm the observation. 'Yes, we was worried about that liaison.'

I turned with justifiable irritation. 'Do you mind, Godber? I'm sorry, Mrs Godber, no offence, but I've warned your lad about this before. Ain't you got any news for him from your home front?'

Lennie's mum stammered: 'I'm sorry, Mr Fletcher. It's my fault. Truth is, I can never think of anything to say to him. It's like visiting people in hospital.'

And Lennie added humbly: 'Sorry, Fletch. Sorry, miss.'

Ingrid smiled like the well-brought-up girl she is and said: 'That's all right.'

I resumed our interrupted conversation. 'So, anyhow, you give Eddie the elbow. Good for you, girl. Just listen to your old Dad in future.'

Ingrid said eagerly: 'Oh I do, Dad. Ain't you noticed how much more discreet I am today?'

I didn't catch her drift and asked: 'How d'you mean?'

'Well, last time I was here I obviously embarrassed you in front of your friends. Well, this time I ain't given you no cause, have I?'

I tried to recall what had occurred at our last meeting but for the life of me I couldn't. 'I don't get you, girl.'

'Oh, dad!' said Ingrid reproachfully. 'Look, I'm wearing a bra!'

And before I could stop her, she reached down, grasped the edge of her sweater and then treated the whole room to a mouth-watering view of her well-filled black bra.

It is possible that I was wearing a self-satisfied expression when I ambled into the old flowery the next evening. Anyway, Lennie looked up from the letter he was writing and asked : 'Swallowed the cream, then?'

For answer, I held up before his eyes a small, smooth object.

'What's that?' he asked.

'Ping-pong ball, courtesy of Mr Barrowclough.'

'Thought it was the crown jewels, the way you're grinning.'

'No imagination, that's your trouble. Don't you know there's a severe scarcity of ping-pong balls in this nick? I'll get a quarter of a pound of snout for this.'

But he didn't seem impressed. He glanced down at his letter again and then back up.

'Fletch, can I ask you something?'

'Feel free,' I invited.

'Well, you know when I was very low the other day – after I got Denise's letter?'

'Yes.'

'When I was worried about the stigma of being an ex-con?'

'Right.'

'Well, will it be a problem for me? I mean, will I be able to work me way back into society?'

'That depends, son. Depends on the breaks.'

'Have there been any problems for you? When you get out?'

'Not for me, no. I've never had to worry about no references, no testimonials. Because I've always gone straight – straight back into crime. It's different with you, Lennie. You're young, you're healthy, you've got an honest face.'

'Is that enough?'

'You've got character. You're a good lad.'

'So you reckon, Fletch, if someone really cared for me,

a girl like – she'd overlook my past misdemeanours, like?'

'Certainly. If she's any sort of human being, of course she would. Lennie, my son, you have to learn to believe in yourself.'

He nodded and a look of relief came into his face, as if a burden had been lifted. 'That's all right then. I'm going to send this.'

He signed the letter and then wrote out the envelope. He handed it to me.

'Fletch, could you get your mucker Barrowclough to post it for me? It's on plain paper so maybe they'll play it for me this time.'

I inspected the envelope. It was addressed to the BBC. 'Oh no,' I exclaimed. 'You're not still trying to melt that slag Denise, are you?'

But he shook his head happily. 'No, not her.'

'Well, who?'

'Ingrid.'

'Oh, Ing – WHO?'

'That's right, Fletch, your daughter. Our eyes met and I knew – I knew – you don't mind, Fletch, do you?'

I shook my head to clear the black mist.

'Mind?' I asked faintly and then more vigorously. 'MIND? You think I'd let my beloved Ingrid take up with the likes of you? A bleeding juvenile delinquent from the back streets of Birmingham? A con, a thief, a – a – a –'

'A chip off the old block,' suggested Lennie cheerfully. 'Now, how about a game of ping-pong, dad?'

Disturbing the Peace

I was rolling myself a fag in my favourite corner of the library, by the radiator, when I heard the sound of a key grating in the lock. That's the way it is in the nick, locks everywhere. If there was any doors on the toilets they'd have locks on the outside – and you'd have to call a screw to let you in. Anyway, anticipating the arrival of a certain Hibernian screw, I hastily crammed my unfinished fag into the hollowed-out copy of Lamb's *Tales from Shakespeare* where I store my snout and sprang into action, stacking volumes onto my trolley and generally conveying an air of dynamic industry and literary devotion. I didn't even look up – affecting to be too absorbed in my duties – until a voice said :

'Right, Fletcher, it's time you were out on your rounds. Hospital and Governor, isn't it?'

A pleasant surprise.

'Oh, hello, Mr Barrowclough,' I greeted the sad-faced officer.

Then I continued stacking volumes but now my mind was racing. I needed a certain signature. I'd never have got it from MacKay – but from Barrowclough?

'As a matter of fact,' I explained, gaining time to plan the crucial move, 'I'm just picking something out special for the Governor. Got a good one here for his wife : "A Perilous Odyssey of Love and Anguish set in Turbulent Tuscany". Very torrid according to the blurb.'

'Not too torrid, I hope?'

'Oh no, it's done in very good taste. They always put the lights out.'

Mr Barrowclough blinked uneasily but contented himself with urging : 'Come on then, let's get along.'

This was the moment. I seized the trolley and made a lunge for the door. Then, as if recollecting something, I snatched a paper off my little desk and presented it to him.

'Oh, could you just sign this before we go? Standard requisition for new books.'

Barrowclough took the paper and began to glance through it. I whipped a pen in front of his face and urged :

'Just sign at the bottom where I've put a cross. I know how busy you are, so don't trouble to read it.'

But he wouldn't play. 'Must have a quick glance through.'

I made a last try. 'Honest, Mr Barrowclough, it's just – '

But he was frowning and shaking his head. 'There's several here quite unsuitable. Good heavens !'

I sighed and waited for it. He went on :

' "The Great Escape" . . . "Nudes of the Naughty Nineties" . . . "A History of Erotica". . . .'

'That's one of them new African countries, isn't it?' I asked innocently.

But by now he was at work with a blue pencil. 'I can't let these through, Fletcher. They're mostly sexual or subversive.'

'Oh, leave "Voodoo Woman",' I pleaded. 'It's a classic, that.'

Barrowclough attempted to eye me severely but the effect was that of a cow with a squint.

'You've got a very privileged job in this library, Fletcher. Take care you don't lose it.'

Oh well, win a few, lose a few. I glanced at the largely-obliterated list.

'I see you've allowed the Enid Blyton Omnibus. The lads'll be chuffed about that.'

'There is a limit.'

'Yes, yes, I can appreciate your point of view. There's always two sides, isn't there? Sort of thing I want to bring out in my forthcoming book.'

That got through. He jerked back like a cow that's been introduced to a milk float.

'Book?'

'Yes. You see, working in the library has rekindled my literary aspirations. So I'm working on this book, see? On prison life. From the man within like.'

'Well, I'm not sure – prison life?'

'Ah, but don't worry, I'm very objective. I haven't overlooked the difficult task which confronts you brave boys in blue and I've sought to shed light on your problems as much as on the ones faced by my fellow felons.'

That reassured him. 'Oh, well, that sounds quite acceptable. What are you going to call your book, Fletcher?'

I seized the handles of the trolley and, as I heaved the load of literary mush into motion, said over my shoulder: 'Don't let the Bastards Grind you Down!'

First port of call was the Governor's office and the first dainty craft I spied as I swung in to berth was Mrs Heskith, the Governor's secretary. Well, to be absolutely candid, the lady was not really in the thoroughbred class, being in her late thirties and spectacles. Nevertheless, when the only women you normally see are two-dimensional and pasted up on walls, the proximity of even a damsel like Mrs Heskith does strange things to a man. Inwardly muttering 'Down! Down!' to my leaping red corpuscles, I edged round her. I was as astonished as the Governor when, as I passed between my judiciously-positioned trolley and her back, the lady let out a sharp yelp, and I hastily cleared my throat loudly and exclaimed : 'Oh, good morning, Mrs Heskith, what a rare treat. I mean, seeing your sunny face.'

She edged nervously away from me. I attempted a little gallantry : 'What a lovely cardigan, Mrs Heskith. Goes with your eyes, two of your best features if I may say so, although I expect – '

But Mr Venables, the Governor, interrupted irritably : 'All right, Fletcher, what is it?'

'Oh – morning, sir.'

He dismissed his secretary. 'Thank you, Mrs Heskith. You'd better go and get me that release form to sign. Now, Fletcher, what is it?'

'Books, sir. New consignment, sir. You always like first pick.'

'It's not a question of first pick. I like to look them over to ensure there's nothing unsuitable for the men.'

His tone was irritable. A little ingratiation was in order. 'I found the book you wanted, sir.' And with that I handed him a thick volume.

He examined it without enthusiasm, finally asking : *Tom Brown's Schooldays?*

'Ah, but the title's irrelevant, sir. The point is it's exactly one and three-quarter inches thick, which is just what you wanted to prop up your wobbly desk.'

He brightened. 'Oh, splendid, Fletcher. Thank you.'

Of course, I could have further ingratiated myself by offering to do the job for him but I had my motives for not being too helpful. These proved sound when he immediately bent down and began himself to remove the oversized phone book which was at present supporting the desk. And that gave me a moment to snaffle from its surface a rubber, a pencil sharpener, a felt-tipped pen, two cigarettes from an open packet and a paper clip. Not a very princely haul, you might suppose, but it's amazing what will find a purchaser in the nick. While at work on the desk top, and still in the brief instant that the Governor was submerged beneath it, I noted a letter laying there. Information is, if anything, more valuable than consumer durables in prison and so, practising an art I had long ago mastered, I read as much of it as I could upside down, before the Governor heaved into view again.

'Yes,' he said with satisfaction, 'that's much better. All right, Fletcher, cut along.'

Naturally, I wasn't sorry to be away with the booty but just at that moment the sultry Mrs Heskith returned clasping a piece of paper. She held it out to the Governor, explaining : 'The release form, sir.'

He, to my faint alarm, remarked, 'Oh good . . . where's my pen?' And started ferreting about for the item.

I promptly offered it to him with the winning remark : 'Use mine, sir.'

He signed the form and handed it back to Mrs Heskith, putting the pen in his pocket. Mrs Heskith and I waited.

'Go on then, Fletcher,' he said irritably.

'Yes, sir, it's just – '

'What is it now, Fletcher?'

'My pen, sir.'

'Oh, I'm terribly sorry.'

'They all look alike, don't they, sir,' I said.

I completed my literary rounds and made it back to the cell with the loot. Lennie, being inexperienced in the ways of penal servitude, was none too impressed by my collection. 'That the lot, then?' he asked, contemplating it moodily.

'Yes – apart from a very interesting bit of information. I always learn something when I go into the Governor's office.'

'Like what?'

'Well . . . apart from the fact that there's something simmering between him and Mrs Heskith – which we'll bear in mind for future reference, won't we? – I also saw a memo on Venables' desk. Upside down, of course, but years of being in the nick have taught me to read memos upside down.'

'What did it say?'

'Eciffo emoh, laitnedifnoc.'

'And what the hell's that mean?'

I grinned. ' "Home Office, Confidential", backwards. MacKay's going on a course.'

That made Lennie sit up, or would have done if he hadn't already been sitting up, your average cell being short on loungers, rockers and deep-stuffed leather arm-chairs. 'When? Where? What course?'

'Easy. I only had four seconds. But I reckon it must have something to do with either promotion or transfer.'

'He's been keeping it very dark.'

'He don't know yet, you nurk. Only me and the Governor knows so far.'

At which point, we both heard a rasping sound from without suggestive of a buzz-saw starting up in the Canadian wilderness. Lennie asked:

'Aren't those his dulcet tones now? Let's ask him.'

'Not on your Nelly! We've got a situation here which I can turn to my advantage.'

Then, hearing MacKay's dainty tread immediately outside, I seized the evening paper I'd nicked from the screws' recreation room and, signalling to Lennie to pretend he was listening intently, I started pretending to read: 'I see here, Godber, that with Saturn passing through your opposite sign of Cancer, this may be an exhausting month for you. Probably means they're moving you out of the kitchens and onto the dustbins.'

As I'd anticipated, the silence behind me was broken by MacKay's heart-warming voice : 'Seeking solace in the stars now, are we?'

I glanced round. 'Oh, evening, Mr MacKay. If you'll excuse me – "As Uranus is one of the most powerful and unpredictable planets – future events will be likewise unpredictable." '

MacKay uttered a dirty laugh. 'I should have thought all your futures were somewhat predictable. Now if that astral bilge was true, Fletcher, it would say : "Little change for the next four years, no opportunities for travel and absolutely no prospect of romance on the horizon".'

I couldn't let that pass.

'It's only a question of scale, isn't it, Mr MacKay? I mean when you're as deprived of romance as what we are, a chance brush with the Governor's secretary is like a naughty weekend in Boulogne with a teenage nymphomaniac. It's only a question of scale.'

At this Lennie, proving a credit to me, chimed in with : 'When's your birthday, Mr MacKay?'

'April the twenty-fifth.'

I pretended to seek out the relevant item in my astrological column. 'Oh yes, Taurus. Not the subtlest of signs. The bull. Ah yes. "Endeavours you have been hoping for come to fruition." And look at this : "A favourable time for a move and seeking opportunities elsewhere".'

'Poppycock,' grunted MacKay.

I shook my head, maintaining a wide-eyed look. 'No, the stars are hardly ever wrong, Mr MacKay. You must be moving on.'

Lennie, again confirming my belief in the lad's essential talent, asked : 'You going on holiday, Mr MacKay?'

'Not till August.'

Lennie looked puzzled. Then he asked : 'And your retirement's not due just yet, is it?'

MacKay squared his shoulders and jerked his chin back as if preparing to launch it. 'Don't be insolent, Godber.'

The last thing I wanted was nap and double, so I said very humbly, shaking my head in wonder : 'But it's very clear in the stars, Mr MacKay, very clear indeed. A move is clearly indicated.'

'Out of the question.'

'I'd bet on it, Mr MacKay.'

'What, on this nonsense?'

'It doesn't do to deride what you don't understand : the paranormal, the psychic. No, the more I study this, Mr MacKay, the more certain I am that within a few days you'll be leaving your familiar surroundings.'

Mr MacKay remarked haughtily : 'Step outside, Fletcher.'

Not quite certain what this development might signify, I asked : 'I hope I haven't – '

'Just step outside.'

With faint forebodings, I accompanied Slade Prison's own Himmler out onto the landing. He rounded on me.

'You have the nerve to offer to bet with a prison officer? In front of young Godber?'

'Oh, I never thought, Mr MacKay.'

'What are you trying to do, disillusion the boy?'

'Sorry, Mr MacKay.'

'How much then?'

'A quid?'

'You're on.'

Well, naturally it all came to pass as the heavens had foretold. MacKay departed on a course. And when young Warren glanced up from his game of draughts with Williams during the fun hour next day, and asked : 'Did he pay up, Fletch?'

I was able to assure him : 'Certainly. With all the ill-grace you'd expect from that charmless Celtic nurk.'

McLaren, the dusky Hibernian, coveting my evening paper, attempted to snaffle it from me when I wasn't looking. But I was too quick for him and left him clutching a pinch of newsprint between finger and thumb. He grumbled in his incomprehensible native dialect : 'Och, you've had it long enough, Fletcher. Are there any nice birds in it?'

'I ain't looking at birds, am I? I'm reading the editorial. I'm not like you lot. All you want from a paper is horses and nudes. There *are* people who have some curiosity about the world. Personally, I like to keep abreast.'

Here Lennie, tastelessly I thought, chipped in with : 'It's true. He's got a dozen pinned up in his locker.'

Williams, the wailing Welshman, remarked : 'Personally, I'm not a breast man. My initial interest is always awakened by the leg.'

'Just one of them?' I asked.

But before he could answer, McLaren asked him : 'They say you're a bit of a ladies' man on the outside, Williams?'

'I've had my moments. I have a large sexual appetite, see. Probably compensating for those years of deprivation in the Bridge End Choral School. Consequentially, I suffer more than most in prison.'

I laid down my paper, allowing McLaren to snatch it up, and contributed : 'From what I've been reading, it seems we're better off in here. This country's on the verge of economic ruin. Yes, our once great nation is hovering on the brink of the abyss.'

'That,' remarked McLaren, his big brown eyes glued to a half-tone bosom, 'is the bosses' fault.'

'No, it's not, Vanessa. It's the average man's fault.

The people who'd rather draw National Assistance than take a job. People who won't do a decent day's work for a decent day's wage . . . people much like ourselves.'

Warren joined in. 'My Elaine says prices keep on rising. No one's got any money.'

Lennie grinned. 'By the time you lot get out, there'll be no one worth robbing.'

'That's what I was trying to say,' I said. 'We're better off inside.'

Warren agreed: 'He's not wrong. I've known worse stir.'

'Right. And with MacKay gone – happy days are here again. Chance to work a few things, isn't there?'

Williams nodded sagely: 'That's true. Old Barrowclough don't exactly rule with a rod of iron, does he?'

I warmed to the theme: 'We can start having a flutter again. What about frog racing? We could revive that. Get them from the farm.'

Williams confided lasciviously: 'I'll tell you something about frogs and it's a fact. Like me the frog has an exceptional sexual appetite. When the frog and his mate mate he's at it for twenty-eight days non-stop.'

'Twenty-eight days?' Lennie gasped.

'Non-stop.'

'No wonder,' I began, 'his eyes bulge out – oh Gawd!'

This exclamation had been torn from me by a hideous sight. Through the iron gates which separated us from more iron gates had strolled Mr Barrowclough in company with another and unfamiliar screw. Unfamiliar in this neck of the woods, that is, but a nurk I had personally encountered in the past. His name was Wainwright.

The others hadn't noticed the new arrivals. Warren asked: 'What's up, Fletch?'

'Happy days? Life of Riley. I think they're over.'

'What you talking about?' asked Lennie.

'You've heard me mention a screw in Brixton? Name of Napper Wainright and nature of a right bastard?'

'Yeah, why?'

'He's just walked in the gate, that's why.'

Naturally this caused a stir, if a discreet one, the lads all being too experienced for blatant rubber-necking. Nevertheless everyone contrived to have a butcher's at the fearsome spectacle.

Warren murmured glumly: 'He looks a right one.'

And McLaren voiced the horrible suspicion: 'You don't suppose he's MacKay's replacement?'

'That,' I admitted, 'is exactly what I do suppose.'

Lennie asked dubiously: 'Living legend, isn't he, in the Prison Service?'

I nodded. 'And he's been promoted. See? Striped like a zebra. We can only hope that success has mellowed him.'

But the unlikelihood of this possibility was speedily demonstrated. A voice from behind us, sounding not unlike a great ocean liner nosing through fog, demanded: 'Something to say to me, have you? Well, my name's Wainwright. You address me as "Mr Wainwright" or "Sir". Now button your lip!'

I glanced round to see a hapless felon cowering back pale-faced from this advice. And the next instant it was my turn.

'Norman Stanley Fletcher, on your feet.'

I rose like a Saturn rocket and confronted the craggy and towering form of Napper Wainwright. He grinned evilly.

'I knew our paths would cross again, my son. The day you left Brixton, I said to you: this is not good-bye, Fletcher, this is merely au-revoyer.'

I nodded agreement: 'It's true, Mr Wainwright. And I said to you – '

'I haven't forgotten what you said, Fletcher!'

'Oh yes?' I asked brightly, since it is sometimes best to beard the bastards. 'And did you manage it?'

Wainwright's eyes narrowed to pinpricks. 'It doesn't pay to come it with me, Fletcher. You remember me.' Then he turned to give the whole group the benefit of his thinking in this matter. 'I have this mean streak, see? I know it's despicable but I'm prejudiced.'

McLaren could not refrain from muttering: 'That'll make a nice change.'

Wainwright offered soothingly:

'Oh, I'm not just prejudiced against your lot, Sonny Jim. No, I'm prejudiced against – ' and his voice again took on the volume and penetrating power of a Concorde taking off – 'Liberals, longhairs, pill-heads, winos, queens, slags, squealers, pikeys and grease-balls!'

He paused to allow the echoes to subside, then rounded on Lennie. 'Are you in there, sonny?'

'Isn't everybody?' I asked.

'Quiet, Fletcher, I was talking to the boy. Well? I said, are you in there?'

Lennie gave it sober consideration.

'I don't think so. I'm Church of England.'

The appreciative titters were obliterated by a single glare from Wainwright's burning orbs. Then he nodded in sinister satisfaction. 'We've only just met and already he's given me a grudge to bear.'

At this cordial juncture, Mr Barrowclough ambled over. He glanced about the subdued assembly and, as is his way, attempted to inject a cheerful note: 'Well, I see you men have been getting acquainted with Mr Wainwright?'

'Some of us,' I remarked, 'have had that dubious privilege earlier in our careers.'

'Oh really?'

Wainwright thrust a finger like Kitchener's towards

me and snarled : 'This one passed through Brixton on a couple of brief but memorable occasions.'

Mr Barrowclough attempted to dribble a little oil on the troubled waters : 'Oh well, it's nice to bump into old faces. I keep telling these men, Mr Wainwright, that our role is to help them ... to encourage them in a programme of self-improvement and rehabilitation. To prepare them for going back into society.'

Wainwright dismissed this drivel with a snort. 'Our role, Mr Barrowclough, is to keep them away from society. Our role is to keep these scheming bastards locked in !'

With which encouraging shot he turned on his heel and strode off for a light supper of scrap iron and broken glass.

The next week was pure hell. Wainwright roared about the nick like a graduate of Colditz. The persecution was on a scale that would have appalled the Romans and finally it became clear to all of us that any measures, no matter how desperate, would have to be used to rid us of this peril. Lennie and I sat debating the situation in our cell while I bathed the bruised hand Wainwright had deliberately trampled all over while I'd been scrubbing the landing.

'What a swine, stepping on your hand like that,' Lennie remarked.

'Be fair. Complete accident. His foot slipped. He was aiming for my head.'

'Your stars never predicted this lot, did they?'

'I never thought I'd feel nostalgia for the muffled snarl of MacKay's – oh hello, Mr Barrowclough.' The screw with the doleful countenance oozed into the cell.

Lennie eyed him with concern. 'You look a bit bushed, Mr Barrowclough.'

'Well, I am. It's that Mr Wainwright. He's been

through this prison like a dose of salts. He's reorganised the entire duty roster.'

'Oh, tough titty,' I sympathised with just a dash of sarcasm. 'Any idea how many curtailments we've suffered? No fraternising in the exercise yard. Shorter telly hours. And he's only commandeered our ping-pong table for your bleeding mess.'

'Only until our billiard table's been re-covered. And after all, Fletcher, it's your fault it needed re-covering.'

'Our fault?'

'A prisoner certainly tampered with it.'

'Really? Can you prove that?'

'It's a strong supposition. When Nosher Garrett went over the wall he was picked up in Blackpool wearing a green baize suit. Anyway, I really came in to say cheerio because you won't be seeing so much of me in the future. He's got me down for a transfer to the farm.'

'No.'

'Says I should just be in charge of trusties. Says I'm not really suited to a cell block. Where I'm at the mercy of infractious and recalcitrant prisoners like yourself, Fletcher – no offence, you understand, these are his words, not mine.'

This was serious. Without Mr Barrowclough's restraining influence, Wainwright was likely to march us all off the battlements.

'Look, Mr Barrowclough, we've got to prevent this.'

'But how?'

'Well – well – you'll just have to change your ways.'

This was a bit like asking a leopard to take his morning stroll wearing a pin-stripe but I couldn't think of any better plan on the spur of the moment. Mr Barrowclough blinked sadly at me : 'Change my ways?'

'Yeah, just so. Don't let people take advantage. Come on strong. Wield the big stick.'

'Put on a bit of a show like,' contributed Lennie helpfully. 'You know . . . mean, moody and magnificent.'

'But I don't see – '

'You will. Some suitable opportunity's bound to crop up. Just wait for it, that's all.'

Just then a sound like a pack of wolves closing in froze our blood. 'Mr Barrowclough ! Where are you !'

Barrowclough winced. 'It's Mr Wainwright. He wants me for something.' And, striving to subdue a bad fit of shuddering, he hastened from the cell.

The following day, in the canteen, McLaren, who is not normally a fussy eater and has indeed been known to devour stewed cockroaches with relish, suddenly took exception to something he found on his plate. He bawled at Lennie, who had just dumped his rations there : 'Hey you !'

Lennie turned, all innocence. 'Me?'

'Yes you, Fanny Cradock. I'm talking to you. There's a caterpillar on my plate.'

'Really?' asked Lennie. 'That could make an attractive pet.' A sinewy brown arm shot out and seized him not too roughly by the throat, while a reedy highland voice complained, 'This food's no fit for swine. We've had enough, lads. Are you with me?'

And within moments, the riot, as previously planned, was in full swing.

A good deal of flying vegetable matter filled the air, reducing visibility, but nevertheless it was one of the most satisfying spectacles I could remember. The lads laid it on big. Tables thundered onto their sides. Benches reared up into crude barricades and, best of all, Wainwright's incredulous countenance, imprudently appearing round the door, was immediately obliterated by a thick layer of mashed spuds, making him look like an abominable snowman. He promptly retreated and, with alarm bells making the jolly old nick ring like a cathedral on Christmas Eve, the lads settled down to a siege. As arranged, I was allowed to depart to organise the next stage of the drama.

Amazing, but the first thing I saw as I entered the Governor's office, pushing my trusty trolley, was Mrs Heskith's rounded posterior. She was bending over the desk and the Governor's head was thrown back for the purpose of ingesting a large assortment of pills.

At that moment, as I squeezed past her, Mrs Heskith once again let out an inexplicable squeal. The Governor made a choking noise and, gulping, looked at me.

'What on earth do you want, Fletcher?'

'Another load of new books, sir.'

'At a time like this?'

'Oh yes, well, I wasn't to know, was I, sir?'

'I'm referring to the riot!'

'Oh the riot, yes. Very nasty situation.'

'It is indeed. There's systematic and wilful destruction of furniture and crockery. Why, they're knee deep in plates down there.'

'Bit like a Greek restaurant on New Year's Eve.'

'Don't be flippant, Fletcher. It's astounding. I'd have thought Mr Wainwright would have been the ideal man to quell the riot but he seems to make matters worse.'

'If the truth were told, sir, it's Mr Wainwright what aggravated the situation in the first place.'

'Really? Well, I suppose I'll have to go down there myself.'

'More than your life's worth, sir. No offence, sir, but there's only one man in this prison who could quell that riot.'

'Who? Who?'

I shook my head sadly. 'Trouble is, sir, he's no longer on the premises.'

'But who is it, Fletcher? Answer me.'

Well, of course, I answered him. And that was the reason why, about an hour later, a van pulled into the prison yard and out of it, resembling as always a bereaved heifer, stepped the familiar form of Mr Barrowclough. He was protesting feebly but, on the Governor's orders, was bustled along to the erupting canteen. Now, of course I was not able to witness the denouement personally but I heard many accounts of it in the weeks to come.

First, the canteen door was unlocked and Mr Barrowclough, eager as a penguin for a hot bath, poked his head cautiously round it. There was instant, magical silence.

Barrowclough cleared his throat and suggested : 'Now – er – why don't we all put those things down?'

He was referring to tables, benches and a luckless screw that had got locked in with the rioters. And his words were as Jehovah's. Every single lag instantly obeyed.

Encouraged, Mr Barrowclough cleared his throat again and asked : 'Wouldn't it be a good idea if we all filed back to our cells in an orderly fashion?'

Apparently it struck those mutinous villains as an excellent idea. They promptly fell into line and trooped out. The Governor goggled. Mr Wainwright nearly, but alas not quite, burst a blood vessel, and Slade Prison's worst ever riot was at an end.

Two days later, with Mr Barrowclough back on the landing, Mr Wainwright left us, doubtless to supervise construction camps in the Arctic.

'So happy days are here again,' said Lennie.

'Normal service has been resumed.'

But of course every silver lining has its cloud. You'll never believe who replaced Wainwright.

'Oh, hello, Mr MacKay. What a nice surprise.'

No Peace for the Wicked

With a mug of tea in my hand and a nearly-intact copy of *Penthouse* under my arm I ambled along the cat-walk towards the cell. Arrived there I paused in the door-way and gazed in. Nothing in the prospect, you might think, to lift the heart or notch up the spirits. I can well believe that to the average law-abiding citizen the view would have been one to cause a shudder of distaste. What was it, after all, but a stone room with a barred window and two bunks? And yet I gazed upon it that Saturday afternoon with practically as much affection as your free man feels when he gazes upon his cosy living room with a fire blazing in the grate and his big armchair ready to receive him.

For a couple of hours I was free to do what I wanted and what I wanted was to get my feet up and relax. Now most cons spend Saturday afternoons indulging in all manner of strenuous activities like leaping over hurdles or punching each other with padded fists. Not me. My idea of true recreation was solitude and a spot of comfort. Usually, of course, the solitude is not that easy to come by since you have a cell-mate to consider, but on that particular Saturday Lennie was still in hospital after having had his tonsils out and so there was no problem.

I placed *Penthouse* on my pillow and my mug of tea on the ledge beside it and prepared to hoist myself up on to my bunk. Just then McLaren slouched into the cell and stood there grinning at me.

'Yes?' I asked, somewhat coolly.

'Got any chewing gum, Fletch?' the dusky Glaswegian inquired.

Since my jaws were working like a thresher I couldn't very well deny it. Anyway the sooner he was satisfied the sooner he'd naff off and leave me in peace. I pulled out a stick of Wrigley's finest and broke him off half.

'There,' I said. 'Don't get your tonsils in a twist or you'll be joining Godber in hospital.'

'Wish I could,' grunted McLaren, feeding the gum into his mouth and showing no sign of departure. 'Going to watch the game, Fletch?'

'What A and B wing? That bloodbath?'

'If we win, we win the trophy.'

'What trophy?'

'It's a silver cup.'

'Correction. It *was* a silver cup. It disappeared from the Governor's office on Tuesday night.'

'Who could have taken that?' asked McLaren genuinely shocked.

'I hear they've narrowed it down to about six hundred suspects.'

McLaren shook his head sorrowfully. 'They'll never see it again. Be melted down by now.'

'Then you'll just have to play for the honour of the wing, won't you?'

'You should cheer us on, Fletch. It's your wing too.'

This kind of sentimental rubbish gets on my box. I said impatiently : 'It's *not* my wing. I just happen to be incarcerated in it at Her Majesty's pleasure, which is a very sinister thought if you come to consider it. It's not your wing, neither. I'm surprised at you coming the Tom Brown's – or, in your case, Tom Black's – schooldays bit.'

'I'm not. When I'm out there I'm playing for Morton. Against Celtic at Hampden. And we stuff them.'

'Well, I've got better things to do than watch people being stuffed at football.'

'What better things? You got visitors coming?'

'No.'

'Got a card game going?'

'No.'

'Gonna watch the box, are you?'

'No. Three times wrong in a row.'

McLaren's face is unsettling because its shape is typically English, or rather Scottish, and its colour is typically African. He looks like a young buck from the Gorbals who's just come down a chimney. Now this peculiar countenance wrinkled into a challenging scowl.

'What *are* you doing then?'

'Going fox-hunting, aren't I?'

Seeing that I was kidding, McLaren's features lightened – well, you know what I mean. 'Seriously,' he urged, 'you should do something. You've got a five-year stretch, Fletch. If you don't do anything it will seem endless.'

I resented his patronising manner. 'Now listen to me, Sonny Jock. Don't tell me how to survive in here. I was doing time when you was running around stealing mangoes on the plantation.'

'What do you mean, plantation? I was brought up in a Greenock housing estate.'

'All right, when you were stealing mangoes on a Greenock housing estate.'

McLaren grinned and went on, 'It's a beautiful day out there, Fletch.'

'And it's a beautiful day in here as well. D'you know why? Because you lot are all out there. That's what I like about the weekend. You're playing football. Others are gambling away their hard-earned money or indulging in their pathetic hobbies. And I ends up with some peace and quiet. So run along and enjoy your game – and don't take any prisoners !'

Whereupon, to my delight, McLaren offered me a cheery wink and departed. I glanced up at my tea, still steaming in its mug, and once more started to mount to my upper berth. 'Bunny' Warren scampered in. I sighed.

'What do you want?'

He smiled ingratiatingly. 'Me and Mini Cooper want to play ping-pong.'

'Don't let me stop yer.'

'Yeah, well . . . there aren't any balls like. Lugless Douglas said you had one.'

'I suppose,' I said sarcastically, 'he just heard. Oh all right – I got one hidden.'

'Would you lend us it then?'

'The word is lease. If you'd care to discuss the possibility of leasing you the ball, Bunny, we might have some basis for negotiation.'

'How much is it then?'

'One snout – ' but then, seeing him pull one readily from his pocket, I added hastily, 'per hour. One snout per hour. Minimum of three hours.'

Warren sighed. 'You're a hard man, Fletch.'

Seeing that he was now undecided, I gave him a little pep talk. 'No, I'm not hard, I'm just taking advantage of something that happened to bounce my way. Now if you was dealing with Harry Grout's syndicate you'd have to leave your wrist-watch as a deposit against the ball being trod on. And if you didn't return the ball your wrist-watch would get trod on – or flogged to one of the screws. So you're lucky to be dealing with me, Warren.'

This had the desired effect. 'All right, Fletch, you're on.' And he produced three crude but smokable fags.

'What's this then?'

'It's good shag, honest.'

'All right.'

'Where's the ball, then?'

'Oh, yes.' I handed over the precious sphere of celluloid.

'Funny colour.'

'I got it off McLaren.'

'You want a game yourself later?' he asked.

'Certainly not. Don't do you no good, exercise.'

'Helps to pass the time.'

'I don't need no help – just the opportunity. Don't forget to return the ball.'

And Warren departed. As I began once more to climb up into my sanctuary, I murmured ironically: 'Next, please.'

And Banyard, the unfrocked dentist, put his huge nose, closely followed by his head, round the door.

'I didn't mean it,' I said hastily.

But he had something on his mind and failed to notice my sarcasm.

'Um, Fletch . . . um, a few of us have formed a drama group.'

'Naff off.'

'I was just wondering – do you have any theatrical inclinations?'

'Yes. I'd like to play Peter Pan and fly out of here.'

'You'd like to act?'

'No.'

'Well, there are other things. You could be prompter or work the lights or operate the wind machine.'

'What you want a wind machine for? You can hire Ives. He's a walking wind machine.'

Since it was becoming clear that I'd never get to drink my Jennie Lee luxuriously in my bunk, I reached up for it and had a sip. Banyard continued: 'We want to do some contemporary plays. We thought we'd start with a thriller. Do you recall "Wait until Dark"? They made a film of it with Audrey Hepburn.'

'I'd never slim down in time.'

But Banyard, who has the sparkling sense of humour of a sheep, said seriously: 'Oh, there's no shortage of cast. What we really want is prompters and lighting men.'

I shook my head. 'Theatre's not really my scene. Now if you was getting up a concert party I could maybe help out. Singing. In the old days I was always round the pubs in North London singing. I was billed as Frankie Fletcher because I thought Frankie sounded more show-biz than Norman which is my real name, if you see what I mean?'

'Quite.'

'I used to be backed by Ted Prendergast and The Organaires. Remember Ted Prendergast?'

'No, I don't think so.'

Memories of those happy days flooded back and, almost without realising it, I burst into song:

'See the pyramids along the Nile,
Watch the sunrise on a tropic Isle...'

I would have continued but Banyard cleared his throat and said firmly: 'But, alas, we're *not* doing a concert party.'

I sighed as the cheerful interior of The Angel, Walthamstow, vanished from my mind. 'Well then, just naff off, Sir Laurence, and leave me to my memories.'

'Are you sure you're not making a mistake, Fletcher? Nothing like theatricals for relieving boredom.'

'The boredom will be relieved as soon as you leave this room.'

'Oh, very well.' And, somewhat huffily, Banyard turned his nose and followed it out.

I looked wistfully up at my bunk, which had by now

acquired all the unattainable glamour of a stroll through Muswell Hill, and then looked hard at the door. It was empty. Stealthily, I put my hands up to get a hold and – a mule popped his head in.

'Welcome,' I greeted it politely, 'to Noah's Ark.'

But instead of all the beasts of the field, Blanco arrived next and I saw that he had hold of the wooden mule.

'It's my Muffin,' he explained shyly. 'It's Muffin the Mule. You know him what's on television.'

If it had been anyone but Blanco I might have had a few choice words to say about converting my cell into a stable but Blanco was a nice old thief who didn't look any too fit and strong. I couldn't find it in my heart to be rude.

'Well, he's very lovely, Blanco,' I said, examining Muffin's teeth. 'Is there any particular reason why you should bring him round here though?'

'Just finished him. I wanted you to be the first one to see him. Taken me nigh on fifteen year.'

I swallowed.

'Fifteen years, eh? Still – worth it, wasn't it?'

Blanco sighed and placed Muffin down on the little table. 'D'you know, now it's done, I'm at a bit of a loose end.'

'Yes, well I expect you are, Blanco. You could always study – improve your mind.'

'I tried that once – I got a book out of the library, on memory training. Studied it for months but then I had to pack it in.'

'Why?'

'I forgot where I left the book.'

'Oh dear,' I said, handing Blanco one of the snouts I'd got for the ping-pong ball. 'Here, try smoking yourself to death instead.'

'Bless you, Fletcher.'

'What are you going to do with Muffin then?'

'Well, I *was* making it for my three-year-old niece but she's an air hostess now and I'm not sure she'd still like it. Fifteen years, Fletch.'

'Yeah, well – time flies when you're having fun.'

Blanco's weary old eyes lighted on my *Penthouse*. 'Can I borrow your magazine?'

'No, you can't.'

'After you've finished it?'

'Better not, Blanco, you know what your blood pressure's like. Try *Radio Times*. Tell you what, will you settle for a jaffa cake?'

'Have you got any?'

'No, but let's see what providence can provide. Come along, Muffin, walkies.'

I walked Muffin and Blanco down to the cubby-hole where Collinson, an evil-tempered screw with a well-known passion for jaffa cakes, was sitting. Blanco waited outside while I went in. I noted with satisfaction that there was a packet of jaffa cakes on the desk and before Collinson could utter a single snarl, I whispered :

'Sorry to disturb you, sir. It's Blanco. He's finished his wooden mule after fifteen years. I thought you'd like to give him a word of praise. Not take a minute.'

Collinson glowered but I had him by the short hairs. Screws have to pretend at least to have the well-being of their customers at heart.

Collinson stepped out of his office and offered Blanco a few words of congratulation and encouragement. While he was gone, I snaffled a couple of jaffa cakes and when he returned I thanked him politely – for being nice to Blanco. Then I joined Blanco outside and gave him both the cakes although I am partial to them myself. Blanco and Muffin toddled off very contentedly to watch

Grandstand and I, with a silent prayer for solitude, returned to my besieged cell.

This time it looked as if I had won through to *nirvana,* if what the pious Hindu craves is to lie on his bunk and read *Penthouse.* I'd actually opened the mag to its centre spread and was studying the lavish anatomy of a young lady from Bude when the faint, discreet sound of a throat being cleared disturbed my concentration. I glanced up and saw Mr Barrowclough standing diffidently in the doorway.

'Oh, hello, Mr Barrowclough. On your way out would you lock me in so's I can get some privacy?'

'On a lovely afternoon like this? I thought you'd be out in the yard, or in the hobby shop. Seems such a waste to be stuck in here.'

'It's not a waste to me. I like to spend my Saturday afternoons in my cell. With my feet up and a bit of reading matter. I don't want to play games or do exercises. Nor do I want to carve toys, take saxophone lessons, form an amateur dramatic group, or watch *The Blue Lamp* on BBC2, a film glamorising that despicable bunch what put me here in the first place.'

Mr Barrowclough tut-tutted. 'Those things are a damn sight better than lying on your bunk reading that lewd lascivious rubbish. If a man puts his mind to it a man can better himself in here. I mean, there's a lot more opportunities now than when I first joined the service. Take Spraggon – you know him in E Block? – Spraggon has made a six-foot space-rocket out of milk bottle tops.'

'Has he now?'

'It's a work of art. Belongs in a museum. He used three colours. The nose cone's in red, homogenised, the bulk of it's made out of ordinary silver top, and the Governor's gold tops provided a nice motif round the centre.'

'When's the launching?'

But Barrowclough ignored my levity. 'There's Rafferty, having his water colours exhibited in a Carlisle art gallery. Not to mention all the professional qualifications that vocational training has given people in this prison. Brickies, plasterers. Even the Tooley brothers left here with a diploma in welding.'

'Yes and what did they do with it, soon as they got out? Welded their way into Barclays Bank in Blackburn High Street.'

'Yes – well – the point I'm trying to make is that we at least gave them the opportunity to do something legitimate with their lives.'

I sat up and swung my legs over the side of my bunk. 'And the point I'm trying to make is that they'll just abuse the opportunity. They're felons, Mr Barrowclough. You get a bloke in here, teach him how to use a printing press. What's he do when he gets out? Does he join the *Northern Echo*? Does he hell! He stays at home and forges premium bonds. Only sensible.'

Mr Barrowclough shook his head agitatedly. 'I won't accept your cynicism. I just don't like seeing a fully-grown man with a good brain – because you're not stupid, Fletcher – wasting his time. You should do something.'

'Is the lecture over? Is that what you come in to say, Mr Barrowclough?'

'Oh, I didn't come in here to lecture you, Fletcher. I just dropped by because I had nothing better to do.'

I gaped at him in amazement. 'Nothing better to do? Well, would you believe it – would you just Adam and Eve it! Your lives are emptier than ours.'

'Nonsense, Fletcher. I have my allotment.'

'Listen, Mr Barrowclough, if the system really wanted to do something constructive for us poor convicts, it would give us more freedom, better grub. Conjugal visits.'

Mr Barrowclough blinked uneasily. 'What kind of visits?'

'Conjugal ones. Didn't you do Latin at school? It's from "conjugo" meaning to have it off.'

'We couldn't possibly – '

'With our old ladies. All above board. Some prisons have 'em – special quarters where the wife visits you and you spend the whole weekend – cementing family ties.'

'I don't know of any such prisons.'

'Maybe not in this country. But they definitely have them abroad, in Holland and America, where they have more enlightened penal systems.'

'They allow the wives to visit, and they spend the whole weekend . . .'

'Conjugating, yeah.'

'That's more than I'm allowed at home.' He shook his head and mooched off.

Now you'll scarcely credit this but, after his departure, I had a really good read! It must have been a good five or six minutes before the next interruption. I'd had a squint at all the poses of Diane from Bude, Deirdre from Liverpool and Francesca, an olive-skinned lovely from Estoril, before I heard a familiar voice just outside the dell proclaiming: 'This is a typical cell in a typical cell block. It is probably unoccupied since most of our inmates are at present participating in the wide range of activities that we provide here at Slade Prison.'

The next moment my heart turned a couple of somersaults because a *female* voice asked: 'Could we peek in this cell?'

I hastily slipped *Penthouse* under my pillow. Just in time because, a moment later, into my cell trooped a young man, an older one and the owner of the female voice that had so captivated me, all three being shepherded by MacKay. Alas, my voluptuous anticipation proved to have been premature. Even in that male desert, where a fleeting glimpse of the Governor's secretary counts as a wildly erotic experience, my uninvited guest wouldn't have released much adrenalin. She was simply too grey and too reminiscent, in build, of a corporation dust cart.

Disillusioned, I stared at the group with distaste, a sentiment obviously reciprocated by MacKay who stared back at me. He apologised to the others: 'Of course, there are always a few who don't cooperate.'

The older man peered up at me as if I was an unfamiliar sausage in a German delicatessen and asked: 'Is this man sick?'

MacKay transmitted the query. 'Are you sick, Fletcher?'

'I'm sick of interruptions,' I growled.

Whereupon the woman, although nothing like Deirdre from Liverpool, endeared herself to me by saying: 'Oh dear, this fellow's probably trying to relax.'

'He never stops,' sneered MacKay. Then, more deferentially, 'As I said, this is a typical cell. Is there anything you'd like to know about it?'

The woman asked: 'Is it a single or a double?'

'Double, ma'am, as indicated by the presence of the two bunks. Prisoners are, of course, allowed to personalise their cells. You will notice the radio, the matches. And, of course, they're allowed to decorate their lockers with mementoes of family and home.'

And the silly nurk tugged open my locker door to demonstrate. The woman gasped and I said quickly: 'Those two are the wife. The other's the wife's sister.'

I hoped she'd assume I'd married into a tribe of

nudists. MacKay hastily slammed the locker door again and suggested : 'Perhaps you'd like to see the recreation room now?'

The older man, revealing a streak of decency, said : 'Yes, we are rather disturbing this man's privacy.'

'Privacy?' I could not help exclaiming bitterly. 'Precious little of that in here.'

MacKay instantly roared : 'Fletcher !'

But the younger man urged him to let me speak and, with this encouragement, I climbed off my bunk and gave it to them. 'Well, have you noticed any signs of privacy on your rounds? Seen a door without a peephole? Seen a shower curtain or a cubicle door in the latrines? Very hard, you know, to retain a vestige of human dignity when you're sitting on the bog and a whole football team clatters past on their way to the showers. Notice the way Mr MacKay barged in here? Not so much as a by my leave or kiss my foot. Paid no more regard to me than he did to the washbasin – in fact, less.'

'Privacy is one of the privileges you forfeit when you transgress the law, Fletcher,' MacKay droned officially. 'This is not a hotel.' And to the others, 'They forget that they're in here to be punished.'

I said indignantly : 'And reformed ! I thought we was also supposed to be reformed?'

The older man, who seemed a kindly old gaffer, said : 'You sound as if you're a Londoner?'

'I am, sir, yes.'

'Long way from home up here. What's a Londoner doing in this neck of the woods?'

'Well, this particular Londoner is doing five years. Might I ask what you lot are doing?'

MacKay began to growl a warning but the older man silenced him with a wave : 'No, no, it's a fair question.

Well, Fletcher, we're all attached to the Home Office in one capacity or another. And it's through these visits that we learn more about our penal system. And only by seeing things for ourselves and talking to people like yourself are we able to make recommendations for change and reform. So have you anything to say?'

'Change, yes. Well, if you can supply a new coat of paint, give us an improved supply of ping-pong balls. But reform, save yourselves the bother.'

Mr MacKay, looking a trifle alarmed, urged : 'I don't think this particular prisoner's opinion is likely to be particularly instructive.'

'Oh no?' I asked. Then I appealed to the Home Office visitors. 'Let me tell you, I've been in more nicks than he has. So who's opinion is likely to be more instructive?'

The woman said simply : 'I should value it.'

'You shall have it,' I promised her. 'Well now, I realise we can't have total amnesty. Got to keep a few hard cases locked away so we normal people can walk the streets at night. But you should do with the rest of us what they do in Scandinavia. Make us work off our debt to society, on farms, building sites, factories, hospitals.'

The woman nodded thoughtfully. 'Well, of course, that is one school of thought.'

The older man boosted my ego a bit by remarking : 'I can see it working with men like you.'

And the younger man asked : 'If you had a choice, what area would you choose to work in?'

'I think,' I said, considering the matter carefully, 'I'd choose a building site.'

MacKay, whose instinct told him what was coming, began to fidget but the woman asked innocently : 'The fresh air?'

'Partly that – but mostly because I could nick myself a fortune.'

'The recreation room!' exclaimed MacKay, urgently.

But as they began to shuffle out, I noticed that both of the men were grinning.

I gave them a few minutes to clear and then I went to the door to establish that at least there wasn't a queue waiting to consult me. There wasn't but there *was* Warren. I groaned : 'What now?'

'I'm sorry, Fletch, it's just that – your ball's got a crack in it.'

'My – oh yeah, the ping-pong ball.'

Warren held it up. 'Cracked.'

Wearily I retreated and Warren followed me into the dell. He said mournfully : 'Spoilt the game.'

'All right,' I grunted, 'I'll have it back then.'

'I'll have my fags back.'

'Not likely. You should have examined the merchandise when the transaction was being transacted.'

'That's not fair, Fletch.'

'Fair?' I exclaimed bitterly. 'Since when was life ever fair? Is it fair that I should suffer this continual intrusion of people who don't know how to occupy their own time and minds? Saturday afternoon provides a few sacred hours when one can enjoy one's own company. It's not much to ask. It don't last long. Only till teatime when we traipse across to have that hideous goo laughingly called cottage pie. When will you blokes learn that surviving in stir is a state of mind? It's an attitude. It's learning to live with yourself.'

Warren bounced the ball a few times and it gave off a dismal cracked sound. I grabbed it on the bounce.

'I like you, Warren. Believe me there are times when I crave your company. I love those action-packed anecdotes of yours of the days when you worked in your father-in-law's ironmongers in Bury.'

'Bolton.'

'Oh the real badlands. Anyway I also have happy memories of those snaps you showed me the other day – of your wife's day trip to Lake Windermere.'

Warren's face brightened and his hand shot into his top pocket. 'I've got some more, Fletch.'

'Have you?' I asked, wondering if Warren could see the faint quiver in my cheek and the way my hands curled involuntarily.

'Only thing is, they didn't come out too well. I expect it was the rain.'

Better not, an inner voice counselled, they give you life. Aloud I said : 'Just – just leave them on the table, Warren, and they'll help me to while away the long evening.'

'Would you like me to explain them, Fletch?'

'That's very kind of you, Warren, but I'm sure I'll be able to harvest their beauties on my own. However, there is just one thing you could do for me, Warren.'

'What's that, Fletch?'

'*Get out and leave me in peace.*'

He must have fled without a word. I didn't see. I only know that when I'd finished trembling and the scarlet flashes had ceased quivering in front of my eyes, I was once more alone. I didn't fall on my knees but I did murmur : 'Dear God, you might think it's a bit of a liberty me asking you favours, but on the other hand there is more joy in heaven when a sinner repenteth – well, I'm ready to repenteth, if you'll just do me one small favour. Could you please, sir, just keep these nurks off my back? Because if anyone else walks through that door I might not be answerable for the consequences.'

For a moment I thought I must have got the hot line

because glancing up I saw a grave figure in the doorway. There was definitely something divine about it but then I realised this was the dog collar. The figure spoke : 'Ah, Fletcher, just doing my rounds. It's quite a long time since we had a chat ...'

It wouldn't be true to say that I have no recollection of anything that occurred until I found myself standing rigidly to attention in front of the Governor's desk, awaiting his arrival. I knew what I'd done but it didn't seem real. It was a nightmare in which I'd become entangled against my will.

'For the chop, you know that,' MacKay offered affably. 'No exit. If ever I had any doubts about the system it's people like you that reassure me. Because in the final analysis your criminal character will always show through like ink on blotting paper.

Mr Venables, the Governor, entered the room wearing a football scarf.

'Sorry I had to fetch you from your game, sir.'

'Not at all, Mr MacKay,' said Venables, seating himself. 'This is a serious matter, a desperately serious matter. These Home Office visitors weren't around when the incident took place?'

'No, sir. Fortunately I had them in the woodwork room at the time.'

'Did anyone witness it?'

'Only old Blanco Webb, sir. And Mr Collinson heard the scream.'

The Governor sighed deeply and transferred his gaze to me. He shook his head and asked : 'Fletcher, what got into you?'

I tried to answer but I couldn't find any words.

The Governor urged : 'I'm talking to you, Fletcher.'

And that gave me a lead. I said bitterly : 'Everyone's

talking to me, sir. End of my tether, see? Think I'm losing my mind, sir. Possibly I should have psychiatric observation in the hospital, sir.'

Venables is not a bad number as prison Governors go. He mused: 'Psychiatric observation? Well, I don't know . . .'

But MacKay wasn't having any of that. He growled: 'No, you don't, sir. An unprovoked assault. And even Slade Prison, which has had its share of violence, has never before seen a chaplain thrown off a balcony.'

'I knew the safety net was there, sir.'

The Governor nodded. 'I daresay, Fletcher, but the chaplain was shattered.'

'I'm sure he'll bounce back, sir. He did a bit.'

'Don't be insolent, Fletcher. I have no alternative but to give you the maximum period of solitary confinement. Then we'll have to discuss the matter further.'

'Yes, sir.'

The Governor contemplated me sadly. 'You've only yourself to blame. You have a very regrettable attitude, Fletcher. Perhaps you'll think it over during the next three days in isolation.'

'Three whole days, sir?'

The Governor said sternly: 'Most certainly!' He turned to MacKay. 'All right, wheel him out.'

But a wild hope had come to me. As MacKay prepared to fill the room with his fearsome bellow, I said quickly: 'Could I just ask one thing, sir?'

'What is it, Fletcher?'

'You couldn't make it a fortnight, could you?'

Happy Release

Not the least of the disadvantages of having to reside in one of Her Majesty's Penal Establishments is that you're surrounded by villains. Practically everyone you meet is some kind of crook. And then they expect you to emerge a reformed man! Don't make sense. I mean, if you want something to be clean you don't trample it in the mud, do you? Would the gentry send their sons and daughters to be educated in Wormwood Scrubs and Holloway? Course not! Too much bleeding sense. I mean, to bring up robbers on the grand scale it's got to be Eton and Roedean, hasn't it? Or am I losing the thread? That's just what I mean about the nick. If you're lucky enough to have snaffled a good bit of thread someone's bound to whip it. And don't talk to me about honour amongst thieves. It's about as plentiful as charity in a snout baron's bosom. Take the case of Norris and old Blanco's legacy. But, I hear you sputter, you didn't expect a nurk like Norris to display even the humanity of a swamp adder, did you? Maybe not, but I had expected better things from Lennie. After all, the lad had by then been exposed for some time to the manganin – the magmanin – to the integrity of my own character.

Well, I'd managed to con myself a temporary berth in the prison hospital – no, hang about! On that occasion it was all fair and square. Yes, now I remember discussing it with MacKay on the first morning I was there.

'You're a lucky man, Fletcher,' he purred.

'I don't see any grapes, Mr MacKay,' I returned

breezily, secure in my status as a medically-authenticated patient. 'And is it official visiting hours?'

'The medical officer told me – but I had to confirm it with my own eyes.'

'Oh, the foot's broken all right, as they verified at Carlisle General. The evidence is irrefootable.'

'I can't pretend I don't find your indisposition a trifle frustrating, Fletcher.'

'Oh, you're wrong, Mr MacKay. It's very gratifying. Better grub in here – better beds.'

'Since you lost your soft number in the library I was all ready to make your life a misery.'

'I gathered that when you sent me up that twenty-foot ladder to clean pigeon droppings.'

'Wouldn't surprise me if you deliberately fell off.'

'No, it was poetic justice, Mr MacKay. You was out to victimise me, and all you've done is to give me a passport to comfort and seclusion. Except that I have to put up with that scroat Norris for the next few days.'

And I gave the rat-faced gink on the other side of the aisle a disdainful glance. He began to whimper but I silenced him with : 'Shut your face, Norris, or I'll hit you with me frying pan.'

He started in again, causing MacKay to roar : 'Quiet, both of you !'

This unseemly bellow had the effect of causing poor old Blanco, the only other patient in the infirmary, to stir and glance about. Blanco was a thin villain with white hair and a white face which, now that I think about it, is probably why we called him Blanco. He didn't look in the best of health. In fact, beside him a plucked chicken would have resembled an Olympic gold-medallist.

'See what you've done?' I reproached Norris. 'You've woken Blanco up.'

Norris appealed to Mr MacKay. 'Fletcher started it. He's been at me all afternoon, Mr MacKay.'

'He has my sympathy, Norris. You're not the pleasantest of men. In fact, you're a horrible creature.'

'That's not fair,' Norris whined. 'I done my bird. I'm being released in two days.'

'And skiving to the last,' commented MacKay grimly.

'Not skiving. I've had surgery – ingrown toenail.'

'Couldn't have waited till you got out, could you?' I put in. 'Had to burden our overworked prison medical service.'

But MacKay, treacherously, and thus in the finest tradition of the prison service, turned on me with : 'Which is exactly what you're doing, Fletcher.'

'Yeah, well, we know who's fault that is, don't we?'

MacKay attempted a silky smile but, as usual, got no closer to it than a twisted leer. 'Four weeks,' he promised. 'That's your lot and then I'll have you up on your foot, Fletcher.'

'Might be longer than that. It's a very bad fracture.'

'Giving you hell, is it, Fletcher? Go on, admit it.'

'No, not – yi !'

This undignified exclamation had been wrung from me by Mr MacKay sadistically giving a tug on the weight which supported my plastered extremity. And before I even had time to threaten him with a full-scale parliamentary inquiry, the Beast of Slade Prison, chuckling softly, strode out of the ward.

No sooner had he left than Norris uttered a groan and proclaimed : 'I'm in pain.'

'Good.'

'I've had surgery.'

'Should be reserved for human beings.'

'I haven't slept for days with the pain. Shadow of my former self I am.'

'Well, your former self wasn't much, Norris.'

'Oh, naff off, Fletcher.'

'Soon as my broken foot's better I'm going to use it to stand on your ingrowing toenail.'

Norris rose above his agony and said nastily: 'Have to hurry, won't you? I'm out of here Thursday.'

At this point a steaming trolley, propelled by my erstwhile cellmate, Lennie, trundled into our vale of tears.

'Meals on wheels!' chirped the white-capped navigator.

'Ah, now cast an eye on this, Blanco,' I advised my neighbour. 'What's on the menu, then, Lennie? Apart from yesterday's gravy stains.'

'Braised steak and carrots, mashed potatoes, bananas and custard.'

'Smashing – and what's for afters?'

'Tomato soup.'

And he began ladling it into three bowls.

'There's a feast for you, Blanco,' I enthused.

But the worn specimen in the next bed failed to match my lusty gusto. In fact, he contented himself with murmuring thinly: 'No appetite.'

'You've got to eat, Blanco,' I urged. 'Keep your strength up. If you don't eat you'll be ill – oh, that's right, you are ill, aren't you?'

A humanoid hiss from across the aisle announced: 'If he won't have it, I will.'

'Not bleeding likely. You leave it by Blanco's bedside, Lennie. Anything he don't fancy now he can have later. And I'll make sure it's not wasted.'

Lennie, under Norris's covetous eyes, began to do as I suggested. He glanced at me and asked: 'How are you then, Fletch?'

'Surviving. How's yourself?'

'Not as comfy as you in those crisp, clean sheets.'

'I'd rather see more of these limp, boiled carrots.'

Norris, who'd been examining his platter with the expression of a thief who has accidentally nicked a Toby jug while trying for a gold cup, squealed : 'I ain't got my full share.'

'Shut up, Norris,' Lennie advised him. 'Here you are, Blanco. I'll leave this here on your locker for you.' Lennie contemplated the old thief critically and then remarked : 'Don't look too chipper, does he?'

I reassured him. 'He's all right. Just a bit depressed, that's all.'

'Looks at death's door to me.'

'Gawd, you youngsters! Don't you know better than to make remarks like that to people? Specially when they're about to snuff it.'

A sound like a very decrepit rattlesnake trying to scare someone attracted our attention and we saw that Blanco was laughing heartily. He said : 'That's a – a good one, Fletch.'

Relieved that he had taken my little slip for a deliberate jocularity, I exclaimed, 'Well, you've got to laugh, ain't you?'

'Anyway, tell me how it's been going, Fletch?' Lennie asked, glancing at the door to make sure it was free of screws. Finding it was, he settled down on the side of the bed for a bit of a natter.

'I had a nice day out, Lennie,' I informed him. 'Went down to Carlisle General and got plastered – unhappily only in the leg. There was some lovely nurses there – kept popping their heads round the door and giggling. The glamour of the convict, see? Mister Menace – handcuffed to a wheelchair.'

'Like Ironside – only bent.'

'Well, yeah – my air of villainy titillated them. Course, some of them had bigger titillations than others.' I beckoned him closer. 'I was in this cubicle, right? With this ravishing West Indian sister and she said – '

'Come on, lad, you've been fiddling around long enough.'

'That's right,' I said, glancing about in amazement at this continuation of my little saga, only to discover that a screw had wriggled in unobserved and was addressing Lennie.

Lennie sighed and manned his trolley. As he began to wheel it away, he said, 'Tell me the rest tomorrow, Fletch.'

'It'll keep.'

And Lennie, with the screw in his wake. disappeared down the corridor. I lay back for a while, inwardly debating whether to have a glance at the 'Pick of Lust Girls' which Lennie had smuggled me under my dinner plate, or take a nap. If it had been a straight contest 'Lust Girls' would undoubtedly have won but there was the factor of Norris's beady eyes and possible ribald comments to be considered. These would, I felt, have robbed the damsels of some of their appeal. So, to pass the time, I had another go at Norris.

'I should think you'll be glad to get out of here on Thursday, Norris? You'll have a better opportunity outside of being even more revolting to a larger number of people.'

Before Norris could think up a snappy answer to this one, Blanco wheezed : 'I'll certainly be glad to see the back of him. You know I never had much, Fletch? Possessions like. But in the last three days, before you came in here, he's had 'em all.'

'How d'you mean?' I asked, shocked.

'He's had me wireless. And me silver snuff holder. Real silver, Fletch. Antique. I kept me snout in it. He had all the snout an' all.'

I fixed Norris with a steely gaze and asked: 'Is this true?'

'Fair and square,' he whined.

Blanco continued the heart-rending list. 'And me musical box which plays Waltzing Matilda when you open the lid.'

'Well now,' I said calmly, 'I can't do much enforcing myself with this leg but there are others who can. You know what Norris is going to do, Blanco? He's going to give them all back, aren't you, Norris?'

'Naff off, Fletch. Fair and square. Cards, wasn't it?'

This was sad news because in the nick a gambling debt is generally considered to be as sacred as it is in the Reform Club or the Unreformed Club or wherever it is that guards officers while away their time dissipating the family fortune.

'Oh dear, oh dear, Blanco,' I queried, 'you didn't play cards with him?'

But Blanco admitted: 'Brag. Nine card brag.'

And Norris repeated smugly: 'Fair and square.'

Well now – a gambling debt's one thing but cheating a poor, sick old thief is another. I fixed the toad with an even steelier look and said: 'You'll give those back, Norris.'

But he refused to be cowed and snarled back: 'Will I hell!'

I turned to Blanco. 'Don't you worry, me old son. I'll get them back for you.'

Blanco sighed. 'It doesn't matter, Fletch. What do I need with a Waltzing Matilda music box where I'm going?'

Pretending not to catch his drift, I said sternly: 'You ain't going nowhere, mate. You've got another two years to do.'

'I'll be out of here sooner than that.'

'You're too old for escaping, Blanco. You've been watching too much Colditz, that's what's wrong with you.'

But Blanco refused to play along and just came back mournfully. 'I'm going out of here in a wooden over-coat.'

'Ah, come on, Blanco! What kind of talk's that?'

'No, me time's about up, Fletch. I'm not going to last the distance. Tired heart, the doctor says. Tired everything more like. I've come in here to die.'

'No you didn't. You come in here yesterdie. Get it?'

'Oh, Fletch, they were cracking that when I was at school. But you don't have to gee me up. I'm not afraid. It's about time I went to that great cell block in the sky.'

'Rubbish. Bloke like you ain't ready for celestial porridge yet awhile. You're not old. I admit you *look* old but that's prison, ain't it? Puts years on a man's appearance. What are you, Blanco, about forty-nine?'

'Sixty-three.'

'Yeah, well – you're not past it at sixty-three. Most of the government's older than that.'

'And look at the state the country's in. Mind you, it weren't much better when I were a lad. Depression. Hard times. No work. Took to stealing. What a waste. Spent nigh half me life in one nick or another. Lost all me family. That's why I'm resigned to passing on. Truth is, I'm relieved.'

'Come off it, there's years of wear left in you yet. Charlie Chaplin became a father nigh on eighty. Winston Churchill was at least your age when he had his finest hour. And so was my Uncle Wilfred.'

'What'd he do?'

'He was only seventy when he married this gorgeous young dental assistant. Admittedly it killed him. But you should have seen the smirk on his face when they laid him out.'

'Died with his boots off, eh?'

'Right. And his teeth out. They couldn't get the coffin lid down for three days. State of mind, age. You're as young as you feel. I mean, take this old boy that goes to see his doctor. The doctor asks "What's wrong then?" And the old boy says: "Well, it's the wife and I – we ain't getting any pleasure out of sex any more." Well, the doc's naturally a bit taken aback. He asks: "How old are you?" "Eighty-one." "And the wife?" "Seventy-nine." So the doctor thinks a minute and then wants to know: "When did you first have this trouble?" And the old boy says: "Last night . . . and it happened again this morning." '

Well, of course, I remember my grandfather raising a snigger with that one when I was listening over the banisters and probably Blanco had heard it before too but it had the desired effect. He laughed, an eerie but re-assuring sound, and then closed his eyes. I glanced across at Norris. The odious nurk, like a satiated python, had curled up on his side and was also asleep. Very softly I pulled the magazine from under my pillow.

It was an uneventful day. About tea-time they came and carted Norris off to the treatment room to disinfect his toes or something and about the same time Lennie wheeled in the nosh. So Blanco, Lennie and I were able to have a pleasant chat without Norris polluting it. After Lennie had gone, what with all the excitement and high living, I very soon drifted off to sleep.

I was woken by Blanco's whisper: 'Fletch! Fletch!'

'What's the matter?'

'Sorry to wake you but I wanted to tell you something – it's important like – while Norris is asleep. He *is* asleep, isn't he, Fletch?'

'Probably – unless he snores when he's awake.'

'I'll keep my voice low. You see, Fletch, I've got something of value.'

'How do you mean?'

'Well, you see, I've got no family – I told you that. And the few things I've got – well, Norris has got them now. But I still got one thing of value. And I'd like to bequeath it.'

'You're getting morbid again.'

'I'm not. I'm being practical. 'Cos if owt happened to me, no one would know about my legacy.'

'If you want to make a will, it's no good talking to me, Blanco. You want a solicitor. We got one on our landing. He'll see you right. Straight as a die, he is.'

'What's his name?'

'Corkscrew Carter. Nice bloke.'

'Trouble is, Fletch, my legacy's not the sort I can legalise.'

'Why not?'

'It's ill-gotten gains. Buried somewhere in Leeds.'

'Oh, ill-gotten gains, is it?'

'Shall I tell you about it?'

'Tomorrow, Blanco.'

'Well, it's like this. There were three of us. And we done this wages van on the way to a fridge factory near Otley. Don't you remember reading about it?'

'Can't honestly say I do, Blanco.'

'It were in t'*Yorkshire Post*.'

'Yeah, but if it didn't make the *Muswell Hill Examiner* or *Titbits* it would have escaped me.'

'Anyway, it were an untidy job. Lot of things went wrong.'

'Blanco, fascinating as it is to stroll down felony lane with you, will this take long? Only my foot's gone to sleep and I'd like to catch it up.'

'But, Fletch, I'm the one who's got the map. I'm the one who knows where it's buried.'

'Oh Gawd, it's bleeding Treasure Island now, is it?'

'Eight thousand quid.'

'How much?'

'Eight thousand quid.'

This was no trifling sum and I allowed my voice to register a sense of awe as I asked : 'Eight big ones?'

'Maybe nine. Used notes. We never had time to count them properly. According to *Yorkshire Post* it was fifteen but that were the thieving company, trying to diddle Lloyds.'

'I must admit, Blanco, I never realised the magnitude of your legacy.'

'The map's yours, Fletch.'

At this moving declaration, I permitted choked gratitude to sound in my reply : 'I – I dunno what to say, Blanco. Words – well, they fail me. Straight up. But I – I shall use the money wisely, Blanco. Rest assured. But let me ask you one question. If you don't snuff it – which we all hope and pray for – that you won't that is, naturally – then on your release you'll presumably want your map back?'

'Oh – well, if I did last the distance, I suppose so, yes.'

'And you'd trust me to give it to you?'

'Of course I would, Fletch.'

'D'you know, Blanco, in all my life I don't think anyone's ever shown me trust like that. Probation officers, Borstal principals, judges. And yet here you are – a man who ain't known me long, or in great intimacy, entrusting me with everything he's got in the world.'

'I am that, Fletch.'

'Blanco,' I said solemnly, 'you must be bleeding barmy.'

I was again rewarded by Blanco's appreciative laugh which sounded this time like a handful of dried peas scattered on a pavement. And ten minutes later the ward was silent again, except for the loud, regular snores of the fink, Norris.

The next thing I became aware of was an unpleasant feeling as of rough hands dancing over my body. Could it be a Lust Girl? I contemplated the possibilities for a moment, wishing she'd remembered to use her hand lotion regularly, and then in a flash I had it! Norris! The nurk hadn't been asleep at all! He'd heard everything that had passed between me and Blanco and now he was trying to lay his thieving hands on the map Blanco had slipped me at the conclusion of our conversation. I sat up with a cry of: 'Help!'

I was just in time to see Norris's scaly form slip back across the ill-lit ward and dive into his pit. I felt anxiously about my person but the precious document was still there. Take more than a Norris to outwit a Fletcher.

At this point, the lights in the ward came on and, framed in the doorway like a painting of The Pride of the Herd, stood Mr Barrowclough.

'What's going on? Who shouted? What's the matter?'

His moos of alarm were augmented by faint twitters from Blanco, who had been wrested from his needed slumbers, and hoarse exclamations from the hypocrite, Norris, who was pretending that he too had been deep in health-giving kip.

'Oh, Mr Barrowclough,' I exclaimed fervently, 'thank God you're here!'

'Will you tell me what's going on, Fletcher?'

'Wish I knew, sir. Someone was poking about in my bed.'

'What? Who?'

'I don't like to say, sir. But Blanco, as you know, can barely raise a finger.'

'Then who was it? I mean, there's only three of you in here.'

'It's a real brain-teaser, isn't it?'

'If it wasn't Blanco – Norris, was it you?'

'Me? I've been sound asleep, ain't I?'

'No you ain't, you lying nurk!' I said indignantly. 'You've been over here rummaging in my pyjamas.'

'Have you got any valuables there, Fletcher?' asked Mr Barrowclough.

'Only what I always keep in my pyjamas.'

'He could have been after your lemon barley water, Fletch,' wheezed Blanco.

'What? In my pyjamas? Funny-shaped bottle.'

'I ain't stirred from my bed,' Norris whined untruthfully. 'I mean, what's he got that I'd want to nick? One orange and a pair of smelly slippers.'

'You've just put yourself right in it there. I got those slippers off Mr Barrowclough. Present they were. My first week in here.'

'Yes, well we don't need to go into that now,' Barrowclough said hastily. 'They were second-hand and I'd happened to be finished with them.'

'Nevertheless, I appreciated and grew to love those, Mr Barrowclough. And I wouldn't like to see them falling into the wrong hands – or feet.'

'I don't want your tatty old slippers,' whined Norris.

'They are *not* tatty,' Barrowclough snapped. 'They cost thirty-two and six in the old currency.'

'Well anyway, I've got me own – fur-lined an' all.'

'Norris,' Mr Barrowclough addressed the reptile sternly, 'you go out of this prison in two days. You must be ruddy mad to risk losing remission by going back to your nasty little habits.'

'Why'd you take his word for it?'

'Fletcher's not the sort of person to scream out in the middle of the night over nothing. Though for the life of me I can't think what there is to steal. You're not hiding anything are you, Fletcher?'

I gave Blanco a quick glance. 'Hiding anything?' I asked innocently.

'You're not hiding a bottle of surgical alcohol?'

'Oh no, Mr Barrowclough. Certainly not.'

But, being a screw, he couldn't take my word for it. No, he has to poke and rummage about my bed and even tap my plaster leg as if it might conceal a compartment full of watches.

However, being essentially a modest man, he never found the map. And being essentially a decent man, when he *did* find my girlie mag. he confined himself to blushing into a startling resemblance to a Jersey and hastily replacing it under my pillow. Five minutes later silence once more descended on the ward.

'MacKay,' announced Lennie, giving us the early news next morning as he ladled out our porridge, 'is in an ever so rotten mood. Villa drew at home. Weather forecast: winds moderate to light.'

'What a shame,' I said. 'Spoil my morning stroll in the park.'

'The hot water's working again,' he continued, 'if you're quick. And it's cauliflower cheese for supper.'

'Dear, oh dear. That's the trouble with being cooped up in hospital. You miss it all, don't you.'

'That's just the highlights. I left out the boring bits.'

'Well, when you next look in,' I requested, 'could you bring me a newspaper – *The Sun*?'

'All right, Fletch.'

I lowered my voice. 'And Lennie, I've finished that book. Could you take it back to our cell? Keep it safe. I don't want any of those thieving nurks on the landing getting hold of it. Understood?'

And I emphasised the instruction with a meaningful wink. However, glancing across the aisle, I saw that Norris was gazing bug-eyed at us and I had a strong suspicion that he might have caught the gist of what was going on.

The eternal screw called from the door: 'Come on, Godber, get a move on.'

'I'll bring the paper, Fletch, and I'll take care of the book.'

He gave me a conspiratorial wink which, quite possibly, Norris intercepted and then pushed his trolley out of the ward.

'Drive carefully,' I called after him.

I then tackled the porridge, an operation which, because of the size and hardness of the lumps, demanded considerable concentration. For this reason, I did not notice Norris rise like a bad smell and waft across the aisle. The first thing I did notice was his nasal whine practically in me ear.

'Listen, I'd like a word with you, Fletch. And Blanco. Point is, I was awake last night. I heard –

Of course, by this time I'd gathered that much. But I frowned in outraged innocence and asked: 'Heard? Heard what?'

'About the map.'

I turned to my neighbour. 'Do you know what he's on about, Blanco? What map's this then?'

'Oh, come on, Fletch,' urged Norris. 'Don't pee around. Listen, you could cut me in.'

'I could cut you in pieces. What are you rabbiting about, Norris?'

'You know damn well, Fletch. The map, the gelt – the buried gelt, in Leeds.'

Probably it would have been difficult to brazen it out in any case but Blanco didn't help by croaking: 'Why should we cut you in?'

'Aha!' cried Norris in reptilian triumph. 'There *is* a map, isn't there?'

I sighed.

'All right, then, there is a map. But like Blanco says why should we cut you in?'

'I'm going out day after tomorrow.'

'So?'

'Well, Blanco ain't out for two years and you're not out for three. Anything could happen. Someone could find it or – or they could build a multi-storey car park on top of it. Well – I could keep it safe, couldn't I?'

'What a thoughtful suggestion,' I enthused. 'Perhaps you'd be so good as to look after my modest savings and all?'

'You don't trust me?'

'Right in one.'

'You're wrong, Fletch. I could – maybe – put it in a building society. Invest it, like.'

'I know what you'd invest it in, Norris. You'd invest it in a brighter future for your despicable self. And by the time *we* come out there wouldn't be a penny left. You'd have squandered it in a vulgar orgy of wining and dining Northern tarts in Northern night clubs.'

Blanco sighed wistfully: 'Yeah. That's what I'd planned to do.'

'Ah, but you're entitled, Blanco,' I assured him. 'It's your money.'

'It won't be if he snuffs it, will it? *You're* going to cop it, Fletch.'

'I happen to be his chosen benefactor. Or the other way round. And you happen to be someone he can't bear the sight of. You're only the bloke what cheated him out of his most treasured possessions. So naff off, Norris, before I drown you in me porridge!'

But for some reason the snake didn't seem too put out. He grinned and said: 'All right, then – both of you – don't say I didn't give you a chance.'

'What are you on about, Norris?'

'You think you're pretty smart, Fletch. It so happens I know exactly where that map is at this moment.'

'Rubbish,' I exclaimed, but there was a note of uneasiness in my voice. 'And even if you did, what could you do about it?'

'I'm only being released from the ward this morning, ain't I?'

And he slithered back across the aisle to his foul lair while Blanco and I exchanged a sober glance.

And now we come to the part of the story that I referred to at the beginning, when I exclaimed cynically: don't talk to me about honour amongst thieves! Yes, it was Lennie, my cell-mate, who by that time I'd come to think of almost as a son and who – well, you'll find out.

Anyhow, it was later that day that Lennie received a visit in his private quarters. The visitor was Nurk Norris and his aim was to separate Lennie from that which I'd entrusted to him. How do I know what transpired? You'll find that out too.

Norris came straight to the point: 'Ere, Godber, when Fletch gave you that book this morning, did he leave a bit of paper in it? By mistake, like?'

'Why?'

'He wants it. He asked me to pick it up. I'll take it straight over to him.'

'Bit of paper, like?'

'Yeah, quite meaningless.'

'Why's he want it then?'

'I dunno. Just doing him a favour. It's just a meaning-less bit of paper.'

'Meaningless is it?'

Failing to secure the desired cooperation, Nimble Norris changed his tactics.

'Look, Godber – Lennie, old friend – how'd you like to make some money – real money? On the outside?'

'Not much use to me as I'm on the inside, is it?'

'All right, but I've got gear on the inside. And there's my back wages.'

'Are you offering me these treasures just for a mean-ingless bit of paper?'

'Ask no questions, son.'

Lennie shook his head. 'I can't do it behind my mate's back. Whatever this meaningless bit of paper is, it belongs to Fletch.'

'Never mind about him. He only thinks about number one. Look, Godber, I'm offering you all my back pay. And my snout.'

'Fletcher's my cellie. My mate.'

'I'll throw in a silver snuff-holder. Antique. Worth a lot of money.'

'He's been good to me, Fletch has.'

'And a music box. It plays Waltzing Matilda.'

But Lennie stuck to his guns. 'Contrary to popular belief in here, we're not all without scruples. Fletcher's shown me friendship. You can't buy that. Without him, I'd have gone under in here.'

But Norris had no finer feelings that could be appealed to. He simply piled on the bait: 'And a radio as well. Japanese.'

'Done,' said Lennie crisply.

So that's how Norris gained possession of Blanco's treasure map.

That evening Lennie wheeled in the trolley.

'Oh, here he comes,' I said, mustering up all my indignation. 'The Judas Iscariot of Slade Prison.'

'Don't know how he dares show his face,' wheezed Blanco.

'You betrayed us, didn't you, Godber?' I hissed. 'You betrayed us to that evil Norris.'

'Yes, I did,' admitted Lennie unashamedly.

'Thank God for that,' I said. 'How did it go?'

'Like a charm,' he said, picking the cover off one of the dishes. 'Now what have we here? One radio. One snuff-holder. And one Australian music box.' And he put them on Blanco's bedside table. 'Lovely idea, Blanco. He really thought you had some money buried.'

'Do you think he'll go straight there?' Blanco asked.

'Oh Gawd yes,' I said. 'The best is yet to come.'

And it was.

The next day, Norris was released and the first thing he did was take a train to Leeds. The second thing he did was buy a spade and the third thing he did was lay low until after dark when, exercising his feeble wits to their limit, he followed the treasure map to the spot marked 'x'. Then he glanced about the great open field to make sure he was alone and then he got down to work.

That evening we listened to the news on Blanco's radio. At last the announcer's voice told us what we were waiting for : 'A man was detained at Leeds Police Headquarters earlier this evening, charged with trespass and causing wilful damage to the property of Leeds United Football Club. He is being remanded.'

So that's the story of our little conspiracy to get Blanco back his possessions. Honour amongst thieves? No way! But amongst friends it can be found – even in the nick!

The Harder They Fall

Who do you think runs the nick? The Governor? Not on your Nellie! It's the snout barons. The thing is the law has to obey the law. The only punishments the Governor can dish out are the ones permitted by the law. He can lock you up in solitary. He can stop your privileges and your pay. He can even get your remissions cancelled so you stay inside longer. None of these are laughing matters but they are trivial as compared to the fearsome power of the barons. I mean, no Governor can spirit away all your precious possessions or duff you up in the bog or tie knots in your extremities. Of course, the barons don't perform these perfidious acts themselves. They get their henchmen to do it. But everyone inside knows who wields the big stick. The proof is, if the Governor or the screws tell you to do something you immediately begin to calculate ways of skiving out of it. If the barons request a favour – you jump!

Now contrary to what is believed on the outside the barons are not just concerned with tobacco. They run all the rackets and if there ain't any rackets they start them. Mainly for profit but sometimes just for laughs. The best thing to do about the snout barons is to steer clear of them but sometimes they insist on getting in the way. That's what happened to me with Harry Grout when Lennie took up boxing.

It started one balmy – or do I mean barmy? – evening when Lennie breezed into the old flowery in his track suit looking like Mohammed Ali might have done if he'd lost two stone and been bleached.

'Oh Gawd,' I exclaimed, 'the athlete.'

'Nothing wrong with that,' Lennie insisted. 'Keep in shape. Better than draughts. You could do with losing a few pounds, Fletch.'

'Thanks to draughts, I just won a few pounds, didn't I?'

'You cheat at draughts.'

'You watch your tongue, Godber, or I'll knock your block off.'

'You'll do what?' And the irritating young nurk started dancing about me, flicking out with his fist. 'Made the boxing team, didn't I. Didn't I? Didn't I? Come on, Fletch, where's your guard?'

'He's outside. Want me to call him in? Look, naff off, Godber. And sit down.' To my relief, he obeyed. I continued : 'Boxing now, is it? You've taken every flipping course in this prison. Arts and crafts, O levels, pottery, Spanish. What are you going to do with Spanish, may I ask, become a bullfighter?'

'Si, si, señor.'

'That's the lot, is it? Six weeks of concentrated study and what have we got : si, si, señor !'

'No tiene vacca, pero tiene uno burro.'

'Flamenco to you, too. All right, what does it mean?'

'I haven't got a cow but I have got a donkey.'

'Oh, that'll come in very handy when you're next on the Costa Brava. Extremely useful, that is. I can just picture you – the pearly beach, the moonlight, the faint twanging of guitars through the palm trees. You slip your arm around the trembling waist of an olive-skinned señorita and whisper : I ain't got a cow but I can offer you a donkey.'

'Vaya con Dios.'

'People like you from Birmingham would be better off learning English. Phew ! I hope this boxing lark don't last long. Because you do bring a terrible smell of sweat and linament into my quarters.'

'Better than the smell of your after-shave. Seriously though, Fletch, I'm dead chuffed about making the boxing squad. Big match next week.'

'Boxing for the wing?'

'That's right.'

'Against another wing?'

'Yeah.'

'Not exactly Madison Square Garden, is it?'

'It's a start. I'm gonna work at this, Fletch. I've got all the credentials of a fighter – deprived childhood, terrible background. Mr Bayliss, the PTI, says I've got natural ability.'

'If you show as much flair in the ring as you show for Spanish, my son, you ain't half due for a clobbering.'

'Que sera, sera.'

'Kiss her what?'

At just that moment, Jackdaw slithered into our chambers. This was somewhat ironic since it was only a few weeks since *he'd* been on the receiving end of a clobbering by Lennie. Ever since, I'd been on my guard for Jackdaw wanting to get his own back. I rose to keep the peace but it seemed Jackdaw was not after vengeance.

'Hey, Fletch,' he addressed me, 'Grouty wants you.'

'Pardon?' I asked blankly.

I'd heard him all right, but what I'd heard was the name of the most feared and powerful snout baron in the nick. It's always as well, when a name like that bubbles up in the conversation, to collect one's thoughts and that's why I'd said 'Pardon?' to give me a moment to collect my thoughts.

'Grouty,' Jackdaw repeated. 'Wants a word.'

'I see,' I nodded assent. 'Are you running for Harry Grout now, Jackdaw?'

'One of his firm.'

My motto is never to show that I'm cowed unless it so happens that I am cowed. So I commented cheerfully : 'He must be scraping the barrel.'

'Watch it,' Jackdaw warned. But I certainly wasn't cowed by Jackdaw.

'Oh, hark at him. Now that he's under the protective wing of genial Harry Grout he's full of bravado.'

Grooves appeared on Jackdaw's brow. I knew he was trying to think up a snappy answer, but since Jackdaw's the kind of bloke who considers counting up to ten an intellectual achievement nothing surfaced and he finally contented himself with : 'Well, are you coming then?'

'I might stroll across in due course, yeah.'

'I'm supposed to take you with me.'

'Brought a shopping bag? Tell you what, Jackdaw, you wriggle back and tell Harry I want to change me socks and cut me toenails. I know the way.'

'On your head be it.'

He departed and Lennie, looking concerned, asked : 'Was that wise?'

'Yeah – he's all right, Harry. I know he has a long past of mayhem and violence but this is his last year of a long, long stretch. He ain't going to come the heavy and cock up his release at this stage, is he?'

'I suppose not.'

'He's happy being the tobacco baron and running all the rackets.'

'Wonder what he wants to see *you* for?'

'Probably wants a slice of my draughts action. Now, where's me nail clippers?'

Lennie wrinkled his nose. 'Oh Fletch, you're not going to cut your toenails in here?'

'Well, I can't let them grow indefinitely, and I ain't tall enough to get me foot out the window.'

'All right, but you always cut them on my bunk.'

'Well, I'm very sorry if it offends your sense of Brummagen propriety. May I ask when you're going to take a shower and wash that linament off? Smells like a Turkish wrestler's jock-strap in here.'

It was amazing! Lennie and I felt it at exactly the same moment, a kind of chill, evil sensation that made us both shiver. It was just like what happens in ancient rectories when one of the long-dead parsons, driven by the undiscovered sins he committed on earth, revisits his old home. We turned in unison and sure enough there in the doorway stood a ghastly apparition. Mr MacKay. It spoke :

'I'm told congratulations are in order, Godber.'

'Oh, the boxing? Thank you, Mr MacKay, yes.'

MacKay puffed out his chest like a mating pigeon and chortled : 'Fine outlet, boxing. The noble art. Teaches you discipline, dedication and team spirit. Oh yes, I was no slouch myself at your age. I once boxed for Midlothian Boys.'

'Against who?' I asked drily. 'Lanarkshire Girls?'

MacKay, with unaccustomed good humour, ignored the sally. 'In the army,' he bragged, 'I boxed for the battalion.'

Lennie, I was sorry to see, seemed impressed by this unverifiable claim. 'Did you, Mr MacKay?' he asked eagerly.

'First battalion, Argyll and Sutherland Highlanders. Great regiment, great tradition. A regiment I was proud to serve.'

'A regiment which is now defunct,' I said brusquely.

MacKay turned slowly towards me, his lip curling. 'I expect *you* were in the Ordnance Corps, Fletcher. Some unit which kept well out of the line of fire. You probably served your time nicking stores in some cushy posting.' And he cackled like a depraved parrot.

'Well, you're wrong there,' I said indignantly. 'I did active service. Malaya. Kuala Lumpur. And I wasn't in no Ordnance Corps. I was in the RASC.'

'What's that stand for?' asked Lennie.

'Run Away Someone's Coming,' I said and laughed. But instead of joining in, MacKay turned back to Lennie.

'National Service would have done you good, Godber. The army's good to its boxers.'

'I don't reckon boxing's such a noble art at all,' I said.

'No?' asked MacKay, sceptically.

That was what I wanted. I launched into my tale: 'I had a friend once – haven't told you this before, have I? He was a light-heavy. Good strong boy. Won a few fights and got the idea he was the bee's knees. Fast cars, easy women. Classic story of too much too soon. And, of course, before long, he blew up – got into debt and ended up in one of those travelling booths. Four fights a night, seven nights a week. Well, of course the body can't take that kind of punishment. His brain went soft. His reflexes went haywire. He was plain punchy and in the end he became like a vegetable, an incoherent, mindless zombie.'

MacKay's face registered concern at this tragic story. He asked: 'What became of the poor fellow?'

'Oh,' I said reassuringly, 'he joined the prison service as a warder. He's recently been promoted.'

And before MacKay twigged that he'd been had, I slipped away to pay my compliments to Harry Grout.

At first glance you wouldn't take Harry for anything

harder than a suburban tobacconist. He was thick-set and greying with the pasty complexion of the long-server. But his cell was certainly far from commonplace. All cons put individual touches to their dells : different nudes pasted on the walls, a radio here, an embroidered cushion-cover there, but to your average free man, passing down the row, there wouldn't seem a lot of difference. Just uniform stone boxes. Not Harry's. At first sight it looked like the interior of a weekend cottage in the Cotswolds. He had a quilted counterpane on the bed. On the locker beside the bed stood an expensive radio and record-player, and also a large lamp made from one of those wine bottles with a straw-covered bottom. There were chintz curtains to shut out the offensive sight of the bars on the window, a rug on the floor and signed pictures of celebrities on the walls. Most startling of all was an ornate, standing bird-cage complete with green, hopping budgie.

When I entered, Harry was seated on a comfortable little armchair gazing intently at the opposite wall. From time to time he nodded and chuckled. I assumed this behaviour was connected with the fact that he was wearing headphones and that these were attached to his wireless set. I approached gently until he picked up my presence whereupon, without glancing at me, he waved his hand to indicate that I should attend his pleasure. I humbly obeyed and, before long, Harry gave a hefty nod of satisfaction, removed the earphones and confided : 'Archers. Never miss them.'

'They still at it, are they?'

'Oh yes. Doris is in a bit of a state. She's got Dutch Elm Disease.'

'Gawd. Are they going to have to cut her down?'

'Her trees,' clarified Harry coldly. 'Don't you follow the Archers?'

'I don't, Grouty. I like listening to the radio, mind. Gardener's Question Time and Desert Island Discs.'

'I like a good play meself. And a Book at Bedtime. Never miss that.'

'Yeah, I've always thought I'd like that. But of course, they don't allow us the wireless that late.'

Harry chuckled. 'Don't they? No one's ever told me.'

'Don't suppose anyone's ever dared. Nice place you got here, Grouty.'

'Do you like it?'

'All the creature comforts. Yeah, I like the lamp.'

'Memento, that is. Of Alassio. That's in Italy.'

It rang a bell. I remembered the headlines. 'Wasn't it Alassio that they extradited you from?'

Grouty nodded proudly. 'I came back handcuffed to Scotcher of the Yard on Alitalia. I paid the extra and moved us both up into first class. Bit of a perk for him. He'd never been south of Worthing before. I bought myself the Chianti, duty free, and got him a bottle of Sambuca.'

I couldn't resist remarking: 'In the light of your subsequent sentence, it might have been better if you'd given the judge the Sambuca.'

'I offered him five hundred quid. What more could I do?'

Jackdaw appeared in the doorway with two cups of cocoa on a tray. Grouty nodded genially.

'You can come in, Jackdaw. Cocoa, Fletch?'

'Don't mind if I do, Grouty.'

'Sugar?'

He certainly lived in style. I helped myself to four spoonfuls from the 2lb bag. 'Thank you, Grouty.'

Jackdaw, who was hovering like an old, bent – and I *do* mean *bent* – retainer, asked: 'Should I feed Seymour, Harry?'

'Yeah, go ahead.'

I glanced about for the invalid and then caught on. 'Oh, Seymour's the feathered friend, is he? Very nice.'

Grouty glanced at the winged chum and shrugged. 'He's company of an evening. When I was in Parkhurst I had a pigeon.'

'Oh yes? Like the Birdman of Alcatraz?'

But the comparison didn't seem to please Grouty. 'Not really, no.'

'No, nothing like, really. Pigeon must have taken a bit more room though, didn't he?'

'Just a bit, yeah. On the other hand, how else could I keep in touch with the bookmakers?'

Harry gave me a meaningful look. I laughed dutifully. 'What did you do with him when you had to leave?'

'I ate him.'

'Oh, very nice. I should watch your step, if I were you, Jackdaw.'

Jackdaw finished serving Seymour and asked obsequiously, 'Will that be all then, Harry?'

'Probably, but hang about. We're gonna be in conference. So do the minding.'

'Yes, Harry.'

Jackdaw withdrew to keep an eye out for prowling screws and suchlike. Grouty leaned back in his chair, touched the tips of his fingers together and remarked, by way of openers : 'Well then, Fletch . . .'

Maintaining the convention, I echoed him. 'Well then, Grouty . . .'

'They're gonna have this boxing match, aren't they?'

'So I hear. Inter-prison championships or something.'

'Well then – money to be made.'

Since it is not always obvious which way Grouty's thoughts are tending, I just looked questioning.

He amplified. 'Sport means competition, don't it? Which means there's a winner and a loser. And that's all right providing you're on the winner.'

Although it was still far from clear what Grouty was driving at something told me I wouldn't like it when he pulled up there. I tried a spot of deflection. 'Forgive me saying this, Grouty, but do you need the funds? I mean, if you want money all you have to do is ask people and they give it to you.'

He shook his head pityingly. 'Where's the fun in that? We're talking about sport, my son. The speculation, the excitement, the tension, the thrill of the outcome.'

'Oh, the thrill of the outcome, yes.'

'That's what I enjoy.'

'I understand, Grouty.'

'That's why I want you to fix the fight.'

I started violently. 'You what?'

'Well, that's putting it a bit strong. What I mean is I want you to feed me certain information so that I get all the thrill of speculation and excitement from knowing I'm on a sure thing.'

'Feed you information, Harry? There's seven fights. Wing against wing.'

'I know that, but as they all have to train in the same gymnasium, it just needs someone with an experienced eye to run over the form. Someone like yourself. As you know, in this nick I have a bit of a rival. Namely, that presumptuous upstart Billy Moffat.'

I smiled at the absurdity of this suggestion. 'That nurk, Moffat? No contest, Harry.'

'Nevertheless, he's running a book without my seal of approval. So I'd like to take him to the cleaners.'

I could feel dark forces closing in on me. I made a desperate attempt to wriggle free. 'I see your point, Harry, but you know me, I'm a loner. I see myself as the Randolph Scott of Slade Prison. I don't like being responsible to nobody, not even a man as distinguished as yourself. So I think really the best thing is for me to say straight off, very respectfully, that I have to decline your flattering invitation. Thanks for the cocoa, Harry.'

I got up and headed for the door. My spirits began to rise as I neared it without lightning striking me down. I was about there when Grouty's low, pained voice spoke from behind me.

'You disappoint me, Fletch.'

A huge shadow, which I recognised as 'Carnera' Stubbins from 'A' Block, materialised in the doorway ahead of me. I spun round with an affable smile and asked : 'When do I start, Grouty?'

For the next few days I haunted the gym. This wasn't an easy thing to do because I had no legitimate reason for being there. In the end, I got to be Lennie's unofficial trainer but before that I had to resort to some very uncomfortable expedients. These included offering myself as sparring partner and, being somewhat out of practice, getting beaten half to death. When I turned up again in Grouty's penthouse, I looked like a failed urban guerrilla.

'Fall over something, Fletch?' asked Grouty solicitously, between puffs of a cigar.

'Been sparring, ain't I?' I explained.

'You should have kept your guard up. I thought you used to be a boxer, Fletch?'

'I used to be a conker champion and all, but they was both a long time ago.'

'So what's the form then?'

'Well, there's not much to choose between any of the matchings, Grouty. Anybody's guess who'll win the flyweight since they're both equally stupid and cowardly.

Question of which one bursts into tears first. I think Big Mac's a certainty in the heavyweight.'

Grouty said impatiently : 'We all know that.'

'The other certainty, in my opinion, is young Godber. Being his second, I've been able to give him a bit extra like.'

'Yes, I heard from other quarters that he's well-favoured. Good strong boy.'

'Whereas his opponent – young Nesbit – just hasn't got it. No contest.'

Grouty nodded thoughtfully. 'Well, that's the one then.'

'You won't get very good odds on Godber,' I pointed out.

'No, but I will on Nesbit.'

I caught his drift and was appalled. 'Oh, now, Harry ...'

'Tell the lad to make it look good. And then go down in the second.'

'Oh Grouty, please ! Not the lad. It means a lot to him.'

'Means a lot to me, Fletch. Billy Moffat will be on your boy.'

'But why Lennie? Why not nobble Big Mac? Get even better odds on *his* opponent.'

Grouty said impatiently : 'Don't be daft. Where's the credibility in Big Mac going down? He put four screws in the hospital last year when someone knocked over his jigsaw puzzle. Can you see Hermiston beating him?'

'But Grouty, I'm not sure the lad will do it. He's young, he's idealistic. He's still got his scruples.'

But Grouty found the perfect argument : 'If he don't do what I ask, he may not have them much longer. So, Fletch, you'd better cut along and tell him, hadn't you?'

On the way back to the dell, I turned over different

possibilities in my mind. But none of them looked good and so I turned them back again. How was I going to tell Lennie? He was heart and soul set on winning his match. On the other hand, if I didn't tell him he was likely to end up with articulated bones. Me too. So I would have to tell him. Yeah, but how?

My soul-searching was not eased by the sight of Lennie doing press-ups on the cold, stone floor of our cosy home, trying to turn himself into a champion. I sat down, lit a snout, and contemplated him gloomily.

'Twenty-five,' he finally gasped, collapsing on to his stomach.

'That's very commendable,' I complimented him.

'And I did twenty pull-ups on the wail bars before I left the gym.'

'Twenty? Really? I can't help wondering, old son, if it's worth it?'

Lennie hoisted himself off the floor and started to tug the upper part of his track suit over his head. When he emerged again, he asked: 'How d'you mean?'

'All these press-ups and pull-ups. All these deep-breathing exercises. And this weight-lifting. It's a bit daft, isn't it? I mean, it's just punishment.'

Lennie, preparing to sluice himself down at the basin, turned and gave me a puzzled look. 'It's for the boxing.'

'I know, Lennie, I know. That's my worry, you see.'

'Why, Fletch?'

'My concern, my very genuine concern, is that you're neglecting your pottery classes. And all those other arts and crafts activities in which you indulged so diligently. I mean, look what's happened to your elementary plumbing? That's gone right down the drain! Boxing's a mug's game, Lennie.'

'But Fletch, this morning you were egging me on. You said I had the makings of a champ.'

'Yeah – a dead champ!'

'Eh?'

I stood up and started pacing about the bed-sit, talking as I went. 'I'm a cynical old so-and-so, which is something I don't have to tell you. I've seen it all. You, on the other hand, haven't seen anything. That's what gives you your naïve charm, I suppose. You ain't had all the idealism ground out of you – yet! But I have to ask you – well *tell* you – that someone has asked me – well *told* me – that is, they was wondering – well really they was insisting – if you could see your way clear – not that you have very much choice – Hell, I don't know how to say this.'

Lennie, who had been gaping at me and drying his face at the same time, which takes skill, said softly: 'What is it you're trying to say, Fletch?'

'Tomorrow night's not going to be your night, Lennie.'

'How?'

'Harry Grout wants you to take a dive in the second.'

He stood there, bare-chested, large eyes widening in his boyish face. He stared at me like a dog that's been kicked. I just couldn't take it.

'Don't look at me that way, son,' I pleaded. 'You're shocked, of course you are – and me – I'm ashamed!'

Lennie finally recovered the power of speech. He shook his head and said in a low, firm voice: 'I can't do that, Fletch.'

'I *knew* you'd say that, Lennie. And I respect you for it. But you have to see the position I'm in.'

'I appreciate that, Fletch. But I just can't do it.'

'Lennie, what does it mean, after all? Wing against wing – it's just kid stuff.'

'That's true, Fletch.'

'Then why can't you do it, kid? For me.'

'Because I've promised Billy Moffat I'll take a dive in the first.'

'I understand, kid, but – WHAT?' I stared at him in open-mouthed amazement. I know it was open-mouthed because after about five seconds a fly flew in and I had a choking fit. Then I gasped : 'You – you – you're gonna take a dive – '

But he interrupted urgently, indicating the door. 'Keep your voice down, Fletch!'

'You're taking a dive for Moffat?' I hissed at him.
'Right.'

I shook my head in sorrow and sat down on his bunk. 'I just don't pretend to understand the younger generation. I really don't. Would you mind telling me *why*?'

'They asked me first.'

'Oh, they asked you first,' I echoed sarcastically. 'So you're in the market for corruption, are you? Case of the highest bidder, is it?'

'Oh, come on, Fletch! I know the score. I may be innocent and naïve but I'm not bloody daft. I know the realities inside. I'd rather be clobbered *in* the ring than out of it. It's the easy way out. No skin off my nose.'

'It's me that's going to get skinned. And not just off the nose neither.' I felt totally disillusioned. 'You've disappointed me, you have. You could have been a contender, you could.'

'But *you* wanted me to – '

'Never mind about that. Things have changed between you and me. I'm bitterly disappointed. I've never been so let down since my son Raymond broke into his school one night and had a prior peep at the exam papers.'

'Did he?'

'Yes, he did, and he still didn't pass.'

And with that parting shot I rose and marched out of

the cell to acquaint the Capone of Slade Prison with the latest development.

When he'd heard, Grouty shook his head as I had done and remarked : 'Well, I don't know what to make of youngsters today. No moral fibre.'

'Men of straw,' I supplemented.

'Poses a problem though, don't it?'

'I don't see that, Grouty. Godber's still going to lose. We're all on Nesbit to win, so there's no conflict of interests is there?'

Grouty shook his head. 'There's no odds neither. All the big money in this nick's on Nesbit. We wouldn't even get evens.'

I again glimpsed the possibility of extricating myself from the whole distasteful affair. 'Well, why don't we just withdraw gracefully from this one, Harry? It's getting ever so complicated. Why don't you just go back to demanding money with menaces?'

But Grouty treated me to the pitying smile once more. 'That doesn't satisfy my sporting instincts. I told you before, Fletch, I like the excitement, the old adrenalin. Only one thing for it. If they've nobbled Godber, we've got to make sure that he wins.'

'How?'

'You nobble Nesbit.'

A very difficult two days ensued. I had to undertake delicate negotiations, involving the exchange of vast amounts of snout, with a number of disreputable criminals. And the worst of it was that I couldn't see myself emerging from it all with credit, or even with operational arms. But finally the dread day came. The cons filed into the gloomy gymnasium. Clustered in the front row were Moffat and his boys on one side and Grouty and his bandits on the other. The early matches passed without incident and then came the big fight: Lennie against Nesbit. So far I'd not thought it advisable to acquaint Lennie with the new arrangements, but now the time had come. As I took his robe and stuffed his gum-shield into his mouth, I whispered to him: 'The fix is on.'

'Well, I know that, don't I?' he asked, somewhat thickly because of the gum-shield. 'I'm going down in the first.'

'Yeah, well don't hang about, because so is Nesbit.'

Lennie gave me a puzzled glance. 'Is he?'

'Which is serious for all three of us. If you win, you're in trouble with Moffat. If Nesbit wins he's in trouble with Grouty. And whoever wins I'm in trouble with both of them. One of us is going to suffer, and it's going to be me twice! It ain't the outcome of the fight I'm worried about, it's the outcome of the outcome. In fact, the only element of speculation in this fight is which of you two hits the flaming canvas first.'

'You should never have got involved, Fletch.'

It was my turn to gape and I was still at it when the bell rang and Lennie and Nesbit danced out to do battle.

It was an intriguing match. For some time the two boys circled each other watchfully, hoping for a hostile move. But both made certain that their feints didn't connect. In the end, it was Nesbit, probably fearful that the round was about to end, who struck first. He suddenly darted forwards on to one of Lennie's feeble flicks, grunted and began to fall. But he'd reckoned without Lennie's superb reflexes. Like a flash, my boy hurled his chin on to Nesbit's carelessly outflung fist and the two killers hit the canvas at the same instant.

About an hour later, I entered the dell after concluding a transaction with one of the screws. Lennie was stretched out on his bunk, looking the picture of health.

He sat up and asked with sombre interest: 'What did Grouty say?'

I tucked something away in my soap bag and replied negligently: 'Couldn't say anything, could he?'

'He didn't suspect?'

'Wouldn't have mattered. He was a bit narked but the bets were void. He didn't gain anything but on the other hand he didn't lose anything. Most important, there wasn't any loss of prestige to Billy Moffat.'

Lennie smiled appreciatively. 'A great solution. Nobody won, and none of us lost.'

'Yeah, well –' I murmured modestly, 'that's not exactly true.'

'How do you mean?'

'There *was* somebody who come out of this ahead.'

Lennie cocked his head on one side. 'You?'

'Confidentially, I made quite a bit of money off of that bent warder who works in the bakery.'

'How?'

'No one else in this nick bet on a draw, did they? Have some chocolate.'

A Christmas Tunnel

Peace in the nick, goodwill towards cons. Yeah, Christmas is a funny time of year inside. On the one hand, there's Christmas dinner which is usually at least edible, a slight relaxation of rules and discipline, a chance, for those who like that kind of thing, to sing carols. On the other hand, there's nostalgia. Even the hardest lag sometimes feels it and can be found with a brooding look on his face recalling happy times outside, even if it was only breaking into closed banks. For family men, like myself, it's more difficult. You have to shut out of your mind the presents and decorations, the excited voices of the kids on Christmas morning, the flaming pudding and turkey.

Still, I try to keep up the grand old traditions. Lennie breezed into the dell and caught me pasting up a Christmas card for my brother George. It was a study of a schoolmistress from Preston that I'd cut out of the paper. When the photographer had visited her, she'd been about to take a bath. Lennie contemplated it.

'That supposed to be a Christmas card?'

'Yeah, for my brother George.'

'Not very seasonal, is it?'

'Well, it is for George. He only gets it about once a year.'

From somewhere down below sounded the voices of the renowned Slade Prison Thieves Choir in a husky rendering of 'Silent Night'. I groaned.

'Shut the door, will you?'

'Don't you like carols?'

'They've been at it for two hours – and they only know four carols. And the words are sometimes a bit suspect. When shepherds washed their socks by night, indeed.'

'But don't you find it rather moving? All those blokes, some of them real tearaways, united in a common exultation of this great occasion?'

'Don't be daft. They're singing, my son, to drown the noise of Tommy Slocombe's tunnelling.'

Lennie looked surprised. 'Tunnelling?'

'That's the great occasion round here. Not the coming of our Lord but the going of Tommy Slocombe.'

'Nobody ever tells me nothing.'

I slipped my Christmas card into an envelope and sealed it. 'It wasn't thought an event suitable for publication. It's a secret between Tommy, six baritones, twelve tenors and a soprano.'

'Have we got a soprano?'

'Oh, there's lots of sopranos in here, my son. And a few of those baritones need watching and all. Don't let those deep gruff voices fool you.'

Lennie went to the door and peered down. Then he came back and asked : 'Where is the tunnel?'

'Where's the choir?'

'Just outside cell twenty-eight.'

'Then it's about three feet under cell twenty-nine.'

Lennie sat down, withdrew a couple of stolen biscuits from his pocket and handed me one. 'Well, I like the singing. At least it brings an air of festivity into our otherwise monotonous existence. I like Christmas, Fletch. There's the carol service, and the concert coming up. And the tree.'

He was referring to the big Christmas tree that is installed every year in the association area and which we are allowed to decorate. I nodded. 'Useful the tree.'

'Useful?'

'For stashing Christmas contraband. All those dingly-danglies hide a multitude of sins. Even the Christmas fairy on the top has got two ounces of tobacco shoved up her tutu.'

'I thought she looked pregnant. Where's the tobacco come from?'

'The Governor's office. It was his present for Mr MacKay. Welsh George made a nifty switch when he was in there doing the floors.'

'What did he switch it for?'

'An identical gift-wrapped box, which Mr MacKay will doubtless open on Christmas Day.'

'What's in it?'

'I'll tell you this much – it's not suitable for smoking. Might come in handy on his allotment though.'

Lennie sighed and I could see that he felt it was a bit raw even for a nurk like MacKay. Then he asked: 'What's Christmas like inside, Fletch?'

'Slightly less horrible than any other day. I mean, the Governor don't dress up as Santa Claus and give us all bottles of after-shave, you know.'

'But we get turkey, don't we? Do we? Do we get turkey?'

'That is the proud boast, yes, but you can't always be sure from either its appearance or its flavour.'

'And we get pudding as well, don't we? Christmas pudding like, with cream?'

'Oh yes, that artificial whipped cream. You'd be better off shaving with that. And, of course, the wheeler-dealers make a few bob at Christmas. Genial Harry Grout grants a few franchises for mistletoe and suchlike.'

Lennie sighed again. 'Sounds just like the outside. People have forgotten the real meaning of Christmas. It's just a commercial exercise.'

'What do you expect? Brotherly love? From Mac-Kay? You'd have a better chance of getting sprung in a sledge drawn by reindeer.'

But Lennie, being young and buoyant, was not to be discouraged. 'Still, the actual day should be a bit brighter, shouldn't it?'

'Not this year.'

'Why not?'

'Because of that flaming tunnel. That tunnel spells disaster for us all. That stupid Tommy Slocombe's only chosen to make his break on Christmas Eve. He'll never get through the traffic for one thing.'

Lennie grinned. 'Only six more digging days to Christmas, then?'

'It's not funny, Sonny Jim. We're all going to be implicated in this escape. Whether we like it or not.'

'But Slocombe's such a despicable nurk. I don't see why anyone would lift a finger for him.'

I explained. 'It so happens young Slocombe is the brother-in-law of a big villain in the smoke. A man who is also a colleague of our own much-loved Harry Grout. Well, he's obviously got the word to Harry: we want our kid for Christmas. So Harry's running this caper. And that means if any of us are asked to assist we've got no choice. Otherwise there might be something else hanging on the Christmas tree. Us.'

Lennie said stoutly, 'Well, I'm not going down no tunnel. I suffer from claustrophobia. Dates back to the time when I was stuck up a chimney for two hours.'

'Oh yes? How'd that happen?'

'I was going to turn over this big house in Sutton Coldfield, you see. The chimney was my only means of access.'

'And you got stuck, did you?'

'It was terrifying. Particularly when my intended

victims came home and saw my legs sticking out the fireplace. They gave a tug and I came down.'

'Didn't they get you?'

'No, I wriggled free and dove out the window.'

'They'd have given the police a description.'

'But I was covered in soot. They're probably still looking for a blue-eyed negro in a coal-black suit.'

'Yeah – well that might get you excused from tunnelling duties. All the same, when Slocombe's well out of it we'll be up to our necks in it. This kind of thing disturbs the equilibrium of prison life.'

'What equilibrium?'

'Them and us. It'll tilt the balance of power which exists between the law and the villain. With this escape we shall have pushed the system too far.'

'There's nothing we can do though, is there? I mean, what can we do?'

'I know what I'm going to do. I intend to be well out of it.'

'How?'

'I'm going away for Christmas.'

'Oh yeah? Majorca?'

'No – everyone goes to Majorca, don't they? I thought this year I'd try the prison hospital for a change.'

'Fat chance.'

I ignored this. 'It's the nearest thing there is to a holiday in here and moreover I shall be far removed from any retaliation by the screws over this escape fiasco.'

But Lennie was far from convinced. He prophesied: 'You'll never get in the infirmary, not with that doctor. Anyway, what's supposed to be wrong with you?'

'It's my knee, isn't it?'

'I never knew there was anything wrong with your knee.'

'No? Well, I've been keeping it up my sleeve. Or, more precisely, up my trouser-leg.'

'What's the matter with it?'

'Cartilage. I've lived with the pain for years. But recently, being on my feet all day in the damp weather, it has escalated to an unbearable degree.'

'Which knee is it?' asked Lennie, taking me off guard.

'It's – er – definitely one of them,' I affirmed, and hobbled out of the cell.

The reason why I'm famous throughout the British penal system is my ability to secure privileges and pull off strokes. But I never push my luck. For example, during one stretch I never try to con my way home for a wonderful weekend, claiming I have to curtail my old lady's passionate involvement with the grocer, more than once. Thus I usually get away with it. Likewise with illness. I'm not one of those who goes whining round to the clinic every other day demanding transfer to Charing Cross Hospital. I think my moves out carefully and carry them out with skill.

Nevertheless, I wasn't too confident about my chances this time. Mole, the new doctor, was reputed to be very tough. It was widely maintained that a germ would have a better chance of getting into a bottle of Dettol than a sick man into his infirmary. And this reputation seemed to be confirmed by my reception when I limped into his lair. Mole was bandaging Bunny Warren's hand, which he had burned on the kitchen grill while trying to nick sausages. Bunny was grimacing.

'Am I hurting you?' the doc asked him.

'You got your job to do.'

'It's a pretty bad burn. What are you so pleased about?'

'Well, doc, if you're going to hurt yourself in here, might as well make sure it's nothing trivial. I mean, there's no way I can go back to work with this hand, is there?'

'I'm reluctantly forced to admit there isn't.'

'I think I could just about make it to the infirmary though, if somebody opens the door for me.'

'You're not going to the infirmary,' Mole said firmly. 'You're confined to your cell for three days.'

'You don't like people getting in your infirmary, do you?'

'And mess up all those crisp white sheets? Certainly not.' The doctor looked up and saw me. 'Out of here, Fletcher.'

'But I've got my white card.' I held it out for him to see.

'Out, out, out.'

'I'm sick.'

'Out!'

'I'm entitled – '

'Years of medical practice, Fletcher, have enabled me to tell at a glance if a man's sick or not. You're a perfect specimen of manhood.'

'It's not my manhood I've come about. It's my knee.'

There was a pause while he put the finishing touches to Warren's bandage. Then he asked, 'What's supposed to be wrong with your knee?'

'Just ask me to stand on one leg.'

'No.'

But Warren, shocked by this blatant example of unethical practice, urged: 'Go on! Where's the harm in that?'

The doctor sighed but realised he'd been outmanoeuvred. 'All right,' he conceded. 'Stand on one leg.'

I slowly raised my left leg and, as I'd anticipated, my right leg buckled under me and I sank to the floor. Then I looked up at the doctor with a reproachful expression. 'And you call yourself a doctor.'

'Get up, Fletcher.'

'I don't know if I can.'

'Make a superhuman effort.' I struggled to my feet. 'Sit in the chair. Now what's the matter?'

'I'll show you.' With my natural flair for drama, I slowly rolled up my trouser leg and pointed at the joint. 'There.'

Warren craned forwards to see the show but Mole merely glanced at it moodily. 'There what?'

'Well – that's my knee.'

'I know it's a knee, Fletcher. I learnt that in medical school.'

'Ah, but you never learned about this kind of knee. You see, the old trouble has flared up again.'

'Laziness?'

'Cartilage. And before you say anything, doctor, it's all in my medical records. You check your files. You'll see I have an official history of knee trouble.'

'I don't believe you.'

'Have to check though, won't you.'

Mole, a pleasant-looking young man notwithstanding his suspicious nature, sighed and went to his files. He murmured, 'I don't know why I'm doing this.'

Feeling on somewhat firmer grounds, I said, 'You're doing it because you know that there's one chance in a million that one day one of us will be telling the truth.'

He pulled open his filing cabinet and, to enable him to get at the files, removed from the drawer a large, wrapped Christmas cake.

'What's that then?' asked Warren.

'It's a Christmas cake. I get one every year for the patients in my infirmary.'

'But you don't allow patients in your infirmary.'

'True. So I always take it home to the wife.'

It occurred to me that a *file* with a *cake* in it was an interesting turn-up in the nick and I was about to share the joke with the other two when Mole, who had apparently found and glanced at my dossier, exclaimed in horror : 'My God, it's true – Maidstone Jail, 1967 – cartilage !'

'Very common with footballers, that. That and groin strain,' said Warren.

'Little chance of groin strain in here,' I offered.

The doc turned to me. 'All right, I accept you have an official record of surgery on your left knee. Nevertheless, it was years ago.'

'Yeah, and I've lived with the pain ever since. Now I never complain, do I, Bunny?'

Warren supported me. 'No, he don't complain.' But then the thick-witted nurk spoilt the case by over-dramatisation. 'Some days he crawls in from work like a wounded bloodhound on his hands and knees.'

'Only when it's really bad,' I said lamely.

Dr Mole asked : 'All right, what is it you're after?'

'The thing is, doc, every so often, when the pain becomes unbearable, I have to lie down with my leg up – just for a week or two.'

'I see. You think a week in the infirmary might do the trick?'

'Might be enough, yeah.'

But then I saw his eyes fill with a hard light and I realised that I'd blundered through over-confidence. 'Let me tell you something, Fletcher,' he began. 'Of all the penal institutions in the North of England, my infirmary has the lowest record of admissions. Donaldson, who's doing a five stretch for grand larceny and embezzlement, has more chance of getting a Barclaycard than you have of getting into my infirmary.'

'Won't be much good to Her Majesty when they have to wheel me about, though, will I, doc?'

'Fletcher, I don't want you spreading malicious rumours about me, such as that I graduated from Belsen, so here's what I'm going to do. I'm sending you to a civilian hospital for X-ray and specialist examination. You'll be there and back in a day. Then the matter will be irrevocably closed.'

This struck me as a poor scheme and I said so. 'Why waste the tax-payers' money? I tell you, I know my knee. All I need is to rest up for a day or two.'

'On your way, Fletcher. You're a liar and a malingerer.'

'Harsh words, doctor, in this season of peace and goodwill to all men.' And I turned and strode haughtily towards the door. Before I reached it, I realised that I'd forgotten something, and so I put on my limp and continued pathetically out of his clinic.

It must have been a day or so later, while I was knocking my knee cap against the edge of the table in order to set up an inflammation, that Lennie burst in in a great state of excitement.

'Hey, Fletch –' he stopped and stared. 'What the hell are you doing?'

'Oh – er – got a slight twitch. Must have been the rhubarb we had for dinner. Often does that to me, rhubarb.'

'Anyway, guess who's on his way here to see you?'

'The Home Secretary?'

'Grouty.'

'What?'

'Straight up – Grouty. On his way.'

My knee started twitching in earnest, accompanied by a sinking feeling in my stomach. I said glumly :

'What did I tell you? Gawd blimey, I knew it. This will be some little favour pertaining to Slocombe's moonlight flit – oh, hello, Grouty?'

The cheerful greeting was prompted by the sudden appearance of genial Harry Grout.

'Hello, Fletcher.'

'This is a rare privilege. You don't often drop in on people. Usually you get people to drop in on you. And if they don't you get other people to drop heavy objects on them.'

Lennie laughed appreciately but Grouty, although he smiled from the bridge of his nose down, didn't seem truly amused. 'You always were a bit of a joker, Fletcher.'

'Yeah, well – what brings you to my humble abode, Grouty?'

'I just wanted to get out of my cell for a while.'

'Change of air? Afraid it's just as foul down this way.'

'A couple of warders are putting up my Christmas decorations.' Lennie demonstrated his impartiality by laughing at this attempt too. Grouty flicked him a coin, 'There you are, son. Go to the pictures or something, would you?'

Lennie blinked but then caught on. 'Oh – sure – thank you.'

'And shut the door after you.'

Lennie ambled off, pulling the heavy door shut behind him. Grouty seated himself on the only chair and, with that graciousness which distinguishes the true leader, said, 'You sit down too, Fletch.'

I planted myself on Lennie's bunk. Grouty extracted

from a case, pierced and lit a handsome cigar. I said wistfully, 'That looks like a nice cigar, Grouty. Wish I had something festive to offer you.'

'Not in the festive mood, Fletch,' and he went straight to the point. 'There's a tunnel being dug. You've heard, I suppose?'

'Only when they leave off singing.'

'Slocombe's a relative of friends of mine on the outside, and they want him sprung.'

'Isn't he the son of Billy-the-Ponce Slocombe? The one that got out of Brixton in seventy-two? Now where did he end up?'

'It seems he emerged on some Caribbean Island where the authorities took advantage of his criminal experience.'

'How?'

'Made him Chief of Police.'

'Yes, he did have a bit of style.'

'My problem is, Fletch, that it's down to me to accomplish the disappearance of his idiot offspring.'

'Delicate, Grouty.'

'Extremely.'

I leaned forwards to share some of the rich smoke from Grouty's havana. 'If only I could help in some way.'

Grouty smiled hospitably. 'You can, my son.'

I tried to look overjoyed. 'Oh yeah?'

'You're having a little day trip tomorrow, aren't you?'

'Only to get my knee X-rayed.'

'Still, you'll be on the outside. And we have friends on the outside who could take advantage of that.'

'How?'

'There'll be a package. Someone. Somewhere. Sometime. No sweat.'

I tried evasive action. 'I'll be under escort, Grouty.

I'm not just getting the bus down there and doing a bit of last-minute Christmas shopping, you know.'

'It's only a small package. A blank passport. Inky Stevens needs one to give Slocombe a more acceptable identity.'

'Wouldn't it be safer for him to pick up his new passport on the outside?'

'Normally, yes. But the finest forger in the country is Inky Stevens, and he's on the inside, isn't he?'

I nodded sadly. Grouty clapped a hand on my shoulder, a sign of esteem for which some of the nurks around here would give a good deal. Trouble was, I was getting a bad deal. 'I won't be ungrateful, Fletch.' He rose to depart. 'Be something in your Christmas stocking for this. Besides your bad knee.'

And heaving gently with laughter at this marvellous quip he waddled out, leaving me to dark forebodings.

Still, I brightened up the next day, especially when I discovered that my escort was to be Mr Barrowclough. Even the rapture of a trip outside the walls tends to be compromised by MacKay's jeering presence.

'Haven't you forgotten something, Fletcher?' he asked as I was climbing into the prison mini-bus.

'What's that?'

'Your limp – ha, ha.'

'Oh yes. Mock the afflicted.'

We hummed along across the moors in the mini-van and swooped down into the noble city of Carlisle. I'd forgotten that the world was so big and beautiful. As usual, I created a small sensation in the hospital. Not every day do they see a man handcuffed to a wheelchair. Admittedly the medical procedures, all the tapping and photographing, lacked true glamour but at the end of it I found myself in the company of an attractive nurse.

'You've really got a very nice knee, Mr Fletcher,' she said.

'Not as nice as yours, nurse,' I returned playfully. 'I bet *they're* going to have a happy Christmas.'

But Barrowclough spoiled the sport. 'That will do, Fletcher. You could be the girl's father.'

'No, impossible, Mr Barrowclough. Never been in these parts before.'

'Anyway,' the nurse said, 'the main thing is the doctor says it's a perfectly healthy knee.'

'Those X-rays prove nothing,' I said indignantly. 'You cannot photograph pain.'

'When did your knee trouble start?'

But before I could reply, Barrowclough said drily : 'Two days ago, when he thought he'd wangle the infirmary for Christmas.'

'Hang about, Mr Barrowclough. My trouble goes back ten years.'

'Anyway,' said the nurse, 'we can't find anything wrong. You can go home now, Mr Fletcher.'

'That's a relief!' I exclaimed. 'We've got friends coming to dinner and we're all going to the ballet.'

The nurse smiled and departed. I glanced about uneasily. So far there had been no attempt to slip me the package Grouty had mentioned. That was all right by me. Smuggling a blank passport into the prison was not going to endear me to the Governor if I got caught. And with Barrowclough glued, or at least chained, to my side, I didn't see how I could avoid getting caught.

'Come on, Mr Barrowclough,' I urged. 'Let's get cracking. You know how Mr MacKay worries if we're out after dark.'

Barrowclough sighed. ' I suppose we had better move,' he conceded.

Just then another girl, a blonde, appeared round the

corner. She was not a nurse but was wearing a white coat.

'Would you two gentlemen care for some coffee?'

'No thanks, we're just going,' I said.

'Do you mind, Fletcher?' asked Barrowclough reproachfully. 'I'd be very glad of a cup of coffee, miss. It's made with milk only here, isn't it? I only get half and half at home.'

'Half and half?' I queried.

'Milk and water.'

'Oh yeah.'

'You sure you don't fancy some?' she asked me, with a smile.

'Not coffee, no thank you.'

'Oh well. I'll get one cup then.' And she pattered off.

'Honest, Mr Barrowclough,' I urged, 'it's a long drive and – '

'What's the matter with you, Fletcher?' he interrupted. 'You seem very ill at ease. Relax. Enjoy yourself. It's Christmas. Don't you think I sometimes get as sick of Slade Prison as you do? Today's been a break for me as well.'

'Why? What would you have been doing today back at the prison, Mr Barrowclough?'

'I was off-duty today. I just volunteered for this trip.'

'You could have stayed at home,' I suggested. 'Spent the day with your lady wife.'

'That's really why I volunteered.'

At this point our conversation was interrupted by the return of the blonde with two cups of coffee.

'Are you sure you won't change your mind?' she asked me.

I grunted and held out my hand, trying not to meet her eyes. Barrowclough frowned.

'You must forgive our friend here. He's a little morose. Not his usual self.'

'Really?' asked the girl. 'Well, I think I've got something here that'll cheer him up. May I speak to him?'

'Certainly, my dear,' Barrowclough simpered. 'By all means. Fletcher, the young lady wishes to address you.'

'The thing is,' she said, 'and I hope you won't take offence, Mr Fletcher, but all of us here know of your sad – predicament. We realise that this can't be a very happy time of year for you and so we – the radiologists – have got together and bought you a little Christmas gift. There.' And she held out a small package, passport-sized.

'Well, take it, Fletcher,' urged Barrowclough irritably. 'What a very nice thought. Good Lord, I should have thought you'd have been delighted.'

'Oh, I am,' I assured him. 'Seventh heaven.'

'Well, open it, then,' he said.

Whereupon the blonde and I exclaimed in chorus: 'No! Not before Christmas Day.'

'It mustn't be opened until Christmas Eve,' she went on. 'Radiologists are very superstitious about things like that. Spoils the surprise.'

'Really?' asked Mr Barrowclough. 'I had no idea.'

About two hours later, I slipped into Grouty's cell and handed him the package, by now moist with cold sweat. He unwrapped it eagerly. It contained a large Christmas card. He opened that and out of it dropped a blank passport. He looked up at me with his most genial expression.

'Well done, my son.'

'Give me palpitations, I can tell you. Right under Barrowclough's nose! Fortunately he was put off his guard by the day out and her legs.'

'Smart bird, that Sandra.'

'Who is she? Does she work there?'

'Course not. Come up from the smoke. All it took was a bit of nerve and a white coat.'

'And about ten years off my life.'

'I'm sorry your knee got a clean bill of health, Fletch. Perhaps I could do you a favour in that direction?'

'How?'

'Couple of my lads could have a go at it. Put it beyond medical dispute.'

'Er – very thoughtful of you, Grouty, but I think I'll pass on that one.'

'Please yourself. I just thought I'd mention it because I need to elicit the help of you and that lad Lennie a bit further.'

I felt entitled to a show of indignation. 'Come off it, Grouty. Ain't I done my bit?'

'Very forthcoming, Fletch. But you see, it's the tunnel.'

'Hang about. The kid's got claustrophobia. And look at the size of me! A ferret I ain't.'

'It's nothing physical. I just want you to join in the choir. They've come up against a very stony bit, and we need all the fortissimo we can get.'

I sighed in relief. 'Oh, my pleasure, Grouty. Enjoy a good sing. Used to do a lot of it down in Maidstone when we worked on the prison farm. Church hymns mostly. Favourite one with the boys was "We plough the fields and scatter". Several of them did an' all. Well, that's everything then, is it?'

'Just one small item – '

I felt the familiar prickling in the scalp. 'Have a heart – smuggling, singing – ain't I doing my share?'

Grouty smiled benignly. 'It's essential to the success of our venture.'

'Yeah well – what?'

'We need a bicycle.'

'Oh, a bicycle? Is that all? I mean, wouldn't an armoured car be handier? Any particular colour?'

'I know you can do it, Fletch,' he grinned, dismissing me with a wave of his arm.

He was right too. We did it. But bicycles aren't like jaffa cakes. If a bicycle goes missing, someone's bound to notice. The following morning Mr Barrowclough paid us a visit in the flowery. In tow was Warren, looking distinctly underchuffed. I leaped to my feet and so did Lennie. We charged towards the door.

'Lunchtime, is it, Mr Barrowclough?' I asked eagerly. 'Nice of you to call us.'

He barred the way. 'Your lunch can wait. I have something very serious to say to you three.'

'Why us?' asked Lennie, innocently.

'Because it was you three who were in the yard to-day when I arrived at work – you three who involved me in a pointless discussion on the 1962 Cup Final. And that's why I want to ask you three one pertinent question. Where is my bicycle?'

Lennie and I exchanged a puzzled glance. Then Lennie and Warren did the same. Warren and I were embarking on the same routine when Mr Barrowclough lost patience.

'Well?'

'What bicycle was this then?' I asked.

'The one I cycled to work on.'

Lennie said wonderingly : 'I didn't know you had a bicycle?'

'I've had one for a month. Ever since the MO advised me to take more exercise.'

'I had a bike once,' Warren offered.

But Barrowclough rounded on him. 'So did I! And I want to know what's become of it.'

'Let me get this straight, Mr Barrowclough,' asked Lennie, like a barrister addressing a feeble-minded witness. 'You are saying that, prior to our conversation this morning, you were the owner of a bicycle?'

'That is correct, yes,' agreed Barrowclough, automatically adopting the appropriate manner.

'And further, that since the aforesaid conversation you are no longer the owner of a bicycle?'

'I am not, no.'

At this point, I came in like Lennie's junior. 'Are we to understand, Mr Barrowclough, that you arrived at work as a cyclist but that you propose leaving as a pedestrian?'

'I don't propose,' expostulated Mr Barrowclough, coming out of his trance. 'I haven't got any choice.'

'You are not, I hope, assuming that there's a connection between our gripping discussion of football history and the disappearance of this alleged bicycle?'

'It was not an alleged bicycle. It was a green bicycle.'

'When did you last see this bicycle?' Warren asked.

'When I dismounted.'

'You sure you had it with you when you got off it?' I offered helpfully.

'Why do you think I wear these?' he said, producing a pair of cycle clips.

'To stop things falling out of your trousers?'

'But if we was talking to you,' Lennie pointed out logically, 'how could we have palmed your bike?'

'It was a well-known diversionary tactic.'

'That *is* one explanation, yes,' I said meaningfully, 'but there are other possible ones, Mr Barrowclough.'

'What do you mean, Fletcher?'

'This kind of thing is not unknown to the insurance companies. Was it carrying a lot of cover?'

'Don't talk nonsense.'

'They get very suspicious at unexplained disappearances.'

'Yes? Well so do I. Come along, Warren.'

'Where to?' asked the hapless Bunny.

'I'm going to start by searching your cell. And if I find so much as a tyre-valve you're all three for it.'

Well, of course, he never found a trace. Grouty had the bike in a hundred pieces by then and stashed away all over the nick. Pity it had to be Barrowclough's but MacKay drives to work.

Over the next few days the tunnel progressed. But I had a feeling we were heading for trouble. MacKay seemed to sense that something was wrong. For instance, I was mopping floors one day and, as he passed with Barrowclough, I heard him growling:

'You should never trust them, not for a minute. Any time a prisoner makes a request, a prison officer must ask himself – "What is he up to?" A prisoner ties his shoelace – question: what is he concealing in his sock?'

'I know all that, of course,' said Barrowclough, 'but I never thought they'd steal a bicycle. They can't conceal that in their sock.'

'Oh come on, man. You know what they're like. Did we ever find any trace of our billiard table? Only the red ball.'

MacKay became increasingly nosy and one day he pounced on the choir, bellowing 'Silence!' Lukewarm didn't even have time to tap a warning on the radiator to the tunnellers. We stood there, numb with apprehension, while MacKay sniffed around. Faintly but distinctly we heard the clink, clink, clink of an improvised pick at work beneath our feet. MacKay froze, like a gun-dog that scents a juicy pheasant.

'What's that?'

'Central heating, sir,' I volunteered. 'Very weird noises it makes.'

'Does it?' MacKay strode to the radiator and favoured it with two hefty kicks. We gave an inaudible sigh of relief. The helpful nurk had only given the 'danger' signal. The clinking stopped.

'I didn't know you was a plumber, Mr MacKay,' I said enthusiastically. 'I think you've mended it. Been ruining our glissando, that has.'

MacKay, still suspicious, prowled about the area. But there was nothing for him to find. Finally he snarled, 'All right. Back to your cells, all of you.'

'But we need more rehearsal, don't we?' Warren pleaded.

'There won't be any more.'

'Christmas, isn't it?' Lennie piped up.

'You've forfeited your right to Christmas.'

'How?'

MacKay, hands clasped behind his back and moustache bristling, strode up and down our little rank like a demented sergeant-major. 'How? Through a series of incidents, culminating in the disappearance of Mr Barrowclough's bicycle. I can't prove anything, of course, but don't think that that technicality will affect my judgement in the least. You were put in here to keep crime off the streets, and I'm not having you bringing it into my prison. You will be advised to remember that we have a solitary confinement area, with which you will become only too familiar if you continue to practise the contemptible habits which brought you here in the first place. Is that clear? Right! Back to your cells the lot of you. Move!'

The following afternoon, I stood gazing at the notice board in amazement. Finally, I tore myself away and hurried along to the cosy dell. Lennie was there making a paper chain. I burst out :

'It's on the bulletin board ! It's official.'

'What is?'

'Christmas is cancelled. It says on the board : there will be no Xmas Eve, Xmas Day or Boxing Day – just the 24th, 25th and 26th of December.'

Lennie absently pulled his paper chain to bits. 'Won't need this then, will we?' he remarked.

I sat down and began to roll myself a snout. 'I told you, didn't I?' I said bitterly.

'About the equilibrium being disturbed?'

'Disturbed? It's upside down, my son. Barrowclough's bicycle was necessary but that bleeding Lukewarm nicking MacKay's wallet and Barrowclough's watch. Talk about daylight robbery. Now we're all in the – mire !'

'Not his fault, Fletch, be fair. He was under Grouty's instructions like the rest of us. They needed MacKay's wallet for petrol for the getaway car.'

'They didn't need Barrowclough's Timex though, did they? Force of flaming habit that was. The whole thing's been a mockery. Ill-conceived, badly organised, and doomed to fail – oh, hello, Grouty –' our friendly, neighbourhood Godfather had unexpectedly entered – 'I was just saying what a shame that your brilliant strategy should come to naught.'

Grouty sat down sombrely and started rolling himself a snout with my tobacco. He sighed. 'Know what they say, the best laid plans and so on.'

Lennie asked hesitantly : 'Should I go to the pictures?'

'No, sit down, sonny – no secrets now. Bad business. My friends in the smoke are bound to bear malice.'

'Oh no – they'd never be so heartless, Grouty.'

'Why not? I would.'

Lennie had a bright idea. 'Excuse me, Mr Grout, but couldn't you re-activate the tunnel at a later date?'

'No. It was off course anyhow. He's an idiot, that Slocombe. He nearly come up in the laundry last week.'

'So the tunnel's now defunct?'

'Except for storing contraband, yes.'

It was my turn to have an inspiration. 'Excuse me, Grouty, something's just occurred to me which may solve all our problems.'

'Oh yes?'

'If the screws was to find that tunnel, it would do two things. One, it would tilt the balance of power back in their favour because they'd be chuffed at their own perspicacity. And two, they'd think that it was the intended escape route.'

'But it was, wasn't it?' asked Lennie, puzzled.

'It was, but it ain't now. It's a red herring. See, Grouty, while the screws are still full of self-congratulatory ardour, you get Tommy away in a dust-cart or something. Wouldn't that please your pals in London?'

Grouty looks heavy, and there's many a mutilated man in the East End of London who can testify that he *is* heavy, but he's not slow. His face lit up. 'Here, you have had a thought, haven't you, Fletch?'

'Save your face, Grouty.'

'That it would.'

'And from the outside it'll seem like a perfectly executed plan,' Lennie contributed.

'You're not wrong, son. What should we do, Fletch? Tip the Governor off?'

'No, I think MacKay should be the one to find it. In fact, Grouty, if you give me the blueprints, I might even arrange for him to drop right in!'

About an hour later, MacKay sought me out in the prison yard. 'I'm told you want a word with me, Fletcher.'

I put a warning finger to my lips. 'Shall we just take a little stroll, Mr MacKay? Away from prying ears? Know what I mean?'

MacKay glanced about cagily. There were one or two cons nearby. He nodded. Keeping my eye out for landmarks, I led him at an easy pace along the route of the tunnel. Meanwhile, I gave him the old patter. 'I know you see me in the role of adversary, Mr Mac-Kay, but we're both old hands at this game. I mean, there's you and there's us. But we both know that neither of us must push the other too far.'

MacKay nodded impatiently. I noted the manhole cover and ambled on.

'For this reason, Mr MacKay, we maintain a tolerable rhythm of life. We must season our mutual contempt with mutual respect.'

MacKay stopped dead, an irritable frown on his face. 'Just what are you getting at, Fletcher?'

I beckoned him on. 'Keep walking, Mr MacKay. Don't want to arouse suspicion.'

Reluctantly, he began advancing again. I led him past the cricket stumps chalked on the wall, to the left of the drain.

'You were about to say?'

'The point is, Mr MacKay, I don't like to see your authority undermined.'

'That's not likely to happen, Fletcher.'

Straight on for four paces, then half-right for ten. 'Maybe not, in the ordinary run of things, Mr MacKay. But there are times things don't run ordinary. See what I mean?'

'Frankly, no.'

'Don't stop, Mr MacKay. Warren's watching us.'

He grunted peevishly, but picked up speed again.

'Have you got something to tell me, Fletcher, or haven't you?'

'I think this is going to come as something of a shock to you, Mr MacKay.'

Three more paces and, yes! – there was the pebble that marked the spot where we'd weakened the roof of the tunnel to a mere wafer.

'Any moment now, Mr MacKay.'

And there he was – on it! But – on it he remained.

'Fletcher, I'm warning you – '

'Now, hang about, Mr MacKay. I've brought you out here at great personal risk because you know the fate of a grass in this or any other nick. Nevertheless, like I said before, there are circumstances which can arise – '

'Fletcher, I think you're trying to divert my attention. I'm not falling for it.'

'No, you're not, are you.'

'All right, Fletcher, you have until the count of three to get to the point. One – two – '

And I couldn't think of another bleeding thing to say.

'Three! I'll remember this, Fletcher.' And he turned to stride off.

In desperation I lunged towards him, pleading : 'Just one more – aaaargh!'

This last exclamation was not part of my attempt to retain the company of Mr MacKay but was occasioned by the ground giving way beneath my feet. I found myself plunging into a great chasm. And when I finally hit bottom, a fierce, wrenching pain shot up my leg and then all was merciful darkness.

I woke up in the prison infirmary with a bandaged knee. It wasn't broken, only well and truly dislocated.

'At least a week!' groaned Dr Mole, grinding his teeth.

And that explains why, on Christmas Day – which had been reinstituted – I had my lunch in a nice, clean, comfortable bed. While I was gnawing the last shreds of meat from my drumstick, Lennie came in. It did not escape my notice that he was carrying a box of ripe Havanas and also a sealed package.

'Morning, Fletch,' he carolled.

'Morning, my son.'

'They've reinstated Christmas.'

'I know. I'm eating it.'

'Here you are. Merry Christmas.'

'Oh dear – Havana cigars!'

'They're from Grouty.'

'Where did he get these?'

'Some things we never know, Fletch. This one's from me. Bit mundane after cigars, but I knitted them myself.'

I unwrapped the package, trying to look eager. As I had feared, it contained two dwarf, misshapen socks. 'Oh, very nice . . . they'll have to wait until I get my bandages off.'

'They're mittens. Grouty says that he's very sorry his directions were eighteen inches out, but that's typical of Slocombe's prowess as a surveyor.'

'I'm not bothered. By devious means, I've achieved my original objective, right?'

'Right. The screws are ever so chuffed about finding the tunnel. Silly nurks, you'd think – and we're going to have the carol concert right after tea this evening. Oh, hello, Mr MacKay.'

The intrepid officer advanced on the bed. I noted that he moved with a swagger, as if he'd just routed Rommel. He spoke warmly: 'Compliments of the season, Fletcher.' Then he turned to Lennie. 'All right,

Godber, cut along. Don't want to miss your Christmas lunch.'

Lennie shrugged. 'See you, Fletch.'

'In due course, son.'

'I'll send you a get-well-slowly card.'

MacKay unbent sufficiently to smile. Lennie skipped off. I contemplated my old adversary.

'Well, Mr MacKay, you look a little – would flushed be the word?'

'Just been to the Governor's sherry party. Everyone was in high spirits. Except the doctor. It seems you've got his cake.'

MacKay held up a tastefully-wrapped package. 'Look at this – a present from the Governor. Pipe tobacco, I imagine. I'm looking forward to opening it.'

'Best part sometimes, isn't it, anticipation?'

MacKay attempted a benign smile. 'Fletcher, I wanted to say that I appreciate what you were up to in the yard.'

'Oh? Seemed to me I was more down than up.'

He laughed pleasantly. 'What I want to say is just between you and me, Fletcher.'

'I can't think what you're getting at, Mr MacKay.'

'Of course you can't officially. But as you said, we're both old hands at the game. I'd like to ask you just one question. What became of the soil that was excavated from the tunnel?'

'Hang about. You would seem, Mr MacKay, to be presuming. Don't get the idea that you've got a new informer in your back pocket. There's you and there's us, and I'm still on the side of us.'

'Oh, come off it, Fletcher. Just a loose end to be tied up. How did they dispose of the soil?'

'I'm afraid I can't help you, Mr MacKay.'

'No?'

He said this very meaningfully and at the same time produced from behind his back a nearly-full bottle of Scotch. He held it up to catch the light and I must confess that its mellow amber sent a pleasant thrill rippling through me.

'Scotland's finest.'

'With a couple of nips out of it, I see.'

'Still, an unexpected treat.'

'Bribe, is it?'

'Christmas present. Now come along, Fletcher, just between you and me.'

I glanced about cautiously. This was not really necessary because, thanks to Dr Mole's loathing of invalids, I was the only one in the infirmary. 'Is that door closed?'

'It is.'

'Christmas present, eh?'

'Christmas present.'

'You want to know where they put the soil?'

'Simple as that.'

'I'll tell you, then.'

MacKay licked his lips and leaned towards me. I whispered: 'They dug another tunnel and put it down there.'

MacKay crowed in glee.

'So that was it! Cunning devils!'

Chuckling, he turned to go. I screwed the top off the bottle, raised it to my lips and quaffed deep. I lowered it again in time to see MacKay, with a puzzled look on his face, turn back towards me.

'But in that case – '

'Merry Christmas, Mr MacKay,' I said warmly and raised the bottle again.

A FURTHER STIR OF
PORRIDGE

adapted from the TV series by
Paul Victor

Contents

The Desperate Hours

It was the night before Christmas and all through the nick, not a creature was stirring not even a tick. Which was not surprising because Slade Prison, while plentifully stocked with cockroaches, mice and screws, does not number any ticks amongst its vermin. To the best of my knowledge, that is. And my knowledge is pretty extensive since I have spent many years within its grand old walls. And if it burned down tomorrow I would not shed a tear. Assuming I was outside its grand old walls. Which is not a very sound assumption since I still have a long time to serve. Moreover, it was not really the night before Christmas which I just said to make the rhyme. Nevertheless, the season of turkey and plum pudding, represented inside by stringy bones and brown goo, was fast approaching. For this reason, and in an attempt to increase the meagre amount of merriment normally available to convicted felons, I had summoned a meeting in the conference hall, otherwise known as the latrines. I addressed the delegates.

'McLaren, Warren, Tulip, Godber, I have gathered you here as representatives of your respective cell blocks.'

'What's all this about, Fletch?' Bunny Warren asked.

'A minute, please. As you know, the festive season is almost upon us.'

'With all the high spirits and jollity which that entails,' McLaren growled.

'Now, come on, Jock, that's the wrong attitude, that is. Let me ask you all, what is the real meaning of Christmas?'

'Robbing postmen?' offered Tulip.

'Not the professional meaning. I mean, what comes to mind when you hear the word Christmas?'

'Chestnuts roasting on an open fire,' Lennie tried.

'Yeah, well – that is one thing.'

'How about MacKay roasting on an open fire?' McLaren suggested.

'Guy Fawkes night, that is,' I corrected him.

Warren wrinkled his tiny brow and then said: 'Crackers? Holly?'

Lennie carrolled: 'Treetops glistening and children listening to hear – '

'That will do, Godber. You can leave out the Perry Como. Look, I'm talking about what the likes of us associate with Christmas. There's one thing above all else which conjures up the very spirit of this joyous occasion.'

'What?' asked Tulip.

'Booze.'

'Eh?'

'Booze, you nurk. Drink. Juice. What does everyone do at Christmas? They get drunk. Bombed. Plastered. Elephant's trunk. Legless. Brahms and Liszt as the proverbial newt.'

Lennie confided to McLaren. 'I've never understood the derivation of that expression myself. Are newts known to be heavy drinkers?'

I held up an irritated hand. 'Time *is* somewhat precious. We are running a security risk.'

'Sorry, Fletch,' Lennie said apologetically.

'Right.'

'Well, what *are* we here for, Fletch?' asked Tulip.

I looked around at them with a proud look and then fed them the glad tidings.

'Wine tasting.'

Tulip goggled very satisfyingly. 'Wine tasting?'

'Yeah. Unbeknownst to all and sundry, and out of charity to our fellow inmates, young Godber and me have been fermenting illicit liquor since last July. We done this so it would reach its peak maturity at this festive season.'

McLaren shook his head in unashamed admiration. 'Fletch, you're a marvel. You're a naffing marvel, you know that?'

I lowered my eyes modestly. 'Yeah, well – '

Lennie said plaintively : 'I helped him as well.'

'And are you dishing the stuff out, like?' Warren asked eagerly.

'You mustn't take that word "charity" too literally, Bunny. This is a business transaction. You are here to obtain a free sample sip and then place orders for your fellow felons. Lennie?'

The lad trotted obediently to cubicle number two, stood on the seat and extracted from the cistern two different bottles of precious liquor.

'We are offering two selections,' I continued. 'We have the five star in the white bottle and two star in the blue bottle.'

At this moment, 'Tinker' Brown, who was minding, stuck his head in and said 'Oi!'. Lennie immediately slammed the door of his cubicle from the inside and the rest of us, like a well-drilled platoon, hit the urinals and stood in a convincing row with our hands in the appropriate position. A screw entered, prowled around for a minute or so and then, satisfied, departed again. The auction got back into swing.

'Now,' I continued, 'as I was saying, the two star is the van ordinairy, though I might say it ain't that ordinary. The five star is our special reserve. We'll sample that first.'

Lennie filled a bottle-cap with the colourless fluid. I

went on : 'I'd like to warn you, gentlemen, that this wine should be sipped delicately, like a fine liqueur. It should not be smashed down the throat by the mugfull. Right.'

I watched critically as the bottle-cap passed from hand to hand. Sheer delight seemed for a moment to rob the tasters of the power of speech. I said approvingly : 'I knew they'd like it, Len.'

Then Warren, surfacing with a strangled gasp, suggested : 'You should have washed the bottle out first.'

McLaren, in a faintly unnatural voice, wheezed : 'Fletcher, are you sure this stuff is fit for human consumption?'

'Candidly, I'm not. That's why I got you three nurks to test it for me.'

'This stuff's evil, Fletcher.'

'Yeah, but don't forget it's got another week to mature. Lennie, give them the two-star. I should warn you, gentlemen, that this one isn't quite so smooth. Be careful, otherwise not only will you lose the flavour and bouquet, you may lose the lining of your throat as well.'

McLaren raised the cap to his nose and sniffed. 'Smells like embrocation.'

I nodded. 'Just a hint of that, yes.'

Tulip protested : 'You could poison the whole prison, Fletcher.'

I sighed. 'It's not all that easy to get the right ingredients in here, you know. I got the potato peelings and the orange pips okay. No bother. But normally I would have avoided boot polish.'

As the howls of dismay broke out, I grinned and said quickly : 'Only a joke, only a joke.'

Warren, with the cap at his lips, asked suspiciously : 'Are you sure?'

'Of course I am,' I said firmly. Warren sipped, as I added : 'It was anti-freeze.'

Well, although the product was not quite up to the standard of the best malts, Lennie and I shifted a fair amount of it, naturally keeping a supply of the least vile batch for our own use. Now, of course, in the nick, making, or attempting to make, illicit hooch is a minor industry. Actually, the problem is not so much manufacturing the stuff as stashing it away where the screws won't find it once it's made. A good deal of ingenuity goes into this attempt. I remember a firm in A Block thought they'd found the answer with a fire extinguisher. They filled it with home-brew and inhaled a gulp from the nozzle whenever they went past. Everything was going fine until a fire broke out in the education room. It was only a small blaze but after the screws turned that particular extinguisher on it, it became a raging inferno. Still, Lennie and I felt we had found a solution to this ancient problem.

Now the Governor of Slade Prison is a strict teetotaller and hates drink worse than a bishop hates sin. He conducts unceasing war against it. For this reason we were not surprised when we returned to the old flowery a day or two later to find Barrowclough turning it over. We paused in the doorway.

'Hello, hello,' I muttered. 'I think we've got burglars.' Barrowclough turned his melancholy eye upon us. 'What's this then?' I asked.

'You're not being singled out, Fletcher. We're doing the whole block.'

'Harassment. Despicable infringement of civil liberties,' Lennie said contemptuously.

But I said politely: 'If you told us what you was looking for, Mr Barrowclough, we might be able to save you all this bother.'

He peered under the lower bunk and said: 'Drink.'

'Drink?' I asked in a shocked voice. 'You mean

alcohol? The demon rum? Mother's ruin?'

Barrowclough straightened himself up and glanced about forlornly. He looked like a cow that's been tethered just out of reach of a clump of juicy thistles.

'That's what I mean, yes.'

I shook my head. 'I'm a strict teetotaller, Mr Barrowclough.'

'Are you really, Fletcher?'

'Oh yes. Never touch tea, never have. You know something, Mr Barrowclough, the pathetic state of this country today has got more to do with tea than alcohol.'

'How do you reach that conclusion, Fletcher?'

'Because tea necessitated the tea-break and that's where the rot set in.'

'You're in no position to point the finger, Fletcher, when you've never done an honest day's work in your life.'

'Oh, that's very nice.' I appealed to Lennie. 'He's added slander now to breaking and entering.'

Lennie said indignantly : 'They've been at it all week. D'you know what they did last night? They come in the hobby shop, where we was making soft toys for orphan children, and with my own eyes I saw Mr Barrowclough disembowelling my panda.'

Barrowclough looked unhappy.

'Don't you think I felt bad about that? Just as I felt bad about sampling your food parcels.'

It was rumoured that Barrowclough had tasted a bit of Christmas cake and inadvertently devoured about three grammes of marihuana. I chuckled and said :

'I heard you felt pretty good afterwards, though.' I informed Lennie. 'They found him standing in a bucket of sand singing the Desert Song.'

Barrowclough blushed. 'Yes, well, I suggest you men get this cell tidied up.'

He hastened out and I said very loudly :

'Exit the red shadow. Charming. They don't find nothing but we get no apologies, no retraction. As you say, Len, a total infringement of civil liberties. An unjustifiable act of mistrust and suspicion.'

Lennie said softly : 'They didn't find nowt, though.'

I also lowered my voice. 'Course not, we hid it too well. Shut the door and fetch your mug.'

Lennie got his mug and I got mine. Then I stationed myself at the head of the bunks.

'Evening, sir,' I said. 'And what will it be?'

'The usual,' Lennie said.

'Large one?'

'Mind your own business.'

'Very good, sir.'

'And have one yourself.'

'Oh, thank you, sir.'

After this chaff, if that's the right word, I got down to business. I unscrewed a particular screw from the bedstead and – lo and cadabra ! – clear fluid gushed from the pipe-frame into Lennie's mug. It was a treat to see it. The screws poke and ferret and check and vet and spy and inspect and here, under their very noses, illicit hooch was gushing as from a sacred spring. I filled Lennie's mug and then my own. We raised these vessels, clinked them together and quaffed deep. When my scalp had landed again and the sound of cannon-fire had abated somewhat, I wheezed :

'Prisoners one, systems nil.'

But my blood, already chilled by contact with our home-brew, now froze into ice-cubes as a sinister voice behind me rasped :

'Not necessarily, Fletcher.'

I spun round, and then, possibly as a result of the fine properties of our poteen, continued spinning for a few revs. When I finally came to rest I saw what I had most dreaded : MacKay's face leering triumphantly at me. He'd got us bang to rights. I groaned :

'Oh my gawd – time, gentlemen, please ! Now then – ain't you got no cells to go to ?'

Thus it came to pass that before many moons, or even minutes, had passed, MacKay was marching Len and me into the Governor's outer office.

'Left, right, halt, face the front. Good morning, Mrs Jamieson, Mr Barrowclough – '

The recipients of these cordial salutations were, in this order, seated at her desk, frowning at a requisition, and seated on a bench cradling a large, and doubtless contraband-containing, Christmas cake on his lap. They both returned MacKay's greetings. The atmosphere seemed friendly and, thus encouraged, I began :

'Good-morning, Mrs Jamieson, you're looking very – '

'Quiet, Fletcher !' barked MacKay, shattering the seasonable mood. He asked Barrowclough : 'Is the Governor in ?'

'Well, I'm waiting to see him. He's indisposed.'

Mrs Jamieson elaborated :

'He's not feeling too well. It came on after he sampled the Christmas pudding.'

'Here, I made that,' Lennie exclaimed miffily. 'Nothing wrong with it.'

I commented :

'That's what you said about your Hungarian gluelash.'

'The word is goulash, Fletcher,' said MacKay.

'I chose the word advisedly, Mr MacKay, seeing as most of us were stuck in the bog.'

'Attention !' bellowed MacKay, and, as we snapped to it, Mr Venables, looking distinctly under-chuffed and definitely below par, tottered cautiously through the outer office towards his lair.

MacKay's countenance became wreathed in a servile smile as he addressed his chief.

'Morning, Governor.'

'Hm? Oh, good morning, Mr MacKay.'

'You're not feeling too good, I hear, sir. Very sorry.'

'Thank you, Mr MacKay. No, I'm not too good. Can't seem to settle down, if you understand me. Have to keep hurrying back and forth.' He turned to his charming secretary. 'I suppose I'd better have some more of that vile medicine, Mrs Jamieson, though it doesn't seem to have slowed me down at all so far. Right, Mr Barrowclough, you can come through, but I warn you I may not be able to stay long.'

The Governor reeled on into his inner office and Barrowclough, bearing his cake before him, followed. Mrs Jamieson produced a bottle of evil green fluid from a drawer in her desk and began pouring a tot for the Governor. I reproached Lennie.

'See what you've done? A stricken Governor. What sort of Christmas is he going to have?'

MacKay chuckled evilly.

'What sort of Christmas are you two going to have?'

I gave him a haughty glance.

'Chuffed, aren't you?' I asked.

'It's your own fault, Fletcher. You know the penalties for brewing illicit hooch.'

'That wasn't illicit hooch. It was a health drink.'

'Poppycock.'

'No, we couldn't get any poppies. Of course, there's no shortage of – '

'Fletcher!' he warned, with an apprehensive glance at Mrs Jamieson. She was still fiddling with the Governor's cocktail and didn't seem to have noticed that anything was amiss.

'I'm just saying, it was a health drink. Me and a few

hundred of the lads saved up a wine gum each. Then we crushed them in the press in the woodwork shop. The resultant extract is a remedy for all known ills.'

Lennie said enthusiastically: 'You should give the Governor some, Mrs Jamieson.'

But the lady responded with no more than a vague smile to Len's kindly suggestion. Then she took her finished preparation and tripped off into the Governor's office. Lennie and I naturally took the opportunity to inspect as much of her shapely lower limbs as became visible. This was not much but, to your imprisoned felon, even a lingering glance –

'Stop that, you two!' roared MacKay.

Lennie said wistfully, 'I've always been attracted to older women. When I was a lad, I always wanted to be seduced by my Auntie Pauline. She was very sophisticated. Worked in a dress shop in Smethwick and wore Evening in Paris behind her ears.'

I nodded sagely.

'Behind the ears, eh? Sure sign, that is.'

Lennie continued:

'I nearly was once.'

'Was what?'

'Seduced. I went round to her house and the radio was on and she said: "Lennie, it's time you learned how to do the foxtrot." Well, even at the naïve age of fourteen, I thought to myself: "Foxtrot? In the middle of the day? Yum, yum."'

I noticed that MacKay was all ears and I cautioned Lennie: 'Is this suitable for Mr MacKay, Len? He's Edinburgh Presbyterian, you know. Sex is only permitted when Hearts beat Celtic.'

MacKay snorted. 'I am not interested in Godber's carnal reminiscences.' He strode jerkily to a chair and sat down.

I said encouragingly: 'Well, I am. So what happened, Len?'

'Nothing.'

'What?'

'Nothing happened. I mean, she held me very close like, but for an hour we just danced round the living-room accompanied by the Northern Dance Orchestra.'

I sighed. 'Godber, your stories have a way of tailing off. You are the master of the anti-climax.'

'I can't half foxtrot though.'

At this point, two small incidents occurred to break the monotony. Mrs Jamieson returned from the Governor's inner office with an empty glass. She replaced it in her desk drawer and then sat down at the desk. A moment later, there was a knock at the outer door, and in came Reg Urwin, a con I knew slightly. Reg was wearing a red band on his arm and carrying a tray full of coffee and biscuits. He started slightly at seeing so many people and then muttered:

'Oh, hello, lads.'

I greeted him. 'Hello, Reg. Trusty now, are we?'

'Er, yes. Replaced Keegan, thanks to Mr MacKay.'

MacKay said piously: 'If a man keeps his nose clean, I don't forget.'

'What happened to Keegan, then?' I asked.

'The Governor had him replaced,' said Reg. 'He didn't like having a poisoner serving him his coffee.' He went on nervously: 'Should I come back later?'

'Not at all, lad,' said MacKay. 'Take the Governor his coffee. Chop, chop.'

Now for the remainder of this true-life saga, you may be surprised to find that I sometimes recount events that occurred simultaneously in the Governor's inner office and his outer office. Since I could not be in both places at once, you will wonder how I perform this feat. Moreover, for one crucial period I was, for reasons that will become clear, deep in slumber. And yet I propose to acquaint you with what was going on as I slept. How do I do it? Exactly the way your Fearless Crime Reporter does it. He spends his days pressing down the brass rail in the Fleet Street boozer. But informants come to him and tell him who's been knifing who. Then he writes it all up and gets the George Medal. I don't expect any George Medal for what's coming but I *can* vouch for its truthfulness, having checked the facts with Lennie, Barrowclough and some of the others who also lived through The Desperate Hours.

Reg Urwin, a mild-looking but somewhat distracted con, doing a very long sentence, passed on into the Governor's inner office. There he placed his tray down carefully on the Governor's desk and said humbly :

'Your coffee, sir.'

'Oh, thank you, er – '

'That's right, Urwin, sir. With a "U". I'm the new trusty.'

'That's a privileged position, Urwin.'

'I know it is, sir. That's why I've been so well-behaved the last few months. So that I could get this job and then get on with my plan.'

Venables, who had been listening in mild surprise, suddenly clutched his stomach and registered anguish. He leapt to his feet, remarking : 'I'm afraid your plan will have to wait, Urwin.'

Then he made a dash for the door. This left Urwin and Barrowclough together in the Governor's inner office. Urwin gazed after the fleeing Governor with some displeasure.

'Where's he gone?'

Barrowclough explained. 'He has a bit of an upset tummy.'

'But he was instrumental in my plan, he was,' Reg said peevishly.

'What plan is this, Urwin?'

Whereupon Reg, thinking aloud as it were, muttered : 'I suppose a screw's just as good. Yeah, I don't see why not.'

Barrowclough, now distinctly uneasy, asked more firmly : 'I said, what is your plan?'

'I want to get out of here.'

'That's what we all want, Urwin.'

'Yes, but you don't want me to get out as soon as what I do. That's why I'm taking you hostage.'

With which, Reg produced from inside his working denims a crude and obviously home-made, but still dangerous-looking, gun. This he pointed at Barrowclough who favoured the weapon with an incredulous stare. Reg explained :

'It's a gun. And it works. And it's loaded.'

Barrowclough recoiled slightly and said, 'Now, just a moment, eh – '

'Urwin – with a "U".'

'Now, Urwin, why don't you put that gun down?'

'What, so you can pick it up?'

Barrowclough gulped. 'You should think very carefully about what you're doing.'

Urwin confided : 'Oh, I have done. Endless planning. Now here's what I want you to do. First, draw them blinds. Second, get me a helicopter.'

Mr Barrowclough merely gaped causing Reg to wave his pistol irritably and urge : 'Well, get on with it !'

Meanwhile, in the outer office, I was trying it on with MacKay.

'Listen,' I urged, 'the Governor's obviously got other things on his mind. So why don't we all come back in the New Year, Mr MacKay, say around April?'

MacKay chuckled out of the corner of his mouth as if afraid that, if he opened it fully, one of us would nick his teeth.

'Fletcher, I'm in no hurry. I've waited a long time for this moment.'

'In that case,' I said resignedly, 'let's take a seat.' With which Lennie and I lowered ourselves to the bench.

MacKay, inhibited by the presence of a lady from unleashing his full bellow, uttered a strangled protest. 'Fletcher, how dare you?'

'I don't mind waiting,' Lennie piped up cheerfully. 'It's almost worth getting busted these days, just for a glimpse of Mrs Jamieson's lovely – '

'Godber!' roared MacKay.

'Smile,' concluded Lennie meekly.

MacKay hastened towards the lady. 'I apologise for these two.'

But Mrs Jamieson was serene and composed. 'That's all right, Mr MacKay. Working in prison I've learned to turn the other cheek.'

'And a very attractive cheek, too,' Lennie offered.

At this point, a new diversion occurred to break the monotony. The connecting door opened and Mr Barrowclough poked a strange pale face through it. He smiled nervously and then addressed the secretary.

'Er – Mrs Jamieson, could you get in touch with the nearest RAF station?'

The good lady gave him a puzzled look and confessed : 'I'm afraid I don't know where it is.'

'Well, the Fleet Air Arm or the Air-Sea Rescue people. The thing is, I want a helicopter.'

'Being a bit lavish with your Christmas presents, aren't you, Mr Barrowclough?' I asked cheerfully.

He favoured me with a distracted glance.

'What?'

'You'll need a lot of coloured paper to wrap that up.'

But MacKay, every inch a screw, had sensed that something was up. 'Quiet, Fletcher,' he snapped, turning to his colleague. 'Is there a problem, Mr Barrowclough?'

'Yes, Mr MacKay, something's come up.'

'Come up?'

'Yes. I'm being held at gunpoint by Urwin here.' And he gestured over his shoulder.

MacKay bridled like an outraged turkey. 'You're what?' he goggled.

Whereupon Urwin materialised behind Barrowclough, waving his handiwork. 'It's true, look.'

Mrs Jamieson uttered a faint cry, whereupon Reg bent solicitous eyes upon her. 'Don't panic, missis. Just get on the blower.'

I sighed deeply and shook my head. 'Reg, have you gone off your rocker?'

'Shut up, Fletch.'

Discretion clearly being preferable to valour at this stage, I said soothingly, 'As you say, my son.'

MacKay, never the man to be intimidated by another's peril, started to advance on the mutinous felon. 'All right, Urwin, give me that gun.'

'You make a move and Barrowclough gets it,' Urwin warned.

MacKay stopped moving but continued to bluster : 'I said, give me that gun.'

'Do shut up, MacKay,' Barrowclough wailed. 'This is no time for stupid heroics.'

'We can't let these people intimidate us.'

'That's all very well for you to say, but it's my head the gun is pointing at.'

Urwin said, 'You just naff off out of here, MacKay. I've got two hostages – him and her – so you go and put the word out, right?'

MacKay squinted at Mrs Jamieson and then at Barrowclough.

'Do as he says, man!' urged Barrowclough.

MacKay finally sighed and nodded. He moved towards the outer door.

'Very well,' he agreed. 'Now, don't panic, Mrs Jamieson, soon have you out of this. And don't you panic, Mr Barrowclough.'

'Can we panic, Mr MacKay?' I asked.

'You two come along with me,' he said firmly.

But Urwin didn't take to this scheme. He exclaimed: 'No. They stay. I can use them. Now naff off, MacKay.'

Whereupon MacKay slipped out of the office and our long ordeal began.

Mrs Jamieson, who had been consulting the phone book, announced: 'I've found the number for RAF Topcliff.'

'Get them then,' Urwin ordered.

She started to dial. Lennie and I exchanged a glance and then I addressed Urwin winningly.

'Listen, Reg, you don't really need us. We're only littering up the place. We'll just be getting back to our cell if it's all the same to you. Busy day ahead.'

But Reg wasn't having any. He waved his do-it-yourself shooter.

'No, I need you two. Lock that door, Godber.' Lennie naturally obeyed. 'Now both of you, move that filing cabinet up against it.'

We started to comply. Mrs Jamieson said: 'I have them on the line, Mr Barrowclough.'

Barrowclough, nervous as a heifer before the cattle show, asked: 'Er – should I – talk to them in the inner office?'

Urwin nodded. 'Yeah, go on.'

Whereupon Barrowclough eased himself through into

the Governor's den while Reg lounged in the doorway, covering both rooms.

'Is that all you wanted us for, Reg?' Lennie asked. 'To move the cabinet?'

'Yeah.'

'Right, well that's done. So we'll just be moseying along then.'

'Let's get this shifted, Len,' I said quickly. And we started to move the filing cabinet away from the door again but Reg, although far from top heavy, perceived something was wrong.

'Hey! Think I'm crackers or something?'

We abandoned the cabinet. I shook my head sadly. 'It *is* possible, Reg. Your behaviour ain't exactly that of a rational man.'

He said stoutly, 'I know what I'm doing. Give me that key. Now, we'll just sit tight and wait.'

Mrs Jamieson remarked: 'I have a dental appointment in half an hour.'

'Then you'll have to bleeding cancel it,' Urwin said impatiently.

Meanwhile, in the inner office Barrowclough had established contact with RAF Topcliff.

'Hello? Yes, this is Prison Officer Barrowclough of Slade Prison and I'd like to speak to your commanding officer. What's that, Flight Sergeant? I realise there's only two shopping days left to Christmas but this happens to be a matter of some urgency.'

Urwin seized the phone from Barrowclough's moist hand.

'Listen here,' he began unceremoniously, 'this is Reg Urwin with a "U". I'm in charge. I've got the gun. I'm holding a man and a woman as hostages. Now, I don't care how you do it, but I want a chopper here in half an hour. And – don't go away. I also want ten thousand quid in used notes. Otherwise I'm not responsible for my actions.' With which persuasive offer, he slammed down the phone and remarked to Barrowclough: 'That's the way to talk to those people. If they ring back and they're still stalling, make believe I'm going to kill you.'

'I'll try to remember that,' quavered Barrowclough.

On our side of the door, Lennie approached Mrs Jamieson. 'Bearing up?'

'Pardon?'

'Under the strain, like.'

'Oh, I'm keeping myself busy. I'm doing those little jobs one's always putting off. Helps keep my mind occupied so that I don't go to pieces.'

'Oh, not you, Mrs Jamieson. I think you're holding up extremely well. Typically British, if I may say so. Stiff upper lip. Calm under crisis and all that sort of thing.'

Mrs Jamieson beamed. 'How sweet of you to say so.'

'To be quite honest, it doesn't surprise me. I've always admired you, Mrs Jamieson. From afar, like.'

'Really? Why?'

'You remind me of my Auntie Pauline.'

'Horny little beast,' I murmured.

'He was just trying to keep my spirits up,' Mrs Jamieson protested.

There was a knock at the outer door. Without thinking, I called: 'Come in. Oh, of course, you can't, can you? Give us a hand to shift this, Lennie.'

Urwin darted in from the Governor's sanctum.

'Here, wait a minute, wait a minute, who is it?'

I transmitted this message, bawling through the door: 'Wait a minute, wait a minute, who is it?'

'It's Mr MacKay. I've brought the coffee you asked for.'

I passed this on to Reg. 'It's Mr MacKay with the coffee we asked for.'

It occurred to me that I had no recollection of any coffee having been requested but Reg, who, as I said, is not a front-runner in the IQ stakes, failed to sniff any rats.

'All right,' he said, 'let him in – but watch it.'

I shouted, 'All right, you can come in. But watch it.'

Lennie and I shifted the naffing filing cabinet once more and opened the door with the key which Reg had handed over. MacKay stood there with a tray, looking like the head waiter in a doss house. He handed over the delicious and, I strongly suspected, doctored fluid and then glanced quickly about to see if bodies littered the floor.

'Is everything all right in there, Fletcher?' he asked.

But Reg, brandishing his improvised cannon, stormed forwards. 'Everything's all right. So naff off, MacKay.'

MacKay, pulling back, remarked, 'I can't believe a thing like this is happening in my prison. And at Christmas.'

I said sardonically : 'It's all right for you lot out there. Just remember it's us what are going through this terrifying ordeal.'

'That'll do, Fletch,' Urwin commanded. 'Lock the door, give me the key and put the cabinet back.'

As I began to comply, I whispered : 'Mr MacKay, one last thing. Could you do me a favour?'

He frowned and hissed back : 'What is it, Fletcher?'

'I left my socks soaking in the basin. Could you wring them out for me?'

And I pushed the door shut on his outraged gasp. Then Lennie and I battened down the hatches again and returned the key to Reg. He took it and went back into the inner office to have some coffee. When he got there, he found that Barrowclough had already poured it out into the mugs provided.

'Here we are, Urwin,' said the tense screw, handing over a mug.

'Ta,' grunted Urwin, taking the mug and quaffing deep.

Lennie and I entered respectfully.

'Fletcher, Godber,' invited Barrowclough, 'take a mug and help yourselves to sugar.'

We helped ourselves and I retreated with the treat to a retreat by the fireplace.

'Well, I must say, this is nice – very nice,' I observed. 'Never thought I'd be given coffee by a screw.'

'In the Governor's office, too,' Lennie added.

Barrowclough shook his head.

'Barriers tend to come down in situations like this.'

'You don't mind if I sit, then?'

'Go ahead,' said Reg.

I seated myself and took a swig. 'Here's to you, Reg. Wherever you ends up.'

Lennie asked : 'Where will you go, Reg?'

'Somewhere a long way away where they don't ask too many questions and don't care who I am as long as I can pay for it.'

'You mean somewhere corrupt where they turn a blind eye if you grease their palm?'

'Like,' I suggested, 'the Isle of Wight?'

Reg mused. 'I was thinking of South America or Mexico – somewhere like that.'

I nodded. 'Oh yeah, funny country, Mexico. Very Mexican. Apparently all the dogs limp.'

Mrs Jamieson looked surprised. 'I didn't know that.'

'Oh yes, well-known fact. Something to do with the food.'

'Food?' Lennie asked sceptically.

'Right. Bloke gets up in the morning, contemplates his horrible breakfast, and kicks the dog.'

Reg frowned, not certain as to how to take this information. 'Really?' he asked. 'I'd always rather fancied Mexico.'

I shook my head. 'No. Contrary to travel brochure myth, they're not a happy people. I suppose any country which has tequila as its national drink is bent on self-destruction.'

Reg nodded, as he finished his cup of coffee. 'I appreciate your advice, Fletch. Maybe I'll think of somewhere else.'

At this point, Barrowclough exclaimed : 'You won't be going anywhere, Urwin.'

Reg jumped and swung round with his Peacemaker. 'What?'

Barrowclough smiled with what seemed on the face of it unlikely confidence. He seized Urwin's empty mug and flourished it.

'Don't you think we have well-rehearsed precautions for emergencies like this? Don't you worry, Mrs Jamieson, you and I will not be going South of the Border down Mexico way today.'

Reg glanced about uneasily. 'What you on about?'

Barrowclough bored on.

'Didn't it puzzle you that I was being so polite, handing out the coffee? That was because one of those mugs was laced with a powerful tranquilliser which acts very swiftly, and in a few moments, Urwin, in a few moments you will be happily asleep in the land of nod.'

This was, of course, exactly what I had anticipated. As if in confirmation of Mr Barrowclough's promise, a loud snore echoed round the room. I smiled. But a moment later, I opened my eyes with a jerk and gazed at Barrowclough in fury. The snore had issued from my own mouth! The blundering nurk had only mixed up the – my eyes sagged shut again. I passed out.

Meanwhile, an anxious conference was in progress outside the main door. Venables, who had just arrived, asked MacKay: 'Any word yet?'

'Not yet, no sir. But everything's under control. The rest of the prison is quiet. All the cells are locked. Cup of tea, sir?'

'No, no. So the men have no idea what's going on?'

'They know something's up. They probably think someone's gone over the wall.'

'We must keep the lid on this thing.'

MacKay glanced at his watch. 'That stuff should have worked by now. I put enough in to knock out a rhinoceros.'

Venables moaned: 'I still can't believe this is happening here. Where did he get the gun?'

'Probably made it. He's spent a lot of time in the machine shop has Urwin, and now one can see why.'

The phone rang. MacKay leapt upon it eagerly.

'Hello? Mr Barrowclough? Is everything – oh, Urwin! Yes – sorry – I meant – *Mr* Urwin. Yes, I – very well. Yes, I'll remember that.'

Grinding his teeth in impotent fury, MacKay replaced the phone. Venables demanded: 'What's happened?'

'Urwin says thank you for the coffee. It perked him up. Fletcher, on the other hand, is sleeping like a rhinoceros.'

In the inner office, where I was slumped unconscious, the phone rang. Mrs Jamieson answered it.

'Hello? Oh – just one moment.'

Urwin darted eagerly through the door. 'Is that for me?'

'I'm afraid not.' Mrs Jamieson rose demurely and proceeded to the connecting door. She addressed the captive screw. 'It's your wife, Mr Barrowclough.'

The news seemed to do nothing to ease the poor fellow's burden. 'Oh dear,' he gulped. 'How does she sound?'

'Same as usual.'

Barrowclough repeated : 'Oh dear.' He asked Urwin, 'May I?'

'Be my guest.'

Barrowclough went to the telephone. 'Hello, dear? What? No, I haven't forgotten but I think I should tell you there's a chance I may be late this evening . . . Now, just a minute, Alice . . . Alice, if you'd give me a moment to explain – I know I've been late three times this week already, but I'm being held at gunpoint as a hostage . . . Yes, I know we're supposed to visit Mrs Wainwright at eight . . . Yes, I admit it's rude and inconsiderate, but I may be going abroad in a helicopter . . . Alice, will you please pay attention – yes, I did say at gunpoint . . . Who? Well, there's Mrs Jamieson, two prisoners and myself . . . What do you mean, "Is that woman going with you?" Of course she's going too. We've neither of us got much choice. Of course I'm not delighted. Oh, look, this is pointless. I'll try and call later but if I don't I suggest you watch the six o'clock news.'

Urwin, although not blessed with a razor intellect, had noticed that, during this conversation, Mrs Jamieson had turned pink and retreated into the outer office. He grinned at poor Barrowclough.

'So your old lady reckons you and Mrs Jamieson have got a little thing going, eh, Barra?'

Barrowclough said firmly, but with a giveaway glance in the lady's direction, 'Certainly not.'

Urwin grinned lewdly. 'I bet she don't believe you've been working all these late shifts.'

Lennie said judiciously, 'Now, Reg, this thing going between Mr Barrowclough and Mrs Jamieson is sheer speculation.'

Barrowclough protested. 'There is no "thing", Godber. Our relationship is purely professional.'

Mrs Jamieson entered briskly and began clearing the desk. She remarked, 'I'll just take these cups out, Mr Barrowclough.'

Reg grinned. 'No need to be so formal with him, love. We know all about you two.'

Mrs Jamieson dropped a mug and turned fiercely on poor Barrowclough. 'Henry! How could you!'

'Dorothy, I never said a word.'

'Well, it certainly never came from my lips.'

And she turned and stormed out of the inner office. As she did so, she inadvertently gave me a light kick on the ankle and this, together with the fact that I have a powerful constitution and was in a very uncomfortable position, was enough to restore a glimmer of consciousness. My eyes flickered open.

'Where am I?' I murmured.

I heard Lennie's voice somewhere a long way off. 'We're in the Governor's office, remember, Fletcher?'

I rose swaying to my feet and saluted. I mumbled: 'Oh yes, sir, about Mr MacKay's allegations. Godber and me weren't drunk. We never drink. I admit we chew the occasional sock but –'

It became difficult to continue because I found I was swaying like a sapling in the breeze. I focused with care and found that Lennie was shaking me.

'Fletch, Fletch – the Governor isn't here. Don't you remember?' And he jerked a finger towards a figure in the middle distance. I readjusted my vision and someone I knew slightly swam into sight.

'Hello, Reg,' I greeted him. 'Are you the new Governor?'

He smiled. 'So you're awake again, Fletch. I'm hijacking Barrowclough.'

'Oh yes? How could I have nodded off and missed all the fun?'

Barrowclough explained glumly: 'The coffee you drank was drugged.'

'Drugged?'

'It was meant for Reg, but Barrowclough mucked it up,' Lennie amplified.

I became aware that my stomach seemed to be trying to do a knees-up and I sagged back in the chair. 'I do feel a bit queer.'

'Could be dangerous, Fletch,' said Lennie helpfully. 'Those drugs on top of all the booze we had.'

Barrowclough turned on us. 'Thank you, Godber, I'll remember that.'

Before I could say anything, Mrs Jamieson tripped in with a transistor radio. 'Listen, we're on "The World at One",' she said excitedly.

A tinny voice came from the tiny set:

'A government spokesman said that the Home Secretary could not be reached for comment regarding the situation at Slade Prison. Details are still confused, but it appears that the Governor's secretary, Mrs Dorothy Jamieson' – at which the good lady blushed with pleasure and lowered her eyes modestly – 'and a prison officer are being held at gunpoint by three desperate prisoners –'

I rose to protest indignantly, felt my stomach make an attempt on the Olympic high-jump record, and sank down again. The ignorant nurk continued: 'They are demanding transportation and a large sum of money. In the City today, shares –'

Urwin clicked the set into silence.

'What's this about *three* desperate men?' I managed to say.

Barrowclough said soothingly: 'They said that details were confused.'

'And the next thing you know, they'll be issuing names.'

'What's my family going to think?' Lennie said in an aggrieved voice.

'What's my wife going to think?' I added.

'I only hope,' sighed Barrowclough, 'that she shows a little more consideration than mine.'

But just then Urwin, who had been frowning in quite a good imitation of a man deep in thought, exclaimed: 'Hey, hey, hey! Never mind your naffing families. What about me? It's on the wireless so everybody knows about it. So why am I still stuck here? Where's my helicopter?'

Reg seemed to be getting a trifle het up. Sick as I was, I knew that someone would have to calm him down and no one else seemed either willing or able. I rose unsteadily to my feet.

'Here, Reg, a word of caution. Don't build your hopes too high, my son.'

'What d'you mean?'

'Well, I think you should get used to the idea that they may not play ball. I mean, put yourself in their shoes. They have to demonstrate to an anxious public that they ain't going to bow down to every nutter with a gun and fly him off to sunnier climes.'

I was aware that this speech was not up to the loftiest standards of diplomacy but then how would Kissinger make out if he had to bring about world peace with a skinful of home-brew and tranquillisers? Reg sputtered indignantly: 'Here! I'm no nutter.'

I said soothingly: 'I'm just taking the Establishment viewpoint, Reg. Nothing personal, you understand.'

'Another thing,' Lennie pointed out. 'Ten thousand is a lot of money, Reg.'

'Doesn't seem an excessive amount for a prison officer with twenty-three years of unblemished service,' Barrowclough said bitterly.

Reg began to get my drift. He said nervously: 'Let me

get this straight. What you're saying like is they're calling my bluff? They haven't been taking me seriously?'

Barrowclough, unwisely in my opinion, declared: 'That's right, Urwin. And there's nothing you can do about it.'

Reg was not in agreement. He remarked: 'There *is* one thing I could do.'

'What?'

Reg levelled his shooter at the dismayed screw. 'I could shoot you.'

Barrowclough seemed to perceive the force of this. He gulped: 'Yes, yes, I suppose you could do that.'

I commented, with what I hoped was just the right amount of emphasis: 'Wouldn't advise it, Reg. Any wave of public sympathy you might be attracting would go right out of the window if you was to maim a screw.'

Lennie supported me. 'You should listen to Fletch, Reg, and just keep cool.'

I pressed on. 'That's the ticket, son. Because I have been through this before, you see.'

'Have you?' Reg asked doubtfully.

Barrowclough gave me a sceptical look. Then, as much to gain time as anything, I spun them a yarn.

'Yeah. First nick I was in. There was this bloke Popplewell. He was a trusty like you, Reg. That's how he come to be on an outside work party. Repainting the Governor's house. Well, the next thing we knew he was barricaded in there with Mrs Bailey.'

'Mrs Bailey?' asked Barrowclough wonderingly, as if I'd said "Mrs Stalin".

'Yeah. Mrs Bailey, the Governor's wife. That was her name. It's a difficult tale I admit but try to follow it. The Governor's name was Bailey and this lady was married to him, so she was Mrs Bailey. All straightened out now?'

Lennie asked brightly : 'Was the Governor known as Old Bailey?'

I sighed. 'Do you want to tell this story, Godber?'

'I'm sorry, Fletch.'

'Yeah, well – '

'Please go on, Fletch.'

'Don't know if I can now. I've lost the thread.'

But Urwin was apparently on the edge of his seat. He pointed his Mauser and urged : 'Get on with it.'

'All right, all right. Well now, before you could say Jack the Ripper the house was surrounded by the screws, and the bogies, and of course there was newspapers and television cameras. If I remember rightly, even Fyfe Robertson turned up. Anyhow, for three days all sorts of people made appeals to Popplewell – the Governor, the Chaplain and the psychiatrist. But there was never a word from either him or Mrs Bailey. You remember Mrs Bailey, Mr Barrowclough?'

'All right, Fletcher. What happened?'

'What happened? On the fourth day Mrs Bailey released him.'

Like I said, Reg would be unlikely to get the point of a joke if it poked his eye out, but I *was* disappointed with Lennie and Barrowclough. They just stared at me blankly.

'You seem to be implying that *she* was holding *him*. Why was that, Fletch?' Lennie asked.

I sighed and admitted : 'Well, to use a catchphrase what was prevalent at the time, she'd never had it so good.'

And my effort had done some good, too. Reg seemed a bit further from flash-point. He sat down and gazed accusingly at the telephone. And we sat and gazed at Reg.

Some twenty minutes later, I nudged Lennie. I rose and ambled into the outer office. He followed me.

'You all right, Mrs Jamieson?' I asked the lady when we got there.

She nodded and then inquired : 'What's happening in there?'

Lennie informed her. 'We've won a small victory. He's extended his deadline till five o'clock.'

We all looked at the big wall-clock. It said half-past four. Mrs Jamieson said briskly : 'That's good. Then I'll probably have time to finish this filing before he shoots us all. Or must I expect a fate worse than death?'

'Is there a fate worse than death?' I grunted.

Mrs Jamieson considered this for a moment. Then shook her head. 'No, I don't suppose there is.'

I glanced at the dividing door, lowered my voice and asked her : 'Are these the prisoners' files? In this cabinet?'

'Yes.'

'Just fish Urwin's out for me, would you?'

'Why?'

'Might be useful. Never know. Have a quick shifty, Len. I'll go and distract Al Capone.'

I ambled back into the inner office as Lennie and Mrs Jamieson began rummaging through the files.

As I entered, Urwin looked up and said wildly : 'Listen, I'm getting bloody angry now. When are we going to get some action around here?'

Barrowclough said quickly : 'I'm still waiting to hear from the Governor, as you know.'

'Well, I can't wait much longer. Just remember that.'

It was clearly time for me to have another go at shuttle diplomacy. I said earnestly, 'Reg, you seem kind of tense.'

He shook his head. He looked desperate. 'I got to get out, Fletch. Can't take any more.'

Barrowclough moaned : 'That's exactly how I feel.'

Reg swung round on him. 'You feel like that after half a day. I've been in stir half me life.'

Barrowclough tried to sound reasonable. 'But you're up for parole soon, Urwin.'

'They won't give it to me. Not a snowball's. They never have and they never will. And I just got to get out of here.'

'But why this way, Reg?' I asked.

'Because if I stay inside much longer, I'm going to top myself.'

'Suicide? You wouldn't do that, would you?'

'I tried it once before.'

I asked, trying to keep the tone conversational: 'Oh yes? How'd you make out?'

'I failed, didn't I? Typical. I was in a supermarket, trying to steal a tin of pork luncheon meat. Suddenly I thought: 'Is this what my life has come to? Stealing luncheon meat?'

'You tried to kill yourself in a supermarket? How?'

'I just put me head down and charged towards the glass doors.'

'And what went wrong?'

'They was electric. I ran head first into an off-duty cop. He booked me for nicking a tin of pork luncheon meat.'

I shook my head sadly. 'There's always one about when you don't need one. What you should realise, Reg, is you're one of those people who just doesn't get the breaks. Not even with glass doors. Today's typical. Obviously you've been planning to hijack the Governor for months. And the day you choose, he gets the runs.'

Just then I noticed Lennie in the doorway. He beckoned. Reg was deep in despair and did not notice me amble out again.

Lennie seemed quite excited. He handed me a file and urged: 'Just read that, Fletch.'

I began to do so. Lennie explained: 'Three times in

the past two years Urwin's been recommended for psychiatric treatment.'

I nodded grimly. 'And he never got it, did he? Well, it's the system what did this to Reg. I'll have to talk to him. Mrs Jamieson, would you come through here a minute, please?'

I led her through to the inner office where I requested : 'Sit down, love.' Then I turned to Urwin. 'Reg, can you come through and have a word with me and Godber? Private like?'

He seemed a bit uneasy about it. 'I dunno.'

'Come on, Reg,' said Lennie. 'These two can't get up to nowt. Well, maybe they can, but I don't think they'd want to with us in the next room.'

Urwin sighed. 'Okay then.'

Lennie dropped the file in front of Barrowclough and whispered : 'Read this – it should interest you.' Then he followed Reg and me back into the outer office.

I said : 'Here, Reg, sit down. You trust me, don't you?'

'Maybe.'

But he sat down. I said earnestly : 'Well, I've got to tell you, son. You ain't going to make it.'

He returned sadly : 'Got to make it, Fletch. I'm a three-time loser.'

I shook my head. 'I swear to you, there ain't no way. They got all the arguments on their side. Worst thing that could happen is if they say O.K. Because you know you'd never make it to that helicopter. They've got blokes out there could shoot a fly's eyebrows off at four hundred yards. Know what I mean? And say you got to Mexico. Where next? Look at you. You think you're going to check in to the Acapulco Hilton looking like that?'

Lennie, not very helpfully, contributed : 'They'd never let you in without a tie.'

I bent over Reg in a fatherly way. 'Reg, me and the

lad could have jumped you over the last few hours. But we didn't. You know why?'

'Why?'

'Because that would have dropped you in even further than what you is now. They have to see that you chucked in the towel yourself. Voluntary, like. Look, I won't lie to you. They're going to throw the book at you. But I've been reading your file. You've got some kind of case – but only if you give yourself up.'

He shifted uneasily. Then he shook his head. 'No, Fletch. I'm going through with it.'

'Think, Reg!'

'No!' He stood up. 'I'm going the distance.'

I sighed deeply, squared my shoulders and planted myself in front of him. 'In that case, you leaves me no choice. I'm going to have to take that gun off of you.'

He gaped. 'You're what?'

He backed away, brandishing the weapon. I said quietly : 'Give me the gun, Reg.'

I closed in on him slowly. I could see, out of the corner of my eye, Lennie goggling in amazement.

Urwin shouted : 'Stay where you are, Fletch.'

I shook my head. 'Reg, you're my mucker. You ain't going to shoot me.'

He aimed the gun, straight at my heart. 'Don't bank on it.'

Lennie said urgently : 'Hey, Fletch, give over! He's serious.'

But I kept advancing. 'Not to worry. Reg and me is mates.'

'Don't push it, mate,' suggested Reg.

I was only a couple of feet from him now. Very slowly I raised my hand – and pushed my finger up the barrel of his home-made gun. Reg gazed at me in anguish. I reached out my other hand and took the weapon from him. He collapsed in a chair, a beaten man. I put my arm round him.

'Now, Reg, on your feet, son. Don't let go. Now's the time you have to be in control.'

'What's the point?' he moaned.

'Every point. Mustn't let Barra think we overcame you. You go in there and tell him this was your decision. And Len and me will back you up.'

'He's right, Reg,' said Lennie. 'It's your only chance.'

Urwin glanced at us dubiously. 'You'd back me up?'

I assured him. 'Course we will. Like I said, we're still on the side of us. There's still them and us.'

Reg shook his head. 'But you two could be heroes. For what you two have just done, you could probably get a free pardon.'

At the words, my brain whirled. He was probably right and all. To march out of Slade Nick, get a train to London, spend Christmas with the family and – I looked at Lennie. From the faraway look on his face, I could see that similar pictures were floating before his eyes.

'What d'you think, Len?'

He sighed and shrugged. 'It is Christmas, after all.'

'Good will to all men and all that swaddling? Yeah.' I turned to Reg. 'On your way, son.'

He nodded. 'Maybe you're right, Fletch. Maybe this is the best way. But I'm still calling the shots, aren't I?'

As he got to his feet and started towards the door, I assured him : 'Course you are, Reg. Main thing is, you didn't shoot the shots.'

He opened the door and went into the other room. 'Mr Barrowclough – ' The door closed after him.

Lennie looked at me. 'Fletch, you are a ruddy marvel. I've never seen anything like it.'

He was gazing at me, his eyes alight with hero worship. It was a very satisfying moment.

'Oh – the gun, you mean? Well, that wasn't really –'

Lennie cut me off. 'No, don't denigrate what you just done. I never see anything like it. Not even in *Kojak*.'

I took up Reg's home-made pistol and weighed it in my hand. Gratifying though it was to have Godber treating me like a mixture of Wild Bill Hickock and Solomon, I knew it wouldn't survive an official examination of the evidence. I sighed and confessed :

'Yeah, well I had an advantage over Lollipop head, didn't I? I knew the gun weren't loaded.'

'Wasn't it?' asked Lennie wonderingly.

'No. I been working in the machine shop with Reg. He's been making that gun for months. It's only a toy.'

Lennie took the gun from me and peered at it. 'You knew that all along?'

'Yes, but as I just said, if I'd mentioned it, I'd have dropped him deeper in the clarts.'

I took the gun back. Lennie shook his head and remarked : 'It looks very authentic to me. Are you sure it's a toy?'

I nodded. 'Course I am. Look.'

I pointed the imitation toy pistol at the ceiling and pulled the trigger. There was a bang like Big Bertha going off and about half the ceiling clattered down on our heads. I damn near fainted.

That evening, I was putting up a paper chain in the cosy dell when Barrowclough strolled in.

'Evening, Fletcher,' he said cordially.

'Oh, hello, Mr Barrowclough.'

He studied the paper chain. 'This is very nice. Is Godber about?'

'No, he wanted to prove that his Christmas pudding was not the cause of the Governor's indisposition. So he ate three helpings to vindicate his reputation.'

'I see. And where is he then?'

'In the bog.'

'Poor lad. And how are you feeling after our terrible ordeal?'

'I'm all right, Mr Barrowclough. But me and the lads are still a bit concerned about Reg Urwin.' I pulled a chair to the right spot, got up on it and added a new bit of paper chain.

'I have been assured that Urwin will be undergoing psychiatric treatment. He will not be punished so much as helped.'

'Yeah – well – not before time.'

'And I had a word with the Governor and in appreciation of your conduct the charges against you and Godber will be dropped.'

I got down from the chair. 'Charges? Oh, you mean those unfounded allegations about us making booze? Well, that's only right and proper, that is.'

'Enough said, Fletcher.'

'Yeah, but we don't get our booze back, do we?'

Barrowclough seemed uneasy as if there was something else on his mind which he was finding difficulty in mentioning. I tried to help.

'Something bothering you, Mr Barrowclough?'

'What? No, certainly not – nothing at all, except possibly that I would like to think that you could forget certain things that may have been revealed during those desperate hours.'

I contemplated the paper chain. It wasn't hanging right. I got up on the chair again. 'Like what?'

'Well, th – er – the rather delicate matter of Mrs Jamieson and myself. I'd like it to go no further.'

I said innocently : 'No idea what you're on about, Mr Barrowclough.'

I descended once more to cell level. Barrowclough seemed chuffed. 'That's the spirit, Fletcher.'

'If you're trying to tell me there's something I'm supposed to forget, I think you're overlooking the fact that I was asleep most of the time. Didn't hear a thing.'

Barrowclough's jaw dropped. I half expected a cud to fall out.

'You mean – you didn't know about myself and Mrs Jamieson?'

'No, sir, I didn't. But don't worry – I do now, Henry.'

A Storm in a Teacup

What's *your* idea of life in the nick? I'm assuming you've never done any bird, that you belong to that happy section of the community which has never been nobbled. Well, how do you imagine it?

When I ask people – during my spells on the outside, naturally – how they think of life behind bars, I always get the same kind of answer: boring, monotonous, routine. And I would never deny it. There *is* a great deal of boredom, monotony and routine inside. But it is not the whole truth! I would like to emphasise that. It is far from the complete Maud and Ruth! You may have had a day or even a week of boredom, monotony and routine and then – kapow! – you find yourself in the middle of an uproar that would make the Battle of the Somme look like a rest cure.

The Great Pill Hunt started like that. It built up gradually, step by step, without my even perceiving, for a long time, that I was getting involved. Then suddenly Harry Grout was on the doorstep and my life was trembling in the balance. Here's how it went and see if you can spot the stages by which Nemesis – or do I mean Genesis? – some bloke with a big meat-hook – or was it a scythe? – began to tailgate me.

'What are you reading, Fletch?'

I sighed. I have a hospitable nature, very similar to those of the Southern gentlemen I was trying to read about, but I do sometimes crave privacy. Unfortunately, the idea that your home is your castle has never caught on in the nick. Villains and criminals tend, between the hours of lock-up, to treat your home as their own and it is considered doubtful manners to request them to depart. So for the last ten minutes, I had been struggling to keep my attention on my book while acutely conscious that Bunny Warren was seated opposite me.

'What are you reading, Fletch?' he had finally asked.

'A book.'

Irony is, of course, wasted on Bunny but it had the effect of easing my own feelings somewhat. He inquired earnestly : 'No, I meant what sort of book?'

'A paperback sort of book. It consists, Bunny, of lots of bits of paper stuck together down the left-hand side.'

'Is it a good book?'

'I won't know that until I've finished it, will I? And that's going to be a hell of a long time if I get these continual interruptions.'

Warren brooded wistfully and then remarked, 'I'd read books too, if I could read.'

'Still, leaves you more time for deep thinking, don't it?' I said encouragingly.

A faint leer stole across Warren's face, making him look like a dissolute hare, and he asked : 'Here, Fletch, is it a dirty book?'

'Yeah, filthy. I dropped it in the mud on the way back from lunch.'

McLaren arrived then. Just like Warren – not a word of : are you free? Or : could I just have a word with you? Or : sorry to disturb. Not a bit. He just slouched into the old dell and gave it the once over.

'Reading a book, Fletch?' he inquired.

'No, I'm ironing.' But the sooty Scot seemed as impervious to irony as Warren. He actually had the once-a-week to come and read over my shoulder. I said indignantly : 'Would you mind not doing that? Height of bad manners, that is.'

But he just shrugged, sat down and studied the soiled cover of my treasure.

'*Mandingo?* What's that about then?'

'Curiously enough, it's about your lot. Slaves in the deep south.'

'Scottish slaves, are they?'

'Blacks, sonny Jock. Your ancestors. Toiling in the cotton fields.'

'My ancestors are from the West Indies. Half of them are.'

'Same kind of thing. This lot picked cotton. Your lot picked sugar cane or bananas. Comes down to the same thing. A load of blacks toiling in the fields under the hot sun picking things.'

Warren, revealing an unexpected streak of scholarship, remarked, 'I thought slaves were in Roman times. In galleys, rowing like.'

I nodded. 'Well yes, them was your galley slaves.'

Bunny shook his head and groaned. It was obvious he was getting out of his depth. 'But they was white. I know they was because I've seen them in films. Set in Roman times. And they always had slaves in them. And Rosanna Podesta. And Steve Reeves. Did you ever see Jason and the Golden Fleas?'

I laid aside *Mandingo* with a sigh. 'Fleece would be the word you had in mind, Warren, assuming you had a mind.'

'Was Tony Curtis in that one? He's often a Roman.'

'You just don't know your history, Bunny. Tony Curtis hangs about in Ancient Baghdad.'

'What was that other film about Jason? A real smasher that was – oh yes, Jason and the Astronauts.'

McLaren and I exchanged a weary glance. Then McLaren growled: 'You dim nurk, Warren. You mean Jason and the Juggernauts.'

I stood up resolutely. 'If you'll excuse me, Philip Jenkinson, I think this is where I came in. It's the bit where Rod Steiger hits Sidney Poitier over the head with a chamber-pot because he wants to read his book *in peace*!'

This time McLaren, whose intelligence, being about average, towers above Bunny's, got the message. He said apologetically : 'Sorry, Fletch – we're just going.'

'No, get your money's worth. Stay for the final shoot-out. With any luck Jason there might get his argonauts blown off.'

I grabbed up my cup of tea and my book and headed out. As I left, I heard a final intellectual exchange between them.

Warren remarked : 'I didn't think they had guns then.'
'When?'
'Well – like – in the days of Kirk Douglas.'

So there I was, banished from my cell and looking for a quiet spot to have a read. Well, of course, there ain't no quiet spots in the nick so I wound up inevitably in that paradise of rest and recreation, the association area, with its festive benches and tables and dog-eared Monopoly set. There I planted myself next to Lukewarm, one of our dear queens, who was knitting himself a winter bra or something, and again opened my book. But – and this is the point ! – fate was already at work. If I hadn't been driven from the dell, I would never have become enmeshed with Grouty and his wayward schemes.

Lukewarm remarked affably : 'Reading a book, Fletch?'

'Oh Gawd, don't you start. Just carry on with your balaclava. There might be another war. In fact, there will be if I don't finish this book.'

But at that point a sound that would have caused a fearless white hunter, accustomed to the hideous noises of the jungle, to freeze in his steps with paling lips, smote our ears. We both looked up at the landing, from whence it had issued. There we beheld that most terrible of predators, the dread MacKay. He was even now closing in on his pathetic prey, little Harris, the slimiest con man of them all. I noticed that Harris still had his arm in a sling as a result of having offended one of the snout barons.

'Stand where you are, Harris!'

'Me, Mr MacKay?'

'Yes, you. Don't move.'

Whereupon the savage creature, eyes glaring and jaws slavering, bore down on the huddled shape.

'Harris, you've been to the medical room.'

'Yes, sir. Just had me plaster changed like.'

'The orderly thinks you may have palmed some pills.'

'Not me, sir.'

'And if you have, by heaven, I'll find them.'

And MacKay naturally started to frisk Harris. I turned to Lukewarm and remarked: 'Never a dull moment.'

Just then a drop of something flew into my eye. I glanced up to see if a half-witted sparrow had come amongst us but all I could discern was MacKay fondling Harris. However, much later in the day I recalled that tiny splash. Enough said?

MacKay, who had had a disappointing grope, snarled: 'Come with me, Harris.'

The one addressed, who had apparently recovered his usual bravado, squealed:

'Listen, I'm clean. You got no right. This is harassment.'

'I'll harass you, Harris, I'm going to strip you down.'

Lukewarm remarked wistfully: 'Some girls have all the luck.' Then he continued: 'He'd whip anything, Harris would. Don't know what he wants with pills.'

'Oh, come on, Lukewarm,' I remonstrated. 'You know

the racket in here. Always someone who wants to be picked up or zonked out. Can't see it meself. Not my cup of tea, drugs.'

This set Lukewarm off. He began recounting an apparently endless tale about his last boy friend's tragic enslavement to some pills known as 'pink whispers'. Still yearning for a read, I picked up my book and tea and stole away back to the flowery, leaving him yarning away to empty space.

'Hello, Fletch,' Lennie greeted me.

I glanced about approvingly. 'They've gone, have they?'

'Who?'

'Warren and McLaren. The Black and White Minstrels.'

'Yes. They've gone to check up on the Thief of Baghdad. They've got a bet about how much he flogged it for.' He went on, 'Hey, I did the lunches on my own today. Did you like it?' Lennie works in the kitchens.

'Yeah. What was the name of that pudding?'

'Tapioca.'

'You couldn't sneak me a dollop back here, could you?'

Lennie beamed. 'You liked it that much, did you?'

'No, but I need something to stick down the sole of me shoe.'

But Lennie was in a cheerful mood. 'I'll ignore that. Tapioca off a chef's back.'

I took a sip of my tea. It was foul. That was only to be expected but by now it was also cold. I shuddered and pushed the cup away.

Lennie asked : 'What was the kerfuffle? I heard Mac-Kay nabbed Harris.'

'Yeah. Thought he'd been pinching pills from the medical officer.'

'Had he?'

'Very likely. But MacKay didn't find anything. Harris must have stashed them.'

'Wish I knew where.'

'Oh? Why? You don't even know what they was.'

'Wouldn't matter to the blokes in here. Could sell them, like.'

'Oh yes? You'd challenge the might and monopoly of genial Harry Grout?'

Lennie shuddered slightly at the thought. 'No, perhaps not. I'd take them myself, then.'

I shook my head sadly. 'Drug addict.'

'Oh, come on, Fletch. Your generation has a lot of prejudices about drugs. It's just fear through ignorance.'

'My generation's sensible enough to know that drugs don't do no one no good no how. They're anathema to me, they are.'

'There's even drugs for that,' Lennie offered.

'What?'

'Anathema.'

'Anathema is an expression, not an ailment.'

'I know. I was only making a joke.'

'Godber,' I said, 'you have used up your joke ration for the month with that tapioca pudding.'

At this point, a hideous scream rent the air. Lennie started. 'What was that?'

'Maybe someone's gone on hunger strike and they're force-feeding him your tapioca.'

'That was a terrible scream, Fletch. Bloodcurdling.'

'Probably one of your drug addict friends taking the cold chicken cure.'

'Cold turkey.'

'Too expensive. They use chicken in here.'

Lennie went to the door and looked out. But he didn't see anything unusual. He returned to his place and remarked: 'You just don't understand, Fletch. Fear through ignorance.'

'Listen, I'm not ignorant. I'm just more aware of the abuses than you seem to be. I've seen it happen. Saw some of my comrades in arms get addicted to morphine.'

'When was this?'

'When I was in the army.'

'Why did they have morphine?'

'To ease the pain of the gunshot wounds.'

'Where was you stationed, a rifle range?'

'You're an impudent nurk, Godber. While you were safely sleeping in your Smethwick crib, some of us was doing our bit for Queen and country. In the steaming Malayan jungle at the height of the terror.'

'You told me you worked in the stores in Kuala Lumpur. There wasn't any fighting there.'

'There was in the stores. Anyway, I'm not talking about that. The point is that two of my best mates got addicted to morphine subsequent to having received gunshot wounds.'

A light of respect dawned in Lennie's eyes. 'Inflicted by the Malayan terrorists?'

'Not exactly. They shot each other in the foot to avoid meeting them.'

Lennie said haughtily: 'Comes as no surprise that that type of person was your best mate.'

'What type of person?'

'Cowards.'

'Oh, it's easy for you to talk. Not being there in the heat and stench. You heard that scream just now. When I was in hospital in Singapore, that would go on all night.'

'It's your own fault. You should have left the nurses alone.'

I reached out to give him a playful clout on the chin and froze. There in the doorway stood the man everyone recognises but no one ever claims a fiver for doing so. It's usually the other way round.

'Oh, hello, Grouty,' I said brightly, hoping my voice didn't quaver.

Lennie sprang to his feet.

'Oh, hello, Mr Grout. Sir.'

Grouty heaved himself into the flowery. 'Hello, Fletch. Goodbye, Godber.'

I could see Lennie hadn't caught on. The kid's a bit dim sometimes and, not wanting to see him provoke Grouty's ire – whatever ire may be – I signalled discreetly at him to naff off. Lennie blinked at me and then caught on.

'Oh – yeah – right,' he stammered. 'I hope you'll excuse me.'

He turned and trotted out of the dell. With a deal more cheerfulness than I felt, I said, 'What's up then, Grouty?'

Grouty seated himself and pressed the tips of his fingers together. 'I just – er – had a word with Harris.'

'Oh yeah?' I asked. Then I recalled the ghastly scream which had rent the air a little while ago. I added : 'I heard you, yes.'

'He whipped some pills.'

'Comes as no surprise.'

'He said that when MacKay frisked him, he dropped them over the landing.'

'Really?'

What Grouty was saying sounded innocent enough but somehow it made me uneasy. On the dashboard of my mind a warning light came on. At Grouty's next remark it flared out like a ruddy beacon.

'Under which there were only two people at the time.'

But I kept my cool and said innocently : 'Yeah, that's right, me and Lukewarm.'

Grouty smiled his special smile which begins just below the eyes. He said gently : 'Well, Lukewarm wouldn't, would he?'

'Wouldn't what, Grouty?'

'Take advantage. Of a windfall.'

Grouty smiled sadly. It made him look fatherly. I once saw him hold that look while Carnera Stubbins, his chief henchman at the time, broke both arms and six ribs of one of his business rivals. He went on :

'I'll explain the problem, Fletch. I want those pills back where they belong.'

'In your pocket?' I suggested.

'Dear me, no. In the M.O.'s office.'

This was a turn-up. I asked warily : 'I didn't know you shared my views on the evils of drugs, Grouty?'

'Not exactly. It's just that despicable pilfering of this nature could mess up my own pill-peddling operation.'

I shook my head. 'I never heard of that one, Grouty.'

'Very few people have. That's one of its virtues. Now, you see the problem? Unless those pills are returned, MacKay is going to ask the M.O. to do an inventory to find out what is missing. Should that happen, they'll find a lot more's missing than they ever imagined.'

I could well believe this. I could also readily grasp the nature of Grouty's problem. What I could not, for the moment, perceive was how I was going to get out of this without acquiring flexible shins.

'Couldn't you replace them from stock?' I suggested.

'I haven't got any stock. I don't keep 'em. I peddle them.'

'Yes, I see your point.'

'Well, we've got an hour.'

'Oh? An hour? We've got an hour, have we?'

'Yes. The doc's over in the married quarters lancing Mrs Barrowclough's boil. That gives us about an hour to replace the pills.'

I tried, without much confidence, a heartfelt appeal. 'Now, Grouty, you and me know each other. I give you my word, which you know is sancro – er sancto – you know it's reliable, Grouty – I give you my word that I ain't got the pills.'

But Grouty contented himself with an understanding nod. 'Not enough time to verify that, Fletch. But what's more to the point is, you're one of the few people in this nick in a position to acquire some more pills.'

'How?'

'Come on, Fletch. You work the admin. block. That means you're in touch with the Governor, secretaries, typists. See, it don't matter what sort of pills they are. Just so long as they're back in the M.O.'s office. Then I'll get the word to MacKay that the matter's been taken care of.'

'Yeah, well that will solve it. But even supposing I can do what you suggest, what sort of pills?'

'Pills is pills, Fletch. Aspirin, allergy pills, slimming pills.'

'Here – those typists are all on the pill. They're all ravers over there.'

'Now steady on, Fletch, there are limits. If you whip those and the M.O. issues them to some poor bloke with toothache, what then?'

'Stop his teeth getting pregnant, won't it?' I suggested, but Grouty didn't smile. 'Oh, I see. It's a serious matter, isn't it. Well, I can't guarantee anything, Grouty, but I'll do the best I can.'

He nodded and his nose smiled again. 'I'm sure you will, Fletch.' He turned to go and then turned back. This time his eyes joined in the fun. 'Oh, if you see any codeine, get some for Harris. It seems his arm has been playing him up.' Chuckling softly, he ambled out of one Englishman's besieged castle.

A few minutes later, Lennie returned.

'What were that all about?'

'Grouty wants me to whip some pills for him.'

'Why?'

'To replace the ones Harris whipped.'

'Well, where are the pills Harris whipped?'

'Precisely,' I said bitterly. 'Where are the peppers that Peter Piper picked? If we knew that, sonny Jim, there'd be no problem, would there? Listen, you know the druggies in here. They're your precious generation. Who's likely to have any pills?'

Lennie looked thoughtful. 'The biggest freaks are those three in the end cell in B Block. One's on pills. One's on grass. And one's on booze. We call them pillhead, pothead and –'

'I can work it out. Listen, you're off duty. Can you get to them?'

'Bit tricky. Them three work in the postage room.'

'Which doubtless explains why our mail deliveries are so erratic.'

'Barrowclough has lots of pills.'

'He has?'

'All sorts. Nerve pills, indigestion pills, and he's also a vitamin freak. I should think when he makes love he rattles.'

'Well, he won't be doing much rattling at present. His old lady has a boil in a very nasty place.'

'Where?' Lennie asked eagerly.

'The screws' married quarters. What's more the M.O. is with her at this moment with his pike or lance or whatever. That's why we've got about fifty minutes to find them pills.'

'We?'

'Oh, come on, Godber. You're supposed to be my mate, aren't you?'

'I am your mate, Fletch. Always have been and always will be, I hope.'

'Then help me get some flipping pills.'

'I'd like to, Fletch, but for one thing.'

'What's that?'

The young nurk grinned. 'You told me not to have anything to do with drugs.'

I involuntarily raised my arm to give him a swift clip on the ear and just then Barrowclough waddled in. I froze. Barrowclough exclaimed : 'Fletcher!'

'What?'

'Do I see a raised arm?'

'I've no idea. Oh, you mean this arm? No, this arm is not a raised arm, Mr Barrowclough. This is a flexed arm. It's set rigid. Muscular stress. A nervous condition. I wish I had something for nerves. A pill or something.'

'I have pills for my nerves.'

'What an incredible coincidence.' I lowered my arm with much difficulty. 'Are you telling me, Mr Barrowclough, you have something which can alleviate my suffering?'

'Well, I don't carry them around with me.'

'You don't? No, I noticed you weren't rattling.'

'They're on prescription, you see. They're only mild tranquillisers, but they help me cope with the horrors of life.'

'Really? How is Mrs Barrowclough?'

'Not too good, I'm afraid. As you know, she's not the easiest of women to live with at the best of times but now that she can't sit down.'

'So that's where it is.'

'What?'

'The boil.'

Barrowclough blinked in surprise. 'How did you know about my wife's boil?'

'Oh, it just leaked out.'

'We're hoping a hot poultice will help.'

'You want to slap a dollop of Godber's tapioca pudding on it. Of course, a lot of these complaints are caused by lack of vitamins. You don't have any vitamin pills do you, Mr Barrowclough?'

'Every morning I take vitamin A, vitamin B, high protein and three hundred milligrams of vitamin C. I've always been a great believer in vitamins. I think that's why I have such a good complexion.'

'That's very interesting. I suspect my nerves are caused by vitamin deficiency. You haven't any to spare, have you, Mr Barrowclough?'

'Oh, I think I have, yes. I'll bring you some in the morning.'

'Be too late then.'

'Well, your nerves aren't going to crumble overnight.'

'I was thinking more of my kneecaps.'

'I don't think I follow.'

'I shan't be able to either with broken kneecaps. No seriously, Mr Barrowclough, the main problem with my nerves and lack of vitamins is the terrible indigestion it brings on. Specially Lennie's tapioca.'

'I do me best with the ingredients I get,' Godber intruded indignantly. 'The chef said my raspberry blancmange was the finest he'd ever tasted.'

I ignored this boast. 'You don't happen to have anything for indigestion, do you, Mr Barrowclough?'

'I certainly do. Where's your mug?'

And the nurk produced from his pocket two giant alka-seltzer tablets, wrapped in foil. I shook my head. 'No use for them. They're too big.'

'Too big?'

'I mean – my digestion's so weak I can't even digest alka-seltzer.'

Barrowclough frowned maternally. He looked like a cow whose calf is running a slight fever. 'I must say you seem in pretty poor shape, Fletcher.'

'I can stand most of it. If it wasn't for the blinding headaches.'

'Fletcher, I think you'd better report on sick parade tomorrow. Get a couple of codeine from the M.O. And now I must get on.'

And he departed.

I sighed deeply. 'That was no flaming help.' Then I turned on Lennie. 'And nor was you.'

'Not talking to you,' he said sulkily.

'What?'

'Not talking to you.'

'Just proved yourself wrong. Why not?'

'Had enough of your derogatory remarks about my culinary prowess.'

'Your culinary prowess is of no consequence compared to the urgent matter at hand. Do you realise I have less than an hour to find some replacement pills.'

'Better get to work then, hadn't you?'

I uttered a bitter laugh. 'I'll not forget this, Godber.'

Lennie shrugged. 'If you can't get any, you can't. Grouty's problem, not yours.'

'Oh right. I hadn't thought of that. And I'm sure Grouty will also take on the problem of finding me a wheelchair. Listen, son, when genial Harry Grout asks a favour, it is with the clear understanding that the favour will be done. If it isn't, he takes it as a personal affront. He sends Crusher Watson round to curtail your mobility.'

'That'll solve your problem then – you'll end up in hospital. No shortage of pills there.'

I was shaking my head, more in sorrow than anger, when Harris slithered into the dell.

'Hello, Fletch.'

'You've got a bleeding nerve, Harris.'

'What?'

'Showing your face round here.'

'Why not?'

'Because you're the cause of all the bleeding trouble.'

'Okay, I took them. But I haven't got them now.'

'What do you want then?'

'I heard of your problem, Fletch. I know that Grouty has given you the favour of getting him some more pills.'

'I don't deny it.'

'I could maybe help you there.'

'How?'

'I know where I could lay me hands on some.'

'Well, why didn't you tell Grouty that in the first place?'

'It's delicate, see. Fact is, today wasn't the first time I nicked pills. But I never knew about Grouty's racket. Well, if he knew I'd taken some before – ' Harris hugged his plastered arm protectively.

'What sort of pills have you been snatching?' Lennie asked.

'All kinds. Always a market in here, isn't there? Uppers, downers, twisters, benders.'

'Let me get this straight, Harris,' I said. 'What you're saying is you've still got the proceeds of previous thefts intact?'

'Could be.'

'Which you will give to me and I will hand on to Grouty, pretending I got them elsewhere?'

'That's right. I think it's a very noble gesture on my part. Get us both out of the clarts, right?'

'Very noble, Harris. Let's have them then.'

'Hold your horses.'

'What?'

Harris smiled like a coy maiden. 'Depends, doesn't it?'

346

'Depends on what?'

'How much?'

At this dastardly remark, I felt the blood drumming in my temples. I repeated : 'How much !'

'Fair do's. I'll give you a fair price, Fletch.'

'Harris, you are – words fail me.'

Lennie said earnestly : 'Has it ever occurred to you, Harris, that there's more to life than turning a quick quid? There's things like comradeship, honour and decency?'

Harris looked dubious. 'Is there?'

I silenced Lennie with a lofty wave.

'Don't appeal to his better nature, son, because he ain't got none. There's only one language that the Harrises of this world understand and that's the language I intend to use in future negotiations.'

Harris shot me a suspicious look. 'What's that, Fletch?'

My reply was to move towards him. He began to back away. Lennie suddenly felt an urgent call of nature and hurried out of the flowery, closing the door behind him. A moment later, the long-delayed echo of the terrible scream we had heard earlier rang round the nick.

'Come in, Fletch,' called Grouty, some time later when I knocked at his palatial door. I entered, marvelling as always at the level of luxury he enjoyed in prison. Carpets, curtains, pictures, lamps, radio – the interior would not have disgraced a charming bungalow in Walthamstow. 'What kept you?'

He grinned at me and I grinned back.

'Well, you said it was a matter of urgency, Grouty. Just for the record, these aren't the original pills, which I have never seen. I had to get these ones using all my ingenuity.'

'Yes, I heard you using it, Fletch.'

'I just hope that this puts me at the bottom of your "favours to be done by" list.'

'No question, Fletch.'

'What a lunch hour. I never even finished my cup of tea. And now I've got to get back to work.'

'No peace for the wicked,' he said, lying down on his bed.

'Don't you have work to go to, Grouty?'

'I'm on light duties, Fletch. They put me in charge of the swimming pool.'

'But we ain't got one.'

Grouty nodded. 'I know.'

'Oh – clerical error, was it?'

'Something like that. That's why time hangs so heavy on my hands.'

'Oh dear me. Well, I'd best be off then. Don't want to interrupt your boredom.' I was backing deferentially towards the door when I saw them : lovely, glowing, coloured things. My mouth watered. 'Aren't those crystallised fruits, Grouty?'

He glanced indifferently at the treasure.

'Yes.'

'My favourite them.'

'Really?' asked Grouty. 'Mine too.'

The delicious edibles slipped from his thoughts. He opened the packet of pills I had brought him. 'Any idea what these are, Fletch?'

'Does it matter? You said yourself : a pill is a pill.'

'Still, you got to be careful with drugs. These could be dangerous.'

'Well, yes, best be on the safe side. Try 'em out in the Governor's tea. See you.'

And with a last wishful look at the tempting sweetmeats, I turned on my heel and departed.

When I got back to the dell, I was displeased to find

Lennie reading my paperback. Not only that but he had ensconced himself in my cosy top bunk to do so.

'What are you doing in my bunk, Godber?' I asked the impudent young nurk.

'More light up here.'

'To read *my* book by. Give it here.'

And I grabbed the volume from his grasp. He sighed and swung himself off the bunk. 'I only borrowed it.'

'Lost my place, didn't you?'

Lennie said dreamily, 'That's a good scene, Fletch, where the plantation owner gets hold of the nubile young slave girl behind the cotton gin and – '

I interrupted him indignantly. 'Just shut up, will you? Blimey, I hadn't even reached that scene. You've had a hard afternoon, haven't you?'

'I'm entitled to my rest. Up at four, me. It's no joke, you know, frying five hundred eggs at dawn.'

'You want to make one vast omelette and let them get on with it.'

I glanced about at the untidy state of the homestead. 'You could have tidied up a bit. I mean, look at this place. You haven't even washed the mugs out.'

I took them over to the sink and emptied the slops. Out of mine fell a small packet. I took it up in surprise.

'Here – what's this?'

'What's what?' asked Lennie.

'Look.' I showed him.

'Where's that come from?'

'It was in the tea.'

'Well, open it.'

I did so and emptied into my hand eight small white pills. I frowned. 'What are they?'

Lennie peered at the hoard. 'Can't be sure. Could be amphetamine. Or maybe Bennies.'

'Whose?'

'Benzedrine. How did they get in your tea?'

But I was no longer listening. I'd got it. The splash! The little splash in my eye in Funland earlier. It must have been the pills, dumped skilfully by Harris, falling into my teacup. A pulse of fury went through me. A lunch-hour of terror and intimidation and I'd had the flaming goods in my hand all the time! I exclaimed:

'These must have been Harris's. And they fell into me tea from above.'

Lennie grinned. 'Bennies from heaven.'

'Oh, belt up, Godber.'

He shook his head. 'When you think of all the trouble you went to and they was under your nose all the time.'

'So – the whole thing was a storm in a teacup.'

Just then an animal bark, readily recognisable as the voice of Mr MacKay, sounded from the landing outside.

'Move, you men! Don't lounge around on the landing!'

The voice was approaching rapidly. And I was holding a handful of terrible contrabrand. Lennie jumped up and pointed at the pills. 'Quick! Get rid of them!'

I gazed about desperately. 'Yeah, but where? If he's doing a search?'

'We'll have to swallow them.'

Just in time I slipped Lennie half and then we swallowed four each. MacKay appeared in the door before they'd even gone down.

'What's wrong with you two? You look like you've swallowed a frog.'

I gulped which helped the pills down some.

'Nothing, Mr MacKay.'

But his head swivelled like a periscope as he inspected us.

'I know when men are acting suspicious. Anything to hide, Fletcher?'

'No, sir.'

'Godber?'

'No, sir.'

There was a faint sound from floor level. I groaned inwardly. The pill container had slipped off the table. MacKay swung round like a gun-dog, only not as lovable. He pointed.

'What's that? What's that?'

'What's what, Mr MacKay?'

'Pick it up, Godber,' ordered Slade's own Führer.

Lennie did so and handed it silently to MacKay. He examined it gingerly as if afraid it might go off.

'Well? What is it?'

'Just a – a thing, sir,' I murmured feebly, wondering if the singing in my ears was a sign that the end was nigh.

'A thing that looks like a container for pills.'

Lennie contributed. 'That's right, sir. Just a couple for Fletcher's indigestion.'

I confirmed. 'I get this terrible indigestion on account of the vitamin deficiency affecting me nerve endings.'

MacKay squinted suspiciously.

'Pills are a dirty word in this prison. I nearly caught Harris with some this morning.'

'What can you expect, sir, from a nurk like Harris?'

MacKay chuckled, the way he does when a new punishment occurs to him. He remarked: 'Well, the doctor told me what they were. I can't help hoping Harris swallowed the lot.'

Lennie and I managed to exchange a glance which was not exactly brimful of cheer.

'What would happen to him, sir, if he did?' I asked.

'Hard to say for sure. They were the doctor's own pills, for worming his spaniel. All right, carry on.'

He spun round on his heel like a drill sergeant gone berserk and marched out.

I tottered to the bunks and lowered myself carefully.

In a small, hollow voice, Lennie asked : 'How do you feel, Fletch?'

'Rowf!' I replied. 'Rowf! Rowf! Rowf!'

Poetic Justice

The nick makes strange bed-fellows. Well, in fact, sharing a bed is frowned on by the authorities and I did not mean to imply anything dodgy. What I meant was that it's amazing who turns up. I know that some noble poet suggested it would be smashing if the lion was to lie down with the lamb. But does it happen? How many lions have you seen kipping with lambs? The only place it would be at all likely to occur would be in one of Her Majesty's correctional establishments if they was both doing bird. Then they would have no choice but to flock together. And that is exactly what happened when Rawley moved in with us. But, you might reasonably be expected to ask, which was the lion and which the lamb? Naturally, I have my own views but, after hearing the facts, you can decide for yourself.

It started one fine day when, apart from being an outcast felon with years of incarceration ahead of me, I hadn't a care in the world. I was strolling along the landing, singing at the top of my voice :

    'Some enchanted evening,

    You may see a stranger – '

I was not distressed by the abusive cries which issued from the cells I passed. I had just won an ounce of snout from a trustee called Turnbull and such small triumphs in the nick lift the heart like a big score on the stock exchange to your free hustler. Since I was so chuffed the blow, when it fell, was terrible indeed. Now I don't mean that some philistine stepped out of his cell and donged me with a slop bucket. Nothing so crude. Still singing, I turned into the happy home and – the song withered on my lips.

The first thing I saw was Harris's face. This was quite bad enough since it is a spectacle which has been known to cause new arrivals, doing their first spell of porridge, to cringe whimpering against the wall. But the next thing I saw was even worse. It was a bed. What, you ask, nothing so terrible about that? Do beds have sharp teeth and knobbly fists? Maybe not. But they have something worse. They have occupants. True, this particular bed was as yet unoccupied but that was, in the circumstances, far from reassuring. Am I making myself clear? In addition to the two familiar bunks in the old flowery, which are the havens of myself and my cell-mate, Lennie, there was now an additional bed. That could only mean one thing. They were putting a third into the dell. Of course, we had had rumours for weeks that, because of general overcrowding, such a calamity was on the cards. But somehow I had never thought it would strike me. The third thing I saw in my ruined home was the bovine face of Mr Barrowclough, quivering nervously in anticipation of my reaction, and the fourth thing was Lennie. I said in a steely voice.

'What have we here?'

Barrowclough bolted for the door.

'I'm just off, Fletcher.'

'Oh no,' I said, barring the way, 'you're not.'

'But, Fletcher – '

I pointed distastefully. 'What is that object?'

'What object?'

'That bed. What is it?'

'Well, it's – a bed.'

'And just why is that bed in my already overcrowded cell? Even more to the point, why is horrible Harris here? There'd better not be a connection between them.'

Harris squealed indignantly, ' 'Ere, I only brung it here.'

I turned on him. 'Good, then you can brung it out again.'

Barrowclough cleared his throat and mooed. 'Fletcher, an alarming rise in crime rates in this country has caused an extra burden on an already overworked penal system.'

'Oh yes?'

'This in turn has meant that prisons have had to stretch their already limited resources to try and accommodate the extra influx of convicted felons, which they're ill-equipped to deal with in the first place.'

I played it very cool. Nodding sympathetically, I murmured : 'Very interesting. Highly illuminating.'

Barrowclough breathed a sigh of relief. 'Well, as long as you appreciate our difficult position.'

I nodded sagely. 'I do, yes. We've all got to make the best of this difficult situation. Now shift that bed out of here.'

Barrowclough drew himself up as if rejecting the advances of some persistent bull. 'Fletcher, a new arrival is moving in here and that's that.'

'It's just not on, Mr Barrowclough. I mean, look at this place. It was designed by the same architect what done the Black Hole of Calcutta.'

'Fletcher, neither of us have any choice in the matter, so you may as well accept it as a fait accompli.'

And, since I'd carelessly shifted a few steps away from the door, he managed to slip out.

Harris glanced at me dubiously. That toad has tasted my displeasure on more than one occasion and he sensed that I was in an ugly mood. He edged towards the door. 'I'll be off then, Fletch. Bit crowded in here. I hope the three of you will be very happy.'

'Naff off, Harris,' I grunted.

As he obeyed, he courted disaster by snarling: 'Naff off yourself, Fletch. With knobs on.'

But I was too downhearted even to aim a kick at his fleeing backside. I sat down and began rolling myself a snout. Lennie remarked: 'I'm afraid the whole rhythm of our lives is in some jeopardy, Fletch.'

'Flaming outrage. What's the word, then?'

'Well, I had a word with Davey Greener who works in reception. He says there's three come in today. One of them's a bit of a mystery. Name's Rawley. He was never documented.'

This was strange. 'How do you mean?'

'The screws just whipped him off some place. No documentation, no mug shots.'

'Really?'

'Me and the lads were speculating. Reckoned he was maybe a hard case. You know, from a firm or something.'

'Not in this nick. They don't have heavies up here. Except for Harry Grout. And he won't stand no competition.'

'I think they whipped him straight up to the Governor.'

'Maybe he's a celebrity. Maybe a rock star on a drug bust and they took him off for a press conference.'

'He was no rock star. Kind of bald and plump with flat feet.'

'Might be Elton John.'

'No, he walked like a pregnant duck.'

'You should know better than that, Godber.'

'Better than what?'

'That. Drawing attention to people's physical peculiarities. I've noticed you doing it a lot recently. I was saying to Taffy, young people today are always taking the mick out of folks because they're too tall or too fat or walk with bow legs or something.'

'Who's Taffy?'

'You know him – bloke in the hobby shop. Fat guy with ears like jug handles.' And I lit my snout.

Meanwhile, back in the old Governor's office – ah but, you are asking yourself, how do I know what was transpiring in the Governor's office? I know because one of the two embarrassed middle-aged men facing each other across his desk was soon to occupy the third bed in my dell and he told me all about it later.

As soon as the orderly had withdrawn, leaving them alone, the Governor did something very surprising. He hurried round from behind his desk and, stretching out his hand, said warmly : 'Steven !'

The newly-arrived convict took his hand and shook it without enthusiasm. He said : 'Hello, Geoffrey.'

'I thought we should have a little chat before we document you. But – what can I say?'

'Perhaps the less said, the better.'

Then Mr Venables, the Governor of Slade Prison, actually got a chair and seated his new inmate. As he did so, he remarked, 'Tragic! How's Marjorie taking all this?'

'As well as can be expected. And how are you, Geoffrey?'

'Oh, I'm all right.'

'And Muriel?'

'Busy as ever. She has her committees. I have my prison.'

'Haven't seen you both for such a long time.'

The Governor exclaimed impulsively : 'You must come round to dinner.' Then he frowned and shook his head sadly. 'Oh no, of course, you won't be able to. Silly me.'

Rawley, his unlikely guest, said : 'Not unless my appeal comes through, no.'

'This whole thing is most embarrassing for me.'

Rawley smiled wryly. 'It's a little worse than that for me. The entire fabric of my life has collapsed.'

'I know, but see it from my point of view. We were at Winchester together. In the Guards together. We're members of the same club.'

'We won't **be** for much longer. They've asked for my resignation.'

'Still, our relationship is going to create a bit of a problem.'

'Is there any reason why people should become aware of it?'

'Perhaps not. There isn't anyone from the old school here, thank God.'

'There's everything else though – officers, clubmen, Rotarians. In the shower, an embezzler came up to me and gave me a Masonic handshake.'

'There you are.'

'I don't want to plead special treatment, of course, but couldn't you separate me in a single cell, with a few books?'

'Fatal. Can't have secrets in here. It would cause speculation. And resentment. Best thing is to slip you into a cell with other men.'

'But I'd be with a bunch of common criminals.'

Mr Venables coughed discreetly. 'With due respect, Steven, since the verdict you *are* a common criminal.'

Rawley said excitedly, 'Surely you can do something. We went through the war together.'

'Only the last three months.'

'Have you forgotten that I saved your life?'

Venables considered this for a moment and then admitted : 'Yes.'

'What, you've forgotten Paris? Armistice night? The George the Fifth hotel? We were both pie-eyed and I stopped you falling down a lift shaft.'

Venables shook his head sadly. 'I don't drink, Steven. Never have.'

Rawley blinked and then sighed. 'I felt sure it was you. Must have been Thunderbox Wallis.'

At this point, the touching reunion was interrupted by a knock at the door, and in marched Mr MacKay. He shot Rawley a contemptuous look and then addressed Venables.

'You sent for me, sir?'

'Ah yes, Mr MacKay – close the door, please. Good. Now, I wanted to discuss a delicate situation with you. This is an old friend of mine, Mr Rawley, who will be with us for a while.'

MacKay, true to his nature, immediately fawned on the bald little man. 'Pleased to meet you, sir. Will you be staying for lunch?'

Rawley smiled faintly. 'If my appeal fails, I'll be staying for three years.'

Some time later, I was sitting in the day room, basking in *The Sun*. With me were Lennie, Bunny Warren and the sooty Glaswegian, McLaren. Before long, the peace and good-fellowship were broken by a reptilian sound.

''Ere, listen,' hissed Harris, ' 'ave you met your new room-mate yet?'

I sighed and kept my eyes fixed to the female form divine. 'Still have that pleasure to come.'

'Hope it isn't Turner,' Lennie remarked.

'Who?' I asked.

'Turner. One of the new arrivals. He's been on remand since Christmas. Sounds a nasty bit of work. Know what he done?'

'What?' Bunny asked.

'He mugged the Santa Claus at Selfridges.'

I shook my head in sorrow. 'What a charmless offence.'

Lennie grinned. 'He paid for it, though. What he

didn't know was that Santa Claus was an out-of-work wrestler known as Abdul the Turk.'

McLaren whistled. 'What happened?'

'Abdul gave him the aeroplane spin. Spun him from soft toys to electrical appliances.'

'Took on a wrestler once myself,' I remarked.

There were sceptical murmurs. I silenced them by saying firmly, 'Truth. I was in a transport caff on the M6. And I got into an argument with this wrestler over whose sixpence was in the jukebox. The discussion became quite heated and in the end we had a real barney.'

Lennie said: 'Straight – you took on a wrestler, Fletch?'

I nodded, the light of reminiscence shining in my eyes. 'It was a tremendous contest – but she beat me in the end.'

They all stared at me blankly. I know that wit is like the Concorde to most cons, about ten miles over their heads, but I had hoped that Lennie – then I saw the lad was gazing past me intently. He exclaimed: 'Here, that's him – the mystery man. Him with MacKay.'

Naturally I turned, and we all had a butcher's at the balding little man now approaching beside Good Deed MacKay. But at the first glance, a shiver of recognition ran down my spine. Not only of recognition but of incredulity as well. It couldn't be and yet – the distant memory formed in my mind. Three years ago – the court-room – Middlesex Assizes – it *was* him! Not the slightest doubt. MacKay barked.

'All right, you men. This is Rawley, who's moving in with Fletcher and Godber. I don't know what you have heard about him but I want you to treat him just like any other prisoner – understood?'

And having thus established that Rawley was different from other prisoners and quite certain to be treated differently, MacKay spun round on his heel and shunted off. Rawley hesitated and glanced at us diffidently. He said timidly, 'Good afternoon.'

Lennie said cheerfully, 'Afternoon. My name's Godber. You're in with us.'

Rawley nodded and attempted a little smile. I could stand it no longer. I rose to my feet and exclaimed, 'God preserve us!'

Rawley drew back a little and said, 'I'm sorry?'

Lennie, seeing that something was up, said quickly, 'Oh, this is Fletch. He's with us and all.'

'Really?' said Rawley.

I shook my head and said loudly, 'You don't remember me, do you?'

Rawley looked at me doubtfully. 'Your face is vaguely familiar, but I can't quite – '

'Middlesex Assizes? Three years ago?'

'Did you two do a job together or something?' Warren asked interestedly.

'Do a job?' I exclaimed. 'No, we didn't do a job together. He's only the judge who bleeding sent me here!'

This naturally produced not a few murmurs from the assembled felons. They gaped at Judge Rawley as a convention of vegetarians might have done if a pork butcher had intruded on them. I continued, with not a little sarcasm, 'The Honourable Judge Steven Rawley! In all his majesty. How the mighty are fallen.'

Rawley blinked unhappily. 'I'm sorry, but I still don't quite recollect – '

'Why should you? I am merely one of a thousand faces who come before you, while you weigh our lives in the balance of what you call justice!'

Rawley's perplexed expression cleared as if by magic. 'It's Fletcher, isn't it?'

'Oh, you remember now?'

He nodded vigorously. 'I remember your rhetoric. I remember your endless protestations of innocence.'

'Which you were deaf to,' I exclaimed bitterly.

'But you *were* guilty, Fletch,' Lennie said diplomatically. 'You've told us that.'

I turned on him haughtily. 'That is beside the point, Godber.'

'It did seem relevant when I passed sentence,' Rawley offered diffidently.

I addressed my fellow sufferers. 'The point is that this man was not fit to sentence me, as his presence here indicates.'

Warren said uncertainly, 'But he's still a judge. Least, he were at the time.'

'Yeah, but obviously a bent one,' McLaren countered. 'When you're sent down it's one thing knowing it's by an upright pillar of society. But Fletcher's been sent down by a fellow con.'

I nodded agreement with these sentiments.

'Thank you, Jock. This man is no different from me. How do you think I feel being sent down by a crook like me?'

'A judge inside. That's worse than mugging Santa Claus,' Lennie murmured wonderingly.

McLaren asked Rawley, a trifle belligerently. 'What did they bust you for, then?'

'Excuse me?'

'What were the charges against you?'

Rawley immediately intoned, like a Clerk of Court: 'I was indicted on three counts for corruption at common law. These were: accepting an illicit payment as an officer of the Crown; party to a criminal conspiracy; and tampering with evidence with intent to falsify, alter or destroy –'

I cut him off contemptuously.

'Yes, yes, we all know. Plain bribery and corruption. Don't camouflage it behind all that legal mumbo jumbo, Judge Rawley.'

'I have no wish to camouflage anything. As I instructed my counsel : "Let light be shed on this whole sorry affair. Let's bring it out into the open. Let there be no half-truths or evasions." '

'Well, that's refreshingly honest,' Lennie said appreciatively. 'So you're admitting you're guilty then?'

Rawley said loftily : 'I refuse to discuss the matter, pending my appeal.'

'You're bound to get off,' McLaren growled. 'Old school tie, top lawyers.'

Rawley sighed. 'If the lawyers were that good, I'd be out on bail now.'

I sniffed contemptuously. 'Listen, it's a token stretch. Most of what you call us common folk never get the chance of bail. Some blokes are inside for months pending appeal.'

'The same law sent him down what sent us down, Fletcher,' Lennie said firmly.

'What are you saying, Godber?'

'I think his presence here is very reassuring. It's a vindication of our legal system. It proves that no one is beyond the reach of the law.'

'Well, I just ask myself, for everyone of his kind they nobble how many's getting away with it? The bloke who sent him up is probably worse than he is.'

Rawley surprised us then by bursting out in an agonised voice : 'Don't you think I have a conscience? Can you imagine what it's been like, to live a lie?'

I put a stop to this sob stuff by saying firmly, 'Course we can. We're criminals. We does it all the time.'

At this point, looking like a fugitive from the stockyards, Mr Barrowclough ambled in.

'How are you lads improving the sunshine hour?'

'We was just getting aquainted with our distinguished friend,' I advised him.

Mr Barrowclough eyed us narrowly. 'Oh, you know who he is then?'

'We met professionally, so to speak.'

'I see. Well, you must treat Rawley no differently from any other prisoner.'

McLaren muttered darkly, which in a sense he can't help : 'We will if you will.'

'What's that supposed to mean, McLaren?'

'Don't show no favours.'

'Rawley will get no favours from me.' The soft-hearted but determined screw addressed the erstwhile judge. 'Whatever you were before, you're just a number now. A statistic. A set of fingerprints. You're a mug shot, like the rest of these men. You'll pay your dues to society the same way they do. Is that understood?'

Rawley nodded. 'Yes.'

Barrowclough frowned. 'Yes, what?'

'Yes, Mr Barrowclough,' Lennie whispered.

Rawley quickly amended, 'Yes, Mr Barrowclough.'

The screw nodded in satisfaction. 'That's better. Now we must see about getting you a job. Could you come this way, please, your honour?'

That night, I returned to the flowery after taking a shower and found Godber making up Rawley's bed. I stopped aghast. In fact, after Barrowclough's kow-towing earlier, I felt I'd stopped two or three ghasts. I said severely :

'Just what are you doing, Godber?'

'Oh, just making his bed up. He couldn't do it himself.'

'Well, I suggest you encourage him to bleeding learn. Either that or get yourself a little frilly apron.'

'Oh, come on, Fletch, go easy on him. He's lonely. He's afraid. Just like I was, me first night.'

'He's the enemy within. Within my cell, what's more!'

'No he ain't, Fletch. He *was* a judge but now he's a con like the rest of us.'

This innocence disgusted me. 'Don't you believe it. He's the establishment, he is. And I don't fancy the establishment breathing down my neck all day and all night. You must admit it's a bit unusual, Godber.'

'What is?'

'Well, when a judge sentences you to five years, you don't expect him to come in with you.'

At this moment, the fallen magistrate entered. 'Oh, you've made my bed up, Godber? That's most kind.'

'Ovaltine or Horlicks, your honour?' I asked solicitously.

'Excuse me?'

'And what colour do you want your brown shoes polished?'

'Leave off, Fletch,' Lennie urged.

But my justifiable resentment at having to kip with my natural enemy would not permit it. I said sarcastically: 'I suppose you've just been having a nightcap with the Governor?'

Rawley shook his head resentfully. 'Look, I have no influence with the Governor. If I had, I'd be in a single cell with a few books instead of sharing a cell with people like – '

His voice trailed off in confusion, as they say. I concluded the line for him.

'People like us – go on, say it! Listen, let me tell you something about people like us. We don't make no alibis. We deserve to be here. But compared to you, there's something very honest about our dishonesty. Because the worst sort of crime hides behind a mask of respectability.

Some people – people like us – have no way of getting things except to take them. People like you had it all, but it wasn't enough. You wanted more.'

He hung his head.

'I have no defence. Everything you say is completely true. I've been a fool and a hypocrite. But it's not been easy to live with. If you knew the sleepless nights I've spent.'

'Oh yes, I can picture you, tossing and turning on that king-sized Slumberland in that palatial mansion. Personally, I could put up with a little insomnia, if I had a croquet lawn and a tennis court and a Rolls-Royce. That would cushion the pain of a guilty conscience, wouldn't it, Lennie?'

But Rawley protested : 'I don't drive a Rolls-Royce. I've made do with the same Mercedes for three years now.'

'Oh, you poor deprived nurk.'

Lennie surprised me by saying heatedly, 'Pack it in, Fletch. He's a criminal now. Are you saying only the poor and underprivileged like us have any right to be one? Don't the rich have a right to be criminals as well?'

'They better not try. The unions would be on to them straightaway.'

'Oh, don't be stupid.'

'You're being stupid, Godber, and also naïve.'

'I'm just annoyed because you're so inconsistent, Fletch.'

'I'm what?'

'Inconsistent in your attitude. Inside is not out there. Inside's another world. And once inside, anybody has the right to prove himself an OK bloke. *You* told me that. That's why we should never ask what a bloke's in for. So we don't prejudice their chance of making it in here. We're all equal. We only have one enemy, that's the screws. And we only have one purpose in life, that's screwing the system.'

Well, naturally I was pleased that my tuition had been so effective but I felt the lad could have chosen a better moment to demonstrate it.

'Very eloquent all of a sudden, aren't you, son?'

'He's one of us now. That's all I'm saying.'

Rawley plucked up his courage to say: 'The boy is right. I know we've always been on opposite sides of the fence. You're the sort of people I'd normally cross the street to avoid. But the fence is down now.'

I sighed and shook my head. 'I still think the gulf between us is immeasurably wide. I mean, Lennie and me, and most of the lads in here, we come from the same background, ran the same streets. They're a little different from your streets. Your streets have rich kids riding round on bicycles waving tennis rackets. Rows of elm trees and hand-carved privet hedges. Don't have no problems on your streets.'

'Yes, we do. I had to spend fifteen hundred pounds last year on Dutch elm disease.'

'Yeah, and I bet you took your elms to Harley Street, didn't you?'

Rawley said humbly, 'Look, I know you're bound to feel cynical. I understand your attitude, but we all have one thing in common – we're in trouble.'

Lennie supported him. 'He's right, Fletch.'

'Okay, I'm just clearing the air, just letting you know my feelings.'

'I promise I shall be as unobtrusive as possible,' Rawley announced.

I looked at his bed which was about as unobtrusive as a helicopter on a tennis court.

'Well, get yourself a hammock then.'

As I started to undress for another prison night, Lennie

tried to reassure Rawley. 'He's a miserable old git. Listen, these are the rules of the house. Top bunk's his. Seniority like. No one reads the paper till he's through with it. It's best to speak only when spoken to, and his is the tooth-paste with the marked tube.'

'I have my own toilet requisites,' Rawley said.

'Just as well,' I grunted.

'Never borrow anything of Fletcher's without express permission,' Lennie urged.

I felt that criticism was implied. 'I am not mean, God-ber, if that's what you're hinting. It's just that I don't believe in giving anybody anything. What one has one keeps.'

'Oh, come on, Fletch,' Lennie protested. 'You *are* mean.'

'No, I'm not. Thrifty perhaps. Frugal. Necessary survival technique in here.'

Lennie, unnecessarily I felt, informed Rawley, 'He unwraps Bounty Bars under water so I can't hear he's got one.'

Rawley said smugly: 'I'll be only too willing to share any of the few things they've allowed me to keep.'

This was too good an opportunity. 'Like I said, bribery and corruption. He's at it again.'

'I only meant – '

'Just get yourself to bed, will you, Judge Jeffreys.'

Rawley made a last attempt at conciliation. 'Well, let me say that whatever rules you make, I will go along with them.'

As I hoisted myself up to my bunk, I heard Lennie explain: 'Oh, we're very democratic in here. Fletcher decides and we agree.'

The screw on night duty slammed the cell door.

I turned to the *Sun*. There was a fascinating story in it about a dog that some villain had trained to nick handbags. They'd caught the dog but not the owner and the police were thinking of bringing the animal to trial. It seemed this was still possible according to some ancient law. How do you plead? Wowf, wowf! As I marvelled, I listened at the same time to the conversation between Lennie and Rawley.

'Want some snout?' Lennie asked.

'Excuse me?'

'Should I roll you one?'

'One what?'

'A cigarette.'

'Oh, I don't, thank you. Only very occasionally.'

'It's currency in here, snout.'

'Really?' He sighed.

'You don't look too chipper.'

'Since the door slammed shut, I've realised what prison is about.'

'I know the feeling. This is my first stretch, you know. But stir's a state of mind and survival's in your own head. His highness up there taught me that. The first year is the worst and – sorry, I shouldn't joke.'

'No, please, you shouldn't feel sorry for me.'

'Oh, but I do. I mean, you had a lot more to lose than the rest of us : position, respect. It's the classic story of a man who had it all and blew it all in a moment of weakness.'

I'd finished the dog story and was now intent on their conversation. I intruded sarcastically : 'This is life, not Peyton Place.'

Rawley confessed : 'My weakness was a younger woman. She was an avaricious, grasping nineteen-year-old go-go dancer.'

'Oh yes, the younger woman – typical case,' Lennie said understandingly.

'One sees it happen so many times to colleagues. What

is it – some middle-aged madness that affects us all? When I first met her, she seemed a sweet young thing. Then over the years, she demanded more and more. Trinkets, trips abroad, a car, a maisonette in South Kensington.'

'I was wrong,' I said sardonically. 'This *is* Peyton Place.'

'How did you meet her?' Lennie asked.

'At our regimental reunion.'

'Oh nice,' I said. 'She was in your regiment, was she?'

'She was part of the cabaret. She was assisting a magician called The Great Alfredo. While he was making cockatoos disappear, my eyes never left Sandra's long, shapely legs.'

'Long and shapely, were they?' Lennie asked wistfully.

'Well, you're paying for those legs now,' I said roughly. 'One glimpse of a young thigh through a fishnet stocking and look at you now.'

Lennie again tried to be diplomatic. 'Well, we're all here because of some form of human weakness. Desire, greed, lust – '

'We're all here, Godber,' I interrupted brusquely, 'because we got caught.'

'All right, but we're all in the same boat. We're all the same under the skin.'

'True. But we don't all wear fishnet tights over it.'

Rawley suddenly asked : 'You'll give me a trial then, Fletcher?'

That tickled me. 'You mean one good trial deserves another? Oh, all right, why not? Like the kid says, we're only flesh and blood. Could work out. I remember in the army they put a rich kid in our billet. He'd been to the best schools. Had all the privileges we so sadly lacked. And suddenly there he was with a bunch of strangers. In fact, in the next bed to him was Alfie Wright, who'd been the leader of one of the biggest gangs of Teds in South London – a real hard case. Well, we treated the rich kid just like everyone else, and you know what? Every week when his daddy's allowance come, he shared it with the rest of us.'

'He did?' Rawley asked wonderingly.

'Yeah. If he hadn't, Alfie would have stove his head in. Good night, your honour.'

The next morning, as I scrubbed the old Hampsteads, I caught sight of Rawley's toilet sundries spread out before me. I rinsed, spat, marked my tube and then commented :

'You can tell we have the upper classes with us. Have you had a butcher's at these toiletries, Len? Mustang talc for men. Rave d'Armour shaving cream. And exhibit C, a badger's hair shaving brush. My God, no wonder you never see a badger these days.'

Lennie attempted to deflect my sarcasm. 'Nocturnal animal, the badger.'

'What?'

'Nocturnal. Only comes out at night.'

'Course they do. They've learnt their lesson, haven't they? If they come out during the day, people make shaving brushes out of them.'

Rawley said deferentially, 'You're more than welcome to use any of my things.'

'No, thank you. And *you* better not use them either, if you know what's good for you.'

'Why?'

'Any idea what effect Mustang will have on the fairies in here?'

There was the harsh sound of bolts being withdrawn. The door creaked open and the hideous, yellow-fanged face of MacKay intruded.

'Good morning, Rawley. How did you sleep?'

'Oh, listen to this,' I exclaimed bitterly. 'All the time I been inside you never asked me how I slept.'

'I know how you sleep, Fletcher. You sleep soundly because you have no conscience, no shame, no guilt.'

'All the things which explain my sleepless night,' Rawley said miserably.

MacKay said briskly: 'You'll have the weekend to settle in. It's Saturday today and you will stop work at noon. Then the rest of the day is your own.'

'I'll take you to the football match if you like,' Lennie offered.

'I'm quite prepared to work on. Helps kill the time.'

'Here,' I protested, 'if you wants to be one of us, you knocks off when we knocks off.'

'Typical prison mentality,' MacKay sneered.

'Wrong. Typical working-class mentality.'

He chuckled evilly. 'Are you saying you consider yourself *working* class, Fletcher?'

'Well, I always used to. Till I went to Glasgow one time. Then I realised I was middle class.'

'That'll be enough, Fletcher!'

Rawley, struggling to blend with his new background, explained: 'All I meant was I rather enjoyed the work you assigned me to.'

I observed: 'Of course you do. Central records. Privilege, that is.'

'No, it's not, Fletcher,' MacKay snapped.

'What, are you saying it's not one of the cushiest numbers in this nick?'

'No, I admit that. But that does not mean it's a privilege.'

'Well, which would you rather do, Mr MacKay, Central Records or latrine duty? Can't sit and read in the latrines, can you? Well, you can but it gets boring reading: now wash your hands, over and over. But Rawley here : one day inside and he scores a job most trustees don't get.'

'He's an educated man. Isn't it logical we should give him a job which requires a clerical aptitude?'

'And since when has logic had anything to do with job allocation? Who was making the blancmange in the canteen yesterday? Riggs, and he's in here for poisoning.'

'Is he?' asked Lennie uneasily.

'Certainly. Cause celebre he was in his home town of Ashton-under-Lyme. Most of his in-laws are under lime now.'

'Is that why they call him arsenic Riggs?'

'No, that's because he once sat on a razor-blade, you nurk.'

MacKay said to Rawley : 'I'm sorry, Rawley, that you're forced to share a cell with riff-raff.'

Rawley said hastily : 'No, they've been most kind and considerate.'

'I hope so. Because I'm aware of the situation, Fletcher, between you and ex-Justice Rawley. But there will be no malice. No vindictiveness. No grudges borne from bitter memory.'

'Grudge? How could I bear a grudge? What has this man ever done to me – except rob me of the best five years of my life?'

With which parting shot I turned and stormed out of the dell.

That afternoon, I breezed into the day room with a copy of *Hare and Hounds,* which I'd just liberated from the screws' common room, under my arm. This periodical was not for reading, since I am not a devotee of the chase, although occasionally a victim of it, but for swapping with a con called Knapton for snout. This Knapton used to be a game warden before he was apprehended in Southampton trying to flog hides to sailors. However,

Knapton proved to be absent. In fact, very few cons were there but those few were arranged in a way which immediately attracted my attention. Four of them – McLaren, Harris and two louts from B Block – were formed in a ring around Rawley who was looking from one to the other of them in a terrified kind of way. Sussing the situation at once, I exclaimed loudly :

'Hello, hello, what's this then? Gunfight at the O.K. Corral?'

Slimy Harris squealed : 'No need to bother yourself, Fletch.'

I replied smoothly : 'Oh, but I do bother, my son. This is my cell block and I'm a long-time resident. And I can tell when something's up.'

McLaren said over his shoulder, while continuing to close in on Rawley : 'He's got it coming, Fletch. And you'll be a prime suspect when he gets it, as he's about to. So get yourself across the yard and out of harm's way. We're doing you a favour, man.'

'Are you about to inflict damage on my cellmate?' I asked.

'Your what?' asked Harris incredulously.

'My cellmate. The bloke with which I share a cell.'

McLaren, still advancing, growled : 'He's no friend of yours.'

'He don't have to be a friend. But he's one of us now, and we looks after our own, don't we?'

McLaren ceased stalking and turned to me with a puzzled glance. 'What are you saying, Fletch?'

'I'm just saying if you takes him on, you takes me on and all. And don't be misled by this bulky torso. It conceals muscles of steel.'

They gaped at me. Then Harris waved something that looked like a deformed butter knife and which he'd probably run up in handicrafts.

'I've got a blade, Fletch.'

'Yeah, well, you'd need one, wouldn't you, Harris? I on the other hand have this rather large volume with which I would happily knock your brains out – if only you had some.'

McLaren sighed. 'Fletch, you're my mate. I don't want to mix it with you.'

'I was banking on that. I hoped that reason and common sense would prevail over your Celtic passion for mayhem and violence.' Judging the moment was right, I said steadily to Rawley : 'On your way, judge.'

He asked nervously, 'On my way where?'

'Out into the yard. Go and watch the football. The word'll go round. No one will lay a finger on you.'

He nodded gratefully and slipped away. Harris brandished his knife in frustration and whined : 'That's a naffing turn-up.'

McLaren said : 'If Fletch wants it that way, that's it. But I would just like to know why. Fletch, what are you doing siding with the establishment?'

'You knows me better than that. It's just that I uses me head. D'you know what this is?' And I held up the large volume I was carrying and winked meaningfully at them.

'What? What?' asked Harris.

'No, not "what, what" – "Who's Who". Now, I've been looking up Rawley. And checking it against the Governor's entry. You want to know something? They only went to the same school, were in the same regiment and belong to the same club. They're life-long bleeding oppos, those two.'

Harris, who has the lightning intellect of a tortoise, wailed : 'That makes it worse.'

'Does it really? Do we whet our appetite for blood or do we agree that what this cell block has always lacked is a life-long friend of the Governor's? Well, Harris, which?'

He gazed at me with furrowed brow. And then, although his eyes did not fill with a wild surmise, a faint nodding of the head made me suspect some glimmer of understanding might be getting through. The others stared at me with respect verging on awe. Then Harris suddenly got the full beauty of it and squealed with delight. Or maybe it was because I'd just dropped "Who's Who" on his foot.

That night, at bedtime, I leaned over the recumbent judge. 'Comfy, your honour? Want another pillow?'

The nurk accepted it and eased it behind his judicial head. 'Oh, thank you.'

'Extra blanket?'

'No, thank you. I'm warm enough.'

'If you're scared of the cockroaches, we can take turns watching out for them,' Lennie contributed.

'You're both very kind. And let me say again, Fletcher, how much I appreciate what you did for me.'

'S'all right. A man in here has a right to prove himself.'

Lennie, sounding faintly aggrieved, protested : 'Here. I said that first.'

'Yeah, but you got it from me, didn't you?'

Rawley said emotionally : 'You, more than anyone, Fletcher, had every right to despise me.'

'No point in that, your worship. No, you just lie back and reminisce about happier times. Tell us about you and the Governor, for example. That should while away a few hours.'

A faint note of caution entered his voice. 'Myself and the Governor?'

I kept it casual. 'Didn't I hear something somewhere that you once knew each other? Or something?'

'Oh, we've known each other for years.'

Lennie said, with assumed innocence, 'What a coincidence.'

Rawley looked from one to the other of us with dawning suspicion. 'I hope this doesn't explain your change of attitude, Fletcher.'

'What?'

'I trust you're not hoping to profit from my past relationship with Geo – with the Governor. Because I must warn you that anything I know about him is in the strictest confidence.'

His tone displeased me. 'Is that so? I'll have me pillow back then.' And I relieved him of it and started to undress.

Rawley sighed and said : 'Fletcher.'

'What?'

'I *am* grateful. I do appreciate what you did today.'

I kept my voice haughty. 'Not all that grateful obviously.'

Whereupon the amazing nurk extended an arm from his pit and invited : 'Shake?'

'What?'

'Shake.'

'Shake what?'

'Hands. No hard feelings, that sort of thing.'

'Why should I have any hard feelings? You're only the bloke that put me in here.'

'Fletcher, I had no choice,' Rawley pleaded.

'Course you did. Several. You could have rejected the jury's verdict. Ordered a retrial. Given me a suspended sentence. Probation. Bound me over.'

'Not in the face of the evidence.'

'And not,' Lennie added, 'with your record, Fletch.'

I thought this over for a moment and then nodded. 'I suppose you're right. But if only I'd known then what I know now.'

Rawley sounded pleased. He said, 'Oh, that is reassuring.'

'What is?' I asked.

'Remorse.'

I leaned over him and my eyes bored into his.

'Remorse? It's nothing to do with remorse. It's just that if I'd known you was bent, I'd have made you an offer you wouldn't have refused. Happy dreams, your honour.'

Rough Justice

I looked up from the letter I was writing and asked:
'What d'you want, Warren?'

The thing is, I had me back to the door. So how did
I know who it was? Puzzles me sometimes. Can it be
that your incarcerated male develops some incredible
sixth sense which enables him to perceive psychic vibra-
tions undetectable to the free citizen? Or is it just that
Bunny has a strong pong? Any old how, I was right, as
the piping voice from behind me confirmed.

'I need a letter written. Home like.'

I sighed and turned. 'Warren, how long have you been
inside?'

'Nigh on ten months now.'

'Well, don't you think you'd have been well advised to
take advantage of the educational facilities here and got
rid of your illiteracy?'

'I'm not illiterate, Fletch.'

I saw no point in sparing the sarcasm. 'Forgive me, I
thought that was the word what described someone who
can't read or write.'

'I'm not illiterate. I suffer from dyslexia.'

Could this, I asked myself, account for the pong?

Bunny jeered: 'You don't know what that means, do
you?'

Honour was at stake. I said carefully: 'It's an offensive
condition connected with acid stomach. But I can see no
reason why it should stop you reading or writing.'

Bunny shook his head vigorously. 'Nothing like. Dyslexia is word blindness. I can't identify words on the

written page. They all get jumbled up in my head, you see.'

'Oh yes? Well there's plenty of room, ain't there?'

'Tragic really. If they'd diagnosed it when I were a lad, I wouldn't be in here now.'

'Oh, here we go. The customary alibi. The hard-luck story.'

'It's true in my case. I had a real tough break. You see, I couldn't read the sign.'

'What sign was this?'

'The one that said : "Warning – Burglar Alarm".'

I shook my head sadly. 'That's much the same excuse as Charlie Dill. He's that burglar in B Wing.'

'How?'

'He's deaf. He didn't hear the dog.'

'Really? I didn't know he were short of hearing.'

'That ain't all he's short of since that Airedale got him.'

Bunny glanced about moodily and retreated towards the door. 'I'll come back later.'

I said quickly : 'No, hang about. I'll do it for you. Usual rates. Half-a-snout a page.'

Warren shook his head vigorously. 'No, I weren't going to ask you.'

This was both displeasing and surprising. 'What do you mean?' I asked.

'I were going to ask your new celly, Judge Rawley.'

My indignation immediately rose. 'Why?'

'Take advantage like. He's a judge. Educated man. Oxford. Public school.'

'Oh, I see.' I shook my head bitterly. 'Suddenly bowled over by his worship's academic pedigree, you've dispensed with my literary services, have you?'

'No offence, like. I just thought he has to be the best person for the job.'

I felt that a little correcting of perspective was in order.

'Bunny, letter-writing is an art. A gift. What sort of love letter is he going to write? "My dear Carol, I am in receipt of your letter of the sixth inst., wherebeit I, the undersigned, heretoforward to be referred to as the party of the first part," and so on. He'd be all right if you want to sue her, not woo her.'

This happy phrase, as it seemed to me, had some effect on Warren. He hesitated. 'Well, I just thought – '

Naturally, I pressed my advantage. 'You just thought wrong as usual. Letter writing is a creative art, endowed only to a few of us. I mean, how many of you nurks in here have my poetic turn of phrase? For example, here's what I'm writing to my nearest and dearest. Just read that. Oh, you can't, can you?' With which, I took up my newly-completed epistle and read to him. 'My Darling, though we have been driven apart by cruel fate, and an inexcusable misdirecting of a jury by a biased judge, who is now sharing a cell with me, I know that our love transcends these grey, grim walls that have driven us apart. You are with me in my heart and this knowledge helps me to wring a few drops of comfort from the limp, damp towel of life. Kiss the baby for me, your own Norman.'

Warren, I was gratified to see, seemed impressed. 'Oh, that's beautiful, Fletch,' he exclaimed.

'Yeah, well – '

'I'm sorry, Fletch. Will you do a letter for me? When you've got a moment?'

I nodded distantly. Now that I'd got him hooked, it would be bad policy to seem too eager. 'When I've got a moment, yes. But first I've got to finish this one off and get it sent. After that, I've got to write one to the wife.'

A faint odour of expensive after-shave wafted into the dell. It was closely followed by Judge Rawley.

'Oh, good evening, Warren,' he said pleasantly.

Warren, as is his nature, immediately cringed. 'Oh, hello, judge. Your honour.' He bowed.

I said testily, 'Don't call him that. Don't smarm up to him. He is not a judge. He is a former judge, an ex-judge. He has been debenched or you might say dewigged.'

Warren shook his head dubiously. 'He's pending appeal, and you never know – '

With which, Warren prepared to take his departure. Rawley detained him. 'Oh, Warren, that matter you raised with me in the canteen. I'll give it a little thought and speak to you in the morning.'

'Oh, thank you, Judge. Night, Fletch.'

And he and his dyslexia departed.

'What little matter was this then?' I asked.

'Oh, just a legal matter. Something to do with his sister's tenancy of her council house.'

'Oh, I see. Setting up shop, are we?'

'Excuse me?'

'Steven Rawley, Q.C., is now open for business? What you charging then?'

'I'm not charging anything.'

I clicked disapprovingly. 'Well, that's daft to start with. If you have any expertise in here which is in demand, then it's saleable. Rule of the house. It's expected. And any philanthropic notions will be taken as a sign of weakness.'

Rawley seemed taken aback by these nick truths. 'I didn't realise – '

'No, well you ain't got the acumen. I'll work out your fees. We'll split 'em fifty-fifty.'

He drew himself up until his shiny pate nearly reached my chin. 'I have no intention – '

I broke in roughly. 'You will do.'

'I will not.'

He was bent but he might not scare easy. I tried persuasion. 'Listen, we could clean up. I mean, there's six hundred blokes in here, all of whom has a legal gripe. We do have an ex-solicitor across the block but he only knows about mortgages and there's not a lot of call for that in here. One thing we *are* sure of is a roof over our head. I tell you where we *could* score heavy. All the poofs in here are getting a movement together. You know, "Equal rights for Homosexuals". You're the perfect man to represent them. Queen's Counsel, ain't you?'

'I am not hawking my legal expertise to the highest bidder.'

'No need to. I do the hawking. You just dispense.'

'Out of the question. I would be mad to engage in anything of that nature until I hear the result of my appeal. Within a month I could be back on the bench. One has to preserve some sort of integrity.'

I sniffed. 'Oh, integrity, is it? I love your high moral tone, despite the disgrace you've wrought on your profession. Do get it into your head, you're now inside. Another world. It's a jungle in here. And you just happen to be fortunate enough to be sharing a cage with King Kong.'

But he stuck to his guns and in the end I let it go – for the time being.

Strange how things go in pairs, ain't it? I'd recognise Warren without seeing him and later that very day, Lennie, as he told me afterwards, had the same experience with Harris. Lennie was alone in the flowery at the time working on a model aeroplane. Why that lad's always making extra work for himself beats me but if it's not Spanish or boxing it's model-making. Anyway, he was just gluing on a fin or something when there was a horrible change in the atmosphere. Now that I come to think of it, Lennie's experience was not identical with mine. It wasn't that he recognised Harris by his pong but that he recoiled from him.

'Is that you?' Lennie gasped.

'Me what?' asked Harris.

'That pong.'

'There's a reason for this pong.'

'There'd have to be. And for your sake I hope it's curable.'

Harris said peevishly, 'They've moved me back on the naffing farm, haven't they?'

'Nice job that. Lots of exercise. Fresh air.'

'Fresh air?' echoed Harris incredulously. 'I'm swilling out the flaming pigs. You know why, don't you?'

Lennie considered it. 'Well, they try to fit people to their most appropriate function. You and pigs – that makes sense.'

'Watch your lip, Godber.'

Lennie protruded it but the task proved beyond him.

'I'll tell you why I'm on the farm,' Harris snorted. ''Cause they've been rejigging jobs round here. To accommodate your naffing V.I.P.'

'Judge Rawley?'

'That's him. And he only went straight into a clerk's job. Trustee's by right.'

Lennie, engrossed in his model building, ignored this. He mused aloud. 'Has its advantages though, the farm. Don't you get outside trips, like?'

'Oh yes,' grunted Harris bitterly. 'Only today I went for a trip in the back of a pig truck that hadn't been cleaned for three weeks, slipping about inside. We picked up six new pigs and clipped back only just in time for supper.'

'Couldn't you have had a bath?'

'This is what I smell like after a bath.'

'But didn't you see anything or anybody?'

'Yes. I'm forgetting the highlight of the day. I caught a glimpse of a woman.'

Lennie whistled. 'A female woman, really? What was she like?'

Harris shook his head in wonderment. 'Well, porridge does strange things to a man. It's the first time I've been turned on by a fifteen-stone pig-breeder.'

At this point, Warren and I arrived at the dell. The discovery that it was being polluted by one of the least savoury inhabitants of the nick did nothing for my temper. I growled, 'What are you on, Harris?'

'Social call,' he replied breezily.

Something hit me. I gasped and wrinkled my nose. 'Dear me, what's that smell?'

'Put me back on the pig farm, didn't they?'

'Yeah. I heard the pigs held a protest march. At least it takes away the smell of Godber's aeroplane glue.'

Warren, to my surprise, had been delicately sipping the air as though it was an unfamiliar but attractive vintage. He said appreciatively, 'I quite like the smell. It reminds me of home.'

'Born on a farm, was you?' I asked.

'No,' said Warren.

I turned back to the Great Pong. 'Clear off, Harris, go on. It's beginning to smell like a Turkish restaurant in here.'

Harris tried a feeble counter-attack. 'If this cell stinks, it's because of His Worship. Don't know how you stomach a bloke like that.'

But I waved him away irritably. 'On your way, Harris.'

He edged towards the door. Then, like a schoolboy, he called back as he darted away : 'We'll have him, you know. In the end, we'll have him.'

I looked after him, shaking my head, and murmured : 'Charmless nurk.'

Lennie suddenly swivelled round and cried: 'Has he whipped my aerofix?' But then his hand encountered it under some diagrams. 'Oh no, here it is.'

He resumed work. I said, with mild reproach, 'I'd be glad if you wouldn't leave that aerofix lying about, Godber. I came back last week from the shower and sat on it unbeknownst. An hour later, I had to be prized out of me underpants. Talk about a stiff upper lip.'

Warren nodded impatiently and said: 'Come on, then, Fletch, let's have me letter.'

'Let's see the snout first, then.'

Warren duly produced the agreed number of fags and, in return, I produced an envelope from under the pillow on my bunk. Bunny asked eagerly: 'Is it good?'

'It's inspired, my son.'

'You reckon Elaine will like it?'

'No question. Did you happen to notice that last night on the box, after our bedtime naturally, they was showing an old Rita Hayworth film? Well, it was called "Fire Down Below". That, my son, is exactly what your Elaine will feel when she reads this.'

Godber, who has large gaps in his education, asked: 'Who was Rita Hayworth?'

'Gawd, Godber, you are ignorant.'

He said cheerfully, 'No, I'm just young.'

'And you missed out, my son. Your deprived generation – what have you got? Twiggy and Tatum O'Neill.'

But Lennie said smugly: 'Since the Olympics, my sexual fantasies are mostly East European gymnasts.'

I smiled pityingly. 'I'm talking about *women*, my son. Your Rhonda Flemings, your Virginia Mayos. And at the top of that glorious heap of pulchritude was always – my Rita.'

'Your favourite, was she?' asked Lennie, peering at the letter.

'Still is.'

'And is that why you've put Dear Rita instead of Dear Elaine?'

I snatched up the letter. 'Have I? Oh well, lend us your pen.'

I was about to cross out the offending name when Warren protested : ' 'Ere, that's not going to look nice. She'll think I've got a Rita on me mind. She'll get jealous.'

There was justice in this. I sighed. 'Okay, Bunny, I'll copy it again for you later.'

At this point we all became aware of a kind of quiver in the air. It was like what happens in courts of justice when the bewigged magistrate is approaching and everyone prepares to leap to his feet in respect. Sure enough, a moment later Rawley strode into the dell. He was not wearing his wig and gown but nevertheless there was something imposing about him. He glanced at us briskly and said : 'Good evening.'

We returned the salutation. As he stowed his washing gear, Rawley remarked : 'In the showers, I ran across that chap from Liverpool – what's his name?'

'Harris?' Lennie suggested.

'Harris, yes. He was most abusive.'

'Take no notice of Harris,' I urged.

'But he threatened me.'

'He's all wind and water,' I explained. 'You know what he's in for, don't you? Snatching an old-age pensioner's handbag.'

'He never !' exclaimed Bunny.

'At least, he tried to,' I continued smoothly. 'She pinned him down till the cops arrived. She kept hitting him over the head with her handbag.'

Rawley looked puzzled. 'And that subdued him, you say?'

'Not half – it had a brick in it. She was on her way to do a smash-and-grab.'

'Good grief,' exclaimed the former judge.

'Don't you worry, your honour,' Lennie said encouragingly. 'If anyone comes on strong, you know we'll always back you up.'

'Yeah, we'll see you all right,' I grunted.

Rawley gazed from one to the other of us, and then said feelingly : 'You already have. I'm most grateful. You men have every right to despise me. Especially you, Fletcher, since I sent you here in the first place. But you have all shown me only kindness, compassion and sympathy. I feel a bond with you men which I know has been forged in adversity, but I think will remain with me always.'

Now this was far from your normal rabbit-and-pork in the nick where any remark more tender than 'shut your face' is likely to be regarded as an emotional outburst. We shuffled uncomfortably and I muttered : ' 'Ere, leave it off, judge. If you go on like this, you're going to make us forget our scruples and like you.'

But there was no holding him. 'I mean it. Who'd have thought a few months ago that I could so much as talk to you. Now I find that I respect you. More than that – I trust you.'

Lennie gulped and I wouldn't swear he didn't flick faintly at the corner of his eye. 'You mean that?' he asked.

'Most sincerely.' And then, possibly to spare us embarrassment, Rawley turned back to his gear. Almost immediately, he said sharply : 'Just a moment.'

'What's up?' asked Lennie.

Rawley turned back and confronted us. His voice was steely. 'Which one of you stole my watch?'

'Your what?' I asked in astonishment.

'My watch. It was there when I went to the showers and it's not there now.'

Lennie was outraged. 'Here, hold your horses. What's happened to that most sincere trust you felt for us?'

'That was before one of you stole my watch.'

This was coming it a bit strong. I moved up for a nose-to-nose confrontation and said : ' 'Ere, 'ere, 'ere, you'd better back off, your worship. We don't rip each other off. We're mates, oppos. We have a code.'

Rawley smiled grimly. 'But I'm still an outsider.'

I shrugged. 'That's true. Give him his watch, Len.'

'That's not funny, Fletch,' protested Lennie. 'I'm no petty sneak thief. Give him his watch, Warren.'

'Pardon?' blinked Bunny. 'I haven't got his naffing watch. I only come in for me letter, which I haven't had read to me yet.'

Whereupon Lennie said reproachfully to Rawley : 'See what you've done, judge? Stirred up mistrust among people who trust each other implictly. Go on, Fletch, give him his watch.'

I said silkily : 'You talking to me like that, Godber? You watch it, my son, or I'll darken your outlook.'

At this, Rawley burst out apologetically. 'I'm sorry. I'm sorry. I was being stupidly hasty. My legal training should have prevented me from making accusations without firm evidence.'

'Never bothered the law in my hometown,' muttered Bunny.

Rawley continued : 'But I swear to you, my watch *was* there when I went to take my shower.'

I saw the answer. 'Harris! How long was he here before I came in?'

'Long enough,' confirmed Lennie. 'He could have palmed it when I was glueing this aileron on.'

'Come on, then,' urged Warren, 'let's gerrafter him.'

I raised a restraining hand. 'Hold on, hold on, you know the crafty git will have stashed it by now.'

The piercing note of the bell which announces lock-up sounded. 'Timed his exit well and all,' Lennie observed. 'Can't go nowhere now.'

'I'll have to be off home, Fletch,' said Bunny. 'Should I not say nowt?'

I nodded. 'Yeah. Shtum, Warren.'

'Should we get him tomorrow, then, and extract a confession somewhere where his screams won't be heard?'

There was a gasp from Rawley. 'Oh no, please!' he begged. 'I've already acted irrationally. I beg you not to do the same. We have no proof – '

I cut him short. 'Just a minute, your honour, d'you mind?' I turned to Warren. 'Okay, Bunny. Saturday tomorrow, football, visitors, lot of diversions. We'll need a quiet room, but we'll also need an eye-out, won't we? Tell you what, ask Frankie Lovelace and Percy the Wrench if they want to make a bob or two.'

'O.K.,' agreed Warren. 'Good night all.'

He scampered off. Rawley, looking dazed, repeated : 'Percy the Wrench?'

I reassured him. 'It's all right. We only want them as minders.'

'But we cannot take the law into our own hands. I shall report the theft to the proper channels.'

I pointed out : 'In here, we are the proper channels. And we looks after our own.'

'Even if "our own" was as impulsively accusatory as what you were,' Lennie added.

Rawley shook his head sadly. 'I've told you, I regret that. And I don't want you people acting in the same impulsive manner.'

'Calm down,' I said soothingly. 'We ain't going to set upon Harris. We're going to conduct a civilised investigation. We're all familiar with the workings of the law, and we're fortunate in this instance to have a guest judge.'

'Guest judge?' asked Rawley, who seemed a bit slow on the uptake.

I elaborated. 'A member of that noble profession what you so recently besmirched. On the other hand, you do know your law.'

'You mean,' asked Rawley doubtfully, 'we're going to have a hearing?'

'A trial, my son.'

'But do we have enough to go on?'

Lennie explained. 'Yes. Harris's reputation.'

Rawley frowned. 'I know he's objectionable, but is he a known thief?'

I rebuked him. 'You should know better than to ask that. We might tell you things which would prejudice your impartiality, know what I mean?'

'Innocent till proven guilty, like,' Lennie offered.

Rawley said hastily, 'Of course. Of course. The less I know about Harris the better.'

'That's right,' I encouraged him. 'Why should you want to know about him? A despicable nurk that would sell his Granny's wintergreen.' I noticed Rawley shaking his head disapprovingly. 'Oh, sorry – let that be stricken from the record, your honour.'

As we started undressing for bed, Lennie asked : 'Are you going to prosecute, Fletch?'

'Certainly. Should be interesting seeing the other side of the fence, like.'

'But,' asked Rawley, 'do you know enough about legal procedure?'

I laughed mirthlessly. 'Been up enough, ain't I? Look, when you choose your living breaking the law, it pays to know the laws you're bleeding breaking. And I've had enough first-hand experience with counsels. Clever men, most of them. Although my last one weren't too bright, as my presence in this nick indicates.'

Rawley cleared his throat and then said hesitantly: 'As the presiding judge at your trial, Fletcher, I thought your counsel argued eloquently against impossible odds.'

I heard Lennie titter.

'Godber!' I warned. Then I turned back to Rawley. 'Listen, my counsel was a loser going in. And I ain't referring to the evidence. I'm talking about his attitude. Before the trial, he comes to see me in Brixton, doesn't he? And you know what the pompous git says? I couldn't believe it.'

'What?' asked Lennie.

I delivered it in the wig-in-the-mouth voice all them barristers use. ' "I should like you to know that myself and my staff shall dispose ourselves with the utmost vigour and dedication in refuting the charges against you. Investigators will pursue a tenacious enquiry into unearthing evidence and testimony. Researchers will work into the night assembling and collating the facts at our disposal, on which I shall marshall a defence which has left no stone unturned, no avenue unexplored and which will culminate in your honourable and justifiable release. In the meantime, please proceed with your escape plan." '

The next day, court was convened in the B Wing boiler room. This place had not been designed with trials in view and a certain amount of improvisation proved necessary. We smuggled in a table and some chairs and shovelled the coke into a heap against the wall.

Rawley gazed about miserably at his new court-room. He commented : 'This is most irregular. I cannot say I'm happy about these proceedings, Fletcher.'

'Yeah, well, happiness is relative, isn't it?' I pointed

out. 'I mean, this is nick. Who's happy, know what I mean?'

Lennie gestured deferentially towards the table and asked: 'Would you like to assume your customary seat behind the bench, your honour?'

As Rawley hesitated, I urged, 'Go on, park your backside.'

Lennie said, 'We should have got him a wig.'

'We could have borrowed one from one of the Transylvanians in here,' said Warren.

I clicked reprovingly. 'The word, Warren, is transvestite. You are a nurk, ain't you? A Transylvanian is someone in a horror film.'

'Which describes most of this nick's transvestites,' Lennie pointed out.

'All right, smarty, but there's nothing very judicial about a platinum blonde wig shaped like a bleeding beehive, is there? Because that is what your ambidexterers wear round here.'

Warren, who was minding at the door, hissed: 'Hey up – here comes the accused.'

'Under escort is he?' I asked.

Warren nodded. 'Yeah. Black Jock's got him in a half nelson.'

I prodded Rawley, who still did not seem completely reconciled to the judicial proceedings. 'Do sit down, your honour. Court is convened.'

As he did so, Harris stumbled into the chamber in the vice-like grip of McLaren. As soon as he saw us, the defendant burst out: 'Here, here, what's going on then? You got no flaming right – '

'Silence in court!' I bellowed in his ear.

'What?'

'Harris, sit down.' McLaren dumped him in a chair. 'Now, Harris, as the prisoner at the bar you are entitled to know what these proceedings are in aid of. We are here to pursue the course of justice and find you guilty.'

There was a groan from the bench. 'Fletcher, please,' protested Rawley.

Lennie said quickly, 'None of us heard that. Well, if we did, it's stricken from our minds.'

Harris bleated : 'What is?'

'The fact that you're guilty.'

'Here, listen – '

I cut in swiftly : 'No, you listen, Harris. A watch has disappeared from our flowery dell, and you are the prime suspect.'

'Why me?'

'Because otherwise it's us and we're above suspicion. Right?'

'No, it's not flaming right – '

But McLaren shook the reptile, snarling : 'Shut up, you.'

Rawley bobbed to his feet and said in a strained voice : 'I must protest these – '

I waved him silent. 'All right, your honour, d'you mind? Thank you. Now, Harris, let me put your mind at rest. You shall get a fair trial. We have a qualified Judge with a long, though slightly blemished, record. We have an eye-witness.'

'Who?' asked Harris.

'Me,' replied Lennie.

I promised : 'And I am going to prosecute you. But to ensure absolute fair play, you will be defended.'

'Oh?'

'By Warren.'

'By Warren?' moaned Harris.

'What's wrong with that?' asked Bunny.

Harris pointed a finger at his new counsel but addressed the rest of us. 'He's flaming illiterate, he is.'

'He is not,' I corrected him. It is a medically-proven fact that Warren is – er – is – '

'Dyslectic,' supplied Warren.

'That's it. Dyslectic.'

Lennie said interestedly, 'I never knew that.'

Warren smiled modestly. 'Yes, for years.'

'Really? Is it contagious?'

I intervened irritably. 'For Gawd's sake, Godber, we're in a court of law.'

'Sorry, Fletch.'

Harris tried again to get his say in. ' 'Ere, listen – '

'Shut up!' urged McLaren menacingly.

'Doesn't a man have a right to speak?' demanded Harris.

I explained. 'Certainly. But in your case only when spoken to.' Then, using cunning forensic skill, I asked him : 'If you're innocent, what you in such a state about?'

'You ask me that – with Warren defending me?'

Warren felt it desirable to set the record straight. 'Here, Harris, I didn't volunteer for the job. I don't like you.'

Harris appealed bitterly to Judge Rawley. 'D'you hear this? D'you hear this?'

I said judiciously, 'It's all right, Harris. He don't have to like you to defend you. You think any of our counsels liked us?'

Lennie nodded approvingly. 'That's a good point, that is.'

'Right, Harris,' I said briskly, 'how do you plead?'

'Excuse me, Fletcher?' Rawley said desperately.

'What? Oh yes, be my guest, your honour.'

'All right then, Harris,' said Rawley to the suspect, 'how do you plead? Guilty or Not Guilty?'

'Not guilty,' affirmed Harris.

I commented sadly, 'I see – a liar as well as a thief.'

Warren called : 'Objection !'

We looked at him in some surprise, never having suspected that there might be a legal eagle buried in Bunny.

Rawley encouraged him : 'All right then, Warren, go on. What is your objection?'

Warren gazed at us blankly, his brow furrowed. Finally, he stammered, 'Er – I don't know.'

Harris prompted desperately : 'Flaming heck. You were objecting to the fact that I was called a liar and a thief.'

But Bunny shook his head resolutely. 'No, I wasn't. We all know you're a liar and a thief, Harris.'

Rawley said sternly : 'That remark should be struck from the record.'

'Unnecessary,' I pointed out, 'since there ain't no record. Now I'd like to call my first and only witness, Leonard Arthur Godber. Take the stand, would you, please.'

Lennie advanced. 'I swear to tell the truth, the whole – '

'Never mind that,' I remonstrated. 'We've got about ten minutes before the screws tumble us. Just tell us about the events of last night, Mr Godber.'

'Well, Mr Rawley took his watch off prior to going to the showers. At the time I was in our cell utilising my spare time in a constructive manner, to wit making a flying fortress. Harris come in. Then Mr Fletcher and the defending counsel entered the room, telling the accused to naff off, which he promptly did. Shortly afterwards, the watch was found not to be there and has not been seen since.'

Rawley turned to Warren, in a very official tone of voice : 'Counsel for the Defence – that's you, Warren – do you wish to cross-examine this witness?'

'Pardon?' asked Bunny.

'Do you wish to ask him any questions?'

'No, I were there. I know what happened.'

'Flaming heck,' moaned Harris, whereupon McLaren shook him again.

Rawley pronounced: 'Let him speak. He has that right.'

'Ta, judge,' said Harris. 'Now, you all know as well as me that this is a mockery. You know as well as me that all this is flaming hearsay. No one can prove nowt. Like, where's the evidence?'

Rawley nodded. 'I have to agree with him. One man's word against another's does not constitute legal evidence. This case would not stand up in a Court of Law, upon which these proceedings are supposedly modelling themselves. In the absence of evidence, there is no prima facie case and I am forced to dismiss the accused.'

Harris beamed. 'Thank you, your honour.'

'Now, hang about, Judge,' I urged. 'Who's side are you on?'

'I'm sorry, Fletcher,' apologised Rawley, 'but you insisted on a proper enquiry.'

McLaren, frustrated by these legal thickets, asked: 'Would a signed confession help?'

'Do we have one?' asked Rawley in surprise.

'I could soon get one.'

'He's threatening me!' Harris squealed.

'Good Lord,' exclaimed Rawley, 'I must protest at this intimidation – '

'Judge!' I said firmly, 'it's best you stay out of this, know what I mean?' I turned to Harris. 'Harris, we don't want no unpleasantness. So wherever you stashed the watch, go dig it out. All right? If you traded it, go trade it back. We just wants that watch back. If not, the consequences to your good self are too dire to contemplate.'

Harris gazed around at the grim faces. He asked: 'Have I definitely been found "Not Guilty"?'

I nodded. 'You have.'

'All right,' he agreed. 'I'll go and get it.'

And he did just that.

That evening, when I returned to the cell after taking three snouts off Bunny at dominoes, I found Lennie hard at work on his model.

'Evening, Fletch,' he chirped. 'Look, almost finished.' And he held up a large, but somewhat tatty, model aeroplane.

'Oh yes,' I complimented him, 'very good. How you going to get it in the bottle, then?'

'Going to hang it on the ceiling. When I was a kid I had planes all over me bedroom. Me dad made them. From the war, like. Hurricanes, Spitfires, Mess of Schmidts. That's how I know what shape a Flying Fortress was. Me Dad told me.'

'Pity he didn't tell you about what shape Rita Hayworth and Rhonda Fleming was and all.'

'No, he didn't talk much about women.'

A thought occurred to me. 'Was he all right, your Dad? Not one of them, was he?'

Lennie shook his head. 'He didn't know they existed in them days.'

'Oh yes. Your poofter just wasn't so blatant then. In *my* father's day, they used to horsewhip them, you know. Now they've become fashionable. What worries me is they might make it compulsory.'

I seated myself and withdrew a slightly greasy copy of the *Sun* from my pocket. Lennie asked: 'See his worship?'

'Heard he had a call to see the Governor.'

'What'll that be about?'

'Have to ask him, won't we?'

'Here, you don't think he'll blow the gaff, do you? About our Kangaroo Court?'

'Nah. He's learned we takes care of our own. He'll respect that.'

Lennie nodded. 'Specially since Harris gave him his watch back.'

At this point Rawley breezed into the flowery. He seemed strangely chuffed.

'Good evening, Fletch, Lennie,' he chortled.

'Evening,' returned Lennie politely.

'I'm glad you're both here because I want to thank you, and tell you that I realise now a lot of what you say is true. There are grave abuses of justice. There is often one law for the rich and powerful, and another law for the poor and oppressed. And the poor usually suffer while the rich get off with clever lawyers. But I want to promise you one thing. I shall remember that lesson when I leave here.'

'That won't be for some time, though,' I pointed out.

'Oh no,' he announced cheerfully. 'I'm going out tonight.'

Lennie dropped his model in surprise and I let the *Sun* sink.

'You're what?' asked Lennie. 'Going out?'

'Yes.'

I caught on. 'Your appeal's come through?'

Rawley had already begun to pack. He nodded happily. 'Certainly. I'm rich and powerful. I have clever lawyers.'

Later that evening, in the Association area, we were privileged to hear the last of Judge Rawley's straight-from-the-bleeding-heart addresses. Not only us but quite an assortment of the lads were there. Rawley, elegantly clad in a Judge's streetwear, was ushered in by MacKay.

'All right, you men! The Governor has kindly allowed Mr Rawley to bid you a fond farewell.'

'Oh, it's Mister now, is it?' I muttered.

'Certainly, Fletcher. If the appeal court judges say his nose is clean, that's good enough for me. They are, after all,' MacKay went on haughtily, 'men of the highest integrity in the land.'

'What are you talking about?' I asked. 'He's *one* of them.'

'Precisely. And he's innocent, which proves my point.'

I couldn't think of an answer to that one, and meanwhile Rawley cleared his throat and began :

'Er – Gentlemen, it's just that I wanted to say goodbye and thank you once more, and to promise you something. Whatever I can do to improve the system, I shall do. This has been a frightening experience for me, but, thanks to you men, a rewarding one.'

This effort was received in uneasy silence. Rawley glanced nervously around at the stony faces. I rose and held out my hand.

'Listen,' I assured him, 'you got a break. No one holds that against anybody.'

This broke the ice. There was a murmur of agreement from the lads and even one or two 'hear, hears'. We all crowded round good old Judge Rawley and Warren actually plucked up the courage to slap him on the back. Lennie urged him : 'You behave yourself now. Don't want to see you back, do we?'

Rawley stammered : 'Thank you, thank you – oh, one more thing.' He turned to me. 'Fletcher, I'd like you to have this.'

And he held out the very article which had been the cause of our show trial that afternoon. I shook my head.

'No, I don't want your watch. No need for that. Besides, only reason they allow watches in this nick is to remind us how slowly the time passes.'

Rawley insisted. 'But surely you could trade it? It's valuable.'

This was indeed a telling argument. I took the item from him and nodded. 'Oh, ta very much, then.'

Rawley smiled at us all. 'Once again then, goodbye – my friends.'

And he turned towards freedom. Lennie suddenly had an idea and detained him with the words : 'Here, Judge. When we get out, we'll come and look you up.'

Rawley hesitated and then turned back to us. I added enthusiastically : 'Yeah, talk about old times, re-establish our friendship, meet your family. Why, we could bring our wives round to meet your wife.'

Rawley's jaw dropped slightly. It was easy to see how moved he was by our suggestion. He nodded weakly.

' Yes – yes, indeed. That would be – nice – awfully nice – really – '

Then he turned and fled.

McLaren shook his head. 'Off he goes – free as a bird.'

'And free to go and find himself a bird, and all,' I pointed out.

Lennie sighed. 'While we remain behind to carry on vegetating.'

I could not refute this. 'True, Lennie, true. But I like to think we've all learned a little from his visit, albeit short. I think we may all have gained something as a result.'

'*You* have,' Lennie agreed. 'You've gained his wrist-watch.'

Bunny Warren said disgustedly, 'Needn't have bothered with that trial. Waste of time.'

'Not in my case. Bunny,' I contradicted him cheerfully. 'As Lennie so rightly remarked, in my case I have gained time – in the shape of this genuine gold-plated, 14-jewelled gents' wristwatch, in full working – ' but as I said the last words I realised that something about Judge Rawley's gift had been bothering me ever since he'd presented it to me. It lacked the dynamic feel of your true chronometer. It seemed light in the hand. I flipped it over and opened the back. Then I looked up and roared : 'Where's that Harris? I'll murder him ! It's got no bleeding works in it !'

Pardon Me

For fifteen years, old Blanco only had two interests in the nick : Muffin the Mule and Monopoly. Then he put the finishing touches to Muffin the Mule and it was all down to Monopoly. Fearing that his outlook would get narrow, I suggested that he have a go at Donald Duck or even Paddington Bear. But he said there wasn't time. Not for a true artist. Muffin had taken fifteen years to complete. Blanco was a long-server. But even he would be released before another fifteen years had passed. So I urged him to have a go at some less heroic work : Dougal, for example, or perhaps just a simple bust of Mickey Mouse. But Blanco didn't seem to think that, after Muffin, these would prove very satisfying. He greeted the suggestion with scorn, as Christopher Wren might have done if, just after he had supervised the completion of St Paul's, his old lady had asked him to run her up a garden shed.

So we all had to take turns playing Monopoly with Blanco. And it was far from bliss. A nice courteous old con most of the time, over the Monopoly board Blanco turned into a fiend. He played Monopoly the way Stuart Granger – or am I thinking of Cary Grant ? – the way one of them played Black Jack in Dodge City – or am I thinking of Stud in Tombstone ? Any old how, Blanco played to win. And he wasn't particular how he did it. He was a very good Monopoly player because of long practice. But he supplemented his skill by such ploys as sneaking houses on to his properties when you weren't looking and snaffling up play money. Has to be said : Blanco cheated at

Monopoly. This did not make for a restful game. And for me the only point of playing games in the nick is to relax. So how did I ever get involved in a four-day marathon Monopoly session with Blanco? By the fourth afternoon, we were playing with gimlet eyes fixed on each other and, if we'd been wearing them, our holster flaps would have been unfastened.

'Ha,' I exclaimed, moodily examining a 'chance' card. 'Would you Christmas eve it – "Go to Jail. Go directly to Jail. Do not pass Go, do not collect – ".'

'I know the flaming words,' Blanco snarled. 'Just get on with it.'

A tiny muscle in his jaw twitched. I said, in a level voice, 'It's your toss, isn't it?'

He tossed. I looked at the dice. 'Four and three. Seven.'

'I know,' he growled. 'I can count. I may be old but I've still got all my faculties.'

'Oh, that's lovely,' I complimented him. 'I should be sorry to think you'd lost a couple.'

'What I have lost is a hotel. Pick it up for me, would you, Fletch?'

'Oh, come off it, Blanco. I saw you work that one last week with Godber. He picked up your dice and you snaffled up half of Bond Street and King's Cross while he was doing it.'

Blanco's body stiffened and I saw his hand creep towards his hip. A voice whispered in my head : he's going to make his play – now. But what he came up with was his snuff box. He took a pinch of snuff, shuddered, sneezed and said : 'It's a flaming lie. Listen, Fletch, I'm not like you lot. With you, cheating is a way of life. But I'm an older man with an older man's sense of values, so if you don't care a rat's about my sciatic nerve I'll get the hotel meself.'

With a groan he began to hoist himself up. Naturally, this affected by tender heart. I urged : 'Hey – hey, hang on. I'm sorry, Blanco.'

He sank back in his seat. I continued : 'You're right. We're all so corrupt in here, we forget there's the odd honest soul.'

Then I rose and began to look for his missing hotel. There was a flicker of movement from Blanco's direction which just might have been his hand snaking out for a couple of houses. But I couldn't be sure. I didn't see his hotel anywhere. Then Blanco exclaimed : 'Oh look, there it is.'

He bent down to retrieve the little red building and, simply to keep fair do's with him, I slipped three five-hundred pound notes from the bank onto my pile. Then the game continued.

About an hour later, I heard two familiar voices behind me. The first belonged to Slade Prison's favourite screw, Mr Barrowclough. It asked :

'Are they still playing?'

This exasperated query was answered by an even more familiar voice, that of my cellie, Lennie Godber. He explained soberly : 'Four days now. Could make the Guinness Book of Records.'

'They're cheating each other into a stalemate, that's why.'

Naturally, I bristled at this monstrous allegation. But I couldn't turn round to remonstrate with Barra for fear Blanco would slash my assets. I called : 'What's that, Mr Barrowclough?'

'I said, you two cheat each other into a stalemate.'

My indignation got the better of me. I turned.

'Who says we're cheating? I'm one of this nick's most honest men. And Blanco's an old man with an old man's sense of – I saw that, Blanco !'

I had turned back to the table just in time to see Blanco's hand in the till. He whined : 'I were only changing a hundred-pound note.'

'Yeah, into a flaming five-hundred pound one!'

'An inspiration to us all,' sighed Mr Barrowclough. 'All right, you two. I think it's time you wrapped up this marathon. Lock up in five minutes.'

Lennie said, 'You two do tend to monopolise that game. Get it? Monopolise?'

Barrowclough gazed blankly at Lennie for a moment. Then he caught on. 'Oh – yes – very witty, Godber.'

Lennie shrugged modestly and asked : 'What's brown, lives in the ocean and attacks young mermaids?'

Barrowclough looked uncertain, like a cow inspecting a bunch of plastic flowers. He shook his head. 'I've no idea.'

'Jack the Kipper.'

This background was not helping play. I was about to suggest that they both naff off and leave us to the final shoot-out when someone new arrived in Funland. It was Lukewarm. He immediately set about Blanco.

'Oh, there you are. You're a naughty old person. You promised me you were going to wash your work shirt. So you'd look presentable for Parole Board.'

'I'm going to, aren't I?'

I was conscious of a distinct feeling of irritation. We only had five more minutes to play. Then I had a butcher's at the game. Blanco had made his pile. There was only a tatty ten-pound note left in the bank. How he'd done it I couldn't tell but if it came to a reckoning, it would cost me a deal of snout. So I turned jauntily to Lukewarm.

'Come off it, me old son. Seventeen-year stretch and you think the Parole Board's going to be swayed by a clean shirt? It's his clean record that counts.'

'Silly to jeopardise it for the sake of a drop of soap and water, though,' said Lukewarm.

'I can't come now. I've got two on Piccadilly. I'll come in a minute.'

'See you do.' And Lukewarm slouched off.

'Worse than me daughter, nagging,' Blanco murmured.

'I thought he was your daughter,' I said.

'Still, he does keep the cell spotless.'

'Well, you soon won't have to worry about that. You're on your way out, aren't you?'

Lennie nodded sagely. 'You're free and clear this time, Blanco.'

'No, nothing's certain.'

I tried to stoke the conversation. 'Of course it is. A doddle. Mere formality.' Barrowclough had eased away a little. I felt it would do no harm to draw him back into the chin-wag. I raised my voice a little. 'Even Mr Barrowclough would bet on that, and you know how middle of the road he is on every flaming issue. If you ask him for a straight yes or no, he'll say : "It depends what you mean by yes or no".'

It worked. Barrowclough perked up his ears. 'What was that, Fletcher?'

'I was saying, sir, you are unwilling to commit yourself on issues. Like to hedge your bets, sit on the fence, know what I mean?'

'I do not. I'm as positive in my opinions as the next man.'

'Oh, well then, you'd agree Old Blanco's release is a formality this time round?'

'Oh – well, I'm not sure. I mean, one has to consider both sides.'

I sighed and shook my head. 'Come off it. It's a disgrace he ain't been free and clear years before now.' Then I gave it to Blanco direct. 'You're on your way, pop. Even genial Harry Grout's giving odds on.'

But Blanco didn't seem overchuffed. He sighed. 'I won't bank on nowt, Fletch. Too accustomed to disappointment.'

He glanced thoughtfully down at the board. I said hastily, 'You know your trouble, Blanco? Always insisting you was innocent.'

'What d'you mean by that, Fletch?' Lennie asked.

'I mean, it's the wrong attitude.'

Barrowclough looked puzzled, something he's good at. 'Wrong attitude?' he asked.

'Look, the Parole Board's like everything else inside. You have to play the game the right way. And that means playing the game their way.'

Barrowclough smiled craftily. 'If you're such an expert on how to play the game, how come *you've* never impressed the Board?'

'Because they wants excuses. And I ain't got none. And when Blanco insists on his innocence, he makes the same mistake. You see, for them, it's better to be guilty and ashamed than innocent and defiant.'

Blanco nodded agreement. 'That's true. You have to show them how you've reformed.'

'Right. In other words, you have to prove you've changed. That you ain't as despicable as what you once was. That's why parole's a piece of cake if you once was an alcoholic or a junkie, or dressed up in women's clothes.'

Lennie asked eagerly, 'So what about a bloke like me who only had the occasional lapse into petty crime? Who otherwise came from a decent home and had an O level in Geography? What are my chances?'

'Lock up!' called Mr Barrowclough.

Later that night, as we were waiting in our bunks for lights out, Lennie returned to the subject.

'Fletch?'

'Yeah?'

'You do figure Blanco's a cert, do you? This time?'

'Need the beds, don't they?'

'What was he originally sent up for?'

I gave a reproving "tsk". 'Now, son, you been inside long enough to know you don't ask that. Take people for what they are, not what they was.'

'I know that, Fletch, but come on. Nothing you could say about Blanco would put me off the old boy. He's one of the nicest people in here. He's kind and gentle and helpful. Don't make no difference to me what he's done.'

'He done his wife.'

As I'd expected, this produced a gasp from the bunk below. 'What?'

'Done her in. Locked her in a deep freeze.'

'And we knock around with a bloodthirsty old scroat like that?'

'What did I tell you? You shouldn't ask.'

'I'm sorry. I admit that was an irrational outburst. Any road – long time ago, wasn't it?'

'So it's okay to refrigerate your old lady as long as it's way back in 1959?'

Lennie struggled to find a way out. 'I mean, he's obviously changed. Had time to repent, like.'

'That's just the point : he's never repented. He always claims he never done it. Says it was her lover.'

'What happened to the lover?'

'They could never find him to ask. He disappeared very smartish – so very probably it *was* him.'

Lennie sighed. 'I suppose there's no way of ever knowing now. It happened so long ago.'

'Right. And a wife can't testify against her old man so there's no point turning to the wonders of modern science.'

Lennie asked in a puzzled voice, 'I don't get you, Fletch.'

'No point in defrosting her and asking what really happened.'

Just then the lights went out, leaving us in eerie gloom. 'Pleasant dreams,' I called cheerfully.

The question of Blanco's chances with the Parole Board was not only being discussed by his fellow prisoners. I learned this when I was mopping the landing outside Mr MacKay's office the next day. Inside were MacKay himself and Mr Barrowclough.

'Sixteen new admissions,' the former gasped. 'Where on earth are we going to put them all, Mr Barrowclough?'

'The Parole Board's here tomorrow. So we'll be saying goodbye to some of our better-behaved inmates.'

MacKay laughed. He always manages to make it sound like a threat. 'That's true. Win a few, lose a few. Well, with the board coming, we'd better make a bit of an effort.'

'Shall I tell the kitchen tinned peaches, then?'

'Yes. And ideal milk, I suppose.'

'Very well. What's your estimate on the releases we might expect?'

'I should think we could count on eight at least.'

'They weren't that lenient last time.'

'If you recall, Barrowclough, the last Parole Board had a woman on it. And she wasn't very receptive to most of the men's pleas.'

'Oh yes, Miss Turnbull. An embittered old battle-axe, wasn't she?'

'She was in a bad mood. Coming into the prison, a work party went by, made certain lewd remarks and jostled her.'

'You'd have thought it would have cheered her up. A woman like that can't get jostled too often.'

'Eight releases will still leave me eight beds to find.'

Barrowclough coughed discreetly. 'I've heard our prison bookie is more optimistic. He's offering odds on ten.'

'Is he now?'

'He's very reliable, Grout, isn't he? He picked all six winners in the boxing bouts.'

MacKay snorted. 'Hardly surprising, Barrowclough. He fixed them in the first place.'

Barrowclough sighed deeply and then asked: 'How does he get away with these things, Mr MacKay? Arranging, fixing, manipulating. I mean, what method can he use on his fellow prisoners?'

The evil laugh sounded again. 'It's called terror, Mr Barrowclough.' I could picture the timid Barrowclough shuddering. 'By the way, which parolee has the shortest odds?'

'Well, my favourite's old Blanco Webb.'

'Oh yes, Blanco.'

'Frankly, I was surprised he didn't make it last time.'

'He was one of Miss Turnbull's victims.'

'Really? How did he manage to upset her?'

'She asked him: after seventeen years, what's the first thing you're going to do when you get out – and he told her. Hell, it's time for inspection.'

And MacKay came charging out of his office.

The next day I was relaxing after lunch in the spacious and well-equipped association area when Lennie breezed up. 'Know summat you don't for once,' he chortled.

'That'll be the day.'

'Well, for starters, I know thirteen across.'

I irritably covered the crossword puzzle with my hand. That is one of the many troubles with the nick. There is nothing – but nothing – you can keep to yourself. I rebuked young Godber.

'Do you mind? Height of bad manners, that is.'

'The word is rook. Type of bird, R, two blanks, K. It's got to be rook.'

This jaunty confidence irritated me, specially since I'd been brooding about the word for ten minutes. 'Not necessarily.'

'Fletch! R, two blanks and a K. What else could it be but – rook?'

'What else? Well, just one example, it could be –er – rilk.'

'Rilk?'

'Exactly. Rilk.'

'There's no such bird.'

'That is just where you are wrong, young Godber. You're not quite as smart as you think you are.'

'What's a flaming rilk, then?'

'A very fascinating creature. Your rilk is, as it happens, a migratory bird from the Baltic shores of Northern Finland. Its most distinguishable feature is that it flies backwards to keep the snow out of its eyes. Ask me another, Magnus.'

'It's still rook.'

I sighed and turned the paper over for future use. 'All right, so what's this piece of knowledge you're aching to tell me?'

Lennie sat down beside me.

'First Parole Board results are through.'

'Oh yes?'

'They've turned down Gibson, who's in for car theft, and okayed Mal Brown who's in for manslaughter. I mean, that's barmy, isn't it?'

'Not really. I should say it was an accurate reflection of society's current sense of values.'

'Yes, but – '

'Think of it this way. It takes one minute to create a

life but ten to make a car. And about five minutes for it
to fall to pieces. Hey up, Nat Mills and Bobbie.'

This last remark was prompted by the spectacle of
old Blanco and Lukewarm ambling towards us.

'Well, the old devil did it this time,' said Lukewarm.

I asked : 'What, worked his parole?'

'He did that. It was that clean shirt.'

I felt a quick pang. Always takes you like that in the
nick. You hear someone else is going out and, just for a
moment, you want to break his leg. Even if he's a mate,
the thought that he's on his way to freedom brings out
some buried demon. Still, if anyone deserved it, old
Blanco did. After *seventeen years*! I pulled myself together and winked at him.

'Told you, didn't I? Doddle.'

'Be a few changes, though. Since 1959,' Lennie remarked.

'I flogged a hot car in 1959,' I reminisced. 'Ford Zodiac
it was. Two-tone with wing mirrors. Took the wife to
Butlins on the proceeds. We won a bronze medal in the
Tea for Two cha-cha.'

Lennie contributed :

'I were in Junior School in 1959. Sitting next to Ann
Podmore. She was left-handed.'

'Bet you got on the right side of her, then.'

Blanco said glumly, 'I remember 1959 only as the year
I were sent away for something I didn't do.'

I remonstrated with him. 'Here, listen mate, you're
casting a gloom on the proceedings. I mean, we're only
trying to be festive.'

Blanco nodded but he looked far from festive.
Curiosity, which I'd suppressed for years, got the better
of me. I leaned towards Blanco and asked : 'Here, Blanco,
now you've swung it, you can level with your mates. Was
you innocent all this time?'

Blanco became animated. He said fiercely: 'I was that! Listen, Fletch, I know you'd like to think I've been screwing the system all this time. But the truth is that the system's screwed me for seventeen years. That's why I've come to a decision.'

'Decision?'

'Aye. For all these years, I've stood me ground. I've proclaimed me innocence. If I accept parole now, you know what I'd be doing? I'd be admitting me guilt.'

Naturally, I tried to deflect this unhealthy line of thought. 'Blanco, parole wipes the slate clean. It says you're free and clear.'

'But it's not a pardon. Parole says we'll let you out now and don't be a bad lad again. Well, I were never the bad lad they said I were in the first place. So they can take their parole – and shove it!' With which, Blanco turned smartly and tottered away.

Well, the next chance I had for a bit of a natter with him was the following day. He was working on his pathetic allotment, raking at the patch of stony dust.

'You haven't, have you?' I asked.

He stopped raking. 'I have.'

'Told 'em to stuff it?'

'Aye.'

'What did Governor say, then?'

'Put the wind up his clappers, I know that.'

I sighed at this barmy behaviour. 'You could be on the streets now, you know. Queuing up at the labour exchange. Standing in the rain waiting for a bus.'

'I waited long enough. Bit longer won't make no difference. Can you pass me the watering can?'

I gave it to him and he sprinkled a few drops on to some feeble green stalks. I said encouragingly: 'Rhubarb's coming on a treat.'

'Can't wait to get your hands on my rhubarb, can you?

Thought I'd bequeath it to you if I got out, did you? In lieu of Monopoly debts?'

'Don't be daft, Blanco.'

'Perhaps you had your eye on me radishes as well? But I'm still here. And this is still my allotment.'

Could it be? I'd heard of cons who go stir crazy and afraid to face the outside world. Was Blanco refusing parole so he wouldn't be parted from his miserable allotment? I said soothingly: 'We'd have looked after it. You know that, Blanco. Till you came back inside.'

His shoulders drooped and he nodded. 'I reckon you would.' He gazed about at the forlorn patch. 'Just like life, prison. You make plans and do sod all about it. Look at this place. I were going to do so much. Caulies, I thought. And spring onions and big ripe runner beans. Maybe even raspberries and goosegogs . . . Never got round to it. In all that time.'

'Didn't one Governor once let you grow grapes?'

His eyes brightened. 'Aye. I read all about vines. I knew I could grow grapes, even in a place like this. And I did too. Bloody marvel, it were. Seeing those ripe, juicy beauties – and then they made me pack it in.'

'Why?'

'Make wine from grapes, don't they?'

'Do they? Always used potato peelings myself.'

Blanco chuckled at old memories. 'They didn't tumble till we'd got about a dozen bottles put down.'

'Nice drop, was it?'

'In the wine stakes, Fletch, I don't suppose it were a classic. But to a man who hadn't had a drink for eleven years – well, Chateau Slade were the finest drop I ever supped.'

'If you weren't such a stubborn old mule, you could be supping champagne now. Out there.'

'Got me pride.'

'Freedom's pride.'

'Want both, Fletch.'

I nodded. 'Right then – we'll have to see what we can do.'

Saturday afternoon, Barrowclough mooched into the association area and found us doing it. He blinked.

'Saturday, and you're all indoors?'

'Crow,' I explained.

'I beg your pardon?'

'These are the central headquarters of our campaign. C.R.O.W.'

Barrowclough looked hard at the sheets of paper in front of me. He asked: 'And just what would that be?'

'The Committee for the Release of Old Webb. You know – Blanco. We wanted to make it the Committee for the Release and Pardon of Old Webb, but that would have spelled Crapow – which sounds a bit rude when you're petitioning the Home Office.'

'The Home Office?' An apprehensive shiver passed across Barrowclough's bovine features.

'Well, eventually. The Governor first.'

Lennie took up the tale. 'See, old Blanco doesn't want to go out free and guilty. So we have to make sure he goes out free and innocent.'

'Which is what Crow is all about,' croaked Lukewarm.

'Already got three hundred signatures,' Lennie said proudly.

'But what are you petitioning for?'

I enlightened him.

'There's two ways it can be done. One, the Governor has the right to request a pardon from the Home Office, under Sub-section twenty-three, part three, paragraph D, Penal Code as amended by the Act of 1972.'

Barrowclough pawed nervously at the ground. 'Really?'

416

'Oh yes. Well known, that is.'

'And the other alternative?'

'Demand a retrial.'

'After all this time? I should think the judge, the jury and the witnesses are nearly all deceased by now.'

'Yeah, well, that may be to the old boy's advantage, know what I mean?'

Warren blew in waving a sheet of paper. 'Here, look at this, Fletch. I've done the laundry and machine-shop since yesterday and got sixty-three signatures.'

'Very good, my son.'

But Barrowclough perceived an objection.

'Just a minute. There's no more than forty people at the most working in those two places.'

'Just goes to show the strength of their feelings, don't it?' I pointed out.

Lennie, who had been inspecting the sheet Warren had handed him, murmured : 'Lot of X's on this sheet.'

Bunny shrugged. 'Lot of folk in this nick can't write.'

'How can you be sure that these X's are the genuine article?' Barrowclough demanded.

I took the paper from Godber and held it under Barrowclough's nose. 'Stands to reason, Mr Barrowclough. Look at the difference in the handwriting. See, one bloke's spelled X with a Y.'

Barrowclough. 'Well, I have to admit it's a praise-worthy effort. My only fear is the Governor's attitude. He has an automatic resistance to any notion proposed by you lot.'

'Well, that's just where you could help us, Mr Barrowclough. Add some weight to our pitch, like.'

'How?'

'We know you for a humanitarian. You're no hard-nose. You've always played fair with us. Seen our point of view. Your example has brought reason and compassion into a world where too often only violence prevails.'

Barrowclough was visibly swelling under this treatment, like a cow that's been at wet clover. He cleared his throat. 'Well, as you know, I consider you men are here to be helped, not punished. I try to understand, not condemn. I respect your rights and if you have a just cause, I'll back it to the hilt.'

There was a discreet murmur of 'hear-hears' from some of the boys. I said solemnly :

'Never doubted it, sir. So would you just add your monicker here?'

Barrowclough shied faintly. 'Well now – hold on – '

I thrust a pen into his hand. 'Just cause, sir.'

But Barrowclough was shaking his head firmly. 'Oh no, you don't. No ruddy fear. I'm up for promotion next month. I'm not jeopardising that by being party to a prisoners' conspiracy.'

And he turned on his heel and strode away.

Lennie said sadly : 'Not quite the humanitarian we reckoned.'

'No, but give him his due,' I said cheerfully. 'He's smarter than we thought.'

'Pity, though. Get his signature and a few more screws might have followed.'

'So that's what we'll have to do, isn't it?'

'Eh?'

'No sweat.'

I took the pen and bent over the sheet. I wrote very carefully. Warren gaped in admiration.

'Can you really forge Barra's signature, Fletch?'

'How do you think we got the new requisition of ping-pong balls last week?'

Lennie was dubious. He pointed out : 'You'll be for it if they trace it back to you, Fletch.'

'More likely to trace it back to you. It's your pen.'

'What?' Lennie seized it and examined it while I chuckled quietly.

It's amazing. When I have to enter the Governor's office in the line of duty, he's never what you might call frantically busy. Usually he's either chatting up his secretary or gazing moodily out of the window as if yearning for freedom. But any time *I* want to see him he immediately gets plunged into activity. We'd been waiting in his outer office with our petition for what seemed the best part of a month. I'd gone into a kind of trance when Barrowclough suddenly snapped :

'Stop whistling, Fletcher.'

'Eh?'

'I said stop whistling.'

I hadn't even realised that I'd lapsed into melody. I sighed. 'Oh, sorry. Against regulations, is it? "Thou shalt not whistle in the Governor's outer office." New one on me.'

Barrowclough turned on Lennie. 'What do you think you're doing, Godber?'

It was obvious what he was doing. He was whiling away the long winter making paper aeroplanes. On Barrowclough's harsh query, he started guiltily.

'Nothing, Mr Barrowclough.'

He unfolded the plane and replaced it in the in-tray on Mrs Jamieson's desk. I remarked : 'Wish he'd hurry up. I've got a busy day ahead.'

Barrowclough said : 'We've all got a busy day ahead, Fletcher. Difficult period this, just after the Parole Board's been.'

'That's true. All the turn-downs get disappointed and bitter. Breeds hostility. Even violence.'

'Yes, it's quite unlike the week before the board get here. You're all on your best behaviour then. Butter wouldn't melt.'

'That's right. Even Mad Dog Hollister didn't hit any-one last week.'

Lennie grinned. 'He's hit a few since they turned him down. And set fire to his mattress. And assaulted the Chaplain.'

Just then MacKay sprang out of the inner office like some hideous clockwork figure. He barked : 'All right, Mr Barrowclough, wheel them in.'

Since they had neglected to kit us out with wheels, Barrowclough had to content himself with marching us in. Once inside, we stood firmly to attention in front of the Governor's desk while Venables pretended to be engrossed in the study of what I could, by using my amazing talent for reading upside-down, see was an old shopping list. Finally he glanced up. Barrowclough said simply :

'Crow, sir.'

'What? Why?'

'Er – no, sir – Crow. You remember? The Committee for the Release of Old Webb, sir. Blanco, sir. I men-tioned it to you, sir – the petition.'

Venables snorted. 'Oh, that, yes. I'm not in favour of prisoners' pressure groups.'

Barrowclough, with a miserable lack of tact, just barged on. 'They have the right, Governor, under sub-section thirteen which clearly states that in the event of – '

Venables held up a peevish hand. 'Don't spout the penal code at me, Barrowclough.'

Since it was clear that Barrowclough was going to be about as subtle as a stampeding long-horn, I said quickly : 'Let us say straight off, Governor, sir, how much we appreciate you seeing us. May I present, sir, for your perusal and consideration this petition for the retrial of Old Man Blanco, sir.'

Venables sighed but accepted the sheets I held out to him. He perused them languidly. Finally, he asked: 'Do we have this many men here?'

Lennie said ingratiatingly: 'The petition, sir, is a sincere expression of the feeling in Slade Prison. And the fact that they have responded in this way is a tribute to your enlightened administration.'

This was heady stuff. Venables blinked. 'Is it?'

I pressed our advantage. 'Oh, most certainly, sir. All them blokes out there, burly felons, putting their names to a piece of paper. In, as the lad puts it, a less enlightened administration, they'd have torn the place apart by now.'

An outraged growl issued from MacKay. 'Is that a threat, Fletcher?'

'Not a threat, sir, no. Just an observation. Based on several years of first-hand experience of the mood of the incarcerated male.'

Venables tapped the petition. 'The mood is really as strong as this?' I nodded. 'Growing stronger ever minute, sir – and uglier. Present company excepted, of course.'

MacKay appealed to the Governor. 'What is the point of this, sir? The authorities have been compassionate enough to offer Webb parole. He should accept it and be grateful.'

I said humbly, 'It's just not enough, Mr MacKay. He has to clear his name, see?'

MacKay snorted. 'The man's an old fool.'

Barrowclough rallied briefly to the cause. 'No, I wouldn't say that. Stubborn, but not foolish. In fact, there's something quite heroic – er – quite – well – something – er – as you say, the man's a fool.'

His sudden indecision has been caused by an encounter with one of MacKay's most corrosive glares. His voice trailed away into silence. Venables turned to me.

'You must remember, Fletcher, that Webb was found guilty by a jury of his peers.'

This was my big scene. I gave it all I had. 'Sir, we know he's innocent. Me and all the lads. I mean, we're all cons, ain't we? We knows when one of our own is spinning the yarn. You lot mightn't, but we do.'

'The case was too long ago, Fletcher, for a retrial.'

'Ah, but there's ways and means, sir. This petition's only the first step in making this a national issue.'

Venables drew in his breath sharply. 'National?'

Lennie dished out the next instalment. 'We want to make old Blanco a national hero, sir. We want to touch the conscience of the nation. We want the spotlight of the mass media on the old fellow.'

Venables actually paled. 'Mass media?'

I came in on cue : 'That's it, Governor, create a folk hero through the television and the newspapers. Why, you'll be a celebrity yourself, sir. Might even get on the Parkinson show. Esther Rantzen's a cert.'

But MacKay said firmly : 'There's no way that this petition could escalate into a national issue.'

I'd been waiting for this. 'You're absolutely right, Mr MacKay. As things stand, there's no way. That's why we need the hunger strike.'

Venables clutched the edge of his desk. 'What hunger strike?'

I said sympathetically, 'Old Blanco's. It would be an ordeal for us all, sir. But don't worry, it couldn't last long. I mean, a man his age shouldn't go more than a week top weight.'

What's called a pregnant silence fell upon the company. MacKay glared. Barrowclough shuffled. Lennie and I gazed upwards as if at the celestial reward that would, if nothing else, be Blanco's at the end of his hunger strike. Venables rallied first. He tapped the petition and, with a

faint gulp, said : 'All right, you can leave this here. Now –
back to your cells.'

I said quickly, 'Can we return, sir, in the knowledge
that you're giving the matter your due consideration?'

But MacKay barked : 'Fletcher! On your way.'

And out we marched.

What happened after we'd gone, as Barrowclough
admitted later, was that consternation reigned. The
Governor, as anticipated, did not relish presiding over
the slow demise of a nice old con who might even be
innocent. But what could he do? What? It was then that
Barrowclough remembered an obscure sub-section in the
penal code, because I'd made sure he would by mentioning it about five times a day for the past week.

'There might be a solution to this problem, sir,' he had
said to the Governor. 'I'm sure you're aware of it, given
your knowledge of the penal code.'

'Er – refresh my memory, Mr Barrowclough.'

'Sub-section 23, part 3, paragraph D.'

'Ah yes . . . Yes, good old sub-section 23, paragraph G.'

'D, sir, paragraph D.'

'D, yes. Of course. Er, jog my memory again, will you,
Mr Barrowclough.'

'Well, as you know, sir, under special circumstances
the Governor of a prison has the right, if his discretion
feels it's warranted – '

'Yes,' the Governor said quickly.

'To request the Home Office for a prisoner's pardon.'

'A pardon?'

'That's right, sir.'

'It would certainly put paid to the news of a hunger
strike being splashed across the newspapers.'

'Well, all round, by and large, it does seem a good idea,'
Barrowclough finished lamely.

'Yes, well, I'm paid to come up with ideas in situations

423

like this. I'll submit a recommendation to the Home Office. Can we get rid of those?' He started to hand the petition to MacKay, when something caught his eye. 'Just a minute. Your signature's on this, Mr Barrowclough.'

'Oh no, sir,' said Barrowclough, looking for his spectacles. 'Some mistake, sir.'

MacKay pointed at the signature. 'Look, man,' he barked. 'Is that not your signature?'

'It must be a forgery.' Barrowclough looked at it. 'No, that's definitely my signature. I must have signed it.'

So that was why Lukewarm was able to amble into our flowery some days later and announce : 'Gentlemen, may I present the best-dressed man of 1959.'

He was closely followed by a vision to delight any nostalgia freak's heart : Blanco clad in a seventeen-year-old grey suit. I nodded approvingly.

'Oh yes. Very elegant. Where d'you nick that, Blanco? Burton's?'

He answered shyly, 'I think it were Fifty Shilling Tailors, January sale.'

'They're back in fashion,' Lennie enthused.

'I think in fifty-nine,' I reminisced, 'I wore Italian pin-stripes and a shirt with a Billy Eckstein collar.'

Lennie admitted. 'I wore grey flannel shorts.'

Lukewarm glanced down at his faded prison denims and sighed : 'I think I wore much the same as I do now.'

'I wore this suit to wife's funeral,' Blanco said.

I was a little shocked. 'Hardly black, is it?'

'Couldn't afford another suit. Only just finishing paying for that damn freezer. Terrible to think she finished up inside it. Mind you, I suppose it were fitting in a way, because all her life she were a cold woman.'

Barrowclough poked his head in.

'Don't be long, Mr Webb. Bus is waiting.'

He withdrew his bonce. Blanco smiled. 'By gum, do you know how good that sounds? *Mister* Webb.'

'When you goes out there, hold your head up high, my son,' I said.

'I will that, Fletch.' The old lag paused and when he next spoke there was a catch in his voice. 'I'm not very good, you know, after all this time like, at expressing gratitude. But I know what you done – and I'll not forget.'

The catch proved catching and I gulped before saying breezily : 'You're away, pops. All that matters.'

Lennie helped out by observing, 'You've got a lot of living to make up for. Don't waste your time nattering with the likes of us.'

Blanco shook his head. 'I don't want much from life.'

'I know,' I said, 'but it's good that justice has been done – albeit a little late. This pardon's for your family name, for your children and your grandchildren. That's why we done it. So's you can walk out of here and look any man in the face without shame or guilt. Life's taken a lot from you, me old mate, but all you need back from it is your pride, right?'

'Right, Fletch.'

'And naturally there's one more thing.'

'What's that, Fletch?'

'You sue the Government for every bleeding penny you can get.'

Blanco said stoutly, 'Too bloody true, I will.'

Lukewarm seized Blanco's hand and said touchingly : 'You always were a cantankerous, stubborn old mule – but I'll miss you.'

Blanco smiled. 'Thanks. I'll try and get that scented notepaper that you want.'

Just then a terrible thought struck me. It was based on knowledge of Blanco's fierce sense of justice. I grabbed him by the arm.

'Here, listen, Blanco. We knows you didn't do in your old lady and that means some other bloke did. Now you've been incarcerated here for seventeen years for a murder you didn't commit. It wouldn't be natural if you hadn't often thought of taking vengeance on the real culprit. But don't do it, my old son, don't do it!'

Blanco sighed. 'I know who did it, Fletch. It were the wife's lover. But I can promise you I won't touch him.'

'How can you be sure, Blanco?'

'Because he's dead.'

'You know that for a fact?'

'Webb!' came the evil bellow of MacKay, for the last time as far as Blanco was concerned. 'Let's be having you.'

Blanco edged towards the door. I said urgently: 'Blanco, do you know for a fact that he's dead?'

He nodded and said simply: 'That I do know, Fletch. I killed him. Cheerio.'

And the old man tottered off to freedom.

A Test of Character

Who won the Battle of Hastings? I bleeding didn't. What happened in 1253? A lot of poor sods were locked up. How do I know? Because that's what happens every year. And always has done. So what use is History? Very little. The only time I thought it might have some value was when me, Charley Ambrose and two other lads hijacked a lorry full of Bacardi rum which turned out, because of a mess-up, to contain about a million history textbooks. But we couldn't find a fence that would even look at them. In the end we dumped them in the River Ouse, where they fouled up the intake of a power station and plunged Goole into darkness. So much for the light of learning. Which was the lesson I'd been trying to drive home to Lennie ever since he'd started his new studies. I mean a dell is not the British Museum, is it?

'Naff off, Fletch !' he urged irritably.

I gazed at him in resentment. A moment before I had been feeling positively chuffed. I had thrashed Warren, McLaren and a timid poofter from D Block called Wiggins in quick succession at draughts. Three quarters of an ounce of good shag in my pocket testified to my triumph. Is it any wonder that I was carolling a cheerful song as I entered our little domain? And what did I get?

'Naff off, Fletch !'

'I beg your pardon, Godber?'

He didn't even glance up from his array of books. But he stopped sucking the end of his pencil long enough to say : 'You heard.'

I sighed and shook my head. 'Shall I tell you something, Godber? Prison's coarsened you, my lad.'

He kept his eyes down but was gracious enough to remark : 'Yeah. Well, it's hardly finishing school, is it?'

'Nevertheless, when you first come in here, you did retain some vestiges of old-world courtesy – such as respect for your elders.'

'When I first come in here, *you* taught me the value of peace and quiet. I'm in agreement with that now.'

'Meaning?'

'Meaning : do not disturb. I'm trying to study.'

This passion for learning was doing nothing for our relationship. It was like sharing a cell with a waxwork, except that a waxwork would not have kept grumbling at the slightest sound. But my motto is and always has been live and let live.

'Very well,' I conceded. 'Not another word.'

'Thanks, Fletch,' he acknowledged, and then muttered some dates under his breath.

I wanted him to feel completely reassured, so I added : 'Not a single, solitary word will emit from my lips forthwith – forthwith my lips are sealed. Yes, sealed are forthwith my lips. I have sealed forth my lips with – '

'Fletch !' he cried in exasperation.

'What?'

'You weren't going to say nowt.'

'And I'm not. Honest. Not a peep. Schtum. With a capital Scht.'

He gave me a doubtful look and returned to his studies. I was about to heave myself on to my bunk when I thought of a good one. Even thinking about it made me chuckle inwardly. The lad would fall about. So I approached him and said : 'Here, Len – '

He jumped and exclaimed : 'Oh, naffin' heck !'

I hastened to reassure him. 'No, no, this won't take a minute.'

'Well, what is it?'

I cupped my hands and held them out to him. 'Guess what I've got in here?' I asked, keeping a straight face.

He didn't seem exactly on fire with curiosity. 'I don't care, Fletch. Go away, would you, please?'

'No, it's a good one this. Have a guess. What have I got in my hands? Go on then.'

He sighed deeply. Still running his eyes along the page, he grunted, 'Okay. A cockroach.'

'No.'

'I give up,' he said unsportingly.

But I wasn't having that. 'You got two more guesses.'

'A walnut.'

'A walnut?' I exclaimed. 'Why should I have a bleeding walnut?'

'All right,' said Lennie, with an air of finality. 'It's a naffing giraffe with a hare lip wearing purple Y-fronts.'

I could not forbear a reproachful look. Height of bad manners, that is, knowing the end of a joke and not letting on.

'Who told you?' I asked sullenly.

'Fletch, naff off!' he exclaimed, a touch of real anger in his voice. 'I've asked you nicely. I have an exam and I need to study.'

'Okay,' I conceded. 'I have no objection to your studying. But this is not the most suitable place for it.'

'Where do you suggest?'

'Well, the education room would seem to fit the bill. Yes, I think that would be most appropriate.'

'Except that there's a lecture in there tonight. The Accident Prevention Officer is speaking on industrial safety.'

'That's been cancelled,' I said haughtily.

'Has it?'

'Yeah. On his way here the Accident Prevention

Officer fell off his bike. He's in Carlisle General now.'

'I wish you were,' Lennie murmured.

'I see,' I said reproachfully. 'Well, just remember there are two people to a cell, Godber. And it's very unsettling for a social misfit like me to have someone sat here who wants to better himself.'

He swung round at this and his eyes blazed. Never seen the lad in such a temper before. 'Yeah? Well, when I get out of here, I may have another "O" Level. What will you have to show for it? Just another stretch done!'

'Is that so?' I asked, with scathing irony. I was trying to think of a follow-up that blended dignity with truth when MacKay bounded into the dell like a jackal.

'Oh yes, oh yes,' he snarled.

'Ah, the town crier,' I exclaimed.

'What's going on here? A heated exchange, is it? Raised voices?'

I was not sorry for the distraction.

'Oh, here it is,' I announced. 'Mother superior.'

'Watch your lip, Fletcher.'

'My lips are sealed, sir. Forthwith my lips are sealed.'

Lennie muttered : 'If only that were true.'

MacKay, adopting his hypocritical fatherly tone, asked the lad : 'What's the problem, Godber?'

But, of course, Lennie was not going to grass, angry though he was. 'Nothing, Mr MacKay.'

'Fletcher getting on your wick?' the screw prompted. 'No, sir.'

'Trying to study, are we? I'm afraid that won't cut much ice with an ageing recidivist like Fletcher.'

Lennie looked up. 'Ageing what?'

'Recidivist,' repeated MacKay smugly. 'A person who pays his penance for performing a crime, goes out and straight off performs another one.'

'He means,' I pointed out sardonically, 'a professional.'

'No,' thundered MacKay, turning to me, 'I mean an habitual criminal. Something which you might have avoided, Fletcher, if you'd got stuck into your education like laddo here.'

I shrugged.

'Yeah, well, I never finished school, did I?'

Lennie sighed and abandoned his studies.

'How come?' he asked.

'War, wasn't it? Always playing truant. Out with the lads, on the bomb sites, collecting shrapnel and that. Learning about sex in air-raid shelters during their off-peak hours. So eventually they sent me to a special school with other kids what was always playing truant. But we never learned nothing.'

'And why not?' asked MacKay.

'No one ever showed up for school.'

MacKay smiled complacently. His chest began to swell as he boasted : 'See me, I had to leave school at fourteen. Help bring a living wage into the house. Hard times in those days in the Lanarkshire coalfields. My father was an unemployed miner with eight children to provide for.'

'Eight kids, eh? He wasn't unemployed the whole time, then?' I commented.

'Let me tell you something, Fletcher, not one of our family neglected education. Even under the most difficult circumstances, like those of Godber here. I've had to pass exams, you know. You don't get to be a warrant officer in the Army without something up here.' At this point the nurk patted the thistle he used for a head. 'As well as something in there.' And he thumped his puffed-out chest.

'And kissing somewhere else?' I queried.

His eyes narrowed to slits. 'Did I hear you correctly, Fletcher?'

'No, you didn't, sir,' I hastily amended.

He contented himself with a fierce glare. Then he shook his thistle. 'You're a lost cause, Fletcher.' He turned back to the lad. 'What subject are you studying, Godber?'

'History, sir. O level like. Already got one O level before I come inside. Geography.'

I exclaimed: 'Gawd, you're so proud of your geography. It ain't got no application in real life, you know? Ain't going to do you no good knowing what an escarpment is. Or what's the capital of Finland.'

'Helsinki,' supplied Lennie promptly.

'Hell's teeth!' I groaned.

MacKay frowned. 'Get out of here, Fletcher,' he ordered.

I looked at him in amazement. 'What?'

'Go on – make yourself scarce.'

This was blatant harassment. I protested: 'I just come in from work. I'm entitled – '

'You're entitled to nothing in here except to obey the sound of my voice.'

I nodded. 'Right,' I said grimly. 'I see. How long am I supposed to absent myself for then?'

'Until lock up.'

I shrugged. 'I'll make it later if you like. Give us the keys and I'll let myself in.'

MacKay took a threatening step towards me. 'Out!' he snapped.

I turned with quiet dignity and strolled out of the dell.

Now in Muswell Hill, if I'd had a tiff with my nearest and dearest, I should just have continued strolling with quiet dignity until I'd reached the saloon bar of The Dragoon. Once there, six or eight pints and the sympathetic ears of a few mates would have rapidly healed the wound. But the architect of Slade Nick had inexcusably neglected to include a bar. So all I could do was take my load of grief to the association area, where all I beheld was a gang of dishonest felons indulging themselves in trivial pastimes.

'Evening,' I remarked, as pleasantly as I could.

Manners in the nick compare unfavourably with those of the average barnyard. No one even glanced up. Since there was practically no room on any of the benches, I asked courteously: 'Is it too much trouble to ask you gentlemen to budge up and give me a seat?'

Oaths and grumbling greeted this civil request. But a slight shifting of criminal bottoms followed. I planted myself on the edge of the plank. I glanced about moodily. That's another difference from your cheery local. In a pub you may chance to make a rewarding new aquaintance. In the nick, every bleeding face is familiar. I spotted Warren and McLaren and Spraggon, who had a paper.

'Spraggs?' I addressed the last-mentioned.

'What?'

'Two's up with that paper, eh?'

'You'll have to wait,' he grunted. 'I'm going to do the crossword.'

'You don't need all the paper just to do the crossword,' I pointed out.

'I do,' he retorted unconvincingly.

I called across to two convicts who were enjoying a game of draughts: 'I'll play the winner.'

'No, I am,' announced Warren rudely.

'I see,' I said. I turned to McLaren. ' 'Ere, Jock.'

'What?' asked Prester Jock.

I cupped my hands. 'What have I got in my hands then?'

A number of disgruntled voices, in ragged unison, bawled: 'Heard it!'

I sighed deeply. 'That is what I shall miss most when I get out of prison – the bonhomie.'

McLaren growled : 'If you don't like it here, naff off to your pit.'

I shook my head and explained politely : ' 'Fraid I can't do that. Can't stay in me own flowery dell in case it upsets His Nibs' concentration.'

Bunny said emphatically : 'Mean a lot to Godber, that exam.'

'Won't open no doors,' I maintained.

Spraggon looked up from his paper. 'Nowt wrong with education. Doing it meself. Writing a book, I am. Manifesting my literary bent.'

I nodded. 'Oh yes, I heard about your literary aspirations, Spraggs. We're all very relieved to hear that you're laying down the sword and picking up the pen. As are a lot of battered night watchmen round your way.'

'Spraggs is right,' insisted Warren. 'If we'd all had some education we wouldn't be here now.'

I laughed bitterly. 'Don't give me that. Us lot was destined to end up in here. If we'd had education we'd have just been in for a better class of crime. Stock manipulation or fraudulent conversion.'

'I know a lot of knowledge,' Warren announced.

'Don't be daft,' I rebuked him, 'you can't even read.'

'Maybe not,' maintained Bunny, 'but I get it from the telly. Schools programmes, University Challenge, Sale of the Century. I learn things and I digest them with my retentative memory. Shall I give you an example?'

'No,' I grunted.

But Warren is not easily discouraged. 'Right,' he said. 'Apparently – 'ere, listen, Spraggs – if every Chinaman in China jumped up and down – at the same moment, like – it would cause a tidal wave which would engulf America.' He gazed about triumphantly.

Spraggon wrinkled his brow. 'Food for thought,' he pronounced.

An anxious look came into Bunny's face. 'Or is it Australia?' he wondered aloud.

McLaren nodded wisely. 'Either way. Secret weapon there.'

I contributed: 'Be ironical, wouldn't it? President Carter gets the world to agree to ban all nuclear weapons. Then, before the ink's dry on the treaty, the Chinks leap up and down and "whoosh" – world domination.'

Spraggon, having run the matter through the mill of his mighty intellect, shook his head. 'Bit unlikely.'

'Not with them Chinese,' I insisted. 'If anyone could pull it off they could. Because they're regimented. Do everything by numbers. Look at the menu in a Chinese restaurant. But it would never work in England.'

'We could do it if we put our minds to it,' Warren declared patriotically.

'Not a snowball's,' I maintained. 'The British working man would never leap in the air in case he spilt his tea.'

'Still,' boasted Bunny, 'that's knowledge, isn't it?'

'Oh yes. May I enquire where you got this fascinating piece of information?' I asked.

'Someone read it to me once from a magazine in this chiropodist's waiting room,' he offered.

'What was wrong with you, then? Toothache?'

'No, I was there with me feet.'

'Naturally,' I said hopefully.

'I've always had these feet, like,' Warren went on. 'It's a good chiropodist, though. They're very quick.'

'Do they do them while you wait?' I asked.

'Eh?'

'I mean, or do they say leave 'em with us, they'll be ready Thursday. Soled and heeled.'

'Get off, Fletch. You're pulling my leg.'

'I wouldn't dare. Your foot might come off.'

'No, listen,' Bunny said, 'I've got some more knowledge. About planets.'

'Oh Gawd – ' I began, but Warren ploughed on.

'If the sun was here,' he announced, holding up his cupped hands to show the position, 'about the size of a football, and the earth was at the end of the table where Fletch is – '

'Oh dear, have I got any on my trousers?' I asked, but he ignored me.

'Now on that scale – where would the nearest star be?'

Felonious brows wrinkled in deep thought. McLaren asked suspiciously : 'Is this one of them trick questions?'

'No, no,' Warren protested, 'straight up.'

But McLaren wanted his reservations put on record. 'Because if it is I'll stuff you, Warren.'

Spraggon held up a hand for silence. 'Let's see. Sun there and earth there. Nearest star? Long way, I know that – I'd say the recreation yard.'

'Wrong,' exclaimed Bunny happily.

'Not by far, I'll bet,' grumbled the humiliated Spraggon.

'Wait and see,' promised the crafty Warren. 'Jock, what do you say?'

'It's further than that,' pronounced Black Jock. 'Married quarters.'

'Wrong,' crowed Bunny. 'Fletch?'

I sighed dismissively. 'I don't care, do I?'

'No, go on,' wheedled the tiresome scholar, 'have a guess. Like I said, the scale – '

I cut him off. 'Yes, yes, thank you, Magnus Magnusson.'

But McLaren, wanting a companion in humiliation, urged : 'Go on then, Fletcher. You know it all.'

'In a minute,' I agreed, ticking off some numbers on my fingers. 'Just doing the calculations, ain't I? Earth – sun –

allow for the speed of light – carry two – plus the hypotenuse – Carlisle.'

'Wrong!' screamed Bunny, insane with delight.

'Wrong?' I asked stiffly.

'Not even close. You all want to know?'

'Get on with it,' growled McLaren.

Warren gazed about at us like a conjurer with his hand in the top hat. Then he pulled out the rabbit. 'Johannesburg,' he announced.

While we were still gazing at him in disbelief, a furrow crinkled his brow and he added: 'Or is it Australia? Well, either way, it's still fascinating.'

This folly had gone far enough. 'Warren,' I said pointedly, 'I can imagine no possible circumstances where that piece of information would mean naff all to no one. It's like Godber's perishing History. Ain't got no application in real life. Now if it were arithmetic he were doing I could see the point in that. He could work out an up and down treble in his head.'

McLaren nodded. 'He could also work out how long the odds were against him passing.'

'Right,' I agreed.

'Specially,' continued the sooty Scot with a peculiar emphasis, 'sharing a cell with you.'

He was getting at something. But what? 'Pardon?' I asked.

'I said, especially sharing a cell with you.'

'And just what's that supposed to imply?'

McLaren shrugged.

'It's tough enough to study inside. But you – you distract him. And you're always putting him down. You're a destructive influence on the lad.'

'That's true,' agreed Spraggon.

'Hold your bleeding horse,' I protested. 'If Godber passes that exam it will be due in no small part to me.'

'How?' asked Bunny.

'How? I've been tutoring him, ain't I? Up all night sometimes. Learning him about the second world war, as told by someone what lived through it.'

Spraggon smiled craftily. 'All very well, but his subject's the Napoleonic wars.'

I shrugged. 'A war is a war. It's all history, ain't it?'

McLaren exclaimed contemptuously: 'My God, if you've been tutoring him, the odds are even longer than I've imagined. You'd be better off having money on a pit pony in the national.'

I began see what he was getting at.

'All right,' I said, 'let's talk about odds then.'

'You'd bet on him passing?'

'With complete confidence. Name your odds.'

'Evens is good enough for me.'

Sarcasm was called for. 'Oh, the odds have been slashed, haven't they? Moment ago he was a rank outsider.'

'I'm not greedy,' maintained the crafty hybrid. 'Money for old rope this.'

'How much old rope you want to bet then?'

'Ounce of shag.'

To my surprise, and slight alarm, two voices came from the other end of the table:

'I'm on that.'

'Me too.'

Still, honour was at stake. 'Very well then,' I agreed. 'Anyone else?'

'I'm betting on Godber,' proclaimed Bunny loyally. 'If Fletch reckons it.'

'Thank you, Warren,' I said feelingly.

McLaren turned to Spraggon. 'Get on this, Spraggs.'

But the literary bruiser shook his head. 'No thanks. Last bet I had got me in here.'

'How's that?'

'Me and my brother, Malcolm, were casing a warehouse in Fazakerley. And I turned to him and I said : "I bet that Alsatian's no bother".' With which he rose and limped away.

It was not long before pressing business called McLaren away too. That left Bunny and me together.

He asked nervously : 'Have I – er – have I done the right thing, Fletch?'

With more confidence than I felt, I asked : 'Bunny, have I ever let you down?'

'No, Fletch, but it's not easy. Slade Prison has a terrible academic record.'

I pointed out reassuringly : 'Bloke got O level in Spanish last year, didn't he? What was his name? Oh yeah, Gomez.'

Warren looked doubtful but he said bravely, 'Well, you really know Lennie. That's what impressed me, Fletch, your faith in the lad.'

'Yuh, well – I have every faith in him, of course. I know the lad. I know his diligence, his application.'

Warren nodded thoughtfully. We looked at each other. I continued : 'Mind you, while I harbour no doubts as to his ability, he'll have to know the right answers before the exam.'

'How could he, Fletch?'

'We'll have to whip the exam paper.'

In pursuit of this scholarly aim, Bunny and I made our way, at a suitable time, to the Education Room. Alas, it was not unoccupied. This was predictable since it is always locked up when not in use. But what I hadn't bargained for was that a screw would be there. Barrowclough was in the midst of a little heart-to-heart with Spraggon. The door was ajar and Bunny and I hovered outside, hoping that Barrowclough would depart. He was saying: 'This – er – manuscript of yours, Spraggon. It's very interesting – brutal but interesting.'

'Would mean a lot to me,' pronounced the Dickens of Slade Prison, 'if I became a writer. Nobody in my family's ever been famous, except for me cousin, Ernie.'

'Your cousin Ernie Spraggon was a notorious tearaway,' Barrowclough demurred.

'Famous, though, wasn't he? He made the top ten.'

'Top ten most wanted men, yes.'

'Made a name for himself, though. Couldn't go in a post office without seeing Ernie's photo, could you?'

Barrowclough sighed. 'Look, Spraggon, writing could be your escape, if you'll pardon the expression, and I would be the last one to discourage that. But I think we should start with some grammatical essentials. For example, on page one, the first paragraph, you've left out the 'k' in knuckle duster. And also in kneecaps.'

'Kneecaps?' asked Spraggon, the reference escaping him.

'Yes,' clarified Barrowclough, 'the ones you break with a cricket bat at the top of page two.'

Spraggon burst out in the exasperated tone of the artist who has no time for petty details: 'Look, I know I ain't put much grammar in there. I know my spelling leaves a lot to be desired, like, but I didn't want to interrupt me stream of self-consciousness, did I? See, I write with me gut.'

Barrowclough agreed feelingly. 'I noticed that.'

'All right, so it's brutal, but I'm writing what I know about and I've led a very full and brutal life. I've been warring with the scuffers all me life. Ever since they found me up a Jigger with a fifteen-year-old Judy.'

Barrowclough asked faintly: 'She was only fifteen?'

'I didn't know. I was only twelve meself. I was big for me age, see.'

440

By this time, it was clear to Bunny and me that this learned discussion might go on indefinitely. We held a hurried conference and put our special emergency plan into operation. First step was to push open the door and barge in. On seeing Barrowclough, I drew back.

'Oh, 'scuse me, Mr Barrowclough.'

He looked up in surprise. The surprise increased when he saw what I was carrying : a football, an orange and a ping-pong ball.

'What is it, Fletcher? What do you men want?'

'We're looking for the Education Officer, sir. The one with the brains, you know.'

'Mr Kingsley's taking a class,' explained the screw. 'I'm just helping him out with some of his more bru – er, basic pupils.'

I nodded sympathetically. 'Well then, Mr Barrow-clough, perhaps you'd grant us a moment of your time – in your capacity as a teacher.'

Barrowclough looked suspicious, like a cow contemplating an electric fence. 'You've never shown any interest in education before, Fletcher.'

'Times change, sir,' I assured him. 'Sooner or later a man acquires a thirst for learning. Right, Warren?'

'Right, Fletch. I'm dead thirsty.'

Barrowclough sighed. 'Well, explain what you want briefly. We're busy in here.'

Warren proclaimed : 'We want you to settle an argument.'

'An intellectual argument,' I added.

'Can't it wait?' asked Barrowclough. 'I'm dealing with Spraggon here.'

'Spraggs is used to waiting,' I pointed out. 'Been waiting parole for four years.'

Spraggon took this in good part. 'Be my guest,' he invited.

'Very well then,' nodded Barrowclough. 'What is it?'

I warmed to the task. 'Well, me and the lads was sitting around our cell discussing the wonders of the universe.'

'You were what?' exclaimed the screw incredulously.

'Yeah, this great and wondrous galaxy what still enthrals man with its magnitude and mystery. Anyway, Warren has a theory what I'm disputing.'

'What theory?'

'I'll show you, Mr Barrowclough,' I promised and I flourished the football. 'What I've got here is a scale model of the universe. You see, this football represents the sun.' I placed it carefully on the floor. 'Now this ping-pong ball represents the planet Mercury, and it goes – one, two, three – here.' And I placed it down near the door. 'Give or take a million miles, that is. Now Venus should come next but we'll skip it 'cos we ain't got a prune. Warren threw it out 'cos it was wrinkled. And this orange is the earth, and it goes – ' At this point I gazed about in bewilderment. I couldn't fit the whole solar system into the Education Room. So I said respectfully: 'Could you just step out in the corridor, Mr Barrowclough? Galaxy won't fit in this room, it seems.'

Shaking his head in exasperation, the screw rose and accompanied me, muttering: 'For the life of me, Fletcher, I can't think what you're on about.'

'All in good time, sir.'

I stepped out of the door. Barrowclough turned to Spraggon. 'Will you excuse me for a moment, Spraggon?'

He nodded. 'Yeah, go on like.'

Whereupon Barrowclough and I vacated the dismal hole. As soon as I'd gone, Warren, as he described in detail afterwards, said urgently to the kneecap-buster, 'Hey, Spraggs, where does the Education Officer keep his keys?'

'Keys for what?'

'Filing cabinet through there.'

Spraggon was puzzled. 'Why? There's nowt in there worth lifting. I looked first day in here.'

Bunny glanced anxiously at the door through which Barrowclough and I had departed. Then he pleaded: 'Ask no questions. Please, Spraggs.'

But the burly author smelled a rat. 'Hey, hey, hey,' he protested. 'He's helped me, has Barra. He may be a screw, but he's okay. Before I knew him, I didn't know a semicolon from an apostrophe. When me book's published, I might dedicate it to him because he trusts me, and you're only asking me to betray that trust, right? Well, naff off!'

Warren wasted no further time on emotional appeals. 'Tell us where the keys are and you've made yourself an ounce of snout.'

'In the top drawer,' said Spraggon promptly.

In no more time than it takes to cry 'stop thief!', Warren was at the desk Spraggon had indicated and had the drawer open. At this point he froze with an innocent smile on his face. His reason for doing this was that Mr Barrowclough, in spite of my attempts to restrain him, had re-entered the Education Room. He bore down on Bunny who, thinking he'd been nobbled, was wondering whether to cut and run. But Barrowclough simply pulled open another drawer and drew out two fine red apples.

'There we are,' he said in satisfaction. 'Jupiter and Saturn.' And he joined me again in the corridor.

Warren then completed his mission. He seized the keys, darted into the inner office, unlocked the filing cabinet and withdrew a sealed, official envelope. He placed this under his jacket and returned to the outer office just as Barra and I came in again through the other door. The screw, who was now fully involved in the stars, was saying : 'I know the nearest one is Alpha Centauri. Bit of a hobby of mine, astronomy.'

I glanced at Bunny to find out if he'd secured the goods. He nodded. So I said dismissively to Barrowclough : 'Right then – '

But Barra was gazing abstractedly at the football. He shook his head doubtfully : 'But on this scale – let's see – I wouldn't have thought it was Johannesburg.'

'Yeah, well, thanks, Mr Barrowclough,' I said with finality. 'If you get the right answer, let us know. You know where to find us. Come on, then, Warren. Sorry, Spraggs.'

Bunny and I made a beeline for the door. On the way, I handed him Jupiter. Barrowclough called after us : 'Just a minute, could you return my – '

We turned, each of us taking a large bite of apple. His face fell. 'Oh well – never mind – '

As we left, I heard Barrowclough ask forlornly : 'Do you suppose, Spraggon, that they enacted that whole charade simply to steal my apples?'

Warren and I lost no time in conveying our treasure back to the flowery. There, inevitably, we found Godber bent over his books.

'Still hard at it, are we?' I asked cheerfully.

The lad groaned. 'Trying, yes.'

'Know what they say?' I chided him. 'All work and no play makes Jack a dull beanstalk or something – '

'Do us a favour, Fletch – '

I could not forbear a wink at Bunny. 'Already have, my son.'

He sighed. 'All right, you left the cell for half an hour. Did you have to come back so soon?'

'Knew you'd miss me, little treasure. Knew you'd be worried if I didn't come back before nightfall.'

He put down his pencil. 'Where have you been?'

'Down the Education Room.'

'You?' he asked in amazement. 'What for?'

'Well, we was inspired by your example, wasn't we, Warren?'

'Oh, aye.'

I continued : 'We want to become educated, like what you are.'

Lennie said wearily : 'Do you know, Fletch, one of the main reasons I want to pass this exam tomorrow is so's I have a chance of *not* ending up like you.'

I frowned. 'I'll have to think about that a minute. It's an insult, isn't it?'

Warren tsk-tsked. 'Ungrateful, that's what. If he only knew.'

Lennie, who had once more applied himself to learning, asked with scant interest : 'Knew what?'

'Knew how much Fletch cares,' elaborated Bunny.

'No, no,' I exclaimed, trying to keep the hurt from me voice, 'don't bother him.'

'Cares about what?' asked Lennie.

'Cares about you,' insisted Warren. 'That's what.'

With a catch in my throat, I murmured : 'One day perhaps – '

'No, go on, tell him, Fletch,' urged Warren. 'Tell his nibs what you just done for his benefit at great personal risk to yourself.'

'You played your small part, Warren,' I said handsomely. 'Though it makes you wonder why we took such dire risks – '

It was beginning to work. Lennie put down his book again and turned towards us. 'What dire risks? Listen, the only thing I ask you to do on my behalf is give me half a flaming chance to pass the exam !'

'Which,' I said triumphantly, 'is precisely what we have done, Godber.'

Warren added proudly: 'We're only going to make sure you pass the exam, aren't we?'

Lennie looked from Bunny to me. 'How?' he asked.

I explained carefully: 'By going over the questions with you so you can prepare the appropriate answers.'

Lennie said, with heavy sarcasm: 'In that case, it would be useful to have the appropriate questions, wouldn't it?'

This was the moment. 'You got 'em!' I exclaimed. 'Envelope, please, Bunny.'

I held out my hand and into it Bunny popped the envelope. I then held it out to Lennie who, with a puzzled frown, took it. 'What's this?' he asked.

'Tomorrow's exam paper. Now shift yourself, Len, 'cos we gotta get it back where it come from.'

Lennie said in a curious, low voice: 'The exam paper?' Then, to the consternation of me and Bunny, he flung it down as if it was red hot. 'No!'

We glanced at each other. I asked patiently: 'What do you mean, no?'

'I mean NO! I don't want to cheat. I want to pass this exam honestly.'

'Well, of course you do,' I agreed, realising that diplomacy was going to be needed. 'But honesty is something you can only afford once you've made it. And passing this exam is going to help you make it.'

But Lennie shook his head decisively. 'Don't you understand? I've cheated all me life. That's why I'm where I am. For the first time I want to do something straight.'

I made soothing sounds. 'Course you do. But once you've passed this exam, no one's going to know *how* you passed it.'

Lennie said positively, 'I'll know. Look, if I fail, I fail. But I'm not going to pass through cheating.'

I shook my head sadly. 'Len, Len, listen, will you?

Cheating, my son, is not a crime.' This did not seem to convince him. I bowled on : 'Course it isn't. Cheating is – getting away with it. World of difference. I mean, everyone cheats. Look, the commercial traveller comes home from the smoke to his local branch office. Puts in his expenses : full week's board and lodging at the Savoy, isn't it? But we all know he's been kipping in a Turkish bath in Hounslow.'

Feeling that reinforcements were needed, Bunny took up the task. 'Listen, Len, you know when you play draughts with Fletch and he says he thinks one fell on the floor and could you pick it up, so you bend down only when you straighten up you find the board's re-arranged. That's cheating.'

I nodded sourly. Warren's support was about as useful as a rubber ladder but I hadn't much choice. Then, to my indignation, the treacherous nurk turned on me.

'Oh, so you admit it?' he asked nastily.

I waved irritably. 'Name of the game, isn't it? Getting away with it.'

Bunny grinned. 'It's not what you do in life – ' he chanted.

'It's what you're caught doing,' I continued.

'And if you don't get caught – '

'You're away, aintcha? Home and dry.'

But the lad still gave no sign of being won over.

'Listen, Godber,' I tried again, 'you sees a television star, like your favourite, Kojak, Telly Savalas, and you think he's such a great actor. Well, why is he always opening filing cabinets and looking at his shirt cuffs? Why? Because his lines are written up for him all over the place.'

'And that's cheating,' Bunny proclaimed.

'Right,' I agreed. 'But who gives a rats? Listen, son, cheating is only another word for conning. Putting one over. And if that was a crime, the whole country would be doing porridge.'

I picked up the crucial envelope and edged it into Lennie's grasp. To my relief he did not hurl it away again. I pressed on : 'I'll tell you what would be a crime – you turning down this golden opportunity we are handing you.'

Warren said earnestly : 'We took a big risk to get that for you, Len.'

Lennie smiled ruefully. 'All right,' he conceded, 'I appreciate your efforts. You want my thanks? Thanks. But I'll still do it my way.'

And the crazy mixed-up nurk handed me back the bleeding envelope.

I shook my head pityingly. 'If you do it your way, you ain't honest – you're just dumb. Because if you do it your way, you'll fail.'

But Lennie stuck his ground. He said sadly : 'There comes a point when the only person you're cheating is yourself. It's like cheating at patience.'

'Fletch does that, too,' Warren said unhelpfully.

I took him by the arm. 'Come on, Warren, what's the use? Let's leave him.'

Sadly, our efforts despised, we turned to leave. At the door, I paused and turned back. In a mournful voice, I gave the lad some last basic truths.

'You're at the crossroads of life, Godber. You make your own breaks, son, because when you get out there, people are going to give you precious few. You can go up for a job one day with all the qualifications in the world and get pipped by some nurk who's never passed an exam in his life. But he's got the right accent, plays for the local rugby club, and he ain't never been in no nick !'

I dropped the envelope on the floor. Then I turned

and, with Bunny, marched with dignity out of the dell. Only we didn't march very far. Just outside the door we paused. Then we peeped. Lennie stood for a long time, staring down at the envelope. Finally he glanced at the door, nearly spotting me as I jerked back. Then he slowly picked up the envelope. He gazed at it for a moment and started to undo the flap.

The next day, while we were playing draughts, Warren remarked : 'Lennie should be out of his exam soon.'

I chuckled. 'Yeah. I wonder how he got on ?'

Warren joined me in the chuckle and, while his head was thrown back, I shifted a piece. I said sternly : 'Mind you, we must never let him know that *we* know the truth.'

'Course not,' muttered Warren, frowning at the board. 'Shtum.'

Warren sighed. Then he rallied and said brightly : 'I knew it would come in handy some day.'

'What?'

'My knowledge.'

I shook my head patronisingly. 'Knowledge in itself, my son, is meaningless. It's how you applies knowledge. Once upon a time some cavemen come up with the idea of a wheel. But he didn't know what to do with it. It was just an idea going "round" in his head.'

I waited expectantly for the laugh but Warren just looked blank. So I sighed and continued : 'The bloke what really cracked it was the bloke who first put one on each corner of a Volkswagen.'

Warren nodded thoughtfully, trying to work it out. While he was thus occupied I flicked a counter on to the floor. 'Oh dear, one's on the floor. Your side, I think, Warren. Could you pick it up for us?'

But a hard light came into his eyes. 'Come off it, Fletch, you must think I'm barmy to fall for that again.'

'What?' I asked innocently.

'You dropped it. You pick it up.'

'How? With my back?'

'Tough.'

I shook my head sadly. 'Gawd, such mistrust in one so young.'

'For once,' declared Bunny, 'I just want to have an honest game.'

He'd outplayed me. Trying to keep my eyes on Bunny and the board, I bent down swiftly and retrieved the counter. Nevertheless, when I rose again the board had an unfamiliar appearance. Warren said smugly: 'Your go then.'

I nodded grimly. 'Is it? Right. Let's see.'

He hadn't been quite as smart as he'd thought. In a lightning swoop I removed all his remaining three pieces. He blinked in amazement.

'How d'you do that?'

'I dunno,' I replied. I wasn't quite sure myself.

But before conflict could erupt, Lennie moseyed into the association area. He seemed relaxed.

'Hello, lads,' he greeted us.

I beamed. 'Oh, Len, son. How did the exam go?'

He shrugged. 'Some questions were a bit tough, but it were not so bad as I thought.'

'No,' I said significantly, 'I'll bet it wasn't.'

He looked thoughtful. 'I was a bit stuck on the Congress of Vienna, but I did well on Wellington's strategy at Waterloo.'

'And we all know what that was, don't we? Put the boot in.'

Lennie smiled. 'I'm going to keep my fingers crossed. But I will admit to being quietly confident.'

I tapped my nose. 'Quietly confident – say no more, lad.'

'Tell you one thing, though,' he said positively, 'pass or fail, at least I have the satisfaction of knowing I did it on me own.'

Now this was on the thick side. I mean, the lad could hardly admit that he'd cheated but he didn't have to be so brazen in his protestations. I couldn't help remarking sharply : 'You what?'

'I did it on me own efforts,' he declared.

Bunny too was outraged. 'Your own efforts?' he repeated incredulously.

I held up a warning hand. 'Er, Godber,' I said tactfully, 'would you like to rephrase that observation. That is, bearing in mind that some of us may know more than you thinks we do?'

But no trace of shame appeared on his youthful face. He said lightly : 'I'm just saying I did it my way. With no help from no one.'

Cheating's one thing but this was dishonest. 'Listen, Godber,' I said earnestly, 'there are many sorts of crimes and we're all here for most of them. But the one thing I can't abide is hypocrisy !'

He never flinched. Looking me straight in the eye, he asked : 'And would *you* like to rephrase that statement, bearing in mind that some of us may know more than what you thinks we do?'

'What?' I challenged him.

Lennie smiled grimly. 'You didn't whip those papers because you cared about my future. You did it because you've got a bet on with half the nick.'

Unlike him, I had the good grace to flinch. But then I rallied : 'Who told you that?'

'No secrets in here.'

I found the answer. 'That bet was an expression of my faith in you.'

'So much faith that you whipped the exam papers.'

'Yes,' I said coldly. 'And which you opened. And don't deny it because we saw you. Which means you certainly qualify for number one in the hypocrisy stakes.'

Bunny said feelingly, 'Worst offence of all in my book.'

Lennie shrugged. 'Yeah, I clocked those papers – but it didn't make no difference.'

'How can he say that?' I appealed to Warren.

'Who actually lifted them?' asked Lennie softly.

'Warren,' I said.

'Well,' suggested Lennie, looking from one to the other of us with a faint smile, 'next time pick someone who can read. He nicked the biology paper.'

And, chuckling softly, the lad strolled away in the direction of our dell.

Final Stretch

Bloke called Harrison. In Maidstone it was – first stretch I ever did. He nicked the key to the stores and locked himself *in*. Since there was no other way out, the screws assumed he was gorging himself in there on tinned peaches and bully beef. Very strong door, naturally, on the stores and it took them some time to break in. When they did, they was amazed to find he hadn't touched a thing. He was just sitting there with his hands pressed to his ears. Turned out that what he was after was simply being alone. He told the Governor it had come over him that if he couldn't be alone, beyond the sight of anyone, for a couple of hours, he'd felt he'd top himself. They treated him decent. Sent him off for psychiatric treatment where he had a trick-cyclist rabbiting at him all day. Never did find out what happened to him. But the point is, I didn't understand it at the time. Now, I do. It comes over you very strong sometimes, the craving for solitude. And never more strongly than at visiting times. Course, at visiting times you don't actually want to be on your tod. You want to be alone with your loved one, beyond the reach of a screw. You wants to forget there's such a thing as cons and warders crowding round you all day long.

Ingrid was saying : 'I know it's only February, but if you book your holiday now it's ever so cheap. So me and Barbara, you don't know Barbara, dad, she's my friend at work – we fancy going to Rimini. That's on the Adriatic. We thought Italy, because your money goes much further there. That's because the lira's the only European currency that's as bad off as the pound. It's either Rimini or Portofino – which is supposed to be rather smart. I believe Rex Harrison goes there.'

I leaned forwards and said in a stage whisper : 'Anyhow, the riot is set for Tuesday. We're going to barricade ourselves in with half a dozen screws as hostages with which we can bargain for better living conditions.'

As I'd suspected would happen, Barrowclough, who'd been hovering at my right shoulder, swung round. I said indignantly to Ingrid : 'I knew he was earwigging.'

'What?'

'Listening to every word he was, of our supposedly private conversation.'

Barrowclough, who'd twigged that he'd been had, protested. 'I was doing no such thing, Fletcher.'

I gave it to him straight. 'Oh yes, you were, Mr Barrowclough. Shouldn't be allowed, hovering.'

He sighed. 'It wouldn't be necessary if we could trust you people not to pass each other contraband.'

'Hear that !' I exclaimed bitterly. I grabbed the packet of cigarettes Ingrid had brought me and suggested : 'Here, check this. There's half a pound of hashish in there !'

And I threw it peevishly towards Barrowclough. As I'd planned it fell short and landed on the floor. He shook his head reprovingly. 'There's no need to take that attitude, Fletcher.'

He stooped to pick up the packet and that gave every visitor in the line a chance to slip contraband across the table to their loved ones. Barrowclough straightened up and handed me back the package. He said haughtily : 'There you are. Now, just carry on.'

'Where was I ?' asked Ingrid.

'Rimini or Portofino,' I reminded her.

'Oh yes, well we was thinking of May, before it gets too touristy and – '

I held up a weary hand. 'Listen, girl, has it not occurred to you that it's a bit tactless in front of your old dad? This conversation about foreign climes?'

'Oh.'

'I mean – you know – '

She patted my arm, causing Barrowclough to peer narrowly.

'You've passed the halfway mark, dad. Less to do than's already done. With parole, only another year. Just under.'

'Oh, is that all? That's nothing, just a mere bagatelle, isn't it?'

'Getting rough, is it?'

I smiled wearily. 'Oh, you know me, I'll survive. It's just every time I see you or Marion or Raymond, I realise you're all grown up a bit more. And without me.'

She pointed out : 'I grew up before you come in, Dad.'

I nodded. 'You had, certainly. Grew up too soon, you did. You somehow bypassed puberty.'

'No, I didn't. You bypassed my puberty by going into Maidstone.'

'Doesn't alter the fact that you was wearing a 36D in junior school.'

Ingrid bridled. 'Not my fault – that's nature.'

'Any road – I forewent my parental responsibilities during your most formative years. Same with young Marion.'

Ingrid sniffed. 'Oh, she'll be all right. Don't you worry, Marion will always end up on her own two feet.'

'If she ever gets herself off her back.' But this seemed a bit raw, so I added hastily : 'No, no, I didn't mean that to sound like it did. I mean, she's a lazy little so-and-so. She got a steady job yet?'

'She don't need one, Dad. Her boyfriend Ricky's ever so well off. He's got three cars. He gave her one for Christmas.'

'I'll bet he did.' Some demon prompted me to add :
'Did she get a present as well?'

'Dad!'

'Well – '

'If she marries Ricky, she'll want for nothing.'

'Oh yes? What's he do?'

'He runs these cheap charter aeroplane trips.'

'What's the firm called? Gullible's Travels?'

But Ingrid has never really had a keen sense of humour.
She just shook her head. 'No, Sunset Tours. It was him
what put me and Barbara on to Rimini.'

'What I'm trying to say is, his three cars was bought
from the deposits scraped together by people like you.'

Ingrid shook her head sadly. 'Dad! I hate to hear you
talk like this. You never give no one the benefit of the
doubt. You're getting so cynical in your old age.'

I said wearily : 'Listen, it ain't no bed of roses in here.'

'You've got nothing to bleat about. You chose to live
outside the law, so you accept the consequences. What
was it you told young Lennie? If you can't do the time,
don't do the crime.'

I was none too pleased to hear my well-chosen words
come back at me from my own daughter. 'How d'you
know I told young Godber that?'

'He said so in one of his letters.'

I turned and favoured young Godber with a glance of
displeasure. But he paid no attention and waved at Ingrid.
She waved back.

'So you've been keeping in touch, have you?' I said
with some slight edge.

'Only pen pals.'

'Yeah, well, he's going out next week, isn't he?'

'Subject to his parole board.'

'Oh, he'll smarm his way past that lot with his naïve
charm, his boyish smile and his one bleeding O level in

Geography. Probably get lost as soon as he's outside the gates.'

'That's why you're so grumpy!' she exclaimed. 'He's going out and you're going to miss him.'

'Miss him? That's not the point. His going out reminds me that I ain't.'

Ingrid gave my hand a squeeze. Barrowclough was mercifully looking in the other direction.

'Won't be too long, dad. Won't be long before you and Mum are going off to somewhere like Rimini.'

I sighed and nodded.

'Yeah, I'd like to think so. 'Cos your mum ain't had an easy life. We never been able to travel, on account of children and incarceration. But now you're all standing on your own two feet, I'd like to make it up to the old gal.'

Ingrid said positively: 'All our mum wants is for you to stay out of trouble.'

'Her and me both, love. This is the last bird I do, don't you worry. And don't tell me you've heard that before, because I know you 'ave. Just that it takes some of us longer to grow up than others.'

Ingrid smiled. She's got a nice smile has Ingrid.

'You've still got a lot of living to do, Dad.'

'Yeah, one of the joys will be catching up on life. Catching up on friends, family, travel – and the repeats of "Upstairs, Downstairs".'

'Tell you what: soon as your release date is set, I'll get in touch with Ricky and he can book you a lovely holiday in the sun.'

'Yeah, well, after Marion and you, why not me and your mum? Then, apart from Raymond, he'll have screwed the whole family.'

So the brief hour passed in fond communing. All too soon it was over and the free ones took wing for the great world while we poor shackled souls trooped back to our dungeons. As I shuffled sadly along I noticed, ahead of me, Lennie deep in conversation with a bruiser called Jarvis. The spectacle did not please me. I was just making a mental note to speak to the lad about keeping bad company when, to my amazement, I saw him suddenly stop and take a swing at the heavy. The next minute they were rolling about near the dustbins.

'Stop that!' called Barrowclough, and that's all I was able to see or hear as the current carried me on towards the old flowery.

I have to rely on Lennie's account for what happened next because I didn't see him again until he slouched into the dell some time later. It seemed MacKay had charged up, bellowing: 'What's all this about then?'

Lennie asked innocently: 'What's all what about, Mr MacKay?'

'Brawling in the yard.'

'We weren't brawling, sir.'

MacKay turned his stern gaze on Jarvis who tried to smile light-heartedly. According to Len it made him look like a wolf with heartburn.

'Just fooling around,' maintained Jarvis. 'Playful high spirits, sir.'

Lennie elaborated. 'We were just re-enacting a big moment from last Sunday's football on the telly. The bit where Peter Shilton dived at Charlie George's feet.'

This delightful picture of innocent frolic did not appear to convince MacKay. He growled: 'I don't recall Charlie George smashing a dustbin lid over Peter Shilton's skull. Not even in the action replay.'

Lennie, slipping out of character somewhat, maintained: 'He would have done if he'd had one handy.'

'Don't be funny with me, Godber.'

'Not trying to be, sir.'

'You two were brawling.'

Lennie shook his head firmly. 'Wasn't, sir, honest. Got me parole board next week. Daft to jeopardise that, wouldn't I?'

MacKay admitted: 'You would indeed, sonny.'

Jarvis had another go. 'Godber's my mate, sir. Him and me are like that.' And he held up two massive digits, lovingly entwined.

MacKay, who hadn't witnessed the affray himself, turned questioningly to his fellow screw. 'Mr Barrowclough?'

'Well,' admitted old Barra, 'I was some distance away, but it did seem to be a vicious altercation.'

Lennie quickly observed: 'Oh, from a distance it could have been misconstrued. But if you'd been close up you could have seen we were smiling.'

He widened his mouth in demonstration. Jarvis did likewise. The effect was unnerving and caused Barrowclough to retreat slightly. MacKay, made of sterner stuff, rounded on the hard man.

'You're no stranger to violence, Jarvis. Your only interest in football was supervising violence at the Stretford End. It's no coincidence that since your imprisonment football hooliganism has declined.'

Jarvis said humbly: 'Didn't know no better then, sir. But thanks to people like Len – '

Lennie supported him. 'It's true, sir. Watch this.' He turned to Jarvis and said firmly: 'Manchester United are rubbish compared to Villa.'

Jarvis swallowed and then returned mildly: 'You could be right, Len.'

Lennie turned triumphantly back to MacKay. 'Doesn't that prove it, sir? It's just that we do sometimes get a bit boisterous in the yard.'

'That's all it is,' insisted Jarvis. 'But to me, sir, Len's family.'

At this moving declaration, Lennie turned to him with quivering chin. 'D'you mean that, Jarvis?'

'Cross me heart.'

'Well, I'm touched. You don't know what that means to me.'

MacKay, who had managed to remain dry-eyed through this performance, sighed and confessed : 'I'm in two minds, Mr Barrowclough. Should I give them solitary confinement or announce their engagement?'

In the end, he did neither, but let them off with a caution. On their way back to the cell block, and when they were out of earshot of authority, Lennie said amicably : 'Got out of that then.'

'Bloody did,' agreed Jarvis.

'Did well in there, us. Abbott and Costello.'

'Morecambe and Wise.'

'We were daft though. Having a go in front of the screws.'

'Should have found somewhere private.'

'We will do,' Lennie promised. 'Because I'm going to punch your lights out, musclehead!'

And with that Lennie turned into his attractive convenience home where I was waiting with an anxious expression.

As soon as I saw him, I burst out : 'I thought I knew you, Godber. What was it all about?'

He sat down and drummed lightly on the table top. 'If someone provokes you, what you supposed to do, back off?'

'If you're up for parole next Monday, most certainly, yes.'

'He made certain remarks.'

'What remarks?'

'Never you mind. Suffice it to say I found them insulting and offensive.'

I shook my head in sorrow. 'If my release was in the balance here, there ain't an insult in the world that would prevent me turning the other cheek.'

'Have to draw the line somewhere.'

'Wrong. You could bring into question the virtue of my old lady, call me a poof, tell me I molest goats – water off a duck's back to me – or off a goat's back, in this case.'

'Perhaps you haven't the same pride as what I do,' he said in a superior way.

'Oh, it's the old pride stakes, is it? The old self-respect?'

He nodded. 'It matters.'

I tried to make him see reason. 'Self-respect is something you preserve on the outside. No such thing inside. When you were sent up you forfeited that. You've ended up just like the rest of them.'

'How?'

'Worried about what they think on the inside. It don't matter. Let me tell you, my son, when you're on the outside, their opinion in here matters naff all.'

He shook his head stubbornly. 'Not doing it for them. Doing it for me.'

I could see I wasn't getting through to him. I tried a different tack.

'I was talking to my daughter today.'

His eyes lit up. 'Ingrid?'

'Yeah, your pen pal. She says, you know, I don't give anyone the benefit of the doubt. Thinks I'm cynical. She's probably right. Know why? Because of people like you.'

Lennie looked puzzled. 'How come?'

'Because if one isn't cynical in this world, one is constantly disappointed by people like you.'

'All right,' said Lennie with what he clearly thought

was irrefutable logic, 'if you're so cynical, why should you give a monkey's about people like me?'

I shook my head wearily. 'Because I had high hopes of people like you. Because people like you could just about make it out there. But – '

'But what?'

'You obviously ain't got the bottle.'

'If I hadn't got no bottle, would I be taking on Jarvis?'

'That ain't bottle – that's stupidity. Tell you what does take bottle in life, knowing when to turn the other cheek. Like Gary Cooper in "High Noon", Alan Ladd in "Shane", er – Gregory Peck in "The Big Country", Glenn Ford in "The Fastest Gun Alive".'

Lennie shrugged. 'Okay, I've seen those pictures.'

'Then you know what I mean.'

'So, tell me something.'

'Gladly.'

'How come those films all ended in the worst fights you ever seen?'

There was undoubtedly some thrust in this observation and it took me a moment to find the correct answer. Then I said firmly: 'I'll tell you why, Sonny Jim. Because Hollywood had to pander to the public's insatiable thirst for senseless violence.'

But Lennie shook his head positively. 'No, you're wrong. Those films raised a moral question, which had to be answered by the last reel. A man has to do – '

'What a man bleeding has to do – yes, yes. Gawd, it's Audie Murphy himself, is it?'

Lennie shrugged. 'There is a basic truth there though.'

'Let me ask you one question.'

'Go on.'

'Would Gary Cooper and all them others have done what they done had they been up for parole next Monday?' This stumped him. I continued: 'And would they have walked into the final shoot-out so willingly had they known their adversary was Reggie Jarvis?'

Lennie said tentatively: 'Alan Ladd stood up to Jack Palance.'

'That was celluloid, not life.'

'It was you brought the subject up in the first place.'

I could see he was weakening. I said sternly, 'Godber, let's have none of your feeble attempts to change the subject.'

'I've forgotten what the subject was.'

But he wasn't wriggling out of it that easy. 'The subject was – is – Reggie, the Red Menace, Jarvis. Listen, Len. There's two sorts of violence inside. One that's born out of frustration and despair, and one that comes from the likes of Reggie Jarvis. Full of Mancunian macho 'cos he's got five years to do and nothing to lose. Now you've got everything to lose. Unless freedom ain't everything. Well then – '

But I still hadn't made any real impression. Stubborn as a mule, that boy, when he wants to be. He said kindly: 'Listen, Fletch, I appreciate your concern, but it's just something that I have to do.'

'I'll make one final appeal to you, Godber. Then I'll wash my hands.'

'Go on then,' he said politely.

'There are three good reasons why you shouldn't take on Jarvis. One, you could jeopardise your parole. Two, it offends civilised sensibilities.' I looked away absently and said no more.

After a moment his curiosity got the better of him. 'All right then,' he asked. 'What about three?'

'He'll bleeding murder you!'

I think it was the next day. We'd finished our stint of backbreaking toil and a few of us were gathered in what we like to think of as 'The Club'. This is a commodious chamber, tastefully furnished with beat-up old tables and benches. Here we indulge in recreational pursuits. Some of us study the daily press to maintain contact with the important social and political issues of the day, such as who won the 3.10 at Redcar. Others prefer mind-stimulating, communal activities such as what Warren and I were engaged upon. He laid down a domino.

'Knock,' I grunted.

Whereupon I sighed deeply and added another match-stick to the kitty. Warren, who was in the midst of a sensational winning streak, laid down another domino.

'Four-five,' he said.

I sighed even deeper, put another match-stick in the kitty and again grunted : 'Knock.'

He laid down another domino. 'Double five.'

I had again to utter the bitter word : 'Knock.

At which point, providentially, Mr Barrowclough plodded up. He tapped me on the shoulder and said diffidently : 'Excuse me, Fletcher – '

'Oh dear, what a pity. Interruption, Bunny, void game.'

And I threw my dominoes face upwards on the table. Warren seemed less than chuffed by this development.

'Hey ! I only had one to play,' he exclaimed crossly.

'It's hard luck, me old son. But we can hardly continue playing when Mr Barrowclough has something to say, can we?'

Barrowclough disputed this. 'You needn't have broken up your game, Fletcher.'

'See !' exclaimed Warren.

'Too late now,' I pointed out. 'Showed me hand, ain't I ?'

Warren, with manifest ill-temper, threw down his remaining domino. Barrowclough bent over and studied the battered tiles.

'Oh, you'd have beaten him hollow there, Warren,' he assured Bunny.

'Matter of opinion,' I shrugged. 'So what's the problem then?'

Barrowclough glanced about cautiously. 'Just a word in your ear.'

I eased my left ear, furthest from Bunny, towards him. 'Try this one, if it's a secret.'

But Barrowclough shook his head. 'Oh, Warren's all right. He's a friend, too.'

'Friend of whose?' I asked.

'Godber's.'

'Him and Jarvis – ' the screw said meaningfully.

'What about Godber?'

I sighed. 'What about Jarvis?'

'You know,' insisted Barrowclough.

'Do I?'

'In the yard. After visiting. You were there.'

I played it cool. 'Was I? Where was this then?'

'I must say,' Barrowclough reproached me, 'you're not much of a conversationalist, Fletcher.'

'What you on about, Mr Barrowclough?'

He tried again. 'Something's brewing.'

'Oh, good,' I enthused. 'Two sugars.'

'You know very well what I mean.'

'Do I? Oh good.'

'I'll say no more.'

'Yes, I think you've said enough.'

'As long as we understand each other.'

I nodded. 'Perfectly, Mr Barrowclough.'

He also nodded. 'Good.' Then he glanced about vaguely and ambled off in search of greener pastures.

'What were all that about?' Bunny asked.

I explained. 'Godber and Jarvis had a barney in the yard. No proof, but they know. Want it stopped before it goes any further. If it does, bad for all of us, specially the lad.' I laid down the first of the new batch of dominoes I'd been assembling : 'My down, double six.'

'I didn't hear him say all that.'

'Read between the lines, son. Your go.'

Warren studied the dominoes I'd shoved in his direction. He shook his head incredulously.

'Would you believe it? I'm knocking.'

'Put one in the kitty.' He did so. I laid down another domino. 'Six two.'

Lennie breezed in.

'Oh, here's Lennie,' Warren exclaimed.

'Hello, Warren. Hello, Fletch,' said the lad cheerfully.

'Never mind him,' I urged Warren. 'Have you got a two?'

Bunny shook his head. 'No, but it's a void game, isn't it? Interruption, like.'

And the impudent nurk went to throw down his tiles. I restrained him with an iron grip to the wrist.

'Naff off !'

'But that's what you did when Barra came up.'

'Different, isn't it? Barra's a screw.'

Lennie pricked up his ears. 'What did he want?' he asked.

'The topic was senseless violence, the prevention of,' I explained.

Lennie pretended to miss my drift. 'If he wants to stop that, he should get the telly fixed. It's been broken for a week.'

'Jarvis broke that,' Warren contributed.

'Only,' I said judiciously, 'because he couldn't get a good picture. I tried to tell him. I said, if the picture gets blurred, you fix it by adjusting the fine tuner with a delicate turn of the knob. You do not chuck the set against the wall. Mind you, that usually does the trick.'

'Can I have a game?' Lennie asked.

'No,' I returned ungraciously.

'Why not?'

'Friendly game, this,' I said with emphasis.

Lennie picked it up. 'What's that supposed to mean?'

'If you was to lose, you might turn nasty, know what I mean?'

'Don't be daft,' Warren protested. 'You know Len.'

'Thought I did. Till this altercation with Jarvis.'

'Change the subject,' hissed Warren out of the corner of his mouth. 'Change the subject.'

'What's wrong with you?' I asked peevishly.

Warren screwed up his mouth even tighter and hissed: 'I said, change the subject.'

I was about to ask him if he was knocking again, when a nasty voice from behind said: 'Godber!'

So that was the reason for Bunny's facial gymnastics. Lennie and I turned.

'Hello, Jarvis,' Lennie said.

'Score to settle, right?' the heavy grunted.

'Any time,' promised the lad.

'Up to you,' maintained Jarvis.

'Ready when you are.'

Jarvis smiled the evil smile of the big gun-fighter confronting the midget farmer. 'What's wrong with now?'

'Why not?' agreed Lennie. 'TV's broke – nothing else to do.'

Bunny gulped audibly and remarked: 'I think I'll go to the lavatory.'

I stood up very deliberately and pressed Bunny down. 'You sit down. Nothing's going to happen, so just hold your horses – or anything else that comes to hand.'

Jarvis frowned at this intrusion, wondering if I might be the local fast gun he'd been hearing about. 'None of your business, Fletch,' he warned.

'It's all our business. A happy nick is a placid nick. Cause a rumpus, you naff it up for all of us.'

'Between him and me,' insisted Jarvis.

'Then, it's between you and me.'

'You don't have to fight my battles, Fletch,' the lad said.

I shrugged. 'No skin off my nose. Few weeks remission won't hurt me.'

Jarvis tried to be reasonable. 'Listen, my gripe's with Godber. But I'll stuff the both of you if you want.'

'Shut your face, toilet mouth,' I said firmly.

Warren leapt like a doe that hears the hounds. 'That reminds me, I really do have to go to the lavatory.'

'I'm going to have you for that, Fletcher,' Jarvis said, and, with disconcerting ease, he picked up a chair.

But I can hold my own. They think I'm slow because I'm a trifle corpulent, and I encourage that belief. But when it's needed I can move. I now moved like a flash to the telly and hoisted it above my head, ready to heave it at Jarvis's ugly mug.

'Everybody freeze !' snarled MacKay, who had popped in unobserved.

Naturally, we froze. 'What's going on in here?' he inquired, unnecessarily I felt.

I explained. 'Oh, we was just trying to fix the telly, Mr MacKay.'

'With the set above your head?'

'Yeah, I was just trying the vertical hold.'

Warren, who had not yet departed for the latrines, gave a startled cry. 'Hey, look – we got a picture.'

I quickly put down the set and the lads all pulled up chairs and began to laugh hysterically at 'The Magic Roundabout'.

After this distasteful incident I took steps to prevent mayhem between Lennie and Jarvis. A couple of days later, I was peacefully darning my almond rocks when Warren moseyed into the penthouse. I glanced at him with displeasure.

'What are you doing here, Bunny? I told you to tag Godber. To never let him out of your sight.'

'It's all right,' the dyslectic felon assured me, 'he's on duty. And Jarvis is in the yard with some of his cronies.'

'Well, we'd better tail Godber when he comes out the cookhouse. Because it's the weekend and this is when it's going to happen, isn't it?'

Bunny sighed. 'I had hoped that you'd have talked Len out of it. If anyone could, you could.'

I shook my head. 'Well, I ain't. Which is a testimony to his pigheadedness.'

'Maybe we should look on the bright side. Maybe the fight won't be tumbled. And maybe Len'll do all right. I mean, he knows a bit. He made the boxing squad.'

I smiled sardonically. 'The boxing squad? Oh yes, the noble art. The Queensbury rules, the fair play and the gumshield. During the time it takes Lenny to proffer his hand for the customary shake, Jarvis will have fractured his groin with his prison-issue boot.'

Warren nodded sadly. 'You're probably right. You can't get odds on Jarvis, because I've tried.'

'Oh, that's charming.'

'Well, fair-dos, Fletch. If there's going to be a fight, and we're powerless to prevent it, it's worth contemplating a flutter.'

There was a certain wisdom in this. 'What odds can you get on Len?'

'Harry Grout's giving a hundred to seven. But I reckon they'll lengthen.'

I nodded. 'I reckon Len will and all by the time Jarvis has finished with him.'

'It's a pity we couldn't get to Jarvis. I mean, if we could put the fix in, we'd make a bloomin' fortune.'

'Fat chance.'

'Could we nobble him? Drugs like?'

'Well, there *is* some animal tranquilliser on the farm. But there's no guarantee it would work on a beast like Jarvis. Not to mention the problem of who sticks a needle in his backside without him noticing.'

Warren tried to be helpful. 'They shoot them into rhinos with blowpipes. I've seen it on the telly.'

I shook my head. 'Subduing a rhinoceros is child's play compared to Jarvis. Anyhow, I think we're getting a bit fanciful, aren't we, Warren?'

'Bit desperate, more like.'

There was gloomy silence for a while. I reached a decision. 'Well then, there's only one thing to be done.'

'What?'

'*I'll* have to take on Jarvis.'

Warren eyed me sceptically. 'You? Do you think you can put Jarvis out of action?'

'No, you nurk. But if I fight him and we're discovered, it's automatically the cooler for twenty-four hours, and he won't come out till Len's passed his parole Monday morning.'

Warren perceived the flaw. 'But hang on, if you're discovered, you'll go to the cooler and all.'

'Yuh, well – ' I shrugged.

'You're going to blot your copy book, Fletch.'

I sighed. 'Yeah, but a few weeks' remission won't do me any harm. But listen, Bunny, I'm going to need your help, 'cos I wouldn't last two minutes with Jarvis. The moment anything happens, you fetch the screws and you better move like greased lightning. Right.'

But Bunny protested. 'Hey, wait a minute, Fletch. If I tip off the screws, that makes me a snitch.'

'If you don't tip them off, son, it could make me a corpse.'

'But, Fletch, think of my reputation.'

'You know the grapevine round here. In two minutes, the true story will be out. That this was a strategic ploy on my behalf, in which you were a vital element.'

Warren considered this doubtfully. 'Well, I don't know – '

'Come on, Warren, naffing hell! I'm the one taking the risk. I'm the one going over the top.'

This reached him. I've always said that, contrary to appearances, there's a streak of humanity in Bunny.

'I'm sorry,' he said humbly. 'You're right, Fletch.'

I stood up. Outside, on Main Street, the bad guys were massing and the time had come when a bloke's got to do what a bloke's got to do. So do not desert me, oh my Bunny, on this my –

'Anything wrong, Fletch?' asked Warren, wondering why I was standing rigid with a faraway look in me eye.

I shook my head. 'He's in the yard then, is he? Come on then, let's get it over with.'

Bunny recoiled slightly. 'Now? Straight away?'

'What's wrong with that?'

'Doesn't give me much time to get a bet on.'

Maybe Bunny is all armpit. Any old how, he accompanied me out into the yard. It didn't take long to spot Jarvis. He and some other thugs were playing pitch and toss. They were about fifty feet away. I set off towards them with a purposeful stride. About five feet away I stopped. I took a deep breath and bellowed:

'Jarvis.'

He turned on the instant – and then smiled affably. 'Oh, hello, Fletch. You want in?'

This was not in the script. Taken aback, I asked feebly: 'What?'

'Want to join in, like?'

I pulled myself together. 'Jarvis. I thought you and me had some unfinished business. From the television room, remember?'

He frowned for a moment but then his face cleared. 'Oh, that? Don't be daft.'

'I meant what I said, Jarvis.'

He shook his head firmly. 'No, you didn't. I know what you were doing – trying to protect the kid.'

With which, the soulless nurk turned back to his game. How would Gary Cooper have handled it? With a definite sense of anti-climax, I called even more fiercely :

'Jarvis!'

But this time he didn't even bother to turn round. He just grunted over his shoulder.

'What?'

'You know when I called you toilet mouth?'

'Yeah?'

'I ain't taking it back.'

That got him. He turned and I felt the adrenalin began to pump into my veins.

'Well, you're right, me old mate. My language is a bit colourful. Me wife's always on at me about it. I try, you know, but I can do sod all about it.'

And he turned back to his infantile pastime. But what he'd said had given me an idea. I said it again :

'Jarvis!'

At last he began to sound a bit peeved.

'Now what?'

'Talking about your wife – '

'Yeah? What about my wife?'

'You're luckier than most of us. I mean, when a bloke's doing a long stretch, you know, his old lady's out looking for nooky, isn't she?'

'Speak for yourself,' he grunted. But at least I had his

full attention at last. I pressed my advantage.

'I am. That's why I'm saying you're luckier than most. I heard your old lady's only been unfaithful to you twice.'

With a distinct sense of triumph, I saw a tiny nerve in his jaw twitch. He asked dangerously : 'Twice?'

I let go with the mortal insult, the one that, in Main Street, would have brought six guns flying out of holsters. 'Yeah, once with the milkman and once with the House-hold Cavalry.'

I braced myself. The muscle-bound nurk glared. Now, a voice whispered in me head, now he's gonna make his play. Then he threw back his head and laughed.

'That's a good 'un, Fletch. Yeah, that's really a good 'un.'

'Oh Gawd,' was all I had the heart to murmur.

Jarvis's laughter seemed infectious. The other players all joined in, slapping their thighs and wiping away tears. Just about then, a neanderthal con called Crusher, who sometimes does little kindnesses for Harry Grout, strolled by. Jarvis, anxious to exploit the fun to the utmost, called :

'Here, Crusher.'

'What?' called Crusher suspiciously. But he lurched over to the group.

Jarvis grinned at him, chuckled and began : 'Listen to this. I heard that your old lady's only been unfaithful to you twice.'

Jarvis paused for some reaction but Crusher just stared at him impassively. So Jarvis went on : 'Once with the milkman and once with the Household Cavalry.'

There were attentive sniggers from the onlookers. Jarvis, his eyes twinkling merrily, waited for Crusher's response. He had to wait some time, since the big man's nervous system is about as active as an old drainage ditch. But finally the jest reached the ape's vital centres. He frowned and then, with amazing speed, smashed his fist into Jarvis's face. I goggled. A moment later and they were rolling about on the tarmac, pummelling hell out of each other. A moment after that and whistles were blowing as screws converged from all quarters. I raised my eyes gratefully to heaven and murmured :

'All right then, I owe you one.'

Then I strolled innocently away.

I can always recognise Lennie by his footsteps. Thus, a few days later, although my back was to the door, the moment he walked into the dell, I exclaimed :

'Congratulations.'

'What?'

I turned and beamed at him. 'Congratulations. On getting your parole.'

He shook his head in surprise. 'I was just about to tell you.'

'Well, I knows, don't I ?'

'How?'

'It pays me to, don't it ?'

'But I only left the Board an hour ago.'

'Son, son, I works the admin. block, don't I ?'

He nodded. I patted him on the shoulder.

'Anyhow, well done.'

'Thanks, Fletch. Here, the Governor was ever so nice about it. He let me ring my mum.'

'I know.'

Again he blinked in surprise.

'How?'

'I listened in on the extension.'

A faint shadow of reproach appeared on his face. 'Fletch !'

'Well, I wanted to share in your moment of elation.'

Another moment and he shrugged. 'Oh well –'

'She was chuffed, your mum.'

'Quite emotional, really. For her. Wish I could tell me dad – if I only knew where the old bastard was.'

'Well, look at it another way. Your dad's absence meant he never knew you went in in the first place.'

'I suppose so.' His face brightened. 'Came in handy today, he did.'

'Oh? How's that?'

'Well, I told the parole board that I thought my father's desertion was a contributory factor towards my temporary diversion from the straight and narrow.'

I nodded approvingly. 'You're learning, ain't you?'

'Thanks to you.'

I lowered my eyes modestly. 'Yuh, well – '

There was a moment of silent communion. Then he said : 'Fletch?'

'What?'

'If it hadn't been for you, I'd have messed this parole up, you know?'

'True.'

'I mean, the fact that you risked solitary confinement and loss of your own remission – well – I mean – well, that's real friendship.'

I said firmly, 'There was no way I was going to jeopardise your parole, son.'

'I realise that now. But I never realised it meant so much to you.'

'Course it did. I had three to one on you getting out.'

Lennie gave this the mental butcher's. Then he shook his head. 'You don't fool me, Fletch. You did that out of the kindness of your heart.'

I shrugged. 'If you believe that, then you are a stupid sentimental nurk.'

But he wasn't put down. 'No, I'm not.'

'Well, you're certainly stupid. As your behaviour over the Jarvis affair demonstrated only too clearly.'

He shook his head positively. 'I promise you, Fletch, I did have a reason for reacting like I did.'

'There was no reason in the world worth risking freedom for.'

'Yes, there was. I can tell you now that it's all water under the bridge.'

'All right,' I said. 'Surprise me.'

'You remember when the affray erupted?'

'Vaguely.'

'It was when we was coming out of visiting hour last Saturday.'

'So?'

'Jarvis came up to me and made an obscene remark.'

I shook my head pityingly. 'Oh, dear me! Did that affront your Brummagem sensibilities then?'

'Yes, it did.' Lennie paused for effect. 'Because the remark concerned what he'd like to do to your daughter Ingrid.'

I absorbed this in silence. Then I asked : 'What?'

'I'm telling you this,' Lennie pointed out, 'so you can understand what you presumed was my stupidity.'

I nodded and asked again : 'What did he say about my daughter Ingrid?'

Lennie shrugged. 'Doesn't matter now.'

I contradicted him. 'It matters to me.'

'Best forgotten.'

'I can't forget it if I don't know it, can I?'

Lennie became paternal, which was a nice turnabout. 'Look, Fletch, I've learned my lesson. Thanks to you. Turn the other cheek, right? I've learned that what the Jarvises of this world think matters naff all, because they're animals.'

These were very sound sentiments, being my own, but I found them a mite irritating at that moment. 'All right, all right. I agree with you. I'm not after retaliatory satisfaction. But for the record, just tell me what he said!'

He decided to oblige. 'To put it delicately, he indicated his carnal desires towards her, then reckoned that he fancied his chances, on account of her sexual proclivities.'

I considered this. Then I nodded reasonably. 'Well, she's always had those. Ever since she was thirteen.'

'Anyhow, best forgotten.'

I looked him straight in the face. 'So. You was defending my family's honour, was it?'

'Seemed a good reason. I owe a lot to you, Fletch. I'd never have made the distance without you.'

'Look, don't make me out to be no hero.'

'I wasn't,' he maintained. 'Father figure, maybe.'

But I shook my head sadly. 'I ain't been no great shakes as a dad. In fact, I ain't been no great shakes as anything.'

'You have to me,' Lennie said positively. 'And I won't let you down, Fletch. I ain't coming back.'

I could not restrain a sigh. 'Oh, we all say that. But you'd better bleeding mean it, Godber. You've got your life before you. Out of the last twenty years, I've spent eleven of them doing porridge. That ain't life, that's marking time. I'm not moaning. What's done's done. But it's a terrible waste.'

'I won't be back. Given the breaks.'

'Make the breaks,' I said fiercely. 'No alibis. No if onlys. You can do it. You're not stupid, and you're not evil. You're a good lad.'

He swallowed. This was turning into one of the slushier episodes of *Crossroads*. So I grunted: 'Enough said. Hope you're leaving me your snout?'

'Only right.'

'Chocolate?'

'Fruit and nut.'

'And first thing you do when you get out, you do for me.'

'What?'

'As soon as you get off the train in Birmingham, go straight into a pub and have a pint of best bitter and drink to your old mate.'

'I'm not going to Birmingham. I was thinking of Rimini actually, with a friend. Or perhaps Portofino. We thought May 'cos it's not so touristy then . . .'

'Godber,' I said calmly, meaning to impart to him some sense of mature values, but suddenly the black mist, cleaved by flashes of lightning, closed in. 'Godber, you lay one finger on my Ingrid's proclivities, and I'll flaming kill you!'

It was a few days later. I was stretched comfortably on my bunk, warming myself in the *Sun*, when a chill breeze, immediately recognisable as Mr MacKay, blew into the dell.

'Fletcher?'

'Good afternoon, sir.'

He seemed surprised. 'Good afternoon, sir?'

'Your title, isn't it?'

He nodded and squinted at me. 'True. But I did not expect to hear it so readily from your lips.'

I shrugged. 'Why make waves, eh? Only eight months to do if I keep my nose clean.'

He chuckled. 'Throwing in the towel, are we, Fletcher?'

I was in no mood for banter. I said simply: 'I just

ced a certain change in your attitude
ase. Our customary ill-feeling seems to
seem to have lost a lot of that brash
Or are you just acknowledging that the
ins?'

ad wearily. 'Nobody wins, Mr MacKay.

That's what's so tragic.' And I turned back to the *Sun.*

I thought MacKay had naffed off but a moment later his Hibernian rasp sounded again. 'Normally, I would have hesitated about putting a new sprog in here, Fletcher.'

'Oh yes? Got some company coming in, have I?'

'In the past year, you have not been the healthiest of influences on first-time offenders. But now I don't think I have much to fear. Got a young lad called Nicholson moving in.'

Without lowering the paper, I asked : 'Not a Scot, is he? I mean, we do draw the line somewhere.'

'He's from Sunderland.'

'Dangerously near.'

MacKay said with relish, 'He's a tearaway. Lashes out. Doesn't think. I have a feeling that the new quiescent Fletcher might be just what he needs.'

'Whatever you think, Mr MacKay.'

'So you'll keep an eye on him?'

'Be difficult to ignore him in a room this size.'

'True, but perhaps you'll show him the ropes. Show him what you've learned.'

I lowered the *Sun.* 'What have I learned, Mr MacKay?'

'That there's no point bucking the system.'

'I see. All right, Mr MacKay – sir – I'll watch out for him. I shall simply tell him three things. Bide your time, keep your nose clean, and most important of all – ' and I raised the paper again, blocking out MacKay's evil face ' – don't let the bastards grind you down !'

479